CUFFED

K. BROMBERG

Cuffed
By K. Bromberg

ISBN: 978-1-942832-09-6

Published by JKB Publishing, LLC

Editing by AW Editing
Cover Design by Helen Williams
Cover Photography Wander Aguiar

PRAISE FOR THE NOVELS OF K. BROMBERG

"A homerun! The Player is riveting, sexy and pulsing with energy. And I can't wait for The Catch!"

—*#1 New York Times Bestselling author* Lauren Blakely

"K Bromberg does it again! The Player is everything you want in a romance; sexy, sweet, and amazingly perfect."

—USA Today Bestselling author KL Grayson

"An irresistibly hot romance that stays with you long after you finish the book."

—# 1 *New York Times* bestselling author Jennifer L. Armentrout

"Captivating, emotional, and sizzling hot!"

—#1 *New York Times* bestselling author S. C. Stephens

"Bromberg is a master at turning up the heat!"

—*New York Times* bestselling author Katy Evans

"K. Bromberg is the master of making hearts race and pulses pound."

—*New York Times* bestselling author Jay Crownover

"Sexy, heartwarming, and so much more."

—*New York Times* bestselling author Corinne Michaels

"Super charged heat and full of heart. Bromberg aces it from the first page to the last."

—*New York Times* bestselling author Kylie Scott

OTHER BOOKS BY K. BROMBERG

Driven

Fueled

Crashed

Raced

Aced

Slow Burn

Sweet Ache

Hard Beat

Down Shift

Sweet Cheeks

Sweet Rivalry

UnRaveled

The Player

The Catch

DEDICATION

To my Mom . . .
She is the one who showed me what strength is.
She is the woman who lifts me up when insecurity weighs me down.
She is my biggest cheerleader, my closest confidant, and my best friend all wrapped in to one.
She is the woman I aspire to be some day.
This book is for you, Mom.
You'll know why, once you read it.
Head up. Wings out.

PROLOGUE

Grant

My tummy feels icky, and if I look at Emmy, she'll know I've been crying. She'll know I told after I promised her I wouldn't.

We even pinky promised on it.

So, I focus on *it* instead.

The glue on my hand and how weird it feels. It's crackly and tight and kind of cold. Kind of like what I imagine alien skin would feel like.

She's gonna be mad at me.

Except their skin would be green. Or purple.

She made me promise not to tell.

Mine would be green. Emmy's would be purple.

She's my bestest friend in the whole wide galaxy.

Her and her yucky purple.

How could I not say anything?

Malone Family Rules: If someone is hurting, you help them.

My dad's temper if I break a rule is much worse than Emmy's, though.

I'm only trying to help her.

The speaker in the room's ceiling crackles, and we all look up. The rest of the class is hoping for an interruption—an announcement for the winners of spirit day, a surprise assembly, anything—but I don't glance up. All I can do is hold my breath and focus on my alien skin.

"Mrs. Gellar?" Principal Newman says through the intercom.

"Yes?"

"Can you please have Emerson Reeves gather her things and come to the front office please?"

"Sure."

Ohhhhh. The whole class makes the collective sound, thinking Emmy's in trouble.

"Called to the principal's office," Cooper says.

But I know the truth.

I dare to look now. To see the worried look on Mrs. Gellar's face as she watches Emmy get her Strawberry Shortcake lunchbox and cram it into her yucky purple backpack. Emmy keeps her head down, but she misses the first time she tries to grab the zipper to close it.

Mrs. Gellar doesn't speak. She doesn't head to the whiteboard or ask us to pay attention like she normally does. Instead, she walks over to Emmy, puts her arm around her shoulders, and bends over to whisper something in her ear. Emmy nods but keeps looking down as Mrs. Gellar gives her a quick hug before standing back up.

When Emmy heads toward the door, I forget all about my alien skin and stare at her from my seat in the last row.

Look at me.

C'mon, Em. Look at me.

She stops right before she walks out the door and meets my eyes. There are tears in hers, kinda like how there are some in mine.

"You pinky promised," she whispers, her knuckles turning white as she clutches her backpack to her chest.

"Em—"

"I hate you. I never want to see you again." She mouths the words and walks out the door.

ONE

Grant

"10-4, Officer Malone."

Her voice, smooth as goddamn silk and full of suggestion comes through the radio. I'm ready for the ration of shit from Nate when I turn his way. His grin is wide as he just shakes his head and chuckles.

"10-4, Officer Malone," he mimics. "Can I give you a side of blow job with that all clear?"

"Fuck off." I sigh.

"Dude, if she talked to all of us like that, the whole force would be walking around with permanent hard-ons."

"Liv does have a great voice," I murmur as a cheer goes up in the crowd to the left of us, drawing my attention. Drunken guys in board shorts, who are all sporting fraternity tattoos, are taking note of a group of tipsy girls with a skin-to-clothing ratio that should be illegal.

"A great *voice*. Yeah. Right. I'm sure that was exactly what you were focusing on . . . because hell if that body of hers isn't a fifteen on a scale of one to ten."

"I'd give it a twenty." I shrug, remembering all too well what she looked like as she straddled me. Goddamn perfection. "You're just a jealous fucker because I won't give you any details."

"You won't give me anything, Malone. For all I know, you're full of shit," he says as he adjusts his bulletproof vest beneath his uniform, both of us constantly scanning the crowd.

"We both know I'm not full of shit."

"Asshole," he mutters under his breath, and I chuckle in response. This is the same conversation we seem to have every time Liv and I interact on the radio.

"I think the hotline tip was wrong. I don't see any of Donnely's gang here."

"Neither do I. Just a whole lotta hot women in teeny, tiny bikinis, and I'm not complaining one bit."

"Pig."

"Well." He shrugs as he points to his uniform.

"Clever."

"Exactly. I'm the smart one. You're not, considering you're the one who walked away from Liv. Just one question, though, why exactly?"

"Too many women, too little time." I lift my eyebrows and grin. "To your right," I say with a subtle lift of my chin as a shoving match erupts between two men outside Hooligan's Bar. Alcohol. Testosterone. All day in the sun. Women to compete over for attention. It's never a good mix.

We shift our attention and assess the situation. Friends take care of it, pulling the men apart before it escalates. "Gotta love the annual Fourth of July pub crawl."

"It keeps us busy, doesn't it? Besides," I say as I glance at my watch, "we have about three more hours on shift in case you want to join them."

"No thanks. Give me a beer in my backyard with the fireworks overhead and I'm good. While the women are nice to look at here, I don't need the chaos of it. We get enough of that on shift." We glance to the left as a woman screams, but then it turns to a high screech of laughter. "You heading over to your dad's?"

"Yeah. Gray and Grady will be there. You're welcome to come if you want."

"*Help me, please,*" sounds off to my left and grabs my attention immediately. It's followed by what sounds like a laugh but is drowned out by the chaos of the crowded street. Hesitant that someone might actually need assistance, Nate and I move toward a group of women in a huddle about fifty feet away.

"Can we help you ladies with anything?" I say and remove my sunglasses as we approach to a hum of giggles.

"My friend here needs help, *Officer Sexy,*" the tallest of the women says, a brunette with a coy smile and legs for days. "She has a real thing for a man in uniform."

Nate snickers beside me as my sense of duty fades when I realize there is no need for help. These are just some women out to have a bit of fun. I stop before them, my thumbs hooked in my duty belt, and pretend like I didn't hear the comment that I sure as hell did. "So, everything is good here, then?"

"That depends," says a voice of the only woman whose back is still to me, "if you're going to give me mouth to mouth and resuscitate me . . ." her voice fades off when our eyes meet.

Holy mother fucking shit. It can't be her.

Can it?

"*Emmy*?"

Her eyes widen, and her lips part. And for that split second, I see the little girl from my memories. The one with the mess of strawberry blonde tangles and emerald eyes. The one who made pinky promises, mud pies, and agreed with me that Batman was far superior to Iron Man when it came to superheroes.

My best friend who told me she never wanted to see me again.

All the emotions come flooding back unexpectedly as I watch the familiarity flashing across her face vanish. Visibly flustered, she shakes her head and takes an abrupt step back, bumping into her friend behind her.

"No. I'm not her. She's not me," she denies.

"Emerson?" It's the brunette again, and hearing that name—*her name*—after all this time is like being sucker punched with a battering ram.

"I'm fine." She shrugs off the hand her other friend has put on her shoulder. Gone is the fun, flirty demeanor she had before turning to see me, Grant Malone—the boy she said she hated. Panic I can't understand, but desperately want to, has replaced it.

"Emmy—"

"It's Emerson," she snaps with a resolute nod before breaking our eye contact and looking at her friends. "I have to go . . ."

"What are you doing here?" I ask a question, but it's so much more than what it sounds like. *How are you? Where have you been? Why are you back? Tell me you're staying around.* But she just stands in front of me and stares as if she can't believe it's really me and, at the same time, frightened that it is me.

"Em?" I reach out, needing to touch her to make sure she's real, but the minute my hand touches her bicep, she jerks her arm back.

"I can't . . . I didn't want . . ." She shakes her head and then looks to the tall brunette before turning back to me with wide eyes as the color slowly drains from her cheeks. "Travis just texted. He needs me to help. I . . . have to go."

Travis? Who's Travis?

And with that, Emmy Reeves—the girl I haven't thought about in years—turns on her heel and walks away.

"No. Wait!" I call after her as she makes her way through the crowd, her mane of strawberry blonde hair the last thing I see of her.

Just like before.

"And you are?"

There's impatience in the voice that breaks through the cobwebs of memories suddenly spinning in my mind, but it takes an elbow from Nate to bring me back to the present.

"An old friend of hers," I murmur to the tall brunette, eyes glancing to the crowd Emmy melted into, as if she were a ghost I was trying to find again.

"An old friend, huh?" She crosses her arms and juts a hip out as her eyes narrow and she decides if she wants to believe me or not.

"From childhood."

"And your name is?" The other women lose interest in our

conversation and begin chatting with Nate, but she's laser focused on me.

"Grant Malone." I stick my hand out. "Nice to meet you."

She stares at my hand for a moment before speaking, "Desi Whitman, and I'm still figuring out if it is indeed nice or not."

I look down to my hand and then back up to her with a lift of my brows, prompting her to reluctantly shake it.

"So, tell me, Desi Whitman, why is it you automatically believe I've done something to hurt Emerson?"

"First off, you called her Emmy. No one is allowed to call her Emmy. She hates it."

"First off?" I laugh. "It's been less than five minutes, and you're already suspicious enough that you've made a list?"

"Not suspicious. Curious. There's a difference," she says as she shifts her feet. "And yes, I like to make lists."

"Okay." I nod, fighting my smile. "Let's continue with that list of yours then. Why else have you assumed I did something to Emmy, er, Emerson?" I glance over to the crowd passing us by, making sure I don't see any signs of Donnely's crew and the rumored trouble they were going to cause before looking back to Desi.

"Because I've never seen her react like that to a man before."

"What do you mean?" Now I'm the one who's curious.

"Hmm." She eyes me cautiously.

"Look, there isn't much eight year olds can do to hurt each other besides steal each other's Legos," I lie, damn well knowing what I did to Emmy was a whole lot worse than that.

"Did you?"

"Did I what?"

"Steal her Legos."

"Jesus. Seriously?" I laugh, but it fades when I see that she is. "Perhaps. I don't remember. Are you satisfied?" She purses her lips. "Now, are you going to tell me why you said you've never seen Emerson react to a man like that before, or are you just going to rake me over the Lego coals for no reason?"

A slight smile curls up one corner of her mouth, and she looks over to her friends, making sure they're preoccupied with my partner before meeting my eyes again. "Em's a confident and in-your-face woman. A flirt. A female who takes no shit and can give as good as she gets. Strong. But when she saw you? It was as if she was a different person all together. Almost like she saw a ghost."

Funny, I felt the same way when I saw her.

"We knew each other in grade school is all. A lifetime ago." I shrug, hoping the explanation is enough for Desi when we were so much more than classroom acquaintances.

"Okay." She draws the word out, but her body language remains on the defensive.

"That's it. I swear." She moves her hands to her hips but doesn't speak, so I continue. "It's been over twenty years since we last saw each other, so I'm sure she was taken by surprise."

"Well, you saw her. She ran away. It seems to me she gave you her own answer whether she wants to continue your little reunion or not."

I nod, wanting to say so much more. Questions. Comments. Memories. All three collide, making me think she had the same reaction and that was why she bolted.

But my past is far different from her past.

Leave it be. Leave *her* be.

"You done chitchatting, Malone? We have a job to do."

"Yeah, yeah." I nod to Nate but hold up a finger before turning back to Desi. "Tell me something? Has she had a good life?" The question is out before I can stop it and is so very different from the one I had intended. I feel like a douchebag for asking, but I *need* to know. "Sorry. Never mind. Nice to meet you, Desi." I smile and walk away.

I take about five steps before she speaks. "From what I know, she has." I stop and look back to her. "The girl is a bundle of perpetual motion and laughter. Maybe it's a cover. Maybe it isn't. But it's how she's been since I met her ten years ago."

"That's good to hear. Thank you."

"Why would you ask that?" She angles her head and takes a step closer.

"When we were little, she was *that* friend. You know, the one who—"

"She's that to me, too. I get it. No need to explain." Her face softens, and her posture relaxes. "I can give you my phone number if you want."

My smile shifts to a grin. "Uh, well—"

"I'm not hitting on you, *Officer Sexy*. Although, while I'm sure you've charmed more than your fair share of women out of their clothes with your smile and uniform alone, you're not my type."

I choke on a laugh, loving this woman I've just met and her brazen personality. "My ego isn't liking you right now."

"Ego, shmeego." She waves a hand at me in indifference before digging in her purse and pulling out a business card. "Go on. Take it." She holds it out to me. "You know, just in case you change your mind . . . or if you want to check on her again."

I take the card she offers, and with one last look that tells me somehow she understands, she turns to her friends and they walk away.

"You ready?"

Nate looks irritated that I'm not reacting. "Sure. Yes. Sorry."

"Who was the woman?"

"Someone I haven't seen in a while."

"An old girlfriend?"

"Nah. We're talking third grade here."

"It's you, Malone. You probably had the girls lined up to play four square with you back then." He chuckles, and I roll my eyes. "Why'd she bail?"

"I'm not quite sure." I look down to where I'm turning the card over in my hand and stare at Desi's name but think of Emmy instead.

One thing is certain, Desi isn't here on vacation. The address on the card and area code are both local, which means she lives here. Does that mean Emerson lives here, too?

Forget about it. If Em lives here and hasn't sought me out, she doesn't want to see me.

But I know I can't forget.

I've never been able to.

She obviously doesn't want this ghost from her past around.

That's the funny thing about ghosts, though.

You can't control when they appear or how they might affect you, but they always haunt you.

TWO

Emerson

THE ENGINE'S ROAR FILLS MY EARS.

I run through my mental checklist. Finish. Then begin it again as the rush of cold air dances around me and whips against my cheeks. My earplugs shift as I slide my jaw out of habit to equalize the pressure in my ears.

I glance over to where Leo is double-checking his own gear. "Head up. Wings out!" I shout over the roar. He gives me a thumbs-up, and with that, I loosen my grip on the door and dive headfirst.

My breath catches. My blood is flooded with adrenaline. My body spirals and hurtles and tumbles in a seemingly endless free fall.

But there is silence in my head. Peace. A bliss I can't find anywhere else as I gain control of my dive, stabilize, and master the arch of my body. The ocean in the distance and the rolling green hills of northern California laid out like a topography map beneath me are as stunning as the first time I saw them like this.

There are no demands from Chris and his bank.

There are no duties left to fulfill for Travis before I can call it a night.

There are no thoughts of Grant Malone and those brown eyes of his that met mine yesterday and surprised the hell out of me.

There are no demons from my past—the ones seeing him again brought out of hiding—trying to weasel their way in.

It's freedom.

It's just me hurtling toward the earth at what feels like a million miles an hour in what could be certain death.

It's my hand deploying the ripcord and my body jolting against the force before rebounding up as the parachute opens and saves me from that death.

Yanking me back to reality.

My parachute.

Saving me.

Grant Malone.

Saved me.

Stop it, Em. Don't think about him.

Look at the fields sprawled out.

I knew it was bound to happen when I moved back here.

At the waves crashing against the cliffs beyond.

He is from before. I'm only about the now.

At the cars on the highway in the distance that look like ants crawling home in the early evening light.

I close my eyes, hating that I'm missing a single moment of my descent, but I use the moment to refocus my thoughts and shift gears.

With another slide of my jaw to re-equalize the pressure in my ears, I open my eyes and force myself to admire the beauty of it all.

After a bit, sometime between the lull of the gliding and the serenity of the silence, I'm able to shut the world out and do just that. Enjoy the moment that will surely dissipate the minute my feet hit the ground.

I think about what I'll do with this place once Blue Skies becomes mine. Fresh paint on the sign. New marketing to tourists and locals. Convert the empty hangar into a clubhouse of sorts to entice the adrenaline junkies to stay longer and spend more money.

I have to get the loan first. Then I can dream.

My mental checklist begins again. The one I use to make sure I don't neglect a single thing. It's too easy to become comfortable when jumping out of an airplane day after day, so I use the repetition as my safety net.

My lone leash to sanity.

Plus it helps me to forget about Grant.

Well, in theory anyway.

"Desi's thinking of having another one of her barbecues again."

My jump coordinator's eyes light up and his lips spread into a huge grin. "Tell her thinking is not an option," Leo says. "She needs to pick a date and commit so my stomach knows when it's going to get treated to the good stuff again."

"No shit." I laugh and shake my head. Friends, food, and relaxation are just what the doctor ordered. Especially when it's *her* food.

"Just promise I won't be forgotten when the invites go out." He holds his hands together as if he's praying.

"I promise."

The phone rings on the desk before me, and Leo goes back to finalizing his schedules.

"Blue Skies, this is Emerson, how may I help you?"

"Emerson! Just the person I wanted to talk to."

"Great. Who's this?" I glance over to Leo, who's sitting at his desk laughing at something.

"It's Chris Severson with Sunnyville Trust and Loan."

"Hi, Chris," I say as I sink down into my chair and glance at the list of reports and paperwork he still needs for the loan. Of the ten items on it, I've only been able to cross two off as completed, and I don't understand what three of the remaining eight even mean or how to go about figuring them out. "What can I do for you?"

"I was just calling to see where you are with getting the information I'd requested."

"It's coming. Slowly." I chuckle because I already feel like I'm drowning.

"I know the list of requirements can be overwhelming, so know that you aren't the only one who feels that way." Sympathy resonates in his voice.

"That's good to know. Since I've never applied for a loan before, I thought I was the only one."

"No. Not at all. Is there anything I can help you with?"

My laugh is part mortification, part reprieve. "Really?"

"Of course. Since you decided to forego having a broker represent you—"

"Only because I know the owners of Blue Skies and they preferred not to use one," I feel the need to explain for what seems like the tenth time. What he doesn't need to know is the lack of a broker was my idea. I simply won't have the extra funds to pay them their fees once the deal is done. I'm stretched thin as it is.

"No need to explain, Emerson. It isn't always necessary to have a broker. Besides, I told you I'd walk you through everything step by step, and I will."

My shoulders sag in relief. "Thank you. I really do appreciate it. You don't know how much this means to me to have found—"

"No need to thank me."

"I still feel I should."

"How about this? How about we meet for a working dinner? It will give me a chance to review everything with you and answer the questions you have."

"I couldn't impose on you like that."

"Nonsense. It's just one of the many services I provide my clients."

I chew my bottom lip, torn between pride and necessity. The silence stretches. "That would be great. I'd appreciate it."

"Good. Then it's settled." He laughs, and I can hear a horn honk in the background. "I'm driving so I can't access my schedule. Let me check it and I'll email you some dates and times that will work."

"That sounds great. Again, Chris . . . thank you."

THREE

Grant

"YOU SMELL LIKE SMOKE." I GLANCE OVER TO MY LITTLE brother Grady and make a show of sniffing the air before bringing the beer to my lips.

"Occupational hazard," he says before lifting his chin to where our dad is attempting not to burn steaks on the grill while he shoots the shit with Grayson, our middle brother. "We were doing drills today over at the old gravel yard. I guess I didn't wash all the smoke off."

"Hmm," I murmur, part listening, part lost in thought.

"So, you gonna tell me why you bailed on coming over on the Fourth? I hope like hell she was worth missing out on Mom's apple pie." He chuckles. "I guess you enjoyed a different kind of pie, huh?"

"You're the firefighter, why don't you go help Dad put those flames out." Diversion intended to get conversation away from my sex life, but I'm not sure he's going to buy it. My brothers are nosey fuckers.

He sits there silent for a moment, and I can feel the weight of his stare as I look at the flames flare up on the old Weber again.

"So, you didn't get laid?" he questions.

"Nah." Another sip of beer. Another push with my foot to rock the porch swing I'm sitting on.

"What's the deal, then?"

"Nothing really. It was a long day, and then I ended up chasing ghosts for a bit and lost track of time is all." I shrug. It's close enough to the truth.

"You should have just told us you got lost in a call. Is it one I know about?"

"Nah."

He chuckles. "Are you being a dick, or are you trying to be vague on purpose?"

I'm not trying to be a dick, but I know that once I say something to him, it will become a Malone family free-for-all topic of discussion.

He doesn't push, which I'm grateful for, but my mind veers back to the ghosts. To the wondering and questioning and wanting to know more.

There's the creak of my swing. The laughter of my dad and brother. The sound effects Luke, Grayson's son, is making as he plays with Matchbox cars on the grass. The squeal of kids a few houses down as they chase each other. The hum of a lawn mower somewhere down the street.

"You remember Emmy Reeves?"

Grady's bottle of beer pauses momentarily on the way to his lips. "Vaguely," he murmurs. "You two were like Mutt and Jeff. She was at the house all the time or you were at hers . . . and then something happened with her family and she moved, right?"

"Something like that," I respond, realizing he was only in preschool when it happened and probably doesn't remember the details. Having a father who was chief of police probably helped keep the facts quiet.

"Why are you bringing her up now?"

"I saw her the other day."

"No shit. How is she? Did she move back? Is she—"

"I couldn't tell you."

"No?" He reaches down and scratches Moose between the ears. The mammoth dog rolls onto his back without a care in the world other than wanting more affection.

"That's the thing, she wouldn't talk to me." I glance up as the screen door opens, and my mom comes out with a basket of buns for the burgers.

"How's studying going?" she asks, saving me from saying any more.

"It's going," I shrug, thinking of the stack of index cards with questions for my detective's exam on them. They are sitting on my nightstand collecting dust.

"Well, let me know if you need any help studying," she says, making me laugh. Once our mother always our mother, even when we're studying as an adult.

"I will."

"Time to eat, boys."

And eat we do. The mountain of food all but gone by the time we finish and sit back in our chairs with overstuffed stomachs.

"How was your night out?" Mom asks Grayson, leaning forward on her elbows, eager to hear that after one date he's ready to marry the girl and give her more grandchildren.

"It was fine." Grayson shrugs. "Nothing spectacular."

"He wore cologne," Luke says and then lifts his eyebrows. "You only wear cologne when you like a girl."

The whole table laughs. "Is that so?" Grayson says as he tugs down on Luke's baseball hat and then gives him a noogie.

"That's what they do on television."

"Are you going to see her again?" Mom fishes, relentlessly, but Grayson turns to me.

"So who do you have on the line now, Grant?"

I don't even have to look to know Mom's rolling her shoulders and getting that sour look on her face. It has become the norm when discussing my lack of settling down and giving her babies to spoil and dote over.

"I don't have anyone on the line." I glare at him.

"You always have at least one, if not four, falling hook, line, and sinker," he continues.

"That's such bullshit. I do not. I—"

"He has Emmy Reeves on the line," pipes in Grady, who then

grunts as my foot connects with his shin beneath the table.

"Emmy Reeves?" Grayson says at the same time as my mom's head snaps up to look at my dad.

"Emmy, Emmy?" she asks.

"Fuck off, Grady," I mutter, knowing he threw me to the wolves to save Grayson's ass.

But when I meet the expectant eyes of my parents, there is a gravity to Dad's expression that I haven't seen since his days on the force. It makes me realize things were probably ten times worse for Emmy than I ever imagined way back when.

As an adult, I can decipher those expressions and understand the things I couldn't comprehend as a kid.

"Yes. Emmy, Emmy."

Mom's face brightens. "Did she contact you on that FaceWorld or InstaGreet everyone is using these days?"

"FaceWorld?" Grady says before letting out an exasperated sigh. "Mom, when are you ever going to catch up with the times? It's Facebook and Instagram. I told you I'd be more than willing to teach you how to use them if you'd like."

"And I told you that I'd rather remain happy and oblivious to all the ways people can stalk me online. I'm a cop's wife, Grady. You keep your personal information off the internet so you can keep your family safe."

"Yes, Betsy." Dad nods, trying to stop this bickering before it starts. "So, Grant," he asks and gives me his investigator's stare, "how did you connect with her?"

"I saw her in town the other day." This has my parents sharing another glance. "What's that look mean?"

"Nothing," Dad responds.

"Nothing?" I repeat.

"Just surprised to hear she was in Sunnyville. Her mom liked to move around a lot." Mom's smile softens. "I used to love that little girl as if she were my own. The daughter I never had. I used to joke with your father that you were going to grow up to marry her someday."

"Of course you would think that." I roll my eyes.

"How is she? Was she well?"

I take a long sip of beer and wipe my hands on my napkin before leaning back in my chair and shrugging. "No idea. I was working the crowd at the pub crawl when I saw her."

"And?" she prompts.

"She saw me, and then she had to leave, so we didn't really get a chance to talk." Emmy's shocked eyes flash through my mind. I'm not sure why I lie to them about it.

"Are you going to see her again?" Dad asks.

"It was so quick, I didn't get her phone number. Besides, if I wanted to, I wouldn't know the first place to look for her. She was probably here for the holiday or something and is gone now."

"You are a cop, dipshit. In case you didn't know." The kick to the shin I gave Grady moments ago is returned to me under the table.

"And your point is?" I grunt, glaring at my brother.

"You have all the stalking capabilities you need at the station."

"Nah, I couldn't do that," I reply, but that doesn't mean the thought hasn't crossed my mind a time *or a hundred*.

"Stick with that thought, Grant," Dad warns. "The last thing you need is to misuse city resources while being considered for the promotion."

"And the chief speaks," Grayson adds to lighten the mood with a laugh.

"Do you have more of that cobbler?" Grady asks, effectively shifting the subject, but not before I see one last glance between Mom and Dad that leaves me lost in thought while the conversation moves on.

I was a kid when everything happened with Em, so it was hard for me to reconcile how nice her dad was with what she said happened to her. Now, I'm an adult and have seen things on the job that have taught me that even the nicest of people could do the cruelest of things.

When I apply that knowledge to the little I know of Emerson's history, I can completely understand why seeing me may have caused some of the memories to rush back.

Chairs shift as the meal ends. The table is cleared. Dishes are washed. Luke helps, but he gets more water on the floor than in the sink. The night wears on.

My hands are on the railing, my body braced as I watch the sun begin to set in the distance.

My mom steps up beside me and slides an arm around my waist. "You're awfully quiet."

"Just thinking."

"About a dispatch or about Emmy?"

I should have known she'd revisit the topic. "A little bit of everything."

"It's okay to be curious about her, Grant," she says.

"Yeah, but for some reason, I don't think she wants me to be."

"What do you mean?"

"She bolted, Mom. She saw me, and I swear the look on her face went from happy to anxious. It was as if she was scared of me."

"You're a reminder of her past she's probably chosen to forget."

"Yeah. I guess." But that still doesn't explain why she's here in Sunnyville or why I can't stop thinking about her.

"Are you going to see her again?"

"Even if I wanted to, I told you I don't have any way to—"

"And I raised self-sufficient, resourceful sons. Don't give me your excuses," she says, putting me in my place before patting my shoulder and walking back inside.

Betsy Malone has spoken.

The only woman who can put the Malone boys in line.

FOUR

Grant

WHAT AM I DOING HERE?

I glance up at the sign that reads: Doggy Style, and I know this is a mistake right off the bat. I knew she seemed quirky, but this already sounds like a bad episode of *COPS*. Police officer stumbles unknowingly into a prostitute parlor.

Walk away.

I take another step up the stairs.

This is a mistake.

I knock on the door and am greeted with the baying of dogs and nothing else. No sound of a normally functioning business. No phones ringing. No customers talking. Just a yellow clapboard house I've probably driven past a hundred times and never noticed before.

Good. She's not here. Curiosity satisfied. Time to go.

And just as I begin to walk away, I hear the pad of footsteps on the raised floorboards followed by the sound of a woman's voice shushing the dogs.

"Officer Sexy," Desi says, giving me a wide smile when she opens the door.

"Ms. Whitman." I nod.

"To what do I owe this pleasure? Let me guess. You came here to convince me that beards and tattoos are out and clean cut and uniforms are in and that we're running away and eloping. Screw our parents and friends, because all we need is each other and the clothes on our backs because love is the currency of life. Is that right?"

I stare dumfounded, trying to process all she just said before laughing and shaking my head. "I was going to say hello, but I think your story is much more entertaining."

"So, you're telling me I can still like tattoos and beards?"

"You can like whatever you want." I turn down my patrol radio as dispatch talks. "Hello, Desi Whitman."

"Hello, Grant Malone. What can I do for you? I know I'm a law-abiding citizen, so I'm not in any trouble, unless you like to use those handcuffs for other purposes." She waggles her eyebrows.

The woman is hilarious. "A real man never kisses and tells," I say with a wink.

"But he does spank and flog," she comes right back without batting an eyelash, making me choke on air.

"Jesus."

"Would you like to come in? I promise all of my clients are locked up tight."

"Should I be worried about that statement?"

"Didn't you know I'm a Dominatrix? Wanna come check out my dungeon?" I just stare at her until she cracks a smile and laughs. "Dogs. They're all dogs. I'm a groomer and pet sitter."

"Ahh, and now the company name makes sense."

"I love a little tongue-in-cheek mixed with innuendo." She shrugs. "It gets clients to call, and why be serious? Life's too short not to laugh."

"Ain't that the truth?"

"In all seriousness, what's up? Although, I seem to think I already know." She motions for me to come in, and I shake my head.

"I can't. Thank you, though, I'm about to start my shift." We fall silent as she stares and waits for me to say whatever I've come to say. "It's about Emerson."

"I assumed." She crosses her arms over her chest and leans her shoulder against the doorjamb.

"Is there any way I can get her number or you can contact her and give her mine? I'd really like to see her again."

"Why?"

"To catch up."

"To catch up, or to pry?" she asks.

"Look, all I want to do is see for myself that she's happy."

"I already told you she is. Why would you think differently?"

"You should be a police interrogator," I deflect.

"Danger and I don't mix unless you consider the jaws of a Rottweiler hazardous."

"Sounds hazardous to me." The woman has a way of changing the topic like no one I've ever met before.

"I'm sorry, Officer Malone, but I can't give you Emerson's phone number without asking her. For some reason, I think if I ask her, she would say no."

"Why's that?"

"Because I saw how she reacted to you the other day. Then, when I asked about who you were, she wouldn't tell me, so now the onus is on you to explain. Who are you to her?"

"I told you the other day. I used to know her back in grade school. Anything else would betray her confidence," I say with a smile to ease suspicion. "I'm sorry, but that's all I can tell you."

"Are you sure that's how you want to play this?"

"I'm not playing anything, just stating the facts, ma'am."

"Smooth one, Malone." She shifts to put her hands on her hips. "My money's on you being her first kiss or first love. Something like that."

"Not quite, but you're getting warmer." My radio crackles to life again, prompting me to look at my watch to see I have a few minutes left until I'm on-call. "Thanks for your time, Desi, but I have to get to work. Sorry to bug you."

"I can't give you her number without asking her, but I could invite you to a little barbecue I'm having tomorrow night. And I might be able to tell you that a certain someone will be there . . . if, you know, you'd like to stop by and say hi or something."

"Or something." After Em's warmth toward me the other day, I can only imagine how thrilled she'd be if I showed up out of the blue.

"She could use a nice guy like you around."

"What's that supposed to mean?" I ask, now curious about the company Emerson keeps.

"Nothing. Oh, make sure you take that uniform"—she gestures up and down my body—"off before you come," Desi says, completely sidestepping my question. "My friends might get a little freaked if you show up in it. They're a little free-spirited, if you catch my drift."

"Seems like most people are these days."

FIVE

Emerson

"PROMISE ME THIS BARBECUE IS NOT ONE OF YOUR elaborate ways to set me up with one of your friends." I take a bite of the carrot dipped in ranch and fight the urge to gag. *Nope*, still don't like vegetables. "Why do people eat this shit?"

"Because it's good for you," Desi says as she hums around her bright pink kitchen with a black-and-white checkered floor like she's freaking Martha Stewart.

"No. Sex is good for you. Chocolate is good for you. Wine is even better for you. They feed the soul. This crap," I say and hold up the carrot, "only serves to make you miserable."

"Says the woman who could eat nonstop every day and maintain her to-die-for figure." She rolls her eyes as she wipes her hands on a dishtowel.

I reach for the dish of M&M's and grab a handful with a grin. "Sucks to be me." I finish chewing them as she mixes something in a bowl. It looks nasty now, but I know will taste like heaven when she's done with it. It always does. "I'm serious, Des. You know I love your cooking, but it isn't enough to keep me here if you play matchmaker again. You try, and I'm gonna bail."

"Pffft. No you won't. My cooking is ten times better than anything you could make on the hot plate at your place."

She isn't making eye contact with me. That in and of itself makes me question whether I believe this whole party isn't a ruse to fix me up with one of the many people that come and go in her life. She's done it so many times, and yet, still has no shame.

"I mean it. I have plenty of men I can call up if I want a good time. I don't need your help in that department."

"Yeah. I'm well aware."

"What's that supposed to mean?" I narrow my eyes and stare at her until she looks my way.

"It means you purposely pick men you don't want to stick around."

Here we go again.

"And there's a problem with this . . . why?"

"Because, at some point in your life, you're going to want a guy who is around longer than just a couple of orgasms, that's why." Her tone is serious when I want to be anything but.

"But damn, those orgasms feel incredible."

"I'm serious, Em. What's so wrong with settling with one man instead of having many?"

I sigh audibly to let her know I'm done with this conversation. "Many? You make it sound like I sleep around. It's one man at a time . . . even I have standards. And nothing's wrong with settling down; it just isn't for me. You know me—no rings, no strings."

"You sound like a guy."

"I sound like me." I shrug. "Promise me, Des."

"Ah look, Leo's here. I'll get the door."

"Don't knock it till you try it, Cassy," I say to one of Desi's friends.

"There is no way in hell you're going to get me to jump out of a plane. No way, no how. I'd have to have about fifteen more of these to even consider it," she says as she raises her empty glass of wine and shakes her head.

"Drink up," I tease. "The offer stands, though. You wouldn't have to do anything other than enjoy the ride since you'd be strapped to me."

"That sounds like a bad porno, but it still won't get me to change my mind," she says through a laugh.

I lean back in my chair as the conversation wears on. Leo talks about his most favorite dive in Machu Pichu. Desi flits between the twenty or so guests, making everyone feel at home with her easy charm. The fairy lights in the trees add a soft glow, there's a welcome chill to the summer air, and the Carne Asada cooking on the grill smells like absolute heaven.

Even better, she's kept her promise. I don't see any unfamiliar faces she can try to set me up with. And while I don't know most of them other than a casual hello, I've at least seen them before. It's the perfect night.

"Don't you think, Emerson?" Leo's voice pulls my attention back from my thoughts, and I find eight pairs of eyes staring at me waiting for an answer.

"I'm sorry. I was in La-la Land. What am I supposed to be opining about?"

"We were talking about—"

I don't hear another word he says because, just over his left shoulder, I see Grant Malone standing in the frame of the door. He's wearing shorts and a cream-colored Henley, and his hands are shoved in his pockets while his eyes are trained on me.

I hate that the sight of him makes my breath catch and causes a flutter somewhere deep inside me. I despise that when I meet his eyes, I want to see the little boy I once knew instead of the achingly handsome man he's become. More than anything, I hate that he needs to go when all I want him to do is stay.

There's an awkward moment where everyone notices my blatant distraction and falls silent. They shift to look at Grant before, almost as one, they turn back to stare at me.

"Excuse me," I murmur as I rise from my seat, a mixture of anger and confusion rioting through my veins.

Desi broke her promise. And not only did she break her promise but she did so with the one man who made the dreams I haven't had in years come back. Last night, I woke in a blind panic: Pillow soaked with sweat, hands gripped in the sheets, and heartbeat out of control.

My rational self knows it isn't his fault, and yet, I blame him for scraping up the past, which is better left dead and buried.

If looks could kill, the one I shoot Desi would put her six feet under. The other guests murmur about who the stranger is as I make my way toward him.

"What are you doing here?" He smells incredible. Like soap and mint and why am I even noticing?

"Hi, Grant Malone. Nice to meet you." Cool as can be, he ignores the irritation in my tone and holds his hand out for me to shake.

"Seriously?" I eye his hand and then look back to him.

"Oh, you're going to remember that we know each other now? I'm sorry. I wasn't quite sure if you were still playing the 'I'm not Emmy, I don't know you' game like you were the other day."

I grit my teeth because I deserve the dig, but hell if I'm going to let him know that. "What are you doing here?"

"Okay, so now we're admitting we already know each other. That makes life much easier, don't you think?" He drops his hand. "Desi invited me. She said she's a good cook, and well, I like to eat." The shrug he gives me is casual, as if there is no other explanation needed, and that smile of his never wavers from its boyish slant. I haven't seen him in twenty years, and all the sudden, I cross paths with him twice in one week.

"In that case, she's right over there." I point to where Desi is sitting, cautiously staring our way. It's only then that I realize most of the guests are also watching us.

"That, *and* I wanted to see you again."

The words on my lips falter as I try to process why him being here has me so irritated, but it does. And just as bewilderingly, I can't stop studying him. I can't stop wondering about him and the man he's become. Is he anything like the person my mind had conjured him to be on the odd occasion I thought about him?

I can feel the weight of everyone's stares on my back and know they are wondering why I'm acting so bizarre. Normally, I'd hug whoever the new person was and welcome them into our transient circle without a second thought.

"Okay . . . well, then . . . beer is over there in the cooler and food is on the table. If you'll excuse me, I need to go to the restroom."

The kitchen is empty when I enter it, and I'm so very thankful for the silence to collect my thoughts. The irony is that the quiet doesn't last long. Someone turns on the radio and music drifts in through the open french doors, along with my friends' laughter and a voice that is unfamiliar yet familiar all at once.

I've come inside to get some distance from Grant so I can think, and yet I'm standing here studying him through the window. His dark hair and five o'clock shadow. How the sleeves of his Henley are pushed up to his elbows to showcase strong forearms. His natural ease talking with everyone and instinctual awareness of everything around him like his dad used to have when we were kids.

He's just like the little boy I used to know and nothing like him at the same time.

That's a brilliant thought, Em. He can't be both of those at the same time . . . and yet, he is.

"Watcha looking at?"

I jump back at the sound of Desi's voice and am shocked to find her standing beside me, admiring the same view I am. I was so lost in my thoughts that I hadn't noticed her come in.

"Nothing. Just thinking." Needing something to do with my hands, I turn on the faucet and begin washing them.

"Uh-huh. That nothing you're thinking of has a mighty fine ass, if I say so myself."

It's then that I realize I'm supposed to be mad at her. "You promised, Des." I drag my eyes from my hands to meet hers. "I said I was going to bail if you did this, so I guess it's time for me to leave."

"Have I tried to fix you up with him?"

"No, but I know that's only a matter of time." I cross my arms over my chest and follow her gaze. He does have a fine ass.

Oh my God. What am I thinking? I can't stare at his ass. Or notice how handsome he is. Or wonder if his hands are as strong as they appear. He was like a brother to me—my best friend—isn't it creepy if I agree with her? He's from memories I erased long ago.

And this is why I came into the house in the first place. All I wanted to do was have a few drinks and relax with my friends, but now my head's all over the place—courtesy of Grant Malone.

"I swore I wouldn't, and I intend to keep my promise." She bumps her hip against mine. "Besides, I made your favorite for dessert, so you can't leave yet."

Dessert? My ears perk up at the same time I try to fight the smile tugging at the corners of my lips. "Which kind?"

Her laugh fills the small space. "You like all my desserts, so does it really matter?"

"No." I laugh. And of course, now my mind is on whether she made a lemon tart or cheesecake or . . . crap, she's right. I'm not going anywhere. Not when her dessert is involved.

"Look, we ran into each other again, and I thought it might be nice for you guys to reconnect. What's the harm in that? He's *obviously* someone from your past. He's *obviously* interested in catching up. He's *obviously* drop dead attractive. He's—"

"You're *obviously* losing your mind."

"I meant no harm by it. I promise. I wasn't even sure he was going to show. We're typically surrounded by all my friends, so I thought it would be cool if you had your own friend here, too."

I eye her, knowing I can't argue since she invited him with nothing but good intentions in mind. "Your friends are my friends," I say exasperated.

"Exactly. He's my friend now, too. That means I was allowed to invite him." Her smile is smug as she expertly maneuvers me into a baseless argument.

"You're exhausting."

"And you love me," she says, refilling my glass of wine.

"Most days." I take a sip but my eyes are still fixated on Grant Malone, and my mind is still on the confusion seeing him again has created.

"All days."

I shrug and agree. "All days."

"Okay, well, I need to get back out there. You coming?"

"In a minute."

SIX

Emerson

"No way in hell." Grant laughs, and I hate that everything about the sound pulls on me to pay attention when I don't want to.

"C'mon. A bunch of us jump. We could teach you," Leo says with more slur than conviction after whatever round of drink he's on.

"I don't trust anyone enough, let alone myself, to jump out of an airplane and rely on them to know the parachute is for sure going to deploy."

Chicken.

I don't say the word aloud, but I think it, and for some reason reverting back to sounding like a kid makes me feel a smidgen better.

"Sounds like you have trust issues," Leo says.

"Yeah, how is that, Grant?" Desi pipes in while I just keep my head down and focus on picking at my nail polish. "You can risk your life every day doing your job, but you're scared to skydive?"

"My partner has my back," he states.

"So, you trust your partner, but you wouldn't trust a skilled instructor to tandem jump with you? They control the jump, pull the chute, and make sure you land safely."

Goddamnit, Desi.

I see the maneuvering going on here, and I don't want any part of the set up. I shift in my seat and try to find an out that won't be so obvious.

"Tell me something, Desi," Grant says as he leans forward and puts his elbows on his knees. "When was the last time you jumped?"

"Me?" She laughs. "You're all out of your minds. There's no way I would trust someone with my life."

"And you just proved my point," he says, and Desi just laughs harder. But that charming chuckle she has, which typically has all the men sidling up next to her, doesn't seem to affect Grant.

Talk quiets some as we finish our dessert and Leo brings another round of drinks for those who are ready.

"I swear every time Desi invites me over, I leave having gained ten pounds," Cassy groans as she adjusts the waistband of her pants and then points an accusing finger my way. "And, of course, you're going to have another helping and grin the whole time you're eating it."

My hand stops mid-cut into another slice of cheesecake, but the guilt is only momentary. It's too damn irresistible to pass up.

"Bitch," Desi playfully comments.

"You always did love dessert." It's Grant's quiet statement that has our friends turning their heads in his direction, the slow realization that he's from the past I never talk about settling over them.

But he isn't looking at any of them. When I glance up, his gaze is on me. Our eyes meet, and for a brief moment, I allow myself to wonder what it is he sees when he looks at me. His soft smile exudes warmth, but it's his eyes that draw me into places and times and thoughts that don't belong in this lifetime.

There's a stirring in my belly that shouldn't be there. The same one that has resurfaced each time the two of us have interacted in some way or another over the past few hours.

I need to stop thinking about the gold flecks in his brown eyes and how he still has the hint of a scar on his chin from when he tried to jump his BMX off a homemade ramp.

Familiarity.

That's what he is, and it's something I'm not used to outside the world I've created.

It's too much. Too unexpected. Too close.

"You're right. I don't need this extra piece," I say as I stand abruptly and begin to clear the dirtied forks that were discarded when the paper plates were tossed into the fire. My avoidance of eye contact only serves to compound the awkwardness and reinforce that I'm not acting anything like my normal self.

Once in the kitchen, I do things to busy myself. Wipe down the counters that have already been cleaned. Restack the dishwasher. Anything to settle the discord I feel.

"Emerson." The deep rumble of Grant's voice cuts through my thoughts. My hands still. My heart races. My feet turn to face him. "Is everything okay?"

Yes. No. *I don't know.*

I meet his eyes and struggle with how to respond. "I worked a long time to make this life, Grant." My voice is shaky, and I hate that it is, but there's no way I can disguise the emotion.

"Okay." He draws the word out as he cocks his head to the side, brows narrowing as if he's trying to understand. "I wasn't trying to interfere."

"Then what do you want?"

"To get to know you again. To be friends. I don't know, you're *my Emmy* . . ."

The endearment from our childhood tears into parts of me I didn't know existed anymore. "You being here . . ." I struggle to explain feelings I'm not even sure I understand. "You're from another place and time I've tried to forget."

He takes a step closer and leans against the counter, but his eyes never leave mine as laughter from outside floats in. He nods slowly, saying, "I didn't know that my being here would upset you. I'm sorry. It's just that since I saw you the other day, I haven't been able to get you out of my head. I thought maybe we could be friends again. That's all, Emerson. Nothing more."

"I can't be who you want me to be." My thoughts explode into words I can't believe I've said and want to take back immediately. For some reason, this conversation . . . *he* makes me nervous.

"Who's that? I don't want you to be anything."

"A victim," I whisper.

Those two words knock the wind from his sails. His shoulders sag, and he roughs a hand through his hair before releasing an audible sigh. "Em . . ."

"I don't need a hero," I explain, thinking of all the times he had talked about someday being like his dad, a hero who saves everyone from everything.

"No one said you did." The gold in his eyes burns bright as his temper surfaces. "I'm confused. Did I do something to offend you? Did I . . . Christ, never mind. Nothing's worth it if it's this much work. Nice seeing you again, Em. Have a nice life."

"No. Wait," I say against my better judgment, causing him to stop in the doorway and face me.

Sadness fuses with the anger in his eyes, and the expression on his face mirrors everything I feel but can't express.

"Am I staying or going, Em? You decide."

Words don't come, and we stare at each other for a few moments before he nods in resignation and leaves.

The front door shuts. Leo turns the music louder outside as Desi begins swinging her hips, but I remain in the kitchen with my chest hurting and my perfectly crafted world spinning off its axis. Even the half eaten cheesecake on the counter holds no appeal to me.

A part of me wants to chase after him and apologize. I was more than rude, and he deserves better. The other part of me has finally recognized the emotion I was feeling but couldn't put a finger on. *It's fear.*

I'm scared to death.

Grant scares me.

Out of habit, I run a hand over the inside of my arm and feel the ridges there. The reminders that fear can be overcome.

Drawing in a fortifying breath, I debate whether I should go back outside, drink some more wine, and waste the rest of the night away.

Something tells me that just might exacerbate the traitorous feelings I'm having. Alcohol, Grant, and fear are a dangerous combination that just might jostle things I've long forgotten and never want to remember again.

I've spent the last twenty years shutting myself off from all emotion—all feelings when it comes to anyone of the opposite sex—and in a span of one week's time, I've let Grant change that.

My black-and-white world has color seeping into its edges.

I love and hate it all at the same time.

It makes me feel alive inside when, until now, I hadn't realized I had been dead.

SEVEN

Emerson

"NONE FOR ME. THANK YOU, THOUGH." I PUT MY HAND UP to cover my glass as Chris tries to pour wine into it. *Again.*

"C'mon, Em. Just because we're working, doesn't mean we can't relax some and have a drink."

His cologne overpowers the scent of food in the restaurant, and there's a soft whistle in his nose every time he inhales. I try not to focus on it, but now that I've heard it, I can't unhear it.

"Where were we?" I clear my throat and lift the profit and loss statement we were talking about before the waiter came with the bottle of wine. This, of course, came after the three glasses he had already had.

"I forget. Where exactly were we?" he says in a playful voice as he scoots closer so we're shoulder to shoulder. *Again.*

Trying the same move I've done several times tonight already, I shift in my seat to put some distance between us. When I do, Chris reaches out and puts his hand over mine.

Alarm bells sound off in my head, but I do my best to appear unaffected. It isn't the first time a man has tried to flirt with me when I didn't encourage it.

I nonchalantly pull my hand out from under his to pick up the income statement. "We were talking about last year's net income of Blue

Skies compared to the proposed loan amount."

"Yes, we were." He reaches across me to pick up an untouched glass of water, his elbow grazes against my breasts. I chock it up to being an accident, but I don't like it one bit. "But I think it's better suited if we talk about you and me."

"What about *you and me*?" I ask, befuddled where this conversation is going.

"You know I'm the only loan officer in town who would take a chance on you, right?" His voice is low, and he's so close that I can smell the wine on his breath.

"Yes, and as I've said before, I appreciate that."

"Nothing is guaranteed though."

"I know." I nod and shift my body again when he leans in closer. "Oh, you know what I forgot to ask about? What's it called? Crap. I forgot. Can you get the other papers off the seat?" I feign stupidity to try to get him to go back to his side of the booth. His excuse that he needed to explain a calculation in order to sit beside me was clearly a ruse.

"Forget the questions, Emerson. I know one surefire way to make certain you get that loan."

"Hmm? What's that?" I ask without looking at him, even though I'm pretty damn sure what he's going to suggest next.

"C'mon." He chuckles and the sound of it makes my skin crawl. "I'm always up for a little game of hard to get, but don't you think we're past that point?"

I choose my next words wisely because I'm in a precarious position. Do I tell him to back the hell off and piss off the only banker who would take a chance on me? Do I do that and risk losing my loan? Or do I just bite my tongue, politely refuse him, and bide my time?

"I'm sorry. I don't understand. " I decide to pick the second option and hope it works when every part of me begs to do the first one.

"This loan process would go much smoother and be a little more certain, if you'd just give into our chemistry."

I turn to look at him and startle when I find his face within inches of mine. His eyebrows are raised and his stare is unwavering.

"Let me get this straight. You're saying that, if I sleep with you, my loan will get approved?" I try to hide the disgust I feel and wonder if he senses it. Then again, it seems he's in an alternative universe if he's interpreted my indifference to his advances as my being interested.

His chuckle rumbles in the small space around us. "Now, now, I didn't say that, did I?" The smirk on his face and suggestion in his eyes says he meant exactly that. "Don't go putting words in my mouth."

"And if I don't *give into our* chemistry . . .?" His shrug is the only answer he gives. "I have a preapproval letter, Chris. The lender has already told me that so long as I get them the information they need and it's accurate, they'll give me the loan."

"Preapproval letters aren't a loan approval," he states, eyes hardening.

"I'm aware," I say with confidence while hating that his veiled threat only serves to intensify my anxiety over getting my loan.

We stare at each other for a few seconds. I refuse to back down or be intimidated by him. The man clearly isn't the type of person I thought he was.

"Oh my. Is it already six o'clock? Where did the time go? I need to get going." I begin putting the papers into a messy stack as a way to show him I'm serious about needing to leave. He doesn't budge. "Excuse me, Chris, can you please let me get out of the booth?"

He narrows his eyes and tilts his head to the side as he studies me. "I need the rest of this information by tomorrow night." His voice is cold when moments ago it was warmth laced with suggestion.

"Tomorrow night?" I laugh as if he's joking but then realize he's not. Panic hits me. It's going to take me all night to pull this together. "I don't understand. You told me I had until next Friday."

"Yeah, well, plans changed. I need it by tomorrow night."

"You're serious." I state the obvious, still dumbfounded by the personality switch he just flicked over to the *asshole* side.

"Deadly. *Unless of course* . . ." He leaves the words unspoken, but his fingertip trailing down my bicep says it all for him.

I yank my arm away and start scooting myself out of the booth, my hips hitting his to try to push him along. He relents but makes sure to stand well within my personal space as I gather the rest of my paperwork. I hate the feeling of him watching me as I bend over to grab my purse and briefcase from the inside of the booth.

All I want to do is get the hell out of here but I grit my teeth, force myself to face him, and sound cordial.

“Thank you for the dinner and for answering my questions. I’ll do my best to get the documents to you by tomorrow night.”

“Don’t try, Emerson. Make it happen.”

With bile in my throat and a film of disgust coating my skin, I walk out of the restaurant as quickly as I can.

EIGHT

Emerson

HOW COULD I BE SO STUPID?

How could I have been so wrapped up in making sure I understood everything needed for my loan that I missed the signs Chris was giving off?

I press the pedal down harder. The speedometer hits seventy miles per hour, but it isn't fast enough.

First Chris.

Then the realization that I have no other options but to deal with him and his creep factor.

The needle hits eighty.

Nothing will ever be enough to outrun that feeling I get every time someone expects me to bend to their will. To be subservient. To play the victim.

Never again.

No way. No how. *Screw that.*

The long road is stretched out before me. Just fields, grape vines, trees, and flat asphalt, making me feel as if I were the only person on the face of the earth.

Hitting the outskirts of town, I push the envelope of safety, but when you jump out of airplanes for a living, that envelope is harder to breach than for most.

With each mile I put between myself and the restaurant, I feel the stress begin to shed. The pressure of making sure all my documents are in order so I don't lose the loan because of some stupid mistake eases. And with the clearing of my mind comes the clarity.

Despite it being so much easier to pick up and move when people started asking too many questions about my past, I let Desi talk me into coming back to Sunnyville. My need to put away the gypsy life I have been living and settle down to plant roots for myself was just a thought back then, yet, I'd been willing to try.

Then I found Blue Skies, which was in desperate need of some TLC, and decided that the girl, who liked to go where the wind blows her, suddenly wanted something permanent. A business. A fixture. Something to be proud of.

My desire to own Blue Skies and make it one hundred percent mine had made me stay to fight for something.

And fighting is what I'm doing.

The sirens come out of nowhere. Blue and red lights flash to tell me my fun—my reprieve—has been compromised and is about to be shut down.

"Shit." I pound a fist against the wheel, knowing this will be my second ticket in six months. The monetary fine. Points on my driving record. The increase in my insurance. All the consequences ghost through my mind as I pull to a stop and wait for Officer Asshole to walk up to the driver side and read me the riot act. I may even pull up the hem of my shorts some so when he's met with an eyeful of tanned and toned thighs, he might be distracted.

It's worth a shot.

"License and registration, please."

I look up to the gravelly voice standing outside my window and am met with my own reflection in his mirrored lenses. "Hi, Officer. How is your day going?" I'll try sweet-talking. I'm not good at it, but at least I'm not going down without a fight.

"License and registration, please, ma'am."

"What seems to be the problem?"

"How about going ninety in a fifty mile an hour zone."

"Oh. Was I really going that fast?" I feign innocence.

"Are you in a hurry?" I stare at him doe-eyed, unable to make my synapses fire so I can come up with some kind of brilliant excuse. "That's considered reckless driving. Endangerment of others. Should I go on?"

With each offense my eyes are seeing dollar signs that my wallet doesn't have.

The radio handset strapped to his shoulder sparks to life, and he responds in some kind of code that sounds like a foreign language. "No, Officer. The thing is I left my house in a hurry—"

"I think we've established that fact."

I look in my rearview mirror as another police car pulls up behind his, and my palms grow sweaty. Am I that dangerous that they need two units to handle this call?

"Anyway, like I was saying, I left in such a hurry that I didn't grab my wallet. I don't have my license."

He angles his head, and even though I can't see his eyes behind the lenses, I can feel them dressing me down. "Then your registration?"

"This isn't exactly my car." I hear the door of the second unit shut behind us.

And the award for Flake of the Year, ladies and gentlemen, goes to Emerson Reeves.

"Whose car is it then?"

"Blue Skies—the company I work for."

"Do you need any help, Off—*Emerson*?"

That voice. *His voice* has my whole body wanting to seize up and melt at the same time.

"You know this woman?" Officer Asshole says as I look to where Grant stands in his dark blue uniform with the setting sun at his back.

"I do."

"You want to handle this call?"

"Sure," Grant says, and after how things went between us the last time I saw him, I'm not sure if I'm relieved or worried.

"Thanks. You'll be saving me from John's wrath, coming home

late from shift again."

"Husbands," Grant plays along and shrugs.

"Exactly." He lifts his chin toward the back of the car, and the two men step back there for a few minutes. They speak in hushed tones, before Grant steps toward me and the other officer climbs into his car.

"Christ, Emerson. Ninety?" There's a disapproving tone to his voice, but under it is something akin to amusement. "Seriously? You're lucky Lyle didn't haul you off to jail for reckless driving."

"We weren't quite done, but I'm sure that might have been an option."

"It *is* pretty serious. And hauling you off is a valid option for the safety of not only you but also everyone else on the road."

"But there is no one else on the road. No harm. No foul. Can I go?"

"You could have gotten yourself killed."

He takes off his sunglasses and hooks them in his shirt. I stare at them hanging from his neck because it's so much easier than looking him in the eyes. But he stands there, hands braced on the frame of my window and waits for me to meet his gaze.

While I had been certain sweet talking would have worked with Officer Lyle, at least until Grant mentioned the other officer's husband, I have absolutely no idea what to say to ease the situation.

"You always had a flair for the dramatic." The words are out before I realize it, and I hate myself for being the first to bring up the past when I don't want him to do the same.

"Dramatic is one thing, Em. Doing my job is another."

"Oh, I see what you're doing here. You're mad at me for the other night when you have no right to be and—"

"This has nothing to do with the other night and everything to do with the law and me enforcing it."

He always was a stickler for the rules. The longer this conversation goes on, the more irritated I become, and a big part of me wants it to continue. If I'm pissed at him, then I'll want him to go away instead of wondering what it would be like to see him again like I have been.

"Are you seriously going to arrest me?"

"Give me a good reason why you're in such a hurry you need to go ninety miles an hour."

Because I can.

The truth almost escapes but I stop myself before it does. Our eyes meet. Hold. Assess. Ask. And then I answer.

"I'm having a female emergency." I ignore the fact that I'm wearing skimpy white shorts no woman on her period would be caught dead wearing and give him the number one response guaranteed to make a man uncomfortable.

His lips quirk for a moment before he leans down so that his elbows rest on the door. "And?"

"Well, I was rushing to the store."

"And that's why you were going so fast?"

"Yes." I nod, hating that he isn't shying away like any man in his right mind would.

"What were you going to the store to buy? Tampons? Monistat? Astroglide?" he deadpans.

If I could die a thousand deaths right now I would. My cheeks burn, and I'd give anything to crawl under the steering wheel to avoid having to make eye contact with him. "Yes."

"All three? That's a feminine emergency if I've ever heard of one."

Already invested in my lie, I have no choice but to continue it. I clear my throat, but my voice comes out in a broken rasp. "Tampons. Just tampons."

"I see." He nods slowly. "Funny thing is, your car is heading in the wrong direction. All the drugstores are back that way." He throws his thumb over his shoulder as I cringe at my mistake. "But being new in town and all that, maybe you got turned around, huh?"

There's a smirk playing at the corners of his mouth while my embarrassment only intensifies. "Yes, that's definitely why." I squirm in my seat to try to sell it when I know he's probably not buying any of this. "Can I go now, please?"

"Go? To the drugstore? Of course you can. I wouldn't want your *situation* to worsen because of all this time we're wasting. Tell you what, Em, if it's such an emergency that you were willing to risk life and limb to get there, I think I should give you a police escort."

"No! That's okay—I—"

"Lights and sirens. The whole shebang all the way to . . . CVS, or is it Rite Aid? Which store has the brand you prefer?"

"A police escort, Grant? Really?" Irritation mixes with disbelief.

"Now that you're a resident of Sunnyville, I'm at your service. Here to protect and to serve." He flashes a grin that tells me he knows exactly what I'm doing and plans to make me pay for it.

And pay for it I do. With lights and sirens. Parading me the long way through town until we pull into the CVS parking lot.

His cruiser parks beside me, and I have every intention of running inside and buying some damn tampons I don't currently need just to get him off my back. So, I'm completely mortified when he climbs out of his car as I get out of mine.

"What are you doing?" I ask, eyes flicking toward the random people who are staring at the flashing lights and the police officer standing in front of me.

"Let's go."

I stiffen when he places a hand on the small of my back and starts ushering me closer to the entrance. He nods and murmurs a few hellos to people who address him by name, all the while I'm trying to figure how far we're going to carry on this charade. He's obviously trying to prove a point while at the same time, willing to make my life miserable in retaliation for my rudeness the other night.

When we enter the store, I immediately begin to scan the directory signs above the aisles to see where the feminine hygiene products are located. Anything so I can put distance between myself and him and this asinine predicament.

"Not so fast. Where are you going?" he asks as he grabs my bicep, keeping me in place.

"To find what I need."

"No worries. I have you covered. It's an emergency after all," he says, leading me to the front of the store.

"What are you—"

"Shh. It's under control." He points to his badge and smiles.

"No. It's okay. I can find them on my own—"

"Excuse me, where are the tampons?" Grant asks the service clerk at the front of the store. Some teenage boys waiting in line snicker, and the young clerk's face immediately turns bright red as he stutters a response. "Better yet, we're in an emergency situation here. *A ninety mile an hour* type of emergency. Can you get on the PA and ask one of your associates to bring up a box for us so this young lady doesn't have to search them out."

Oh. My. God. Is he seriously going to do this?

Yes, he is.

That irritation I was hoping for just hit full force.

"I can get them myself," I grit out between clenched teeth.

"Oh, no need to. He's got it under control." He lifts his chin to the cashier, who looks less than thrilled to be asked to do this. "Go on," he urges the clerk.

"Can I get some assistance to the front please?" the clerk asks, his teenage voice cracking on the overhead speakers. "I need a box of tampons brought up."

"Tell them it's an emergency," Grant says as the kid looks over to me and then down to my pelvis before realizing what he's doing and snapping his head up, more flustered than ever.

"It's an emergency." His voice booms over the PA system and draws the eyes of some of the customers waiting at the photo counter.

"Thank you." Grant flashes a huge grin his way. "Oh, wait. What brand do you like, Emerson?"

"You're joking, right?" I sputter.

"Only if you're joking." He lifts his eyebrows as he throws down the gauntlet to see if I'm going to come clean or keep lying. The problem is that I think if I don't continue, he might really haul me off to jail to prove a point. "I don't think generic will do for such a dire situation. Brand?"

"Tampax," I say defiantly.

"Tampax," he relays to the clerk, whose cheeks are burning brighter with each second that passes. When the clerk continues to stare at Grant as if he's crazy, which I'm beginning to think he is, Grant points to the phone in his hand. "Go on. Let them know so they don't bring the wrong one and then we have to start this whole process all over again."

The clerk goes to protest and then realizes that it's in his best interest to relay the message. "To the associate in the, er, woman's aisle . . . please make it Tampax."

I stare at Grant and his smug grin and know there is no way I'm going to let him get away with this. Funny thing is, I'm a woman, tampons don't embarrass me . . . but I know something that sure as hell will embarrass him.

"Are you still having that problem?" I loudly ask Grant, getting the blank look from him I was banking on.

"Problem?"

"Yes. You know . . ." I cringe and give him a sympathetic look before turning to the clerk. "While your associate is at it, can they grab one more thing for Officer Malone?"

The clerk's eyes widen. "Can't he go and get it himself?"

"No. He can't. He has a suspect in the car, and department policy says he can't be more than one hundred feet away from him at all times." I push Grant back as he tries to step forward and interrupt. "Please?"

"Yeah. Sure." The clerk looks at Grant and then back to me, uncertain how he became the ball in our ping-pong match.

"He needs his Viagra."

"Viagra?" The clerk's voice is suddenly soprano.

"Emers—"

"Don't be embarrassed, Grant. A lot of guys have trouble getting it up." I pat Grant's arm and return the smug smile as the muscle in his jaw clenches.

"Em," he warns.

"Viagra," I reiterate to the clerk ignoring the hand Grant squeezes on my bicep. "He's really embarrassed. I mean I wore lacy lingerie, high heels . . . everything, and he still couldn't get hard."

If the clerk's cheeks could get any redder, they would. "Th-that's a prescription. The phar-pharmacy—"

"Emers—"

"The urologist already called it in." I cut Grant off again, smile sweetly at the clerk, and point to the phone. "So just get on the PA and tell the pharmacy that you need the prescription of Viagra for Grant Malone to be brought up to the front."

Grant's hand tenses, and I swear I hear him mutter *son of a bitch* as the clerk stares at me as if I've lost my mind. I nod in encouragement to him.

He picks up the phone and keeps his eyes on mine the whole time he speaks on the PA system. "Uh, pharmacy, I need the prescription of Viagra to be brought up to the front."

"For Grant Malone," I say.

"The Viagra is under the name Grant Malone." His voice booms overhead.

Snickers of laughter from somewhere in the store echo up to us. The teenagers in line shift their feet and try to hide their smiles. The older lady standing at the Hallmark cards glances my way and then shakes her head in sympathy. I can only wonder if the sympathy is because I'm having a period emergency while wearing white shorts or because my assumed boyfriend can't get it up.

"Nice try, Malone, but I think I won this round," I mutter under my breath.

"Excuse me, Brian, is it?" Grant says to the clerk after looking at his nametag.

"Yes."

"Can you tell your associate that Emerson here needs the largest box of tampons you have?"

"The extra-large size box on the tampons?" he asks and looks at Grant with wide eyes.

"Yes." Grant smiles.

"Associate, please make that an extra-large box of tampons." Brian hangs the phone up and is about to turn his back when I speak.

"Brian, one more thing."

"You're joking right?" he asks exasperated.

"No, it's important. Pretty please?" I turn on my charm and bat my lashes.

"*What*?"

"The Viagra, can you make sure it's the extra strength?"

Poor Brian looks at Grant and then back to me for what seems like the tenth time. "You two are crazy. I don't want to be in the middle of your weird fight. Use the PA yourself if you need anything else." He holds the phone out to me. I'm more than tempted to make my request but figure we've caused enough of a scene, and by all accounts, I think I won this round.

"Thank you for your assistance, Brian, but we're good now," Grant says as he eases his grip on my arm and slides his hand down to the small of my back. I step away from him with the low hum of his chuckle in my ears.

Asshole.

The awkward tension only builds between us as the seconds tick by. Grant chats amicably with the cashier about how nice the weather is while the poor kid fidgets restlessly and refuses to meet his gaze. I glance around the store, waiting impatiently for the associate to bring the Tampax to the counter and wondering what is going to happen to my Viagra request.

Finally, the associate makes her way down the main aisle with the familiar blue-and-green box and holds it up to the male clerk. "Is this what you were looking for?"

Poor Brian blushes a darker red as Grant steps forward and takes the box from the associate. "Thank you, Eileen. You're looking wonderful as always," Grant says, prompting her to pat down her mass of gray curls. "How are the grandbabies? Is little Mario still as rambunctious as ever?"

Impatient to get the hell out of here, I force myself to watch the exchange between the two. Grant is holding the box of tampons in his hand, casual as can be, which is both surprising and unnerving. Not only am I privy to his personable skills with the nice lady who works at CVS but also I'm in the position to notice how perfectly well Grant's uniform pants hug his ass.

And what a mighty fine ass it is.

Stop it. Here he is dragging me through this stupid charade, and instead of being mad at him, I'm checking out his ass? Again.

But it's not just his ass. I'm also admiring the way his uniform sleeves hug his biceps and how broad his shoulders are.

But this is Grant Malone. He's the little boy I used to giggle with and play cops and robbers with. He was like the brother I never had . . . so how is it possibly okay to find him this damn attractive?

It isn't.

That's the plain and simple answer. I can't find him attractive. I can like him, but he's off limits. He knows too much. Him just being here reminds me of *before* too much.

He's too close when I've never allowed anyone to be.

I can be mad at him. I can be pissed as all hell that a little while ago he was threatening to haul me off to jail because I was a *smidgen* over the speed limit. I can also be livid that he called my bluff.

That's all I can be.

Oh, and I can be damn proud that I just met him tit for tat with his little plan to embarrass me.

"Right, Em?" His gravelly voice cuts through my thoughts—*of him.*

"Right, what?" I must look like a deer caught in headlights, and Eileen just smiles softly.

"He's such a good boy, isn't he?" Eileen says as she pats my arm.

I smile with so much saccharine that my teeth are going to rot. "He is."

And then she steps into Grant and lowers her voice. "No need to be embarrassed, dear. Having trouble getting an erection can sometimes be caused by stress." She pats his arm much like she did mine. "Try some good old fashioned pornography. I may have experience in knowing it does the trick." She winks and gives a knowing smile that leaves me biting back my snicker before she walks off as if she didn't just talk about porn.

Way to go, Eileen!

Grant blushes for the first time during this whole charade and blinks as if he's trying to make sure he actually heard her say what she said. I take his stunned silence and use it to my advantage by pushing a ten dollar bill across the counter to Brian. The poor kid is standing there trying to act like he didn't hear the exchange when he clearly did.

"I got it," Grant says with authority, taking my money off the counter and shoving it back in my hand.

"I can pay for my own—"

"No one said you couldn't." His lips quirk into a cocky smile, a clear indication he's regained his footing. "But it's the least I could do to help out with your . . . situation."

"Apparently, porn is what will help you with yours," I say nonchalantly, needing to get one last cheap shot in, before I turn and walk outside to wait for him in the fading daylight.

Within minutes, Grant strolls out of the drugstore with a bag in his hand and stops before me. We stare at each other for a moment.

"Viagra, Emerson? Really?" he asks, disdain owning his tone.

"I can go back in and wait for your prescription, if you'd like?" I bat my lashes.

"Cute. Very cute."

"You're not the only one who can dish it out."

"So it seems."

A new set of looky-loos slow their pace as they walk by, curious what crime I committed, and despite my little show inside, I'm not a fan of being the center of attention.

"Are we done now?" I huff as I hold my hand out for the bag.

We wage a visual war on the sidewalk in front of CVS. The lights on his squad car are still flashing and lighting up his face as he looks down at my hand and then back to me. "You tell me, Emerson. Are we done yet?"

"It's just a box of tampons."

"Oh, this is about so much more than *just a box of tampons*," he says, voice serious, eyes locked on mine. We stare at each other for a minute more, both of us wondering who will give in first. My wanting to believe the lie I tell myself that this is only about feminine hygiene products against his waiting for me to realize I'm wrong.

"May I have the bag, please?"

"Of course you can, so long as we get one thing clear." He steps closer to me and leans in. "Nothing's changed, Em. Don't you remember? I can always tell when someone is lying. Especially you. That's one thing about me that's still the same, so it's best you don't forget that. Otherwise, next time will be a whole lot worse than a box of tampons you don't need."

I grit my teeth as he leans back, those brown eyes of his laden with humor as he places the bag in my hand. "Is that a threat, Officer?"

"No. It's a promise."

NINE

Grant

I GLANCE AROUND THE QUIET CUL-DE-SAC AS I STEP OUT OF MY cruiser. The street is a perfect picture of fictional Mayberry with its pristine cut lawns, blooming flowerbeds, tidied houses, bikes left on driveways, glimpses of swing sets above the tops of backyard fences.

Nate eyes me as we double-check the address of the house in front of us: 12662 Serenity Court. It's tan stucco with brown trim, above average in size. A minivan is parked in the garage with the door open, and an SUV is parked behind it. The garage is clean but cluttered with toys on one side and a table saw and drill press on the other.

Normal.

But that's the problem. Sometimes it's the normal that's deceptive.

Nate runs the plates while I keep an eye on our surroundings. When the check comes back clean, we exit the vehicle. I glance over to the neighboring house to the right and nod at the woman peeking out the window from behind the curtains.

"Is she the one who reported it?" Nate asks as we cautiously make our way up the driveway.

I nod to tell him yes but don't confirm it aloud. "The caller wishes to remain anonymous."

"Mm-hmm."

It isn't surprising considering the call is a 10-16—possible domestic disturbance with a minor involved.

The pathway is lined with river rocks. Interspersed into the multi-colored gray stones are some that are painted. There are a few that look like ladybugs, others have indiscernible drawings on them, and still others with words written across the top, all obviously done by a child.

For the briefest of moments, I flash back to being a kid and making fun of Emmy for painting the rocks on the side of her house. Just like a thousand other kids have done. There's no correlation. Yet, I find it funny how she's been gone for so long but, in the last few weeks, it's as if she's everywhere and there is a memory of her in everything I see.

Nate's knock on the door is loud against the afternoon quiet. Standing about ten feet back with one hand on the butt of my gun, I wait for someone to answer, listening for the slightest sounds of distress inside the house as my eyes scan back and forth over my surroundings.

"Who is it?" a male voice asks on the other side of the door.

"Sunnyville Police Department. We'd like to speak with you for a moment," Nate says.

"About what?"

"Just want to make sure everything is all right in there. Neighbors heard some screaming going on, so we're going door-to-door around the cul-de-sac checking each house to make sure everything is okay," Nate lies in perfect good-cop fashion.

"Everything's fine here. Thanks for your concern."

"That's good to hear, sir, but I need you to open up so we can check for ourselves. It's a procedural thing."

There's movement to the right of me that catches my eye. A blonde-haired little girl peeks over the windowsill so all I can see is from her nose up. I smile softly to try to let her know we're here to help. She stares at me before ducking out from beneath the curtain and disappearing from sight.

"Jesus Christ," the man on the other side of the door mutters before the deadbolt slides and the door opens about a foot. "Everything's fine. See? Are you happy?" His voice is loaded with irritation as we get a glimpse of him for the first time. I take a mental rundown: Dark hair, blue eyes, a drip of sweat sliding down his temple. He's wearing a dress shirt with the sleeves rolled up to the elbows and tie loosened around his neck. His shirttail is untucked, and as hard as I try, I can't get a clear view of his hands so I can see what his knuckles look like.

"Thank you, sir. Your name please?"

"Ren Davis, but people just call me Davis."

"Thank you, Mr. Davis," Nate says, taking a step closer and placing a hand on the door to open it a little farther.

The man grunts in disdain. "You think I'm lying?"

"No, sir," Nate's smile is broad and disarming. "I'd just hate to lose my job for not crossing all the T's and dotting all the I's, if you know what I mean?"

"Goddamn government workers," he grumbles.

"Exactly." Nate moves his free hand from the butt of his gun and holds up two fingers behind his back.

There are two other people he can see in the house.

"I didn't hear any yelling."

"I didn't ask if you did," Nate responds, making sure the man understands he's on our time; we're not on his. "May I see the rest of the people in the house?"

The man's head startles at the request. "I'm home al—"

"I just saw a little girl run by," Nate interrupts. "I'd like to speak with her."

Davis exhales loudly, his irritation written all over his face before he steps back to reveal more of the scene behind him. There is a dark stain on the carpet where it looks like the plant sitting on the pony wall at his back had been knocked over and the dirt has yet to be vacuumed. From what I can see of it, the house seems clean, which makes that smear of dirt stick out.

"Keely, get over here," he yells, feet shifting, jaw clenched. With his movement, I can see one of his knuckles has blood on it and the others look a bit red. Nate notices it as well, and he slides a glance my way as I take a step forward.

"And your wife, too, please."

"My wife isn't—"

"There are two cars in the driveway, sir," Nate explains. "So I'd like to make sure she's okay, too."

"Was it that damn lady next door who called?" he asks. "She's so goddamn nosy. Always getting in our business. Last year, our dog pissed on her begonias and killed them so now she's out to get me back."

"No phone call," Nate says. "Like I said, we're just going door to door and checking to make sure everyone is okay."

Davis eyes both of us. His skepticism is etched in the lines of his face, but he shakes his head and calls back into the house. "Amelia. The police are here and want to make sure you're okay. Can you come down here to show them you are?" He steps back. "You happy?"

"Thank you, sir," I say, entering the conversation for the first time just as the blonde-haired girl peers out from the corner of the wall behind him. "What's your name?" I ask softly as I kneel to get on her level.

The poor thing is scared to death. Her eyes flicker to her father and then to me and then back to her father. She waits for him to nod before she responds. "Ke-Keely."

"Can you come here for a second, Keely?" I ask as her mother comes up behind her and places a protective *and* trembling hand on her shoulder. Keely looks back to her dad and waits again for him to consent before she slowly approaches the door. She reaches the threshold and just stands her hand clutching the arm of a worn teddy bear. There are matching smears of dirt on her cheeks that tell me she's been wiping away tears.

Her mother comes forward also but seems much more timid than her daughter. Amelia's hair is a mess and her red-rimmed eyes have black smudges under them from where her makeup has run. She crosses her arms over her chest to steady the shaking of her hands. Even though she remains several feet behind her husband, she never looks at him.

Alcohol or abuse.

It's my immediate assumption. It's definitely one of the two.

"Did you paint those super cool rocks over there?" I ask Keely, using the same soothing voice as before in an effort to earn her trust.

"Me and my mommy did." She barely nods, but it's enough for me to try to coax her away from her parents to make sure she is okay and not in danger.

"Can you show me which ones you did? I bet I can guess because they are so pretty like you."

She gives me a ghost of a smile, and the fleeting glimmer of happiness in her sad eyes breaks my heart. She looks up to her dad, who does not seem to be too pleased with my request. Those are the breaks, *asshole*. "Can I?"

He nods at her before shooting a glance over his shoulder to his wife.

Keely wrings her hands as she takes a few steps before looking back at her dad as if she's going to get in trouble. I gently place my hand on her shoulder to try to lead her over to where the majority of the rocks are—far enough away that I can ask her questions to make sure she's okay. My gut tells me she is—*for now*—but her mom's well-being is a whole other story.

"Which ones did you paint?" I ask as I squat back down.

She angles her head to the side and stares at me without responding, the willingness to talk to me moments before suddenly dissipating into the distance I put between her and her mother.

"I bet you painted that caterpillar there," I say, pointing to a rock and hoping I'm correct in my guess. The corners of her mouth softly turn up and her back straightens with pride. "And that one there?" I wait for her eyes to find what I'm pointing at. "That butterfly is so pretty. Is pink your favorite color?"

She nods but still doesn't talk.

I glance over to where Nate is talking to Mr. and Mrs. Davis, who are still standing in the doorway, and hope he is able to get Mrs. Davis alone for a moment.

"Ahh, there's a K on that one. I bet you painted that for your name."

"Yeah." Her voice is so quiet, and yet, I can hear the fear woven through it.

"That's what I thought. That definitely looks like a ten-year-old painted it."

She laughs, but there is no sound. "I'm not ten, though."

"How old are you then?"

"I'm five."

"No. Way. I thought for sure you were already driving. Are you sure the car in the driveway isn't yours?"

Another crack of a smile is followed by an adamant shake of her head.

"And that rock there . . . is that one of your teddy bear?" I ask, pointing to the rock and then her ratty bear.

She nods. "His name is Nemo."

"Nemo?" I smile. "I thought Nemo was a fish."

"Nemo can be whatever he wants to be."

"You are very right." Schooled by a five-year-old. "Do you know why my friend, Officer Nate, and I are here, Keely?"

She shakes her head, but her quick glance over my shoulder to her dad tells me she knows exactly why we are here.

"We're here to make sure you and your mom are okay."

"What about my dad?" Her brow furrows, and she wraps a finger in the hem of her shirt.

"Your dad, too. We're the police. It's our job to make sure everyone is safe at all times."

"Hmm." She twists her lips as if she's getting antsy, and I know I need to get to the point. It's only a matter of time before Mr. Davis gets smart and tells me I can't speak to Keely without a parent present.

"If you weren't safe, you could tell me, you know? Like if your mommy and daddy got into a fight, and it scared you, it's okay to tell a police officer like me. They're not going to get into trouble for it, but it would help me understand why you seem so upset." Her eyes widen.

"Were they fighting earlier?"

"Mm-hmm." There is so much shame in her little expression that this hard-ass wants to pull her into my arms and give her a hug.

"When you get in trouble, does your mommy or daddy ever spank you?"

"Only when I've been really bad," she whispers, eyes downcast to watch her fingers, which are still twisting in the hem of her shirt.

"What's really bad?" Her eyes flash up, and then she shakes her head and bends over to pick up one of the painted rocks. She turns it over in her hand as she finds the words her innocent mind wants to use.

"When I come out of my room when they're fighting. Or if I spill my milk." She shrugs as if it's not a big deal but everything else about her posture says it is. "Or if I tell anyone about how they fight."

Fucking Christ.

"Well, I won't tell them that you told me anything if you don't. Okay?"

She stares at me with tears welling in her big blue eyes as she tries to figure out whether to trust what I'm saying or not. I slowly nod to reinforce what I've said. "Okay," she finally whispers, her eyes looking back to where her mom is speaking to Nate with her dad lingering close by.

"Does your mom ever get in trouble with your dad?" I ask, clocking her quick intake of breath.

"My mom doesn't spill her glass of milk." She breaks our eye contact and looks at the rock in her hand to avoid telling me more.

"Okay. Maybe she gets in trouble for other things though, huh?"

She nods subtly and then lifts her chin in pride as if she refuses to admit her mom is weak. She has no clue that her mom putting up with this might be a sign of weakness, but it is also a sign of strength to protect her daughter from the brunt of her dad's anger.

"Did anything happen earlier that you want to tell me about?"

"Keely? Tell the officer goodbye now," her mom says from the doorway where she stands with Davis's arm wrapped possessively around her shoulders.

Keely nods, her little blonde curls bouncing with the movement before she looks back to me. "I have to go now."

It's my turn to nod, even though every part of me is screaming to pick her up and put her in the squad car with me until I know for sure she's safe. "Can I give you something?" I ask.

She glances at them, torn between loyalty to her parents and the safety of a police officer, before looking back to me. "'kay."

I reach into my pocket and produce a sticker badge. It's left over from the elementary school appearance Nate and I made earlier today, and it's perfect. "I want to give this to you and make you a deputy officer."

"You do?" Her eyes widen and voice escalates with awe. Her innocence and willingness to trust is so palpable it breaks my heart.

"I sure do." I hand it to her. "I don't give these out to just anyone, either. It's an important job I know you can handle. This gives you the authority to call the police, dial 9-1-1 on the phone, if you ever get scared or are hurt or need help."

She stares at the sticker for a few seconds and speaks without thinking. "What about if my mommy needs help?" Her voice is back to being so quiet that I almost don't hear it.

"Definitely use it for that, too."

I hold my hand out for her to shake it. She giggles for the first time, and although I welcome the sound, I loathe it at the same time. Right now, I'm going to have to let her walk back into that house without knowing anything more about what happened other than the neighbor heard yelling.

"Nice to meet you, Deputy Keely."

She smiles again as she shakes my hand before turning on her heel and walking back to her mother, who ushers her inside and shuts the door on us without a second glance back.

Nate turns to meet my eyes and shakes his head as we walk down the front walkway.

"She walked into the wall," he murmurs with resignation, and I know he's referring to a bruise the mom must have had.

"She wouldn't give you anything else?"

"Nah," he says as he stares at me over the cruiser's roof. "She wouldn't step away from him so I could ask more. What about the girl?"

I know he isn't using names to keep the emotional distance, but for some reason, I can't do that this time. "Keely?" I reassert. "I didn't see any bruises, nor did she say she'd been hit. Daddy spanks her for telling anyone about mommy and daddy fighting, though. Or for spilling her milk. And probably just for breathing."

I grit my teeth as I rein in my anger. I can't stay detached. Not from a little girl with big blue eyes and soft blonde curls, who has most likely seen more than her fair share of adult things.

"Fucking prick."

"If only we could get Mrs. Davis alone to talk," I think aloud.

"We can try another time. Stop by for a well check when he's gone. Maybe she'll talk then."

"Perhaps." It isn't good enough. "He better not lay a hand on that little girl."

Nate eyes me for a second before nodding and sliding into the car to continue our day.

TEN

Grant

"WELL, THAT WAS CRAP."

I glance over to Nate as I crack the top of a Coke open and nod. "Sure was."

"And yet, we have shit to show for it. No arrests. No nothing."

"Makes for a long-ass day." I take a sip as I lean back and put my feet on the desk I'm currently occupying in the squad room. "If you want twenty-four hour lights and sirens, Nate, then you should move to San Francisco. I'm sure the guys there would kill for the slower beat we have."

"True. But I bet they're adrenaline junkies. They wouldn't be able to live without it." I nod at his statement. "Speaking of which, the fun stuff always seems to happen when I'm out sick."

"What are you talking about?"

"Lyle was just telling me in the locker room that you had a ninety five mile an hour-er the other day, but I don't see it on the reports anywhere." He leans his hip on the desk beside me and crosses his arms over his chest.

"It was an emergency situation. Lady speeding to get somewhere," I explain as I nod a hello to a few more guys coming in to roll call to grab their assignments. "I was trying to be nice and just gave her a warning."

"So, in other words, she was a hottie and you got her digits."

"Whatever." I roll my eyes and take another sip while thinking of Emerson. Her damn defiance and that haunted look she gets in her eyes every so often that makes me want to ask more questions than I know she's willing to answer. And then there were those little white shorts she was wearing the other day that make me think thoughts I shouldn't be thinking but can't help.

"Earth to Grant."

"Sorry. I was just thinking about that first call today—"

"The asshole husband and sweet little girl? Yeah, they got to me, too."

We both fall in silence for a second, and I hate that when I picture little Keely, an image of Emerson leaving school that day superimposes itself over it.

It's just because she's on my mind more than she should be. So much so that I'm projecting her situation onto another little girl when I know better.

"How about we liven up our day a bit and get some action?" he suggests.

"I get enough action. Thanks, though." I chuckle just to irritate him.

"Fucking, Malone. *Playboy cop*. One of these days a woman's going to come along and put handcuffs around that cold heart of yours, and then you'll be whipped like the rest of us fuckers."

"I'll be cuffed, huh?" I run a hand over my jaw and shake my head. "Sorry, I just don't see it . . . but if it makes you feel better about the white picket fence you'll be locked behind, then by all means."

"Some days I hate you, you know that?"

"Yeah, but you also love me," I tease as Liv, the dispatcher, walks down the hall and gives me a coy smile that makes parts of me regret walking away from her.

"Shit. I told you she still wants you," he murmurs as we both watch her hips sway.

"Me and my cold heart." I laugh.

"You sure you don't want to go out after shift is over?"

"Nah, I told the chief I'd stay and do some desk work." Like that's a fun way to spend the rest of my afternoon. "I'm reviewing the cold case files for him. Trying to prove how great of a detective I'd be. You know, gotta put a good foot forward if I want that promotion."

"You're kissing major ass with the extra hours you're putting in," he taunts.

"And I'm loving the OT pay. I can see a new patio and built-in barbecue in the near future."

"The offer stands. A bunch of us are meeting at seven o'clock at McGregor's if you get done in time."

"Thanks, but I have other shit to do."

"Ha," he says as he pushes away from the table. "Just make sure you remember her name in the morning."

"Whatever." I shoo him away as I sit up in my chair to play the role of desk jockey and tackle updating the stack of case files in front of me.

I shouldn't be doing this.

I shouldn't have let that old case file I went through get to me.

I shouldn't have looked at the picture of the victim and thought about both Keely and Emerson.

I shouldn't have let my finger hover over the search button on the file archives site where I had typed in "John Reeves, Emerson Reeves" and debated whether I should hit "find" so I could see what exactly it was that happened to her all those years ago.

And I definitely shouldn't be driving out to Miner's Airfield to where Desi said more often than not I could find Em.

But here I am, looking at the airstrip with hangars lining one side of the field and the airplanes parked to the right of them. On the far side is another parking lot and Blue Skies, an old skydiving business. It's been there as long as I can remember, owned by the Skies family, who last I heard, no longer had any family members in town to run or even care about the place. The lack of attention shows in the aged building and faded sign.

Why am I here?

Why am I chasing after someone who is clearly pushing me away?

Because I want to apologize to Emerson for the Tampax stunt? Yes *and* no, since she clearly beat me at my own game with the Viagra request. Or is it because every time I thought of Keely today, I kept seeing Em's face when she was little and I know it isn't going to go away any time soon.

More likely than either of those is the notion that if I see her, make sure she's okay, befriend her, then it might just ease the guilt I feel over breaking my promise to her when we were kids. My adult self knows it was the right thing to do. The little boy beneath the surface still feels the guilt every time I picture the look on her face as she walked out of Mrs. Gellar's classroom.

Em's always been there in my mind. Sure, it's been a long ass time since third grade, but in some sort of way, I knew I'd see her again. She isn't someone I could easily forget.

Great, now I sound like some goddamn Hallmark movie.

I scrub my hands over my face, and when I look up, there she is in full living color, walking across the tarmac as if she owns the place. In a flight suit with the sleeves tied around her waist and a purple tank top beneath it. If jumping out of airplanes is what she likes to do to relax after a long day, I can't imagine what else excites her.

As if sensing my attention on her, Emerson turns her head to face my direction, and I swear she knows it's me. It's the way she angles her head. It's the immediate straightening of her shoulders. It's the sudden stalking of her feet my way with a definite purpose.

I grin, can't help that I do. I love seeing her all worked up. After the day I've had, I'm more than ready for a good fight.

But fuck if she's not trying to distract me in other ways. Like that damn flight suit of hers. It should be the most unattractive thing on the face of the earth—dark blue, baggy, manly—but . . . goddamn. I'm a red-blooded male and would have to be dead not to notice how her tits bounce beneath that thin tank she has on.

I scrub a hand over my face to try to stop my thoughts from going where they shouldn't, but hell if they don't have a mind of their own.

They go there.

Oh, how they go there.

When she's about twenty feet away from me, she stops and plants her hands on her hips before calling out, "Airstrip's closed for maintenance. No one called for the police. You can turn around and leave now."

I stare at her behind my sunglasses with my elbow propped on the open driver's side window. "I'm off duty. And it's good to see you, too, Em." I grin just to irritate her.

"It isn't good to see you."

"Aww, now you're just trying to win me over with kindness."

She rolls her shoulders. "Sorry, we're all out of tampons today. You can take your emergency elsewhere." Sarcasm drips from her voice and only serves to antagonize me to draw this out.

"No emergency," I say as I climb out from my truck and lean against the door. "Just out for a drive and somehow ended up here."

"Convenient." She snorts. "You came. You saw. You can leave now because you won't conquer." She flashes me a dazzling smile that just might serve to warm that cold heart that Nate swears I have.

"And you used to be so sweet."

"And you used to not be so annoying."

"All this fire from you and I can't remember doing anything wrong."

There's a quick flash of something across her expression but between the distance and how fast it disappears, I can't read what it means.

But it's enough to know my comment got to her.

We stare at each other, both of us stubborn enough that we'd hold the line until someone looked away. While it might be fun to push her buttons, I know it isn't going to get me anywhere. That I know for certain.

"Is this where you jump from?" I jut my chin to the tarmac behind her.

"What's that?" she asks as she takes a step closer and furrows her brow.

"The other night at Desi's house, a bunch of you were talking about skydiving."

"And your point is?"

It takes everything I have not to tell her to stop when she begins to put her arms through the sleeves of her flight suit and zip it up. There's no need to cover up the perfection I was just admiring. And when I meet her eyes again, her knowing expression says I've been caught checking her out.

Can she blame me?

"Well?" she prompts drawing me back to our conversation.

"I assumed you guys are on a dive team or something."

She cocks her head to the side and chews on the inside of her cheek. "What do you want, Grant? You weren't just on a drive, and you just didn't happen to end up here . . . so what is it specifically that you want?"

Good question. It's one I need to ask myself.

I take a few steps toward her as she does the same to me until we're standing a few feet apart on the desolate tarmac.

"I'm not sure," I murmur, more to myself than to her, wishing she'd take those damn aviator sunglasses off so I could see her eyes. At least then I might have a clue as to what's running through that mind of hers.

"That's helpful. I'm sure the chief taught you that if you don't know what you want, there's no way you can get it . . . so, uh, good luck figuring it out. Like I said, the airstrip is closed." She lifts her eyebrows and turns as if to walk away.

My hand is on her arm in a flash. "What is your problem?" I snarl the words, and fuck if this woman can't rile me in a flash.

Why the hell am I chasing a ghost? Why do I even care?

She jerks her arm from my grasp but doesn't walk away. At least she's not running. "*You*. You're the problem."

"Why's that? What's so wrong with being friends?"

"I have plenty of friends, Grant."

"Not like me, you don't."

"Charming." She rolls her eyes and shakes her head. "Arrogance gets you nowhere with me."

"What is it, Em? What is it about me that irritates you so much? What did I do that was so wrong that when you saw me on the Fourth you already figured out you hated me?" I step into her, my thoughts flying and temper flaring even though I swore I was going to try to calm the situation.

"I'm not irritated," she sneers.

"Then what do you call it?"

"Hostile." She gives me a ghost of a smile.

"I call it being defensive." That one hit home. For a split second, her expression falls before she reins in whatever nerve I've hit.

"If you don't like it, then why are you here?"

"I keep asking myself the same damn question."

"Seems like we're at an impasse." It's that blasé tone of hers that irritates the fuck out of me. It's nothing but a mask she's hiding behind, and I want to rip it off so I can examine what's beneath it.

"I'm gonna wear you down."

Fucking brilliant, Malone. I went from swearing she was too much trouble to now vowing to wear her down.

"No you're not." Those hands of hers find her hips again.

"I know your type, Emmy. You're used to pushing people away the minute they get too close. You're used to calling the shots and being in control. News flash, I don't budge when I'm pushed and no one controls what I do."

"For the record, behind my sunglasses I'm rolling my eyes at your macho bullshit tantrum."

"You always did love to roll your eyes."

"Stop!" She clenches her fists and fights to regain her composure. "I told you, I'm not the same girl you used to know."

"Good thing," I say as I take a step toward her, "or else we'd be having this discussion while making mud pies in my parents' backyard and eating those gummy worms you used to love." There's a crack in her armor, a slight curl to one of her lips.

"There's nothing wrong with gummy worms."

I cringe in mock disgust. "And just like you're not the same girl, I'm definitely not the same boy. I won't try to sweet talk you into pouring salt on snails or covering your hand in honey to see how many ants we can collect. Bugs aren't my thing anymore."

She fights her smile, her ice melting. "What is your thing then?"

We stare at each other for a few seconds from behind the protection of our tinted lenses. I know I should walk away. This is complicated, and I don't do complicated, but instead of doing the smart thing, I dig in the front pocket of my uniform shirt for my card. "Here's my number should you ever want to call it and . . . I don't know . . . hang out at CVS with me."

This time, I'm granted her smile. "Thanks, but I'm all stocked up on drugstore supplies."

I deserve that. "Take the card, Em. I'd love to do something—as friends—and catch up on the last twenty years." I realize my mistake mentioning the past the minute I say it, but she saves me from fumbling with how to correct the statement when she takes the card from my hand.

"I'll take it, but I won't use it."

"Yes, you will."

"So sure of yourself, are you?"

"You've never been able to say no to me, Emerson."

"Oh. Please. Take your card back." She shoves it back at me, but she's laughing and that's a good thing.

"Nope." I take a step back. "You'll call. I know you will."

"I won't."

"You know you want to find out what happened to Miles O'Neal."

Her head startles as she remembers the little boy who used to have the biggest crush on her. "Whatever," she says as she slips the card into her pocket without looking at it. "For the record, Malone, I don't fall for sweet talk anymore."

"Then what do you fall for?"

Em freezes momentarily as she gets an odd look on her face that I can't read before shaking her head. "I have to get back to work."

Whoa. What? "*Work*?"

"Yeah. Work. I'm in the process of buying this place."

"The airport?"

"Blue Skies, the skydiving school."

"You are?"

"Yep." She turns her back to me and tosses over her shoulder, "Later, Phony Maloney."

So she is sticking around. Permanently.

Huh.

I watch her walk across the tarmac until she disappears inside the door of Blue Skies. Then I climb in my truck and start the engine but don't leave.

Fuck if I know why I'm working so hard for this woman.

But I am.

After a bit, I reverse, pull out of the parking lot, and smile.

She didn't correct me when I called her Emmy.

I guess I'll take any victory I can get, because I have a feeling when it comes to Emerson Reeves, they are hard fought and few and far between.

The question is, what the hell is the victory for?

ELEVEN

Emerson

"You really need to clean this place, Em."

I glance around the loft and shrug. I have a stack of clothes piled on a chair in the corner that I need to wash, there is a mess on the counter of the kitchenette—if I can call it that—and my bed's unmade, which is usual.

"You're the only one who visits, and since you already like me, it isn't like I need to impress you," I say to Desi as I pour some wine into her plastic glass.

"That's highly debatable," she says with a shake of her head and then begins to stack the paperwork on the card table, er, kitchen table—in some sort of order. "This place isn't exactly spacious. I'm sure it would look bigger if it were clean."

"Yes, mother." I lean back in one of my mismatched chairs and prop my feet on an opposing one. "Do you know how freaking exhausted I've been lately? Between Travis and Blue Skies and the loan, I feel like I don't have time to breathe."

"Then quit one of them."

"Easy for you to say. Travis manages the airfield. The odd jobs I do for him give me this glamorous roof over my head and the car to use. My job at Blue Skies pays the other bills. And the loan is going to hopefully be approved for enough so I can buy Blue Skies."

"And then what?"

"And then I can make it what I want it to be. Pull the rest of the money for the improvements out of my ass or something, but I have to have it first to be able to make it mine." I can see it all so clearly in my mind, but reality makes it hard to believe it just might happen.

"I have faith that you'll be able to."

"In the meantime, I'll deal with the exhaustion."

"But not too exhausted for sex."

"Huh?"

"Who's the flavor of the month?"

I nearly choke on my wine. "Who said there's a flavor of the month?" I laugh.

"Hmm . . . well the black pair of boxer-briefs over there in the corner tells me there was definitely a flavor—whether it be for the night or the week or the month is up for debate."

"Where?" And sure enough, when I look to where she's staring, there is a pair of Shawn's underwear bunched in the far corner of the flat.

"Which hot stud do they belong to?" she asks, holding her hand up to jokingly go through the possible names by ticking them off her fingers.

"Those would be Shawn's."

"Shawn? As in three months ago, Shawn?"

"Apparently." I bite my bottom lip and wonder how they got left there. "He hasn't stepped foot in here since asking if I minded feeding him a bottle while he wore a diaper."

"Shouldn't those be a diaper instead of undies, then?" We both snicker at the thought.

"Uh, yeah. I'm fearful of what else you might find when you actually do clean this place."

"It isn't that bad—" The lift of her eyebrows stops my response. "Okay, it is."

"Admission is half the battle." She laughs, but it's her eyes flashing and that mischievous smile sliding across her lips that gets my attention.

"What?"

"Nothing." Cue her cat-ate-the-canary grin.

"*What*?"

"You saw Grant, didn't you?"

And here we go again . . .

"Why would you say that?"

"No reason." She shrugs, but I don't believe her. "But you want to see him again, don't you?"

"Why would you say that?" I repeat.

"Because if you didn't want to see him again, you would have gotten rid of this." She lifts his card between her two fingers and hides her victorious smile.

"Uh, look around my place, Des, I obviously keep things I have no use for—case in point, Shawn's underwear. It's the same thing with Grant's card." I lift my eyebrows and hold her stare because I know she won't back down from this unless I do.

"I disagree."

"Great. Good for you." I rise from the chair, needing to move and think. My place is small, and all of a sudden, it feels like it's closing in on me. "He stopped by that airfield a few weeks ago. Gave it to me. If I cared, I wouldn't have thrown it in a pile of junk mail, now would I?"

"And if you didn't care, you wouldn't be so aggravated right now."

She's right, and she knows it, but I try to play it off as I grab a pile of clothing and toss it into the laundry basket. "I'm irritated because you won't leave this alone. He's become the main topic of conversation between us for the past few weeks. Why? Why is that?"

"You tell me."

"Don't give me your calm psychosomatic bullshit, Des."

"Remember when I came out to visit you on the skydive-my-way-around-the-country-I'm-a-gypsy tour you took?"

Her change of topic gives me whiplash. "Where are you going with this?" Annoyed with her and this conversation when Grant already bothers me enough.

"We went to that bar in Podunk, Maryland. Remember that place?"

Of course I remember. Too many drinks and constant laughter. How good it was to see Desi again after meandering around the country for a few months while I got my head together after the death of my mother. "God, yes. We had fun that night, didn't we?"

She nods, her smile growing. "There was that bachelorette party there."

"Oh my God. Yes. They were so raunchy. And then the stripper showed up. We laughed so hard at how cheesy his moves were." I can still hear the hoots and hollers in my ears. "We thought he was a police officer coming to kick them out, and surprise, surprise, he was the entertainment."

"Yep. But he was sure nice to look at."

"Yes, he was."

"Remember when you saw him and said that there was something about a man in a police officer's uniform that you found super sexy and couldn't resist?"

Bingo. She just got to the point of this detour in conversation.

I stare at her from across the space where I've started to collect some of my clothes strewn about. "Desi," I warn.

"What?" she asks, voice feigning innocence as she blinks rapidly. "You can't resist a man in a police officer's uniform. Grant is a police officer. *In a uniform*. And yet, you're resisting him."

"There are a shitload of issues with your statement."

"Like?"

He lied.

And just like that, everything I've been fighting when it comes to Grant—every excuse, every bit of irritation, every bit of wanting him near but push him away—is summed up in those two tiny words. They have never before crossed my mind, but now they make perfect sense of why I've acted the way I have.

I'm immediately brought back to the pinky promise he made me. The tears in his eyes when I looked at him before I walked out of the classroom. The pressure in my chest that felt as if an elephant was stepping on it as I made my way to the principal's office.

Feeling like I'm suddenly lost in a fog I should have seen coming, I forget that Desi is sitting there staring at me and walk a few steps to sit on the edge of my bed.

It's stupid really. To hold that much resentment for so long over something. It's ridiculous to think that of all the shit I've been through, that is the one thing I've harbored subconsciously.

But it is.

He lied. He was the one person I trusted in that whole teeny, tiny world I had back then. He was the one place I felt safe. And normal. I believed him when he said he'd keep my deepest, darkest, most shameful secret, but he didn't. Instead, he told and tore my whole world apart.

Sitting here at the age of twenty-eight, I know what he did was right. Sitting here a survivor because of him, I know I should actually seek him out and thank him.

But it's so much easier to blame him.

It's much more palatable to pretend that he was the one who hurt me instead of the man I was supposed to trust above all others, my dad. It's so much simpler to blame my lack of trust or want for any kind of intimacy on the little boy I left behind.

"Em?"

The softness of Desi's voice is enough to make me blink. I'd been sitting and staring blankly at the dirty pair of Shawn's underwear for I don't know how long, and I look away. Panic claws its way up my throat as I try to process my epiphany without letting her get a glimpse of the past she knows only the gist of.

"Yeah. Sorry." I shove off the bed and begin collecting the rest of the clothes and shoving them into the hamper like a mad woman as I try to hide the trembling of my hands. "I just was remembering when we were kids is all. How his hair used to stick up all the time and how much I loved hanging out at his house after school."

"Hm," she murmurs, and I don't look up because I haven't quite gotten ahold of my unexpected emotions yet.

"I lost the train of thought. Where were we?"

"You were going to set me straight as to why you're resisting the hot guy in a police uniform. Then I was going to reiterate just how damn good he looks in said uniform and how if you're not going to let him get frisky, er, *frisk you*, then I'm willing and able to take your place. Then you were going to roll your eyes and tell me I'm jumping to conclusions and that he only wants to be friends, which we both know is a load of horseshit. I'd tell you when he looks at you, it's obvious he wants more than to meet you for coffee at Starbucks. You'd tell me I'm making it up, that you'd never meet him at Starbucks because you can't imagine spending that kind of money for a cup of coffee, but you know damn well you've thought about him in that way too and when he walks into the room your lady bits go all tingly . . . even though you won't admit it." She takes an exaggerated breath. "What have I forgotten?"

I laugh. Somehow, she has given me exactly what she didn't know I needed, her quirky and lighthearted sense of humor. It's drawn me back to the world I created for myself. One where the past is black, and day by day, I make my own future.

"Then I'd ask you why you're so invested in this person you just met and why you keep pushing him on me, your *best* friend, who prefers to keep shit with the opposite sex simple." I lift my eyebrows to challenge her.

Desi purses her lips and shrugs. "I'd tell you that he's nice and obviously safe. Besides, why is it so bad for me, your *best* friend, to want you to have another friend to count on should I walk out the front door and, I don't know, get struck by lightning."

"And out comes the guilt card," I say with gusto. "You forgot something, though, there isn't a cloud in the sky."

"It could be heat lightning."

"Whatever," I laugh. "You're just as irritating as he is."

"Oh, he's irritating, is he? That's a good thing. Pray tell." She props her chin on her hands like an eager child.

"A good thing? I call it a pain-in-the-ass thing," I say, playing along even though I'm the one who has been creating the friction with Grant. Then again, he did do the whole CVS stunt . . . so, I've earned the right to be pissed at him.

"But *why* does he irritate you?"

"Because he's a man. Because instead of writing me a damn ticket for going ninety miles an hour he called my bluff when I told him I was speeding because I was having a feminine emergency and took me to CVS to buy Tampax for me," I explain, fully expecting her to understand. When I look up, the sympathy I expect on her face isn't there. Instead, she's grinning ear to ear.

"Oh. *Wow*. So the guy saves you from a reckless driving ticket, a possible trip to jail, and is considerate enough to buy you tampons when he thinks you're having period problems. Man, he sounds like a *real* bastard."

"I assure you, it wasn't out of the kindness of his heart."

"You know what they say about boys who pick on you . . ."

"No. What?"

"It means they like you. And be careful, you're rolling your eyes so hard they just might get stuck there."

I do it again for show. "You forget, I knew him in third grade. He was much sweeter then."

"He still looks pretty damn sweet to me," she murmurs, her lips sliding into a mischievous smile.

"I told you, I'm not disagreeing with that . . . but he's *Grant*."

"Yeah, and I'm sure *Grant*," she says, mimicking the way I said his name, "wouldn't say no to a little fun with you." She rises from her seat and makes a show of tossing his card on the table before resting her hands on her hips and sighing.

"Uh-oh, should I assume you're going to finish the rest of our conversation for me?"

"You mean the one where you start making lame-ass excuses about why you can't call Officer Sexy back? Like how you think it's creepy to go out with a boy you knew in third grade, to which I'd counter with how there is *nothing* boyish about him now and who fucking cares? Is anyone keeping tabs? So what? You guys hung out, colored pictures of rainbows during class, and swung on the monkey bars together. None of those things matter when we factor in his hotness, his uniform, and his handcuffs, which I'd put a million dollars on him knowing exactly how to use. I reject that argument. It's moot. *Next*?"

I use a pair of tongs to pick up Shawn's underwear and put them in the trash while hating and ignoring the fact that everything she said makes perfect sense. But she doesn't know about how he fits into my past or the particulars. My mom is gone, my dad is out of jail and somewhere I don't care to know, so that leaves Grant and his family as the only ones who do. What about that? How does that make me feel?

I just don't know.

"I think you've pretty much covered the bases." I turn to face her.

"Good. Then my work here is done." She dusts her hands off as she grabs her purse, picks up the bag she set beside it, and holds it out to me. "I cooked for you."

My face lights up and my tummy growls. She really loves me. "Is there dessert?" I ask, skeptical as to why she had the forethought to bring me bribery. She nods. "You're forgiven for the inquisition."

"That's what I thought."

TWELVE

Emerson

"EMMY, SWEETIE, YOUR PARENTS HAD TO CANCEL THEIR plans. Your mom was called in to work. Your dad said he'd be by to pick you up in about an hour."

That icky, weird taste fills my mouth at the sound of Mrs. Malone's voice. "Okay." The word barely makes a sound when I speak it.

Grant nudges me. "That stinks, but at least we have another hour to play."

"You okay, Em?" Mrs. Malone asks from the porch. She has a funny look on her face that makes me want to cry and get one of her awesome hugs. But I know that will cause questions. According to Daddy, questions cause trouble, and trouble is punishable.

I don't like his punishments.

"Yeah. I was just looking forward to spending the night."

"I asked if you still could, but your dad said no. I guess you now have plans early in the morning, so it wasn't going to work. I'm sorry."

"'Kay." I shrug and lean back against the tree trunk next to Grant as she disappears inside.

My tummy doesn't feel good, and my hands are sticky with sweat.

"C'mon, Emmy, we can finish making our wine before you have to go."

I look at the mess we've made. The two bowls are full of smashed grapes Mr. Malone let us take off the vines growing in the backyard.

My fingers ache from trying to mash the juice out of them. They made it look easy on our field trip to the grape vineyard last week, but for some reason, I don't think the clear juice will taste anything like the red stuff my mom drinks from her bottle.

"Nah, I don't want to make anymore."

"How come?"

Because I don't want to go home.

I close my eyes for a minute and just feel the cool breeze on my cheeks. I fight back the sting of tears burning against my eyelids and the sound of my heart beating in my ears. "Just cuz. I'd rather hang out with you."

"You never want to go home." He knocks his knee against mine. "How come?"

"This is our little secret, Em. You can't tell anyone or else it will hurt your mommy very badly."

My dad's whispers fill my ears and make my throat burn. I try to swallow over it, but I feel like I have one of the grapes stuck there, and it hurts.

"Just cuz." I pick up one of the rocks on the ground beside me and absently rub it against the inside of my arm until my skin starts to turn red. "Your house is much more fun than mine. You have brothers and a dog and stuff."

"Yeah, I guess. Stop it, will ya?" He takes the rock from my hand and tosses it. "We could always play at your house next time if you want. I'm sure we could find fun things to do there."

"Thanks, but . . ." I take a deep breath as I run my fingers over the red mark. "My house is kinda scary."

"You're just a girl. Girls are scared of everything. What's so scary about it?"

I shrug. "I don't know."

"You don't need to be scared, Emmy. I'm taking karate now. I could protect you."

There's laughter from inside his house, and we can hear it from where we're sitting in the backyard. The sound makes me smile even though my eyes are blurry with tears.

"My mom's drinking wine," he says. "You know what that means."

"Uh-uh, What?"

"Kissy, kissy."

"Ewww, gross."

"Yeah," he says as he picks up an escaped grape and throws it into our bowl. "She gets all giggly and then my dad will dance with her in the family room and sing horribly and then the grossness happens—they kiss."

"Ick." I giggle but hate that feeling in the middle of my belly that loves the idea of dancing and laughing. "My parents never kiss."

"They had to have kissed at least once because that's how babies are made and they have you, right?"

"True." I lean forward and grab a bowl as I try to forget what will happen when I go home in a bit. "But if your mom and dad kiss now, doesn't that mean they're going to have another baby soon?"

"That's not how it works, silly."

"Then how does it work, then?"

"I'm not quite sure."

THIRTEEN

Emerson

The asphalt bites into my shoulders as I lie down on the tarmac in the chilly, early morning air. I needed to escape the loft and the fear that hung in the air from first my nightmare and then from the confusion I felt after the memory resurfaced of Grant and me as kids in his backyard.

"You don't need to be scared, Emmy. I'm taking karate now. I could protect you."

Guess I should have known he'd end up like his dad, protecting and serving—being the hero.

It suits him. The question is, does he suit me?

It's a tricky question, and one I'm not sure I'm ready to know the answer to. I've lived my life escaping my past, hiding it from anyone and everyone so that no one can ever look at me and blame my lack of success on *it.* Or just plain look at me differently.

But he knows.

He knows more than I might even know, and that's scary as hell to me.

So yes, I've blamed him unfairly, but it's so much easier to believe that truth—that he is more at fault than my own flesh and blood.

I've always thought of myself as a fair person.

There's no reason not to believe he isn't a good man.

And, as I sit here on the closed runway with the sun slowly rising in the east, I know I need to step outside the box I've carefully constructed and fortified around myself. I need to listen to Desi and her whacked logic and remember what Grant said to me when we were nothing but kids.

I need to do the one thing I do every day in my professional life but can't seem to ever do personally: Leap before looking.

I need to follow my motto: Head up. Wings out.

FOURTEEN

Emerson

Me: For the record, I still think it's a bad idea, but you're right. You wore me down. Maybe we can get together sometime for a few drinks. Your call.

Grant: I knew you'd see my ways. How about tomorrow at six at McGregor's?

Me: That works.

I stare at the string of texts and feel as if my throat is closing up on me. At the same time, I'm excited and nervous and more than anything, afraid. My interactions with men are fleeting. I don't use them for their conversation skills. Sure, we go out and have a good time, but on my part, things are superficial. The first time they lie, they're gone. And if they can make it past that first test, then when they start wanting more . . . when they want to talk about our pasts and have that kumbaya moment where we realize we are meant to be together forever, they stop being of interest to me.

I only live in the now. I only live in tomorrows. I can only cope with the future I make for myself.

But there is something about agreeing to meet for drinks with Grant that is making me nervous.

"You are *not* chickening out. I will *not* let you," Desi says as she applies another coat of mascara to my eyelashes.

"I'm not chickening out. And I don't need all this makeup. It isn't as if he hasn't seen me before without it."

"Shush. Every woman needs to act like she cares on a first date." She takes a step back to admire her handy work. "If you don't act like you care, then you're not setting the standard of how you expect to be treated."

"But this isn't a first date, and I think you're off your rocker."

"You *are* hoping to be frisked and handcuffed at some point, aren't you?" I just raise my eyebrows at her when she gives me that motherly look. "Then shush and let me finish my masterpiece."

She busies herself with curling my hair when throwing it into a ponytail would be fancy enough for me. There's no use arguing with a determined Desi so I let her have her way.

"I may have done something in a knee-jerk reaction."

"What did you do?" She sets the curling iron down, plants her hands on her hips, and looks at me with warning in her eyes.

"You remember Paulo, don't you?"

"Hmm, that Latin lover you had fun with for a while."

"That's him." I begin to bite my lip, and she squeezes my cheeks to stop me from messing up my perfectly lined lips.

"Why are we talking about him, and why are you nervous to tell me?"

"Well, I kind of agreed to meet up with him tonight."

The reaction I expected is immediate: Brow narrowing, lips parting, eyes blinking, nostrils flaring. "Why in the ever-loving hell would you do that?"

I shrug, because now that I've admitted it out loud, it does sound ridiculously stupid. If I'm not afraid of meeting up with Grant, then why did I go and give myself an out for this evening should things get too serious? I don't shrink from her stare even though I want to.

Her eyes narrow as she pins me immobile. "You just showed your cards, Em." A broad grin slides across those heart-shaped lips of hers.

"My cards?"

"Yep. You wanted an out because you know tonight is going to be epic, and you're not used to epic. You're used to good sex with a pretty face but nothing behind it."

"I beg to—"

"Shush." She picks up my phone from the table beside me and tosses it onto my lap. "Tell Paolo thanks but no thanks. You're all Latin-lovered out for the time being and you're handcuffed to other obligations tonight."

"Fine." I huff out a breath as I pick up the phone.

She's right, but hell if I'll admit it aloud.

"Is this seat taken?" I ask as I slide into the booth across from Grant. Nerves idle within me, only serving to reinforce Desi's assumption that I'm already treating Grant differently from how I treat other men.

I'm not exactly sure how I feel about that.

"Hey there." Grant's face transforms with the warmest of smiles that makes parts inside me that I wasn't aware could tingle come alive. We stare at each other for a moment, almost as if there's a silent acknowledgement that the defensive banter we're used to has no place here tonight. "You look beautiful."

Uncomfortable with compliments, I blush. "You clean up pretty nice, too. Although, you can never go wrong with your uniform."

Did I really just say that?

"So I've heard." A smile plays at the corner of his mouth, referencing back to the first time we ran into each other, but his eyes hold so much more amusement in them.

A waitress comes and takes our drink order. There is ample chatter in the bar but an awkward silence between us. I play with the cardboard coaster, uncertain what step to take in the uncoordinated dance.

"Emerson."

"Hmm?" I meet his eyes.

"There's no pressure here. I just wanted to spend some time with you, have a few drinks, and catch up on what you've been up to. That's it."

Our eyes hold as I struggle with laying down my defensive shield and not running away at the mere mention of catching up. Catching up means talking about the past, and my past is dark as hell. And while he may already know the gist of my dark, it's hard not to be defensive over something I've always protected.

"I'd like that." I don't remember telling myself to say the words, but there they are, out in the open, making his grin widen and his shoulders relax some.

"Good. That's good. Because as stupid as it sounds, I've really missed you."

FIFTEEN

Emerson

B*ECAUSE AS STUPID AS IT SOUNDS, I'VE REALLY MISSED YOU.*

Every time Grant laughs, I hear him saying those words. Every time he smiles, I hear him saying those words. Every time I want to clam up at a seemingly benign question, I remind myself that I only have to tell him as much as I want to and think of him telling me he missed me.

Those are words I don't think anyone has ever said to me.

"So tell me something . . ." Grant laughs as he slides next to me in the booth and then pushes a fresh drink in my direction. His eyes are a little glassy, but his smile is still kind and his humor is becoming of him. "What's a girl who's scared of heights doing jumping out of airplanes?"

"Who said I was scared of heights?"

"Oh come on," he says, patting my thigh with a tipsy flourish and then absently leaving it there. "This is coming from the girl who refused to climb Old Man Conner's tree because it was too high off the ground. You threw up all over his daisies just thinking about it."

I stare at him, flustered by his hand. *Warm*. On my thigh. *Contact.* When I should really be freaking out that Grant is talking about a memory I have no recollection of, but I can't. All I can focus on is the ache currently simmering a few inches from where his fingers reside.

"I don't remember that," I say and shift to face him in the booth.

He moves his hand back to his drink and shakes his head.

"You don't? I made fun of you for weeks, calling you Daisy until you got so mad you told me you weren't going to come over to play anymore unless I stopped."

Daisy. The taunt ghosts through my mind, but I don't recall it. What I do know is that, even back then, we played games with each other. Sure, they were different games, innocent fun, which is a far cry from the one we are playing now. But just like then, I still feel the same sense of ease with him. The same level of comfort. I can't remember a single time I didn't want to go over to the Malone house to play. It was safe there.

I felt safe there.

"No. It's been a long time." I take a sip of my drink and hate how my fingers tremble ever so slightly.

"But skydiving, Em?"

I shrug. "It's my peace. For a few seconds, everything is there, laid out before me. It's calm. There's no noise in my head, just the wind in my ears, and I'm forced to only think of the present."

"The present is good."

"Mm-hmm." There's a look in his eyes that says a million things at once, and I can't pinpoint any of them, so I don't try. "So, a cop, huh?"

"Yep." He places his arm across the back of the booth, and his fingers automatically toy with a strand of my hair, as if it were the most natural thing in the world to do.

"I could have figured. All those hours playing cops and robbers on our bikes. You always had a hero complex, wanting to save anyone and everyone . . ." I'm stepping too close to no-go territory for me. Panic tries to find a foothold, but I ignore it and smile at Grant. "Remember that time we found—"

"The bullet shell smashed in the street, and we swore someone had broken into the Parker's house and robbed them?" His eyes light up.

"Yes! And we called 9-1-1 because we thought we were real detectives." I smile wider, thrilled to remember this memory and not draw a blank and feel stupid.

"Yeah good ol' Chief Malone read me the riot act for distracting officers from legitimate calls." He shakes his head and laughs.

"How is your dad?"

"He's good. Real good. He retired about eight years ago, and I think it's driving my mom crazy that he has nothing to do. Occasionally, the force asks him to consult on an old cold case, which keeps him occupied, but other than that, he's just busy being a grandfather to Luke. That's Grayson's son."

"Oh, I didn't realize any of the infamous Malone boys were hitched," I say with a wink.

"We're not. Gray's is a long story. Too long for right now."

"So no aspirations to be chief and follow in your dad's footsteps?" I suddenly want to know everything about him.

"In time." He shrugs and takes a sip of his beer.

"Give up the routine of sitting in The Donut Shoppe's lot and doing paperwork?"

"I actually despise donuts, and I'm more of a sit-in-the-parking-lot-of-Starbucks-on-Main-Street-and-do-my-paperwork routine kind of cop."

"A cop who hates donuts?" I hold my hand to my chest in mock horror. "Isn't that sacrilege? No wonder you haven't been promoted yet."

"It is. Actually, I'm up for detective right now. I debated for the longest time whether I wanted it—more responsibility, more politics, and less being on the streets, which is what I love doing the most. But, we'll see. It's a long process, and I'm not sure who else has applied for the position. Time will tell . . ."

"You're a Malone. In this town, that's gold, isn't it?"

"Depends who you ask." He angles his head and stares at me for a beat, curiosity owning his eyes. "So tell me, you're buying Blue Skies? Why that? Why now?"

I take a long sip of my wine and marvel at how easy it is for the words to want to spew off my tongue. It's unsettling; yet, I find myself wanting to tell him. I find myself wanting him to know I've been okay.

"My mom was a gypsy at heart. We wandered around a lot, moved from one town to the next the minute she started to feel too settled." I smile softly as I think of her. Her crazy, colorful clothes. Her unconventional ways. Her fierce protection of me from everyone.

"That must have been hard with school and—"

"She homeschooled me for the longest time. Trust was hard for her." *As it is for me.* "If I was learning about American history, we'd take a road trip and live in Washington, DC for a while. We were fluid."

"That must have been hard, always moving around."

"It was isolating in a sense because I didn't have many friends, but it was rich in so many other ways." I shrug. "One year, we went through Missoula where the fire jumpers are based. It was hot and humid, but I sat and watched them practice their jumps for hours. I knew right then I wanted to try it."

"Did you?"

"Not then. I was too young, and if my mom wasn't willing to trust a babysitter watching me for an hour, she sure as hell wasn't going to trust an instructor to get me safely back to earth."

"True." He traces the line of condensation on his beer bottle with his fingers.

"I had to wait until I was eighteen for my first jump."

"That's a long time to wait."

"It was."

"As non-traditional as it was, it sounds like she taught you a lot."

"It was all I knew." I smile softly at him, the memories of my mom and the life she created for us so clear despite all the time that has passed. "We stopped moving around when I was a senior in high school. I could have easily taken my GED and opted out, but my mom refused to let me. She wanted me to experience high school for at least one year."

"That had to have been brutal."

"Yeah, well, when you live in a bubble, sometimes you don't have the cognizance to notice or even want to care. It was definitely an experience. Gone were the lazy days where we'd finish our lesson and then take a tube and float down river wherever we were to celebrate another day lived to the fullest. I fought her on it, but she wanted to settle for the first time in almost ten years. Little did I know it was because she was sick."

"I'm so sorry, Em, I didn't know." His hand covers mine and gives it a squeeze.

"How could you have?" I squeeze his back, loving that he keeps his hand there even when the moment is over. "She was fine for a while, but after I graduated, I spent most of my time taking care of her. She fought hard, but the years of being ill finally took their toll. During it all, the one friend I had made in high school was my moral support. That was Desi." I lean back in my seat and lift my eyebrows. "This is all a little too depressing, isn't it? Let's change the—"

"It's okay. I want to know."

I stare at him for a moment, hesitant to talk about one of my deepest sadnesses, but realize he loves his mom just as fiercely as I loved mine. He'll understand why the grief robbed me of so much for so long. And some days still does.

"When my mom died, I took to her ways to cope. The day she passed away, I headed to a local skydiving school and jumped. It was the only way I thought I could be free of all the grief I felt. At first, I couldn't concentrate, but then I hit this moment in my jump where there was silence in my head. It was almost soothing, and it forced me to think of what was next and where to go from there. It was liberating and sounds ridiculous . . . " I look down to where my fingers are fidgeting with the coaster. It's weird how easy it is to tell him about it when it's something I don't think I've ever given a voice to before.

"It isn't ridiculous at all."

I clear my throat and drop the coaster before continuing. "So, I said goodbye to Desi, packed my belongings, and traveled all over the country, going from jump site to jump site until the grief stopped drowning me."

"How long ago was that?"

"Eight months."

Grant lifts his eyebrows, obviously surprised that it happened so recently, and I laugh. "By some weird twist of fate, while I was on my adventures, Desi ended up moving to Sunnyville. It shocked the hell out of me when she told me. And then I found out Blue Skies was up for sale. I felt like all roads were leading me back here when it was the last place I ever thought I'd return to."

"Plus there was me," he says, adding a flash of a smile and tip of his beer against my wine glass.

"Plus there was you."

His finger twirls absently in my hair again, and I hate that it sounds so cliché, but my heart really does beat faster.

"I'm glad you came back, Emerson. I know it was probably hard, but I'm—"

I press my lips to his to shut him up. I don't want to think about how hard it was stepping foot in this town or how I expected everyone to point fingers as I walked by and remember me as "that girl."

I just want to feel now.

And I know I take him by surprise. It's in the hesitancy of his lips at first. It's in the tightening of his finger wrapped in my hair. But it only takes a split second for him to react, to part his lips and give me the taste of beer on his tongue. For him to consume my mind and shift it away from the hundreds of thoughts I don't want to be thinking.

He's heat and warmth and soft fingers on the underside of my jaw. A hand demanding more on the small of my back.

His kiss is thunder and lightning, a tornado and a tsunami, all in one fiery package that makes me forget about the here and the now, makes me want more when more with Grant scares the shit out of me.

The noise of the bar slowly seeps into my conscience as the kiss ends and we move apart. Grant's eyes are hazy, but his lips are turned up in a cocky but adorable grin that makes that sweet ache our kiss ignited burn bright. He shakes his head, and it mimics how I feel: *Holy shit, I just kissed Grant Malone.*

Our eyes hold for a beat as the bar carries on around us before I suddenly feel shy under his unwavering gaze. I look down to my empty drink and stare at the scars on the wood tabletop as I try to process the sensations running through me. Desire, surprise, and euphoria mix and meld as heat creeps into my cheeks as he studies me.

The realization hits that I have no idea what to do now.

Cue the nerves and unexpected panic.

Typically, I'd make the next move. We'd decide whose place to go back to and have some unapologetic fun.

But this is Grant.

Didn't I already know this—the emotion, the sensation, the fallout—would be different before I kissed him?

"Hey, Em?" Grant's voice calls through the haze of my overthinking. "I'm going to save you from the panic that's written all over your face." He scoots closer and lowers his voice. "I had a great time tonight. I'd love to do it again sometime—*soon*, but I think it's best if I go home now. I've had a long and crappy shift, but you were the highlight of the day."

He leans in, and I suck in my breath, thinking he's going to kiss me again. The ache in the delta of my thighs only deepens with the scent of him near, but he bypasses my lips and goes straight for my ear. "While I appreciate a forward girl as much as the next guy, you need to understand that you're not in charge here. I know you want to be so you can control the pace and set the standard—make sure you maneuver me into the next move so you can stay one step ahead and on the run—but that's not how I operate. I'm flattered you wanted to kiss me because, hell, if I haven't been staring at your lips all night long wanting to do the same, but next time, I make the first move. A man only has so many firsts in life, and I'm sure kissing you is going to be a damn good one that I plan on taking."

Without another word, he scoots out of the booth and stands to full height. I stare at him, fully expecting those flecks of gold in his eyes to be amused, but they are anything but. They are dead serious with a mix of temper and concern that I don't quite get. He smirks before looking over to the waitress and holding a finger up with a nod.

"Question is, Emmy, are you still stubborn? How bad do you want that next kiss? How long are you going to hold out just to make a statement while denying your body what we both know it wants?"

"You bast—"

"Next round's on its way. Have a drink on me, will ya? At least when you put your lips on it, you'll know it's from me."

And with another flash of that cocky grin of his, Grant turns and strides out of the bar without ever looking back.

"Arrogant son of a bitch," I mutter, angry at more things than I care to count. That he rejected me. That he maneuvered me. That he just put me in my place. That he called me out.

That he's leaving and all I can think of is how I want more.

"Thank you," I murmur as the waitress slides a fresh drink in front of me.

What exactly just happened? My head spins at the turn of events and my logic tells me I should be pissed off at him.

But I'm not.

Because as much as it pains me to admit, he was right. I am panicking. I am trying to figure out why everything seems so damn different when it comes to Grant. I don't do different. I run the opposite way from different.

Yet here I sit. I haven't run away. I didn't even protest. I just let everything that happened happen, and I know damn well I'd do it again . . . because that kiss of his felt like none I've ever experienced before.

And I hate that I love it.

And I detest that I want more of them.

The bar buzzes on around me as I focus on being angry with him. It's so much easier to be pissed off than to accept the fact that he scares me. And the good kind of scare.

So I look at the drink he left me in consolation. I fixate on that cocky smirk of his that makes me want to strangle him and kiss him at the same time. And I tell myself I need to stand my ground. I need to be the strong girl I've tried to be instead of allowing myself to fall prey to the way he makes me feel.

He's crazy if he thinks I'm going to drink this. I won't just out of pure spite.

No one handles me.

No one tells me what I can and can't do.

And no one walks away from me unless it's on my terms.

Lost in thought, I pick up the glass and take a sip. "*Shit.*" I just fell right into that one. I stare at the dark red liquid for a long moment before shaking my head and tilting the glass all the way up until it's empty.

SIXTEEN

Grant

"YOU HAVE A LIST OF CASE FILES ON YOUR DESK. THERE ARE a dozen highlighted and the remaining not. Do you need me to do anything with them?" Nate asks as I pull up in front of my house and sigh when I see Grayson's car there.

I'm not in the mood to deal with my brothers. Not after my sleepless night complete with requisite cold shower after thinking about Emerson and her damn kiss.

"Earth to Grant?"

"Sorry. I just pulled up and the assholes are here." Nate chuckles in my ear, knowing how much it annoys me when my little brothers show up unannounced and help themselves to my beer and food. "Um, the list of case files . . . do you have time to pull them up and request the rest for me? The non-highlighted ones. If not, I can do it tomorrow before shift."

"Nah, I'm killing time. Today's quiet as fuck. This will give me something to do. When's the test?"

"Written is in a few weeks. The interview, I'm waiting on the chief to decide. Stetson is making noise, though, and bringing up that crap with my dad—"

"Old fucking news that should have never been news."

"I hear ya." I roll my shoulders as I prepare myself for the onslaught of my brothers. "Thanks for your help. See you tomorrow."

I hang up the phone and push open my front door.

"Ah, look, asshole number one is here," Grady says as he lifts up a beer in greeting.

"And he looks grumpy," Grayson chimes in.

"What are you two pricks doing here?"

"It was a rough little league game," Grayson says, shaking his head.

"Seriously? That's what you two have to stress about? Get out." I throw my thumb over my shoulder but then realize Luke is nowhere to be found. "Should I be concerned that Luke isn't here?"

"Nah, he's with Mom and Dad. We were given a warning to go cool our jets because we were showing him a perfect example of what poor sports look like." Grady grins, and I can only imagine what happened to get that rebuke from our mom.

"So you decided to come here and crash my party?" I head to the refrigerator to grab a beer and grit my teeth over the stash they've already depleted.

"You were having a party?" Grayson sits up like a damn meerkat.

"No. No party. Go home." Shaking my head, I unholster my weapon and walk the few strides to place it in the gun safe before turning back to my brothers and lifting my eyebrows. "I don't see you moving."

"Oh, that means Grant has a *lady* coming over," Grayson harasses, drawing the phrase out and earning a laugh from Grady.

"No, it does not mean I have a *lady* coming over."

"Good thing," Grady says, "because she'd be sorely disappointed in your skills." He makes a show of trying to thrust his hips.

"Says the man who could fuck a cheerio without breaking it," I reply, just to shut him up, but I chuckle when Grady holds a fist over his mouth, points at me, and yells, "Burn!"

He never takes anything seriously.

"You really let him around Luke when he's like this?" I ask Grayson. "No wonder mom took him for a while."

"It's nothing like that," Grayson says, always one to defend whichever one of us is being picked on. "We treated the team to pizza after they won. We had beer and mom asked Luke if he wanted to spend the night. Of course he did—*it's Mom*—so we figured we'd come over here and bug the shit outta you."

"That is, unless you have a *wo-man* coming over," Grady chimes in.

"No, I don't have a wo-man coming over," I say and throw a pillow at Grady. "Get your feet off the table."

Grady laughs, tucking the damn pillow behind his head. "He so has a woman coming over if he's telling us to get our feet off the table and shit."

"You guys are fucking idiots." I plop down on the love seat and glare at Grady until he plants his feet back on the floor.

"So, big brother . . ."

Nothing good ever comes from Grayson starting off the conversation with those three words.

"It's been a long day, let's not start whatever it is you're trying to start," I warn.

"Why do we come here? It's nothing but abuse with him," Grady says as he takes another sip of his beer.

"Exactly. If I'm so abusive to you little shits, don't let the door hit you on the asses on the way out." I know they're not going anywhere, but I do our typical song and dance anyway.

"Not until we hear the scoop." Gray sits forward and rests his elbows on his knees. "Rumor is you were at McGregor's the other night with Emerson."

"And?"

I can still taste her kiss.

"Well, obviously, you tracked her down, so what gives? You bumping uglies yet?"

I can still see that panicked look in her eyes.

"What is it with you guys? Can't I go out with a woman for a few drinks and just be friends?" I ask.

I can still see the determination in her scowl when I walked away.

"No," they both say in unison, and it prompts me to sip my own beer because I have a feeling it's going to be a long-ass night.

The wood porch creaks as I sit on its steps and breathe in the fresh night air. It's the first time I've had a chance to think all day, and considering Mutt and Jeff are inside catching up on the Giants game, I'm taking the liberty.

It's fucking ridiculous that I have to go outside of my own house to relax, but it isn't like they've listened to me the thirty other times I've kicked them out in the past three hours.

"Needing a break?" My father's voice startles me.

"Dad?"

I look up to find him walking up my driveway. I was so lost in thought I didn't even notice when he pulled up across the street.

"I figured you might need help kicking your brothers out. They were quite the pair earlier." He steps closer, and his silver hair looks pale yellow under the porch light.

"I heard mom wasn't too thrilled with them."

He shrugs, as if to say boys will be boys. "You know your mom. She'll take any excuse to get Luke alone for a few hours so she can spoil him rotten."

"Thank God for him because that means she lays off me."

"True," he muses before taking a seat beside me on the steps. "What's troubling you, Grant?"

I glance over at him, and even though his face is etched with perpetual lines of worry every retired cop seems to have, he still has the impenetrable stare. A proud and defiant angle to his chin and jaw. "Who says something is wrong?"

He raises his eyebrows, as if to ask me if he's misinterpreted my demeanor, which prompts me to blow out a sigh, lean my head against the railing behind me, and close my eyes. He gives me a few minutes to gather my thoughts without pressing me.

"I saw Emerson the other night." It isn't much, but it's a start.

"So I heard." He nods but doesn't look my way. Damn nosy people already talking. "What seems to be the problem? Did you have a bad time?"

I chuckle. "Just the opposite, actually." His silence tells me he isn't following me. "It's complicated."

"Most things are. If they were easy, they wouldn't be worth figuring out."

Father logic is not what I need right now, and yet, I find myself needing to talk through everything.

"She kissed me."

It's his turn to chuckle. "And that's a problem, why?"

I push up from the step and walk back and forth on the sidewalk before shoving a hand through my hair. "Because . . . because I don't know how to handle it."

"You've never had trouble handling a woman kissing you before if I recall correctly."

"But this is different."

"Why?"

"Because it's her, and it's . . . everything she's been through and . . ."

"How do you know what she's been through? Has she told you? Has she talked about it with you?"

"No."

"Then how do you know?"

"Because I was the one who told Mrs. Gellar, Dad. I'm the one who turned her life upside down."

"You mean that you're the one who saved her." His voice is even but serious, and it stops me in my tracks. I stare at him with hands at my side and every part of me confused about one goddamn kiss amidst a million other kisses I've had.

"She saved herself, Dad."

"Good. I'm glad you know that. Because you're right. She did. But let me ask you this, son, if she hasn't said a word to you about what happened before, why does it bug you? How do you know it bugs her?"

"How can it not?" I raise my voice without meaning to. It's just that this is like talking to a brick wall instead of talking to the one person who should be able to give me insight on how to handle this.

"If you met her on the street, you would have no idea about what she's been through. So, if she doesn't tell you, then that's how you have to treat her."

I look at the moon above and shake my head. "Easier said than done."

"It is, but it's her past, Grant. Sometimes you have to accept the other's history and just leave it there—as the past. It isn't fair if you use it against her when she's never even brought it into the equation."

"I would never hold it against her."

"Aren't you already, though?"

"What are you talking about?"

"You wouldn't be out here stressing about Em if you didn't know her history . . . so that in and of itself says you're already using it against her."

I reject the idea immediately, but the longer he just sits there quietly and stares at me the more his reasoning makes sense.

"You're right." I walk to the end of the pathway and then walk back before throwing my hands out. "Never mind. This is just my crazy talking. A few drinks and a kiss should not amount to me stressing this much about a woman."

He gives a non-committal noise.

"What's that supposed to mean?" I snap.

"It doesn't mean anything," he says cool as can be.

He thinks I'm wrong. I take a sip of my beer but refuse to acknowledge he's right.

Because I am wrong. This is Emerson we're talking about. Of course, I'm going to think harder and be more careful with her.

Fuck.

"You don't understand. You wouldn't get it."

"Try me."

"There's this look she gets in her eyes. It's like she's perfectly fine.

She's funny and outgoing and God is she feisty . . . but every so often, there's this sadness, this uncertainty that flashes in her eyes, and it fucks me up. I don't know how to make it go away."

"You always did want to save people."

"Not that again." I roll my shoulders and walk over to the bucket of ice on the porch and grab a new beer. I need it. This conversation is way more in-depth than I ever intended it to be.

"No. I'm serious. It bugs you because you want to fix it. You want to swoop in and take the pain away, but I'm sorry, that's something for her to deal with. You can't save her from something that happened twenty years ago."

"I know . . ." I hang my head and resign myself to this bullshit feeling I have. When I look back up, I meet his eyes with more certainty than I feel. "How bad was it?"

The widening of his eyes tells me my question takes him by surprise. "That's not for me to tell you, Grant." He glances back to the house were Grayson and Grady shout inside at the game, and he gets a ghost of a smile on his face hearing my brothers. "I'll tell you this, though. If it had been one of you, I would've stepped on the other side of the law."

Our eyes hold, and I know he means it. For Chief Malone to even utter the statement, it had to have been bad. Worse than I thought. Worse than I could even stomach considering. He slowly rises from the step, his still-fit body moving a little slower these days, and pats me on the back.

"You've always liked Emmy. I'm not surprised all these years later that you still do." He takes a few steps toward the screen door before turning back to look at me. "Tell me this. Is there any time you've been with her when she hasn't gotten that look?"

"Yeah." I laugh. "When she's mad at me." I think of the fire in her eyes when I left the other night. Her temper was hot, but it put color in her cheeks and made her spine stiffen some.

He smiles. "Seems fitting. She always did have a stubborn streak."

"She sure did."

"So how'd you leave things with her?"

"With her pissed off at me. She wants to be in control so she can keep her distance."

"Kinda like you," he muses and draws a quick glare from me that doesn't faze him. "And let me guess, you let her know you were the one who was going to set the pace?"

"Damn straight."

"Your mom would disagree with your line of thinking."

"So, don't tell her."

"I won't." His laugh rings out, and I know my brothers have heard him so our time is limited. "You already have your answer how to handle her, Grant."

"What?" I tip the bottle up again.

"Make her mad at you. It might be frustrating. It might not be pretty, but then again, matters of the heart never are."

No one said anything about hearts.

SEVENTEEN

Emerson

He's still there. I can feel his eyes on me.

I huff as I lay the first of six canopies out on the ground and inspect it for any sign of tears or any seams that might need to be re-stitched before I can repack it in its rig.

"Who pissed off Malone?"

I look over to where Travis stands with his sleeveless shirt on, his baseball cap bent at the brim, and a red rag fisted in one hand, and I am thankful that my sunglasses hide the glare I shoot him. The sweet, old man who manages the airstrip doesn't deserve my vitriol, and yet, his comment has fanned the flames of the irritation Grant is causing.

"How do you know Grant?" I ask.

"Everyone knows the Malones in this town. They're as much a part of Sunnyville as the grapes that grow on the hills around here." He adjusts the brim of his cap.

"For the record, I didn't piss off Malone." I walk to the other side of the canopy, which is starting to billow from the breeze, and force myself not to rush through the inspection. These chutes stop our falls, so it definitely doesn't pay to be hasty.

"If you didn't piss him off, why's he been sitting at the end of the runway for the past hour?"

"He is? I didn't notice." I don't even venture to look the way of his police cruiser where it sits blaringly out of place because I refuse to give either man the satisfaction of knowing I have been paying attention.

"Yep. Right out there." He lifts a chin and eyes me as he tries to figure out if I'm lying or not.

"Humph." At this point, the less I say the better.

"D'ya want me to go find out? Maybe he's interested in jumping. Having a Malone jump here might be good for business."

"Nah. He's not worth the wasted breath. Thanks for the offer, though." I squat and begin the methodical process of packing the first canopy into its pack under the scrutiny of both men. Each minute that passes only serves to annoy me further, until I'm huffing every few seconds to show some kind of resistance.

"Well then . . ." Travis's boots scuffle against the pavement until they are in my eyesight, prompting me to look up at him. "I put a to-do list on your desk. It isn't too long, but . . . it has to get done."

"I'll take care of it in a bit. Thanks." I focus again on the task at hand. After a minute, I hear him turn and head back inside, leaving me alone to ignore Grant.

Over the next hour, I work on the next five packs, well aware of Grant's presence. Reminded of the kiss we shared. Of the demands he laid down. Of the frustration I feel every time I think of him—*which is a lot*—when I don't want to think of him at all.

I don't get handled. I don't get played.

Even being firm in those beliefs, the scene from the bar plays in my mind over and over again. By the time I'm done, I'm hot, I'm tired, and I'm irritated to all hell.

"Whoa, where's the fire?" Leo asks as I slam into the front office of Blue Skies, stomping my feet like a tantruming toddler.

"Don't ask," I grumble as I walk right past him and into my office, shutting the door behind me. He stares at me through the glass door, completely confused, so I turn to stare out the window, which of course directly faces where Grant is parked.

For the love of God.

My phone is in my hand, and I'm pushing send without thinking this through.

"Officer Malone."

"Don't give me your 'Officer Malone' bullshit. How about Officer Stalker? Or Officer Asshole? It looks like you're a real crime fighter, sitting out there at the end of an empty runway."

His chuckle fills the line and grates on every nerve that isn't already shredded. "You never know where a crime may occur." There's a slow, relaxed drawl to his voice.

"Huh."

"Like it sure is a damn crime how good you look in that flight suit when you bend over and fold those parachutes."

I click end on the phone and stew as I pace the short distance of my office like a caged animal. He's going to sit out there for over two hours and that's all he has? *The jerk.*

I hit send again and grit my teeth harder with each and every ring. He finally picks up on the fourth one, right before it goes to voice mail.

"Seriously? That's the best you can do? You've gotta work on a better line than that."

"I knew you'd call back."

"You're infuriating."

"Perhaps."

"Definitely." I sit in my chair and then stand again, too antsy to stay still. "Why have you been sitting out there all day? If it's just to annoy the hell out of me, you've succeeded. Whatever else it is you're trying to do, it isn't going to work," I lie.

"Mmm."

"What's that supposed to—Oh . . ." The light bulb comes on. "I see what you're doing here, Malone."

"What's that?"

"You're trying to get the upper hand."

"I am?"

"Quit answering everything I say with a question, damn it." I throw my hands up in exasperation.

"Why does that bug you?"

"Grrr. You just did it again!"

"Do you think I don't know that?" he says, and I can hear the smile in his voice, but I'm not going to play into his question carnival again.

"I'm not letting anyone control me or any situation regardless of what one particularly annoying male may think."

His chuckle fills the line again, and I hate that with as mad as I am at him, it's still sexy as hell. "You sure about that?"

"Damn sure."

"You might want to double-check that hill you're willing to die on."

"Why's that?" I narrow my brow as I stare out at his cruiser.

"Because I've already gotten what I came for."

"Yeah? What's that?"

"You to be thinking about me."

The line goes dead.

And before I can make it out of the building, temper leaving smoke in my wake, his cruiser is already pulling out of the driveway onto the main highway.

"You to be thinking of me," I mutter in disgust.

Because he's right.

I am.

And hell if he didn't just get the upper hand.

EIGHTEEN

Emerson

"HELLO?"

Crap. Why did I think calling him would be easier than texting him? That deep rumble of his voice. The memory of his kiss on my tongue. The thought of that smile that makes butterflies take flight in my stomach.

Get a grip, Em. It's Phony Maloney.

"Will you stop trying to win my friends over to your side?" Impatience owns my voice as I look through the sliding glass door into Desi's kitchen, where she is flitting around oohing and ahhing over the delivery.

"Come again?"

"The Williams Sonoma basket. The gift certificate for a cooking class. I mean, really?" I huff and put a hand on my hip.

"What? I'm not allowed to send a thank-you gift for having me over the other night? You know my momma, Em. She's real big on manners."

"Manners, my ass."

"What was that about your ass?" He starts with the questions as responses bit again.

"Nothing. Never mind."

"Were we hanging up now?" The humor in his voice sparks my temper, and I hate that he's getting exactly what wants from me—a response.

I can't help it.

"I forget. Were you always this annoying when we were younger?" I grit out as Desi pulls out a bottle of some kind of olive oil and holds it to her chest as if it's the Hope Diamond. I roll my eyes as I wait for his answer.

"Not that I know of, but I do remember you being a pain in the ass."

"I was not."

"Hmm, you sure about that?"

I hate that his comment gives me pause. That it leaves me standing in Desi's backyard, scouring my memories and wondering if he's right. I can't recall any one situation to disprove him.

"You there?" he asks, his voice full of humor and feigned impatience.

"Stop trying to distract me and stop trying to buy my friends."

"That's a steep accusation."

"What else do you call it?"

"Positioning?" He chuckles.

"This conversation is over."

"Okay." There's silence except for his breathing on the other line. "If it's over, why haven't you hung up?"

"Because you need to hang up first." Oh my God. I'm reverting to being a teenager here. Why does he make me act this juvenile?

"Ladies first."

If the phone was old school, I would have slammed it down, but it isn't, so I can't. There is absolutely no satisfaction in pushing end.

"This is absolute heaven," Desi calls from inside the house. "Come look."

"I'll pass," I say drolly as I move to the open door to watch her fawn all over what really is a gift tailor-made for my best friend. I can't be blind to his consideration, but I know deep down he's doing it to irk me and *position* himself in my life.

"Isn't this the sweetest thing? And all for having him over the other night. They don't make men like him anymore."

It's the second time I've heard that, but it strikes my ear differently from when she said it before. "The other night?"

Desi looks up, doe eyes blinking rapidly before looking back down to sort through the bagged pasta and gourmet sauces included. "Yeah. The barbecue."

"But that wasn't the other night." I step forward and brace my hands on the counter across from her.

She waves a hand my way. "Semantics, Em. The other night, a few weeks ago, it's all the same thing."

No it isn't.

And as she prattles on about this and that and truffle oil and terms that sound cook-ish but I'm not certain, the phrase "the other night" continues to replay in my head.

Have they gotten together another night to conspire about me? Desi told me she was busy last week when I asked her to go get some sushi, but she wouldn't tell me with what. Did she and Grant meet up so she could help him plan ways to win me over?

Correction—annoy the hell out of me.

Winning me over would mean he has a chance, which he doesn't. Okay, maybe he has a tiny one, but that's beside the point.

Another cry of pleasure from Desi comes at the same time a thought crosses my mind that makes my stomach drop. What if they weren't conspiring ways to win me over? What if I pushed Grant away enough that he moved on to Desi, and now they're seeing each other? My mind stumbles over the thought.

I'd like to say good riddance. That I don't care.

Not about how he delivered pizza to the crew at Blue Skies unannounced and for no reason. Or how a box of tampons with a blue ribbon tied around it somehow ended up on the hood of my car parked in the airport lot. Admittedly, that was so not cool, and while I'm sure every guy working that day thought it was strange, I still might have sat with it in my lap, fingers playing with the bow. I might have remained there, watching planes take off and land until sunset because I was so lost in thought and at peace that I hadn't noticed the day slipping away. I hadn't felt that way in the longest time.

My gut churns because as annoying as everything he's doing is, I hate the thought of him just . . . moving on. Would Desi do that to me? Would Grant?

"Nothing's worth it if it's this much work."

His words from the barbecue ring in my ears and cause a slight flutter of panic. But then I see Desi smile a mile wide and know she'd never do that to me, but that doesn't rule out a plotting session. And still, I hate that the thought of him charming someone else—because that is what he's doing to everyone else while he does nothing but provoke me—doesn't sit well with me.

Then I realize that . . . his plan has worked. He's maneuvered me. He's making everyone around me like him so when I tell him to take a hike, they'll all tell me I'm crazy.

Goddamnit, I've been handled. Positioned. Whatever he wants to call it.

Screw him. I'll find a way to outwit him. To put the ball back in my court. To take back control of the situation. The question is, when it seems he's always a few steps ahead of me, how do I do that?

I guess I could have started by accepting Josh's invitation last night to meet up for a little late-night rendezvous. But I didn't. I told him I was busy when in reality it was me, my hot plate, and *Big Brother* on television.

Did I seriously give up what I know from experience to be an incredible orgasm for Grant Malone? Or let's get real, multiple orgasms? It is Josh, after all.

I sure as hell did.

This is not good. He's already winning, and I haven't even read the damn rules yet.

"Em, look at this." Desi holds up some kind of kitchen contraption in glee.

Is that basket a bottomless pit of bribery?

"If you don't snatch that man up, I will."

Apparently, it is.

I groan.

How can I compete with this? How can I fight back when he is single-handedly persuading everyone around me to take his side?

He may think he's in the lead, but he hasn't seen me in action yet.

Now I just need to rewrite his damn rules and figure out a plan of attack of my own.

NINETEEN

Grant

"ARE YOU TRYING TO GET OFFICER OF THE YEAR OR something?" Nate asks with a laugh.

"Huh?" I look up from where I'm lacing my boots to see him hauling two file boxes stacked on each other into my family room. "Are those the archived files?"

"Yep. Your patio cover."

"Ain't that the truth?" Those are some serious boxes.

"There are two more in the car, but please, stay where you are and sip your coffee," he says, holding his hands out in the stop motion. "I have nothing better to do than haul your shit around."

"I knew you were good for something," I say with a laugh as I make a show of sitting back into the couch, propping my feet on the coffee table, and making a loud *mmm* sound as I sip my coffee.

"Asshole."

"The one and only."

He laughs as the screen door shuts behind him while I get up to move the boxes out of the way. I have the lid off and am running my fingers over the tabs of the files to make sure they are the ones I asked for when he comes back in and drops the remaining two boxes with a *thud*.

"You got some dust on your uniform," I say as I point to nothing on his chest.

Nate lifts his middle finger as he makes his way to my coffee maker and pours himself some as if he lives here.

Cold Case File #865593: Jensen Darby Homicide - 6/12/2001
Cold Case File #628336: Mimi LaRuby Missing Person – 1/04/1995

"Make yourself at home. Oh wait, you already have." I say, only half paying attention as he opens the fridge and pulls out the creamer.

Cold Case File #458899: Matthew Larsho Homicide – 9/10/1992
Closed File #713920: Emerson Reeves – Sexual Abuse – 10/23/1997

Nate says something, but I don't hear him because I can't tear my eyes off the label on the file.

"These files . . ."

The green folder is several inches thick. Unfortunately, I know from experience on other case files I've looked through what it will contain. Evidence. Physical exams. Testimony. Psychological evaluations. Pictures.

Fucking Christ.

Pictures.

"Yeah, what about them?" Nate asks as my stomach revolts at the thought of what is contained in between the covers. The coffee that tasted like heaven minutes ago, feels like acid eating a hole in my stomach. "Is something wrong? They were the ones on the list on your desk."

"The list?" I ask absently but can picture it perfectly. The list of names where I was so preoccupied with curiosity about Emerson's past—what happened to her father and how bad it was for her—that I wrote her name down at the top of the paper. I can see it clearly. Her name in block letters with two lines beneath it. How Nate could have assumed it was for emphasis when it was nothing more than me doodling as I thought of her.

"Is everything okay, man?"

"Yeah. Sorry. I thought I forgot one, but I see it here," I say to distract him from coming over and inspecting the files.

"The boxes were ready to go when I picked them up, so if something is missing, blame the admin who pulled them. Not the messenger."

"No worries. I'm sure they're all here."

I had never intended to look up her case. Obviously, it had crossed my mind, but I had decided it was a line I wasn't going to cross. Now that the file, and the information inside it, is at my fingertips, I can't stop staring at it.

I can't stop wondering.

"Earth to Grant." Nate stands in the middle of my family room with his cup of coffee in hand and makes a show of looking at his watch. Our shift is about to start.

"What? Sorry." I shove the lid on the box and walk away from it.

For now.

I don't think any type of distraction is going to prevent me from thinking about the closed file nestled in the box.

"Something wrong?"

"Nah. I'm good." I force a smile and walk over to grab my cell and wallet so he can't look too closely.

"You ready?"

"Yeah. Sure. Let's go."

But as I shut the door, I give the box one last look.

Fuck.

TWENTY

Grant

"OFFICER MALONE?"

"Yo." I shove my chair out and wheel across the aisle so the receptionist can see me.

"Delivery for you."

Nate eyes me from across the aisle of desks, and I shrug. "For me?"

"Who's subpoenaing you now?" he asks.

"Beats the hell outta me," I say as I grab the manila envelope and turn it over in my hands. There's no return address on it.

"Hey, Sue?" I call to the receptionist before she retreats back to her desk.

"Yeah?"

"Who delivered this?"

"Some guy. Kinda cute if you like the tall, dark, and handsome vibe." She flashes me a smile.

"Yeah, sounds just like my type." I roll my eyes and get a few laughs from the guys as I slide a finger beneath the flap and open the envelope.

There are waivers filled out with my name and yellow "sign here" tabs everywhere a signature is required. At first, I'm confused as to what all this is. Then the gift certificate works its way out from between the papers.

"Blue Skies Skydiving School Gift Certificate: Good for one tandem flight with lead instructor, Emerson Reeves. Unless of course you don't trust her . . ."

Look who just stepped onto the playing field with a Hail Mary right off the bat.

Took her long enough.

I chuckle, which has Nate narrowing his eyes at me. "I gotta make a call," I say as I stand and make my way out of the station away from the other officers who like to gossip like little old ladies.

"Blue Skies, this is Emerson, how may I help you?" Her voice sounds like goddamn sex. And she's doing it on purpose because her caller ID tells her exactly who's calling.

"You tell me. How can you help me?"

She murmurs a sound that I swear to God sounds like how I imagine her fingernails scratching over my balls would feel, and that thought alone tells me I'm so far fucked when it comes to her it isn't even funny. "I see you got my gift."

"I did."

"Just thought I'd pay a little token of appreciation to our officers who protect and serve."

"I think I'm the only one here who received a gift certificate, though."

"Yeah, well, you're a special case." She laughs. I can picture her standing on the tarmac with that damn flight suit on, her baseball cap pulled low as she peers down the stretch of runway from behind her aviators. "Are you calling to schedule your flight time?"

"Not hardly. I told you, I don't trust anyone, especially when it comes to jumping out of an airplane."

"Not even little ol' me?"

"Especially not little ol' you." I laugh, imagining she has a dartboard somewhere with my picture on the bull's-eye.

"What's wrong, Malone? Should I call you *Daisy*?"

"Touché."

"What then? Are you that afraid of a woman being in control?"

Her voice is coy, playful, but I can hear the underlying tone of curiosity in it.

"Not in the least, Em. I actually think it's sexy as hell. What's even sexier is a woman who demands control from everyone else except for the one she's with behind closed doors because she trusts him implicitly. Now that? That's a turn on."

I hear her suck in a breath in reaction, and I love knowing that I've gotten to her somehow. "Well, I guess we both have control and trust issues we need to work through, don't we?"

"I thought that was what we were doing."

With a chuckle, I end the call and let out a long, controlled sigh.

Fuck. I may be getting the upper hand, but hell if I'll take any hand about now so long as it's hers.

TWENTY-ONE

Grant

"HELLO, ARE YOU OFFICER MALONE?"

What the?

I look out the open passenger side window to see a fresh-faced kid, late teens, dark features, about five foot eight, two hundred pounds.

"Can I help you?" I eye him. My immediate hunch is that he's harmless, but I don't like that I can't see both his hands.

"Yeah, I have a delivery for you."

"You what?" I sit a little taller in the driver's seat and study him closer.

"A delivery. Here." He shoves a pink box through the window. "From The Donut Shoppe."

"The Donut Shoppe?"

"Yes. There's a note on the top."

I eye him warily. "'Kay. Thanks." The kid starts to walk away. "Hey, wait." I dig into my wallet and pull out some ones to give him.

"Thanks," he says, but I'm already looking at the top of the pink pastry box. "Donut think you've won this battle – Emerson"

I stare at the writing and do the only thing I can, laugh.

"What's that?" Nate asks as he slides into the car.

"Emerson."

"She's sending you love notes on donut boxes now? I thought you were the one trying to get the upper hand."

"I'm trying, dude. Believe me, I'm trying."

"Well, try harder. If you play this game any longer, your balls will become bluer than your uniform."

"Fuck off."

He smirks. "At least someone would be getting some then."

"Whatever. Dude, you wish—"

"All units. 10-16 at 12662 Serenity Court."

I don't even have to glance over to Nate to tell him to respond. He already has the radio in his hand as I throw the car in gear and flip the lights and sirens on.

It's Keely's address.

We make it there in minutes, and I turn the siren off but leave the lights on as I turn into the neighborhood. We're parked in the driveway and out of the car, my fist banging on the door in seconds.

"Sunnyville Police Department, open up." I pound a few more times as Nate steps on the planters to try to see inside the front window.

"There was yelling and screaming." I round at the sound of a feeble voice, my hand automatically going to my weapon, but I ease off when I see the elderly neighbor from across the street.

"What else?" Nate asks as he steps forward, leaving me to man the front door. I hear words such as "shouting" and "threatening," but when it comes down to being a witness to anything, she didn't see much.

I pound again. "Mrs. Davis, open up. We just want to make sure you and Keely are okay in there."

Glancing around, I note that a few other neighbors are home from work already, a few even nosing out of their houses to see what the problem is. More rocks are painted in the entryway—hints of a normal, creative child or signs of a little girl escaping the fighting inside her house.

Just as I'm about to pound again, I hear the deadbolt slide, and the door cracks open. Amelia Davis stands there, tears staining her face and hair a mess.

"Mrs. Davis? Is everything okay in there?" I ask, voice gentle. I'm well aware that Mr. Davis might be on the opposite side of the door, judging her every answer and the according punishment.

"Yes. It's fine. Everything is fine," she says unconvincingly as she widens the door without my asking so I can see inside. My eyes scan her person for bruises, but she's wearing long sleeves mid-summer. "He's not home, if that's what you're worried about."

"Momma? Is everything okay?" Keely's timid voice calls from inside.

"Yes, sweetie. The nice officers from the other day stopped by. They wanted to see the new rocks you painted." She lies easily, and I'm not sure if I respect or detest her for protecting her child.

"He did? He is?" Awe fills her voice as she peeks her sweet face beyond the corner wall, blue eyes wide as a smile spreads on her lips.

"I did." I nod and play along with the mother as I eye Nate to take over the questions while I separate Keely from their conversation.

"I'm sorry, Officer. It was just a fight." I overhear Amelia say to Nate as I walk Keely down the path and away from the front door.

"Are you here because my mom and dad were fighting again?" she asks and breaks my heart.

I nod, not wanting to lie about the obvious and needing her to trust me. "Mm-hmm. It's our job to make sure everything is okay." I kneel so I'm eye to eye with her. "Is everything okay, Keely?"

She stares at me with eyes that have seen way too much, and her bottom lip trembles some before she nods ever so slowly.

I could kill the bastard for putting that look on her face. Wring his goddamn neck.

"You sure?"

She glances back to her mom and then down to her fingers, which have found their way to twist into her shirt. "Yeah." Her little shoulders shrug. "Mommy had me go in my room and be quiet. I don't know what happened."

"Okay." I nod. I can face down a six-foot suspect and know if he's lying or not, but give me a five-year-old little girl, and I'm lost in fucking translation. "What were they arguing about?"

"Stuff." She shrugs again. Twists her fingers. Shifts her feet. "Money and just stuff."

"Okay. Were you scared for your mommy or daddy at all?"

She finally lifts her eyes to meet mine, and I can see her fighting wanting to betray her parents. "Yeah. I don't like when they fight. Nemo and I hide under the covers and sing 'You are My Sunshine' so we don't hear them."

"That's my favorite," I say, thinking of how my mom used to sing it to Luke when he was a baby. "And a very *smart* move on your part."

"Did you really want to see my rocks?"

"Yes. Of course. That was why I came to talk to you. I've found some new favorites." I glance over to Nate to see where we are in the call, and his slight nod and stiff expression tell me he's getting no-fucking-where. "The poop emoji one is my new favorite," I say, trying to keep a straight face.

Her giggle makes me smile, though. "You know what a poop emoji is?"

"Of course I do. Don't let the uniform fool you. I know poop emojis like the best of them."

And every time I say "poop," I get another giggle, a sound that should be a norm for her but probably isn't. Déjà vu hits me in the moment, much like it did the last time I was here. I shake it, along with the image of the strawberry blonde little girl in my memories, away but come up with an idea.

"Tell me something, Keely, do you like to keep secrets?" I ask in a hushed voice.

"You mean like secrets that will get you in trouble or secrets like a super spy?"

"Like a super spy."

She nods, her smile widening. "I can keep super spy secrets. Of course I can."

"I thought so. I mean, I gave you the badge last time, but I was pretty certain you were spy worthy."

"I am. I am."

"Sometimes, when you're a secret spy, you have to leave coded messages for other secret spies so they know what's going on."

"You do?"

"Yep." I nod, knowing I need to wrap this up but also needing to get this point across. "Sometimes the littlest of signs tells other spies that things are okay or they're not okay."

"Really?"

"Definitely."

"So what does that have to do with me?"

"I need you to be a super spy for me. It's my job as a police officer to know that you and your mom are okay at all times." I can see her little wheels turning, and I speak before she can question it too much. "So, I'm thinking that we use your rocks as our secret code."

Her eyes and smile both widen, pride in her work replacing any skepticism she had seconds ago. "My rocks?"

"Yes, but you can't tell anyone else or else the secret spy code will be broken, and then we'll no longer be spies."

"I can keep a secret."

I eye her as if I'm doubting her, but then when I smile, she knows I trust her. "Good. I think we should come up with a certain picture or word, and if you paint that on a rock, then I know you're afraid and need help for you or your mom."

Skepticism is back, but it isn't as deep when she asks, "What word or picture?" Her voice is barely audible.

"You can pick it."

"Hmm." She twists her lips and thinks so hard it's adorable. "Watermelon."

"Watermelon?" I laugh, not expecting that answer in a million years.

"Yeah, watermelon. I'm not that good at painting, though. I know you're just saying it because I'm a kid and you're an adult so you have to say it so you don't hurt my feelings . . . but I promise I can really paint a good watermelon."

"I believe you." I love the little glimpses of her personality that are starting to shine through her fear. "Will it be green and—"

"No. It will be red with black seeds; although, mommy only buys the kind without seeds and those are no fun because there are no seeds to see how far you can spit."

"Got it. A red rock with black seeds." I glance at the painted rocks already there and know I'd be able to spot it in a second. "Good choice. Now, we need to decide on a place to put our secret signal. Where do you think?"

She bites her bottom lip and looks around. "How about right there at the corner of the sidewalk?"

"I think that's an excellent choice. See? You're already proving what a great secret spy you're going to be."

"How often are you going to check for the code?"

"As often as I need to," I say, not wanting to overcommit but needing her to understand she's safe.

"What are you two talking about?" Amelia asks as she comes up behind Keely and puts her arm around her daughter's shoulders.

"Secret spies and watermelon," Keely says.

"Is that a show on Nickelodeon?" Amelia asks.

"Yep." Keely looks back at me one last time with a soft smile before her mom ushers her to the house and shuts the door without another word.

"Did you get anywhere?" I ask Nate as we climb in the cruiser.

"You mean did she admit that the bastard hits her so she wears long sleeves in summer to hide the bruises? No. No matter how many times I told her that we'd protect her, that all she has to do is press charges to protect Keely, she kept denying anything was wrong."

"Son of a bitch."

"'Bout sums it up."

I pound my fist on the steering wheel. "I'm sure we'll be back again."

"We can't help her unless she wants the help."

"And in the meantime, the girl is in the crosshairs. That seems fair," I say, frustrated disgust edging my tone.

"Yep." He blows out a sigh. "At least we have donuts."

"No, you have donuts," I say, hating their smell currently filling my car.

TWENTY-TWO

Grant

"Call Emerson and tell her you're running late and then turn your car around and go home."

Desi sputters on the other end of the phone. "You're cute and all, but that doesn't excuse you for being a bossy asshole."

I glance over to where Emerson is sitting at the bar about fifty feet away. Her strawberry blonde hair is tucked behind her ear, her fingers twirl the straw stuck in her drink, and those long, tan legs call to every man in here. The thought alone has me itching for a fight or any excuse to get my anger over the Keely situation out of my damn system.

"I'll owe you one," I say between gritted teeth as another man sits beside her and offers small talk she doesn't encourage. But still, she smiles. Still, she's goddamn gorgeous.

"How do you know I'm meeting her for a drink?" Desi asks.

"Because I'm sitting in a back booth at Davenport's, drinking away my shitty day, and I'm watching Emerson sit at the bar and ignore every man who dares pull up a stool next to her."

Desi snorts. "So, in other words, you're pissed at every man going near her, and the sight of them has started the testosterone-laced caveman part of you to finally make your goddamn move instead of sitting on the sidelines, playing games like you have been."

"I am not playing games, Desi. I am making sure she knows she can't control this like she's controlled every other relationship she's ever had . . . at least according to you." I let that dig sit there to let her know if she talks about our conversations to Emerson, then I'll talk, too.

"Are you blackmailing me, Officer Sexy?" she teases.

"Just stating the facts, ma'am."

Another man. Another clench of my fists.

"Well, it's about damn time. I was getting dried up over here waiting for you to act."

"Yeah, yeah."

"Just so you know . . ." The four words every man cringes when he hears. "You're I'm-in-control shit doesn't fly with me any more than it flies with Em. I'm only calling her and doing what you ask because you two need to get over this cat-and-mouse game and eat the damn cheese already."

"Goodbye, Des."

The call ends, and I sit back and wait for Emerson to pick up her phone. As if on cue, the moment I think it, her phone rings. She looks at her watch while talking to Desi, and she shrugs, flinging one hand up as if to question Desi when she's nowhere in sight. She may be irritated, but that only serves in my favor in the end.

As soon as she sets down the phone, I'm already ringing her.

"Hello?"

"Hey, I'm heading out to you right now for my jump."

There's resignation in her sigh over the connection, and I physically watch as she slumps her shoulders back against the chair. "Not today. I can't."

"I thought you said any time, though." I push her buttons.

"Yeah, well, any time is not right now. Besides, I'm not even there."

"Where are you?"

"I'm meeting Desi."

"What's wrong?"

"Just a shitty day all around."

"You and me both. Wanna talk about it?" She's silent for a moment as a man sits too closely next to her and she shifts to regain her personal space. "Tell him to back the fuck off, Em."

It takes a second, but I can tell the moment awareness hits her. Her spine stiffens. Her fingers tighten on her drink. But ever cool, she takes her time scooting back and looking around the bar. She finds me right away. Our eyes lock. A smile flickers and fades before I hear her sharp intake of breath on the phone.

"Tell him, Emerson. Tell him you're with me."

Her brow narrows, but she doesn't move. "I'm meeting Desi," she says into the phone instead of taking the ten steps to tell me face to face.

"No, you're not. She isn't coming. I called her and told her to turn around and go back home." Temper stews on that gorgeous face of hers. "*Tell him*."

She doesn't say a word to the man next to her, who is still eyeing her, but rather slides some cash across the bar, pushes her chair in, and then stalks over to me, phone still held to her ear.

She stands in front of me, and every part of me begs to kiss her. Fuck her. Anything with her because it feels like forever since we kissed and a lifetime of foreplay that has in no way been satisfying.

"You don't get to tell me what to do."

Okay. This is how she wants this to go. "Have a seat."

"No."

"Have a seat, Emmy."

"It's Emerson." She glares, her feet shifting as she lowers her phone from her ear. I eye the seat next to her and then look back to her.

"Sit."

"You're an asshole, you know that?" she sneers.

"Yeah. Probably. But I've had a shitty day, so fucking sue me if I want you to sit and have a few drinks with me and maybe see why your day was so goddamn crappy too . . ." I shrug. "Sit."

Her emotions wage a war across her face, but I can see reluctance flash through those eyes of hers before she lowers herself to the seat across from me. Without looking away, I lift a hand to the bartender and motion for another round. We don't speak until the drinks arrive, tension mounting between the two of us for some odd reason.

Foreplay.

I smile at the thought, and I know it pisses her off.

"Since when did you become such a stalker?"

"Me? Stalker?" I laugh, and this banter is just what I need.

"Yeah, word has it that you've been asking about where I live."

"You mean the one question I asked Desi?"

Her lips quirk as she fights a smile. "Yeah, that question."

"If I'm going to stalk you effectively, don't I need to know that info?"

She's still trying to make up her mind whether she likes this idea, just like I'm still trying to figure out if I like her living in the loft of a hangar doing odd jobs in exchange for rent and transportation. Even if it's for the harmless caretaker, Travis Barnhardt, it's still another thing on her plate to do when she already does too much.

"Being a cop and all, I figured you had better means than loose-lips Desi."

"I happen to have a soft spot for loose-lips Desi," I say just to irritate her.

"No shit. Give the girl William Sonoma, and she'll sing like a canary."

I laugh, which draws looks from others around us. "I'm afraid to know what else she confessed."

"That's for me to know and you to never know." Her eyes glance up from her drink and hold mine.

"So, you had a shitty day, too?" I prompt.

She shrugs. "Something like that. What about you? Why was your day so bad?"

"I had a donut delivery even though I hate donuts. My cruiser still smells like them."

There's her smile. "Must have been donut torture."

"Yep. It was. Waterboarding and the smell of donuts are right up there together." I lean back in the booth and take a long sip of my drink before pushing the bowl of pretzels and nuts across the table toward her. "A call we had today got to me."

"Want to share?"

"Can't . . . I just can't," I explain, when what I need is to talk about it. But not now. Not with her while I keep seeing her face in Keely's. Not until I can separate the facts from the past. "What about you?"

"You know what, let's not and say we did." She laughs and takes a sip, averting her eyes from mine. It's a gesture that only serves to remind me of Keely again.

"Nah. I'm not biting. What's going on, Em?"

She sighs and concentrates on picking through the bowl to steal all the cashews from it. I give her the time and smile at the prick who's glaring at me from across the way because she's talking to me and not him.

Maybe I'm taunting him because I'm in the mood for a fight. Maybe I'm just being an asshole. Then again, maybe I just want to kiss Emerson and know this is bad timing to be thinking about it.

"I told you I'm trying to buy Blue Skies, right?" I nod. "Well, trying is the operative word. In fact, my loan officer is a total prick."

"Is he not responding?"

Her laugh has my back up instantly. "He's responding, all right. I think the only reason he's responding and considering me for the loan is because he thinks he can get in my pants."

I don't like the fucker already. "Who is it?" I demand.

She eyes me and twists her lips. "He's a loan officer." She deadpans. "I can handle it myself."

Bullshit.

"Then go to a different bank." Simple.

"I wish," she says in a way that makes me want to move to her side of the booth and slide an arm around her. I'm not quite sure we're at that stage yet. "But they were the only bank even willing to consider my application. When my mom got sick, money was tight, so we used her credit, my credit, anything we could to pay for treatments. I've worked my ass off to pay it all back, took odd jobs everywhere I traveled to, and have sold off everything I own to do so."

"So, you have no collateral."

"Nope." She sighs, and I hate seeing the sadness in her eyes. "It's all paid off, but that doesn't mean my credit score has recovered. I just need a fresh start, and Blue Skies is my chance."

"Everyone needs a fresh start now and again. Besides, I find what you did—paying off the debt instead of declaring bankruptcy—very admirable."

"It is what it is." She rolls her neck.

"So, who's the prick?"

"I told you, none of your business. I've dealt with a lot worse than a handsy loan officer, Malone."

"Handsy?"

"Chill out. I'm a big girl."

TWENTY-THREE

Emerson

"Chill out. I'm a big girl."

A look comes over Grant's face that makes every part of me come alive. It was an innocent comment on my part, and yet, the look in his eyes is suggestive as hell and perfectly fitting for this darkened, back corner of the bar.

"I'm well aware that you're a big girl, Emerson. You've gone out of your way to make me acknowledge it."

I'm not sure if it's a dig, but it's true, so I don't take it as anything other than that.

"I heard you dropped the donuts by the homeless shelter." His eyes flash up, and I'm immediately reminded of how I felt when I found out through the grapevine about what he did. "I have my own stalking capabilities."

"So I see."

"I think it was a super cool thing for you to do."

"Besides meeting you here, it was the easiest decision of my day."

I can see sadness in his eyes as he goes away from me momentarily. Back to his call? Back to the reason he is here, drinking in a bar by himself, perhaps?

"Tell me about your call," I prompt and reach out and put my hand on his. "I'd like to know about it."

His hand stiffens momentarily, and I know he's battling with whether he should talk or not—a blue blood through and through. He picks up his drink with his free hand, takes a sip before setting it down, and then laces his fingers with mine. But he still doesn't look at me.

And as the silent seconds tick by, my mind begins to wander. To how we just officially held hands and I'm not freaking out over it. To how it feels natural and pretty damn good. I think I'm more freaked out over that than the notion that we are sitting in a bar and looking like a couple.

"I used our rock thing today," he finally says as he meets my eyes, but I'm completely clueless as to what he's referring to.

"Our rock thing?" I ask, head angled as if it would help me understand.

"Yeah. It came to me today when I was on my call. I thought it might be a way to connect to a little girl, and I told her about it."

I'm so lost. Rock thing? What am I missing here?

"I don't understand."

"Yeah. Our rock thing. You know what, fuck it. Forget I said anything."

"No. Please. I want to know."

"My call today. It was a 10-16 . . . sorry, a domestic disturbance, and it wasn't the first time we'd been called out there. I think the dad is abusing the mom, but the mom is making excuses to protect him. It's a classic case of him beating her down enough, grooming her, so that she thinks he can't live without her and vice versa. I don't know. I don't get it, but I know it's real because I've seen it more times than I care to count."

"I'm sorry." It's all I say, but I squeeze his hand to lend him silent support as he thinks about something I can't even fathom.

"So am I." He sighs, the sag of his shoulders a visible manifestation of the toll the call has taken on him. "I want to help the mom, but I can't help her until she wants it, and I hope that it isn't too late. But what's even worse is that they have a daughter. She's five, and the sweetest little girl who is caught in the middle of a shit sandwich. She's defending a dad, who isn't nice, and loving a mom, who doesn't defend her. All this little girl wants is just to be a kid."

"That's rough. I don't know what to say other than I'm sorry. I can't imagine the things you see every day. The things you deal with," I say, really wanting to go back and find out what he meant about the rocks. Something is niggling at the back of my mind. I'm not sure what it is, but I'm too scared to ask.

"You know what? I think we should stop talking about our shitty days and go get ice cream."

"Ice cream?" I laugh. "We've gone from drinking away our sorrows to ice cream?"

"Yep. Do you have something against ice cream?"

"Umm . . . no. Who could hate ice cream?" My stomach growls at the thought of food, reminding me just how long it's been since I've eaten. "But then again, after my crappy day, this alcohol isn't so bad, either."

"There's my Emmy." He flashes me an irresistible grin that freezes when we both realize what he said.

I'm not going to lie and say those words don't make me want to give in on this silly game we've been playing—control be damned—and kiss him. Right here. Right now.

Our eyes hold and try to read what the other is saying. It's then that I feel his hand tighten around mine and realize our fingers are still interlocked.

"I know a way we can mix both ice cream and alcohol," he says, eyes never leaving mine.

"How?"

"Mudslides. They have them here." My stomach rumbles. "You want one?"

"Like you have to ask." I laugh when he raises his finger to the bartender before I even finish the sentence.

"I'm a big girl, Grant. I don't need you walking me home," I say and then giggle when I realize that I'm nowhere near the airstrip. But still. Saying it is like meaning it, right?

He swings our joined hands as he walks beside me. "I'm not walking you home. I'm walking you to my home since we aren't sober enough to drive." He veers off the sidewalk and up a short little path.

"Grant?" I ask as I take in the wood porch of the house in front of us.

"I know you're a big girl, Em. I'm well aware of it."

His words hang in the air, hitting my slightly fuzzy mind as I follow him up the steps to stand under the porch light. "Is that flirting, Malone? Are you flirting with me?"

He yanks on my hand, and I land solidly against him. It takes a minute for our minds to register what's going on—that our bodies are pressed together—because we're too busy making sure our wobbly feet don't give out.

But when we're steady, everything registers for me. The heat of his body against mine. The hardness of it, too. The hitch of his breath, answering the gasp of mine. The darkening of his eyes. The tensing of his hand on mine. The flick of his tongue across his bottom lip.

And, oh, how I want him to be flirting with me.

Better yet, I want him to be kissing me. All of me.

The thought makes me giggle as we continue to stand body to body, a lot a bit tipsy, beneath a dim porch light on an empty and darkened street.

"We shouldn't do this," he murmurs more to himself than to me. It cues the panic inside me, screaming that this insane display of foreplay between us needs to have the match lit before I combust from sexual frustration.

"Why not?"

"Because you're Emmy." He brings his free hand up and runs a finger down the side of my cheek.

That touch, skin to skin, is like a mainline of electric current to charge that slow, sweet ache burning inside me. It only serves to make me want more.

"And you're Phony Maloney."

"Exactly."

He steps back, and I tighten my hold on his hand and step forward with him. "Are you telling me there is nothing here? No lust? No attraction? No anything?"

He gives me that sly smile of his again, the one that lights up his eyes and does funny things to my insides. "I never said that."

"Then what are you saying?"

"I'm saying . . . Christ, Em, I don't know what I'm saying." He runs a hand absently up and down the plane of my back.

"Maybe you're saying we need to get each other out of our systems." I utter the words before I think them and then feel ridiculous.

"What?" He laughs. "Are you saying what I think you're saying?"

His body is against mine. His cologne is in my nose. His laugh is in my ears. He's everywhere all the time.

Too much talk right now. Too much *saying*. Not enough action.

"*Yes.*"

A few seconds pass as he gauges whether I'm serious, and I wonder if he's going to take the bait. "And then what?" He angles his head to the side, silently asking a million questions my body wants to ignore.

"And then curiosity will be satisfied, and we'll be out of each other's systems."

"You think that's going to work? You think we've just met again after twenty years and it'll be that easy?"

He has a point, and I don't want to think about that or semantics or reality. I want to think about him. And me. And his mouth. And his hands.

So, I lean forward on my tiptoes and press my lips to his. "Enough talking, Malone."

He laughs, his lips vibrating against mine, but I don't relent. I want him. I want this. I know we're both buzzed, but maybe that's the best way for this to happen so I'm not nervous and overthinking and neither is he.

For a minute, I think he's going to reject me. It's in the way he stills for a brief moment, the way his lashes lower for just a second too long. Then he frames my face and leans back to look at me. Our breaths feather over each other's lips as an unspoken conversation passes between us. I can't put words to it, but somehow understand each and every syllable of it.

And then his mouth is on mine in a savage greeting of lips and tongues and hands on skin and history reconnected.

"Grant."

"Shh."

"Wait. I have rules."

He laughs with exasperation, a man being denied what's sitting at his fingertips. "Of course you do."

"No sleeping over. I don't do the sleeping together thing."

"No one said anything about sleeping, Em."

His smile sidelines me. The kiss he leans forward and brushes ever so tenderly against my lips makes me want to sag into him, even more so.

"No promises."

"I thought this was a one-night thing, right?"

"Yes, but no promises."

"I'm going to make you come. Can I promise you that?"

Another kiss. This time I take the lead and lick my tongue against his until I pull back and nip his lip. "I'll accept that promise."

"Good. Can we stop talking now because there are much more important things I want to be doing with my mouth, and every single one of them involves you and no words."

My teeth sink into my lower lip as our eyes meet. The door unlocks behind us. Our feet move in reflex. Our fingers link together.

Once over the threshold, we kiss again—his lips beginning their masterful assault of everything that is good and sexy and arousing and needed.

"God, yes."

His lips find my neck as my hand finds the door to push it shut behind me. As soon as the lever clicks, Grant has me up against it with one hand on my breast and his tongue licking its way up the line of my neck.

He laughs as he stumbles. I giggle as I grip his shoulders to steady us. But even when I do, the earth is still tilting beneath my feet from his desirous assault. Every sensation is welcome and wanted. Each touch of his another reason to temporarily ignore my history.

But he doesn't.

For some reason, the minute the thought crosses my mind, I can feel the sudden hesitancy in Grant's otherwise all-consuming and libidinous demeanor and know we are on the same page.

He is remembering.

He is wondering.

He is worrying.

"No," I gasp out in a desperate plea for him not to go there.

"Em." Regret. Fear. Uncertainty. All three meld and mesh in that one syllable of my name.

My hands are on his jaw, forcing his face up so that he has to meet my eyes through the dimly lit entry to his house. "No," I repeat. "I am not her anymore. She is not me. Don't do this, Grant."

With that simple statement . . . that simple devastating statement, I press my lips to his. I need him to see that I'm not a victim and that I refuse to be treated like one. I need him to know that he has no clue what I do or don't need, and therefore, I am going to show him.

As if he knows this is what I need, he allows me to take the reins. The man hell-bent on proving to me that he's in control, lets me take the lead in this dance that is uniquely ours.

"Show me," he murmurs, those two words as seductive as his touch.

And so, I show him.

With my hands and my tongue and my words and my touch.

This time, we start slowly. I tease and taunt him with the gentlest of caresses while my hands find the hem of his shirt and pull it from his pants. With the slightest of breaks of our lips, the fabric passes over his face and falls to the floor. I do the honors for myself next as we move slowly backward in that awkward dance of kiss, touch, retreat, repeat, until the backs of his legs hit the couch

"What do you need from me?" he whispers against my lips, unknowingly giving me the question I need and the willingness to take it.

I've never been shy about taking what I wanted from a guy before. I've never worried about what they thought because, in the end, we were both there for the same thing—pleasure. With Grant? I care. His ability to give me the things I need without even questioning is unnerving and comforting and makes me want this all the more.

"You. I just want you," I say as he hisses a breath when my hand slides inside the waistband of his jeans to find him hard and stiff and ready for me.

"Take me, Em."

And then our mouths crash together again in a torrent of desire that warns of its irreversible damage to my body and *my heart*. I push it away, focusing on his hands undoing my bra. The pads of his thumbs brushing ever so softly over the tips of my nipples. His fingers tugging at my zipper. The palms of his hands as they run down my sides and push my pants down over my hips.

My body reacts in every imaginable way to him. It wants and needs and begs and pleads. He pulls me against him so we're body to body. Skin to skin. Mouth to mouth.

"Christ, I want you," he says as he shoves his pants off and steps out of them.

"Then take me." I give his words back to him because control has given way to need, and hell if every part of me isn't ready and willing.

My hands are around his shaft, stroking him gently. I cry out as his fingers part me and find me wet, muscles vibrating, nerves stimulated and waiting to respond to his onslaught of touch.

He falls backward onto his couch—our laughs filling the room before they morph into drawn-out groans. There's the telltale rip of foil and then I straddle his lap. Our mouths meld again as I grind atop of him so that my arousal coats his cock, and the feel of him steals my breath.

Urgency becomes the name of the game.

I lift my hips so his hand can find its way between us, and his fingers press into me. I moan. My nails dig into his shoulders and score his skin. He doesn't seem to notice or even care as his fingers keep their even tempo.

"Grant. *God.* Yes. *Please.* I need. *Oh.*"

His chuckle is a murmur amidst the sounds I make, and at some point, I begin to beg. At least I think I do. Or maybe he does. I'm so caught up in the machinations of his fingers and the crest he's slowly building within me that I've lost all semblance of time and place. As long as he doesn't stop, I don't care where I am.

And in a practiced move that's both impressive and havoc inducing to every nerve within me, Grant withdraws his fingers from me and replaces them with the girth of his cock.

If I thought I'd felt pleasure before, I was dead wrong. This—his cock in me, his tongue licking against mine, the sexy groan in my ears—is pleasure. Pure, unadulterated pleasure like I can't ever remember feeling before.

"*Fuck.*"

It's one word, but it's long and drawn out and almost a growl as we begin to move together. He thrusts up as I grind down, allowing the base of his shaft to hit the nether part of my clit in a way that sends shockwaves to where his crest is working within me.

We don't speak, we react.

His exhale, my next inhale.

His curse—*fuck*—my want.

His tempo, my pulse.

We move in unison, each taking and giving and feeling, until every part of me burns bright with a desire I never knew possible.

His fingers press into my ass. My hands grab his biceps. The sounds of skin on skin fill the room with the constant undertone of our moans and groans and praise and pleas of bliss. His dick swells. I grind harder. My breath hitches then catches then gasps as the orgasm swells and surges. It hits with such forewarning, but I still lose myself as it drags me under its possessive haze, only to toss me up again just as Grant groans my name and loses himself to me.

My forehead rests on his shoulder. His fingers trail up and down the line of my spine. Our heartbeats bang against each other's through our rib cages. Our breaths remain labored. My mind too hazy from being overwhelmed by everything that is Grant Malone to think about next steps and what the hell line we just crossed.

"That promise wasn't so bad, was it?" He chuckles as he brings his lips to the top of my head, his breath heating my hair.

"No," I murmur.

He definitely made me come, all right.

At least I know he keeps his promises now.

TWENTY-FOUR

Emerson

THE ROOM IS BRIGHT, AND THE RAY OF SUN SLICING BETWEEN the blinds hits me perfectly in the eyes. I snuggle deeper into the comforter, and then awareness hits.

My eyes flash open.

I'm not home. In my loft. In my bed.

I'm in Grant's bed. A bed that is way more comfortable than mine. And it's way past my typical six thirty wake-up time.

Grant's also nowhere to be found.

It takes a moment before it ghosts through my mind. *"Em. I have to go to work."* The gravel in his voice as he presses a kiss against my temple. The sound of his duty belt clinking. The metallic sound of the gun safe closing. The rumble of his chuckle as he runs a hand down my bare spine and makes me snuggle deeper into the bed that smells like him and is just as warm. "Stay as long as you like. Just lock the door on the way out."

Then falling back into an oblivious sleep.

I broke one of my rules.

Shit.

I'm here when I should be at work. I'm wrapped in the scent of him when I should be in my flight suit and focused on this afternoon's clients. Instead, I want to nestle back into this softness and remember every delicious thing he did to me last night.

No.

Get up.

I shouldn't do this. I don't get to throw my rules out the window for one man. One hotter than hell and more than skilled man named Grant Malone, but a man nonetheless.

I make myself sit up in his bed, the comforter held beneath my armpits to cover my nakedness, and take a look around. The room is classic and clean, light walls with dark gray and blue accents. Very male, but not in the bachelor monochromatic way. It's tidy and there aren't any clothes strewn about. He even took the time to fold my clothes on the chair in the far corner.

The walls hold a few black-and-white photographs of the ocean and cliffs—stoic, powerful, and moving. There are very few personal effects in his bedroom, but it's cozy and inviting.

Determined not to want to know more, I force myself from the bed. My debate whether to take a shower is short lived. One, it isn't my bathroom and that might be a little awkward just making myself at home. And two, I can still smell his cologne on my skin and I'm not certain I want to wash him away just yet.

If per my rules, I only get one night with Grant Malone, I ridiculously want to make it last a little longer. So, instead of thinking too much about how this is so unlike me, I force myself to get dressed in last night's jean shorts, tank top, and unbuttoned overshirt.

It's just when I finish making the bed—because as messy as I am, there's no way I can leave an unmade bed for Mr. Nice and Tidy—that I hear voices.

At first, I think maybe they are from next door and Grant left a window open, but after a few more seconds, I know for certain there are at least two other men in Grant's house.

"Dude, check it out," the first voice says. It's followed by a low hum of a chuckle.

"Looks like someone got lucky last night." There's a low whistle.

"Well, it looks like whoever it was, didn't want this nice setup of coffee he left for her. So, I don't mind if I do."

Coffee? Did he just say coffee? My ears perk up and my mouth waters at the thought of it. Did Grant really leave me a coffee cup and all the fixings? There is a God.

I just need to figure out how to walk out of this bedroom, surprise whoever the two guys are in the family room, and retain my dignity. But, then again, there is no dignity lost considering we were two consenting adults. Plus, who cares what they think?

My shoes. I don't have my sandals. They are most likely in the living room where I kicked them off last night. I look around Grant's spotless bedroom and change my mind. They are probably sitting side by side by the front door.

"Hey, Grady," the one voice says to the other.

It's the same time the voice says those two words that I know who is on the other side of the wall. It may have been a long time, but I would know that voice anywhere. Grant's brothers, Grayson and Grady, are in the other room.

"Shoes."

Crap. They noticed them.

Cue the panic. And not the run-of-the-mill, walk of shame type of panic, either. More like these men used to run around in their underwear with me in their sprinklers when we were little. We share a history of getting sticky from eating Big Stick popsicles that we bought from the ice cream man.

I snicker at the thought of Big Sticks and how that has a whole different connotation now.

Should I just stay here and wait them out instead of face them? But then what? They walk in here, find me, and I end up looking like a damn heel?

The longer I stand here and listen to the two of them bicker like kids, the worse my nerves hum with the thought of what they're going to think when they see me—little Emmy who suddenly up and disappeared years ago. That's the kind of attention I don't want or like.

So I react.

With a glance in the bathroom mirror, I grab some lipstick from my purse, do a quick fluff of my hair so I don't look like a complete disaster, and then suck in my breath. When I'm fairly certain I don't look like a hot mess anymore, I waltz out of the bedroom with my head held high and a smile on my face.

"I knew he was hiding something when I called him this morning. The son of a bitch."

"Hey, that's mom you're talking about," the other says.

"Whatever, dude. You know what I mean. Grant went and got himself laid last night. I wonder—"

"Actually, I was the one who got laid last night," I say as I enter the room and draw two pairs of eyes my way. I love the shocked O's their mouths fall into. Slack jaws on hot men are always a good thing—whether it's from some lacy lingerie or from putting them in their place. I walk right up to one of them—because they look too damn similar for me to venture which one is who after all these years—and grab the piping cup of coffee from his hand. "Thanks for making this for me. I appreciate it."

His eyes widen, and his lips sputter into a shit-eating grin as I take a tentative sip of the steaming heaven without breaking eye contact. "Hello, Emerson."

"Hi. And you are . . ." I feign ignorance to set the precedence that I have no past with them. It's hard enough as it is with Grant, so I need to make sure we start this off on the right foot.

"Grady Malone," he says and then lifts his chin toward Hot Malone number three. "And that's Grayson."

"Ah, the infamous Malone boys. Now, I've met you all again." I narrow my eyes and study both of them in the same way they are studying me. I can see the similarities. The little boys they were beneath the men they have become. "Thanks for the coffee. A little light on the creamer for my liking, but now you know for next time."

I flash a dazzling smile as they laugh. "He was right," Grayson says to Grady as if I'm not in the room. "She is feisty as hell."

"Always." I wink and walk over to where my sandals are perfectly lined up side by side near the front door. "I need to run so I'm not late for work. Grant asked me to lock up. Since you obviously have the keys to help yourselves as you please, can I trust that you can handle that instead?"

"We'll lock up. No worries," Grady says and then smirks. "It's the least we can do."

"Thanks. I'm tired." I turn the handle on the front door before adding, "Your brother really knows how to keep a girl up all night."

With that, I walk out the front door, shut it behind me, and don't spare a look back as I stroll down the street toward the bar where my car is still parked.

The ringer of my phone comes through my speaker on my car, and I know who it is before I even glance at the screen. I contemplate not answering. If I pick up, it will sound as if I want to go back on the rules I made last night. We shouldn't feel as if we need to do the obligatory *morning-after* call to make sure things aren't awkward.

Then again, if I avoid him, doesn't that just prove to him—and me—that I can't handle what happened when following my own rules.

"Get a grip, Em," I mutter as I jab my finger at the car's display and answer the call.

"Hello?" I say as if I can't already see it's him on the Caller ID.

"Good morning." I'm not sure why I expected there to be a smug sound in his voice, but there isn't. "Hey, I know you're probably on your way to work, but I just wanted to apologize for my brothers. Sometimes they come over and steal my coffee. Other times they just want to harass me for no reason. I didn't expect them to stop in this morning."

"It's okay," I say with a smile, remembering their shocked faces.

His chuckle fills the line. "I don't know what you told them, but somehow you managed the impossible."

"What do you mean?" I make a right turn onto the highway and smile when a police cruiser passes me. It isn't Grant, but it still feels like it is since his voice is in my car.

"The two of them can never agree on a single thing, and yet, when I talked to them earlier, they both decided they are head over heels when it comes to you."

"What?" I laugh.

"Yep. I believe *gutsy* was their word of choice."

"That's a good word." I let the word roll over my tongue and gladly own it.

"It is, and it suits you to a T."

"I may have played them a little bit." I chuckle.

"Oh really?" he murmurs. "I wouldn't know anything about that."

And there's something in the way that Grant makes the statement that catches my ear and puts my mind into overdrive. "What's the supposed to mean?"

"Nothing." I can hear the smile in his voice. "Break's over. I have to get back to work. Bye, Emerson."

TWENTY-FIVE

Grant

"YOU WANT TO EXPLAIN WHY YOU'RE IN SUCH A GOOD mood?" Nate asks.

I glance his way and then look back to my computer with Emerson front and center on my mind. "No reason. I'm always in a good mood."

"Bullshit." He snorts. "You got some action, didn't you?"

"Are you telling me I'm only in a good mood when I get laid?" I can see other guys tune in to our conversation.

"No, but it does help."

"True . . ." I muse as I request another cold case file from the archives to help Chief Ramos keep his promise to the public that the Sunnyville Police Department never backs down on crime, old or new. It doesn't hurt that it looks good for the promotion plus that patio cover I've been itching to build.

"So?" he asks in a verbal nudge.

"So, nothing." Much to his annoyance, I blow him off. None of the guys in the place need to know about my personal life more than they already do.

But that doesn't stop me from mentally reliving every single moment spent with Emerson. Every kiss. Each lick. All the moans. The groans. The orgasms. And every damn thing in between.

I shift in my chair, knowing I need to stop thinking about her or

I'm going to be sporting wood.

But as I ignore the bullshit puppy-dog eyes from Nate and focus on calling up more cold case files from the archives, all I think about is Emerson. How sex with her was a mixture of familiarity and new and unforgettable all at the same time. Her rules she needs so she feels like she's in control but that I know I'll peel away one by one until it's just her and me and nothing between us.

And to add the cherry to the sundae that is most definitely her, she put my brothers in their damn place.

The woman is a force to be reckoned with and hell if I'm not sitting in the middle of her windstorm and waiting to be hit with everything she has.

"Malone."

"Yep." I look up to where Dyson is standing at the front of the squad room.

"Chief Ramos needs to see you."

I throw a glance to Nate, curious as to why he's asking for only me and not the two of us. He shrugs as I stand, make my way down the hall, and rap on the glass door. "What do you need, Chief?"

Chief Ramos lifts his eyes from the open file on his desk and motions for me to come in. "Shut the door, Malone." *Uh-oh.* "Take a seat."

"Sure." I sit in the chair across from him and wait for those dark eyes of his to study me. Nothing says a dress down is coming like the Ramos stare.

"How is the studying going for your exam?

"Good," I say with caution. "Most of the stuff is second nature, but I'm reviewing it anyway."

"Do you have a test date yet?" he asks, glancing at his wall calendar before settling the intensity in his eyes back on me.

"End of the month," I reply. Twenty-two days. It should be more than enough time for me to spit shine my knowledge and ace the test.

"I'm sure your dad told you the test is the easy part, right?"

What is he getting at?

"So I've heard."

"Good. Good." He nods and leans back in his chair as he looks through the glass walls of his office and into the squad room. Even with his focus off me, he's still intimidating as hell when he wants to be. His sigh tells me there is more.

"What's the problem?" I finally ask.

"Your dad is a good friend of mine. You're important to this department. I just want to make sure you're prepared."

"Okay." I draw the word out, still lost to the purpose of this conversation.

"Stetson threw his hat in the ring a few days ago."

"What?" I feel like I've been hit by a two-by-four. "Fucking Stetson?"

"Yes. And I only have one opening."

I nod and clench my fists to hide my reaction. "Understood."

"You'll both pass the test easily. It's the interviews that are going to be tough. You each have friends on the committee, so the vote will be split . . . and—"

"And I have the bullshit lies Stetson and his dad spread about my dad and me to contend with." I finish his unspoken thought for him and hate to even have to say it.

"There's that." Another sigh. When he clenches his fists atop the file on his desk, it's just one last visual directive to have my shit in order. To not take any of this lightly.

"I knew it wasn't going to be a cakewalk," I say. "But I didn't expect to have to contend with a past I had nothing to do with."

"I know, Grant. It's bullshit, but it's shit nonetheless, and at some point, we're all forced to stand in it and try to wipe it off our heels."

"Thanks for the head's up," I say and stand, needing a moment to process this.

"Let me know if I can help with anything."

How about kick the fucker off the force?

I nod again and offer a tight smile before turning and walking out of his office. Nate catches my eye as I stride through the precinct without stopping. We've worked together long enough for him to recognize I'm about to lose my shit, and I know he'll be ten steps behind me as soon as others stop paying attention.

Once outside, I walk to the edge of the lot and try to calm the fuck down.

"Grant?"

"The asshole is coming after my promotion," I grit the words out to him.

"Stetson?"

"Fuck yes, Stetson." I roll my shoulders and walk a few feet away from him before turning and walking back. "He can't let it go, can he? His dad was a piss poor cop on a total power trip just like his bastard son is."

"I'm not going to disagree with you. But why now? He just up and decided he wanted to be detective?"

"Apparently." I laugh, but it's void of humor. "Is he trying to avenge dear old daddy?"

"Fuck that, Malone. His dear old daddy was crooked, so your dad kicked him off the force for misconduct and marred his reputation."

"Yep. And then he started spreading bullshit rumors about my dad to get back at him. *Fuck*." I run a hand through my hair, the anger eating me raw inside.

"I know, man. I know. It was fucked up all around, but anyone who knows your dad knows the accusations are crap."

"Does it matter? He still stepped down over it and gave them the satisfaction of thinking they had won." The thought alone makes my body vibrate in anger. I know he didn't step down to avoid the smudge on his incredible career but rather to remove all drama so his son, who wanted to follow in his footsteps, could do so with a clean slate in front of him.

Yeah, I'm the selfish bastard who let him do that—not that anyone could have stopped him.

"Don't let your head go there, man. He stepped down because he had already planned on retiring, not because of you. We both know that."

"Yeah, well . . ." How do I go from the high of last night with Emerson to this shit? "Now I get to deal with Asshole Jr."

"He's doing it just to spite you."

"But he has friends in high places."

"So do you, my friend."

"Let's hope so."

TWENTY-SIX

Emerson

"Are you avoiding me?" Desi's voice rings out through the red hangar, prompting me to lift my head without thinking and rap it smartly on the underside of the Cessna's wing.

"Shit." I rub a hand over the top of my head.

"Now, I know I was poking pins in the Voodoo doll I have to punish you for avoiding me, but I didn't think it would actually work."

"Very funny," I say as I roll my eyes, step away from the plane, and wipe my hands on a rag.

Desi stands with her hands on her hips, head angled to the side, and a scarf that looks like a rainbow threw up all over it wrapped around her neck. It's ridiculous and bright and girly, but she pulls it off and makes it look uniquely fashionable.

"So, are you?"

"Am I what?"

She huffs, as if she's trying to explain thermonuclear dynamics to a kindergartner, and takes a step forward. "Avoiding me. Not taking my calls. Not returning my calls. Pretending like Grant never called me two nights ago and told me not to show up at the bar because he was going to otherwise occupy your time. You know"—she shrugs—"that kind of avoiding me."

"No." I avert my eyes and finish wiping off the windshield of the plane with Windex to—*yes*—avoid her. "I've just been busy."

Her laugh is rich and bounces off the concrete floor and echoes back to me. "Like bow-chick-a-wow-wow kind of busy?"

I level her with a glare. "You're so childish."

"And you refuse to admit you slept with Grant." She'd be a really good interrogator. I don't plan on telling her that.

"Who said I slept with Grant?" I feign innocence, trying to keep the act up for some reason.

"You did."

"I did not."

"Uh-huh."

"If I haven't spoken to you, then I obviously haven't told you I slept with him."

"Your silence speaks volumes." She purses her lips as if victorious, and all I can do is attempt to follow her messed-up logic.

"Silence doesn't speak."

"Ah, but that's where you're wrong. It can scream sometimes, and honey, yours is louder than a sonic boom." I lower my hands from where I've moved on to the side windows and just shake my head. "Admit it. I need to hear it."

Another glare. A repeated sigh. A confession that I'm not sure why I'm keeping so close to the vest when I usually share everything with her.

"Yes, I slept with Grant."

"Woohoo!" She pumps her fists and jumps up and down as if I just completed an Ironman. "I knew it. He had sex all over his voice when he called me. It was so damn hot I almost had to get myself off."

"You're incorrigible."

"And you got laid. So . . ." She pats the makeshift bench of a two-by-six piece of wood sitting atop two spaced out sawhorses. "You better not leave out a damn bit of detail."

"You really want a blow-by-blow?"

"Ohh, you naughty girl!" She screeches. "You blew him, too. I love it!"

"No—I—oh my God, I can't believe we're having this conversation."

"So, you didn't blow him?"

"Desi!"

"Yes, that just means there's going to be another time to explore all other avenues you haven't ventured down yet."

"Slow down, Turbo," I say as I put some of my supplies back on the cleaning cart before taking a seat beside her. "It wasn't like you're thinking."

"It wasn't?" she asks, her smirk only growing wider. "Was it more swing from the chandeliers or more gasp for breath because your face is pushed into the mattress because he feels so good from behind?"

"Jesus," I choke out but shouldn't expect any less from her.

"Did you satisfy your curiosity then?"

"You know what they say about curiosity . . ."

"It killed the cat, yeah, yeah. But honey, by the grin on your face, I know your kitty meowed. *A lot*."

"How about you stop or else you don't get any details."

Her face falls, and I know I've hurt her feelings when I didn't mean to. I love the woman to death but subtlety is not her forte and overboard dramatics definitely are.

"Okay. I'll shut my mouth so you can give me the 4-1-1."

I laugh. We'll see how long that lasts. "I don't know," I begin. "We had some drinks. We talked for a few hours. We were too tipsy to drive so we walked back to his house. On the way, we decided that if we got each other out of our systems, we might be able to stop this nonsense competition we seem to be in over who has to be in control. A one-time romp with no strings attached."

"Get each other out of your systems?" She guffaws and just barely manages not to laugh at the idea. "Because that's what normal childhood friends do when they reunite after twenty years."

"*Reunite*? Is that what it's called?"

"I am trying to be good here. What word should I use to describe it?"

"How about 'fucked'?" She isn't the only one who can deliver the shock value, and by the way she just choked on her next word, I'd say I was successful at it.

"*Fucked*. I can approve of that word." She laughs. "But the question remains: Did it work? Did you get each other out of your systems?"

I stare at her as I try to figure out how to answer.

Of course it didn't work. Being with him once only left me wanting more. Pride prevents me from acknowledging that every time my phone rings, I jump to see if it's him, only to chastise myself that it doesn't matter if it is.

One time. That's all it can be.

My rule. Not his.

And I hate that the only time we've talked was when he called to apologize for his brothers showing up unannounced.

"So, the *one-time thing*," she continues on, well aware that I haven't responded to her last question. "Was this his rule or yours? My bet is on you."

"You'd be correct. Don't act so surprised." I swat at her arm.

"I'm not surprised by the rule, I'm just surprised you fell for it." She swats my arm right back and gives me a look that makes me think she's privy to some type of knowledge that I'm clearly not.

"What does that mean?"

"You guys have been playing Control Wars for what? Two, three weeks?"

"Yeah. So?"

"Don't you find it awfully convenient that, all of a sudden, he let you call the shots when he's been vying for the top?"

"Are you saying he played me?" I hate that the coin she's just put in the slot drops down and hits with a loud, ricocheting *clank*.

"You're damn straight he did. Damn brilliantly, too."

She laughs, and her face has an incredulous expression on it I don't really feel like recognizing.

The smug bastard.

"Are you complaining about the outcome?" she asks after I sit quietly for a moment.

"Uh, no," I finally say. How could I complain about the skill of his hands and lips and marvelous cock?

"No?"

"Absolutely not," I assert.

"Then why do you look like you're about to call him and chew him out?" And she's right. I feel like doing just that even though there is no reason to because we both got what we wanted out of our little rendezvous, didn't we?

"I'm not," I concede.

"Good. You shouldn't be mad because he one-upped you."

"Are you trying to rub my nose in it?"

"Nope." She blows a bubble with her gum and it pops with a *smack*. "I'm just thrilled that someone finally beat you at your own game."

"I do believe that's rubbing my nose in it."

"Semantics." She grins with a shrug. "So . . . was all this trouble worth it?" She lifts her eyebrows, and the blush on my cheeks and laugh on my lips tells her all she needs to know.

"Definitely worth it."

"For a girl all about the orgasm, that says a lot." There's the sound of a plane's prop starting in the distance, and she waits a moment to continue. "We always get sidetracked when it comes to Grant and talk about all the swooniness that is him . . . are you ever going to tell me why the two of you stopped being friends in the first place?"

"No reason." I rise from my seat and head to the cart where I fiddle with things that don't need to be fiddled with.

"C'mon. There has to be a reason."

"I moved away." It isn't a lie. "It doesn't matter. He and I would never work anyway."

"I didn't know you wanted it to."

"I don't. I mean—It wouldn't—" I stop talking because I sound like a bumbling fool.

"Why wouldn't it work?" she asks. All I want her to do is drop it, which I know she won't. She's sunk her teeth into the point she's trying to make and won't let go until this conversation has played itself out.

"He's a player, Des. I'm a player. There's disaster written all over that," I say as I turn to look at her.

"You two could *play* together." I roll my eyes at her lame sense of humor. "But he chased you, Em. Players don't chase."

"Ha. They chase until they get what they want and then they're done. Besides, he didn't chase."

"Keep thinking that, sister, and I'll sell you some ocean front property in Arizona." I level her with a side-eyed look. "Fine. I'll be quiet. Tell me how you guys left things."

"Other than saying it was a one-time thing, we really didn't leave it any way."

"There was no goodbye. No walk you to your car afterward? No, call me later?"

"No." I shift my feet because she's going to see right through this in a heartbeat. "He left for his shift at the break of dawn."

She leans forward, eyes wide, and full attention on me. "You were sleeping? In his bed?"

Yep, I knew she'd call me on how I broke that rule in a heartbeat. "It wasn't like that."

"Oh, so it was more like he sexed you up so good you fell into a sex-blissed coma and then he left you—a woman he doesn't really know—alone in his house when he went to work? Was that how it was?"

"You missed the part where he kissed me on the top of the head in the dark and told me to stay as long as I like."

She makes a show of shaking her head in mock disgust of my breaking my own rules, but I know she's secretly fist pumping beneath the surface. "Yeah, just minor details. Like sweet and endearing details."

I can't help the uncharacteristic smile on my lips or the warmth that spreads within me. I don't do tender or intimate. Hell, I don't do anything near the sort, but then again . . . this is Grant we're talking about. There is some level of comfort with him that I'm not used to.

It's only one night, Em.

"He obviously trusts you," she muses.

"Well," I laugh the word out, "it doesn't go both ways."

"What the hell do you mean?"

"Drop it, Des."

She angles me a look that says she's confused, and it matches how I feel inside.

It's amazing that no matter how many strides I take forward—how normal my life is—a simple thing like the word "trust" can force my past to come back and slap me.

Grant doesn't deserve it.

Then again, neither did I.

TWENTY-SEVEN

Grant

"Hot damn." Nate smacks his hands on my kitchen counter and scares the shit out of me. "I knew you got laid last week."

"What?" I look up from where I'm tying my boots.

Where the hell is this coming from?

"There's lipstick on this mug," he says as he lifts the coffee cup he was just taking a sip from.

"There is?" I mutter with a shake of my head. "My fucking brothers."

"Gray and Grady are wearing lipstick now? Wow. I thought they'd go for more of a red than a pink." He laughs as he dumps his coffee into the sink and grabs a new mug.

"No. They washed the cup after Emers—"

"I knew it!" Nate shouts from the kitchen. "You did get laid." He flashes a knowing grin that I ignore as I move to my other boot.

"I sure did."

"See? You can't hide shit from me."

"You're a real detective. Maybe you should put in for a promotion," I deflect.

"Nah, there's only room for one of us to steal center stage at a time. I'll leave it to you to put that fucker Stetson in his place."

I glance at my watch. "C'mon. Fill your cup. Our shift's about to start and there's somewhere I want to stop before we clock in."

"Sure thing." He puts the creamer back in the refrigerator. "And you can fill me in on all the details on the way."

"Humor me, will you?" I say to Nate as I pull the cruiser along the curb and put it in park.

His deep sigh fills the car. He doesn't have to say a word to let me know he thinks I'm way over the line.

He'll get over it.

The street is silent as I exit the car. The garage door is closed, and the driveway is empty. But there are new rocks painted in the planters along the walkway to the house.

One looks like a flag. Another is black and white like a cow's spots. One has a K in bright blue on it.

But there is no watermelon. Nothing red with black seeds.

No cry for help disguised as secret spy code.

I'm there for no more than a minute before I turn on my heel and head back to the cruiser.

"Everything okay?" Nate asks as I slide behind the wheel, his voice full of concern.

"Yep. Everything is okay."

For now.

TWENTY-EIGHT

Emerson

SLIMY BASTARD.

I can still feel his hands on my shoulders and smell his obnoxious cologne. I can still see the snake oil behind the lunch he brought with him to Blue Skies to conveniently offer to share. I can still hear the implied threat that if I don't acquiesce to the prick, then my loan might not be approved.

Or funded.

Or maybe if I dated a sturdy man of industry such as himself, the lenders would look favorably upon his stability and be more willing to bargain.

I'm well aware this is all total bullshit. He's out of his mind if he thinks I don't see that he's most likely holding back my loan from approval to string me along. To try to extort a date from me before he tells me if I've been approved or not. I've provided the correct documentation—a business plan, financial statements, an audit of the company—and yet I'm still dependent on him.

Dependent but not desperate.

No date. No way.

I may be a gypsy in his eyes, but this gypsy is smarter than he gives me credit for.

And then, of course, his departure was followed up by a phone call from the owners. Their weekly questions about our latest sales figures that segued into why I don't have the loan yet. That was followed by the casual mention—*threat*—that regardless of how hard I work for them currently, if the sixty-day escrow falls through, they already have backup buyers in place *just in case*. Oh, and naturally, the backup buyers are offering a higher buying price, which I find to be total bullshit. But if I call their bluff and don't play their game, too, do I risk losing out on my dream?

I slam around the training room, moving chairs back in place, resetting slideshows, wiping off the dry erase boards. Anything to calm my temper and rid the room of the slime Chris's presence left behind.

Everything about me is itching to put my gear on and jump.

"You okay?" Leo asks from where he stands outside the doorway. More than aware of my mood and prepared for a running start should my temper flare.

"Yeah. I'm fine. I'm just . . ." I stop talking, the frustrated tears threatening to make their presence known when I don't want them to.

"He's a prick, Em."

"Yeah, I know. I just wish I could tell him what I really think of him, but I can't risk the loan."

"My mom used to tell me never to wrestle with pigs. You both get dirty and the pig really likes it."

"Smart woman."

"Just know we all see it and admire you for dealing with him. It shows just how much you want Blue Skies to be yours."

"Thanks." I nod but avert my eyes, hoping it will prevent the sting of tears.

"You know Sully is taking one more flight up in an hour, right?"

He has my attention, which I'm sure was his hope. He knows me well enough to know that a jump is just about the only thing that will make me feel better. I've been so bogged down with loan stuff and instructing clients, that I need the release . . .

"He is?"

"Yeah. A fun run for some of the crew to get rid of some of the mid-week all-we-do-is-instruct-and-not-jump blues."

I laugh. "God bless him. What time is he going up?"

"In about an hour. Everyone's heading out to get a bite to eat and then meeting back here at seven. You want to come?"

I glance at my watch. That gives me seventy minutes to fill out a few reports for Blue Skies and complete the last few things on the new to-do list Travis gave me this morning.

"I can't go out to eat with you guys," I say, "but I'll be geared up at the plane at seven."

"Cool. It's been a long time since we just jumped for the hell of it."

"Amen."

Leo leaves me be, but I can still hear him rattling around and gathering his things in the office before the bells on the door ring as he shuts it behind him.

I'm not sure how much time passes before the bells on the door go off again.

"Sorry, we're closed," I call out to the front of the shop and mentally chastise myself for not taking the time to lock the door.

Then the thought hits that it's Chris coming back while I'm here alone.

"We're closed," I call again just as I turn the corner to the front office and run smack dab into someone.

"Whoa! Where's the fire?" Grant's hands are on my shoulders, holding me steady as I look up at him. I hate that I sigh in relief that he isn't Chris.

"No fire," I say as I catch my breath. "We're just closed."

"So you said." Grant's eyes narrow as he studies me, and I know he sees fluster. "Everything okay, Em?" Concern laces his tone, and the sound of it makes me step back quickly.

"Yeah, fine."

"You sure?"

"Nothing I can't handle."

Why am I suddenly so nervous?

"Em?"

"It's nothing, Grant. The loan guy was here earlier, and he was just . . ."

"He was just what?" The muscle in his jaw pulses as he clenches his teeth.

"I told you, I'm a big—"

"Girl who can take care of herself. Yeah, yeah. That doesn't mean that prick has the right to treat you how he does. Who is he, Em? I can take a quick stop by his house and—"

"No. You're not doing anything."

"All it would take is some asking around, a little detective work," he says, flashing me a smirk as he points to his shiny badge pinned over his heart, "and I could fix the fucker."

"Thank you for the chivalry. I really appreciate your willingness to be my knight in shining armor, but I'm a big—I have it handled."

He stares at me for a beat, our eyes warring over his hero complex and my independence. On any other day, I'd smile at the trait and think it was cute . . . but not right now. Not with my loan at stake.

"This is off your beat, isn't it, Officer Malone?" I ask with a smile and try to switch gears.

"You keep ignoring me." There is just a bit too much accusation there for his statement to be casual.

"No, I don't," I lie. "I've just been super busy."

"Too busy to return a text or answer a call?" He angles his head to the side, and his brown eyes pin me motionless as they try to read my body language and unspoken words.

"Just busy. I have a lot going on." A lot as in I'm trying not to want to talk to you as much as I've wanted to. I take another step back but bump into the wall behind me. "Did you need something?"

"I wanted to see you."

I've never known just how fine a line there is between want and need until this moment.

"That wasn't the deal, Grant." I reject his words immediately because they hit too close to home.

I wanted to see him, too.

"What deal?"

"The deal we made the other night."

"Oh, you mean your rules?"

"Yeah."

"Didn't anyone ever tell you not to believe any promises spoken when in the heat of passion?"

Heat of passion.

I level him with a glare. "Haven't you realized yet I'm not your normal woman?"

"If by 'normal' you mean the type of woman who jumps out of airplanes, loves to eat food without shame, gives as good as she gets, and has no problem wanting sex for sex. Then, no, I'm sorry. I didn't notice." His face is stoic, but his eyes hold the humor and sarcasm his voice is lacking.

"Funny."

"Perhaps, but it's true."

"The other night was a mistake." Lie. Lie. Lie. I'm just so unnerved that he sees me so well when most days I can't see myself.

"Nice try, but I call bullshit."

"You can call *it* whatever you want, Malone, but *it* isn't going to happen again."

The corner of his lips curl as he shakes his head. "I'm glad you have this all figured out."

"He chased you."

Desi's words come back and hit my ears as I stare at him and realize that he has the patience of a saint and she was right—he did chase me. He's still *chasing* me.

So, why am I pushing him away again?

Because rules are rules. Now, I just need to stick to my guns.

"Look, I'm far from typical. Anything you might need to do out of obligation after sleeping with someone is not needed when it comes to me."

"Like?" he asks as he folds his arms across his chest, leans a shoulder against the wall, and tucks his tongue in his cheek to fight from smiling.

"Like I don't require the phone call afterward to make sure we're both okay with the one-night stand thing. I don't need flowers or apologies when you move on to the next woman. I don't need empty promises or whatever else it is you guys do to soothe your egos. It's all crap."

"Every woman likes those things."

"I'm not every woman."

"So we've established." He holds his hand up when I start to protest. "But no worries, I don't do that. Just don't tell my mom."

"Good to know."

"Is there a reason for so much hostility, Em? I'm sensing you're mad at me, but if these are your rules, then how can you be?"

Silence falls in the small space as my tongue-tied thoughts spin and shift the conversation. "Look, we're attracted to each other. There's nothing wrong with that. We wanted out of each other's systems. We screwed. We're good."

"So eloquent." He lifts his eyebrows as his smile spreads.

"I'm serious. I barely have time to breathe most days, never mind have the time to deal with this kind of shit."

"Wow. Way to knock a man's ego—*and dick*—in the dirt."

I growl in frustration when I realize how he took my comment. "We're not talking about the sex part." I backpedal. "That was top notch. It's just . . . you're Phony Maloney. And I'm Emmy Reeves . . . don't you think we should let the past be the past and just be happy with knowing we turned out okay? With accepting our chemistry is great but that it will never work between us."

"What wouldn't work? The *screwing* part?" he asks, eyes narrowing as he mimics the way I said the word.

"Yes. That."

"But we already did that part, and what were your words? Top notch? So, I believe that did work." He knows he's irritating me and is enjoying every second of doing it.

"What about this?" I motion to the space in between us. "Isn't this weird?"

"It didn't feel weird the other night. In fact, it felt pretty damn amazing, so lay your next excuse on me. Why can't you pick up the phone and take my call, Emerson? I'm not buying whatever logic you're trying to sell. And frankly you're making absolutely zero sense, but please, continue. I'm enjoying this immensely."

"You're exhausting." I sigh.

"And you're infuriating, but we already knew that twenty years ago . . . so what's your excuse going to be now, huh?"

"I don't trust you." I know my comment is a low blow before it even comes out of my mouth, but I can't stop it any more than I can stop the sun from setting.

He staggers back as if I've physically assaulted him, and I can see hints of our past flicker through the anger sparking in his eyes.

Regret is immediate. How do I tell him not to think of the past when I just threw it in his face? I'm a goddamn mess. He doesn't deserve this. He has to know that much at least.

"You fooled me the other night," I say with a smirk, trying to make amends for the lingering effects of my childhood grudge.

Way to get my head straight. Tell him there was nothing to the other night and then admit to him that I'm thinking of it.

"Why ever would you think that?" He feigns innocence, but a smile plays on his lips.

"The agreeing to my rules but then turning around and saying I shouldn't believe anything said in the heat of passion. That type of thing."

He shrugs. "I agreed to your rules. We had sex. We got each other out of our systems," he says, but the way his eyes run up and down the length of my body has me shifting my feet to abate the ache the hunger in his look causes. It's like he's remembering every line and curve and flavor. "And now I'm here because I wanted to see you."

"But why? I've been nothing but bitchy to you."

He shrugs again. "Your words, not mine."

"I know, but they're true. We squabble like brother and sister and—"

"Not exactly like brother and sister, or else that would make the other night a little more awkward than you're already making it."

"You're a bucket full of laughs today, aren't you?"

"Always." And there goes the panty-dropping smile of his that makes me weak in the knees when I don't get weak in the knees. "I'm sorry. You were saying? Brother and sister . . ."

My concentration is lost amid his interruptions, leaving me to fumble with where I was going with my point. "Just why? That's all. Why would you want to come see me if I've been nothing but rude to you?"

"Because despite it all—or maybe because of it—I like you. And seeing as we got each other out of our systems, maybe I want to be friends."

"Friends with benefits," I retort.

"Not gonna deny the thought hasn't crossed my mind." His eyes lock with mine, those gold flecks dancing as my thoughts swirl, whirl, and tumble out of control.

"You're serious."

God, please let him be serious.

"As a heart attack."

Thoughts of us in the dim light fill my mind. The warmth. The pleasure. The comfort. The praise.

The breaking of rules.

"C'mon, Em. You know it's a good idea. We'll both be the beneficiaries of good sex—sex we've already proven to be *top notch*—and we don't have to deal with the complications of afterward. The clingy one who suddenly wants more. The frantic phone calls to make sure we're thinking about them. The randomly showing up where we like to hang out to make sure we didn't forget them."

I chuckle because it's as if he's repeating every scenario for why I've deleted names from my phone.

"See? You know what I'm talking about. You know that's all a pain in the ass."

"Kind of like you?"

"Yeah, but I'm a cute pain in the ass."

I can't stifle my laugh because he's wearing me down, not that I've put up much resistance.

"I have to think about this . . . without you in my face, badgering me like a little kid." Because I know he's playing me right now, and I'll be damned if it isn't a pretty brilliant play.

His laugh fills the room, and I know he knows he has me.

"Meet me here tomorrow after work. Like seven-ish. We can talk then."

"Deal." His grin is back and as disarming as ever.

And when he turns to go out the door, I hate that every part of me is relieved that I have an excuse to get to see him again. Whether I agree to his plan or not, at least I know he'll be here tomorrow. I spent the last week avoiding him, and I would never admit it aloud, but I'd missed him.

Friends with benefits.

Humph.

Way to stick to your guns, Reeves.

TWENTY-NINE

Emerson

STEP.

There it is again.

Step.

I dig my fingers into my stuffed bunny.

Step. The jingle of Rex's collar.

Don't make a sound.

Step.

Don't move.

Step.

My tummy hurts. I want to throw up.

Step.

Mommy. Come home. Please.

Step.

I can hear him breathing. I know if I open my eyes he will be standing there with his shoulder against the wall, watching me. Waiting.

I squeeze my eyes shut even tighter.

Please, God. If you make him go away, I promise to be a good girl from now on.

Step.

I promise not to sneak the M&M's hidden in the back of the pantry.

Step.

I swear I won't talk back and will make my bed every day.

Step.

Pretty please, God. I mean it this time.

The bed dips beneath me. His breath hits my face. The cold metal brushes against my arm.

I know what comes next.

"Emmy."

I want to throw up.

He moves my hair from my face.

"Emmy."

Runs his hand over my shoulder. Down my arm.

The sheets become wet as I go potty.

"Emmy." Angrier. Upset. Disappointed.

I've been a bad girl.

I know what comes next . . .

I jolt up out of bed, the sound of my voice filling the room. I'm disoriented and petrified. Confused. Sick to my stomach.

My heart is racing, and my pulse is pounding in my ears. There are tears on my cheeks, and my hands are shaking.

I don't remember anything about the dream.

Not a single thing.

Except the fear. I can still taste it on my tongue. I can still smell it clinging to my skin.

I know it has to do with *him*. I may not remember a damn thing from the dream, but I know this feeling. I've lived this feeling.

But it's been forever since I've felt this way.

Clutching the comforter tighter around me with one hand, I reach over and turn on the light on my nightstand. I don't like the dark.

The boogey man lives in the dark.

So does my dad.

Trying to settle the anxiety rattling around inside me as sure as the blood flowing through my veins, I stare out the window to the airfield beyond. To the yellow and red and green lights and pretend they are the lights on a Christmas tree. Something. Anything.

My fingertips run absently over the scars on the inside of my upper arms.

Over.

And.

Over.

And.

Over.

It's the only thing I can do to process the dream I can't remember and the nightmare I lived through.

THIRTY

Emerson

Staring at the box cutter in my hand, I ignore the contents of the open box in front of me. Its weight is as comforting as it is torturous.

My sleep-deprived mind drifts off and begs me to give into a need I haven't had in years.

Cut.

Feel the pain my mind has closed out.

Cut.

Take the blame I don't deserve.

The blade calls to me.

My skin begs to be scored.

To bleed out the guilt.

Cut.

My fingers itch to do it.

"You have a visitor, Em," Leo calls from the front of the office, making me drop the knife from trembling fingers. A quick glance at the clock tells me I've been standing here in La-la Land for way longer than I should have been.

"Okay," I say, but before the word is even out, Grant is standing in the doorway, looking like my own personal Heaven and Hell—a reprieve from the thoughts that have stolen my focus all day and the reason I think I had those thoughts. His smile is genuine, and I hate that every part of me craves to walk straight up to him and wrap my arms around him.

Comfort.

Distraction.

The need to feel anything other than what I'm feeling right now.

"Hey," he says.

"Hi." I infuse confidence into my voice when really I'm scared shitless over these emotions I'm not used to having.

"I'm early." He shrugs, his smile turning sheepish. "Can you blame me?"

My brow pinches, and I stare at him for a moment before what he's talking about dawns on me. The time and place I set. The offer he made that has, unbeknownst to him, been overshadowed by my issues he has no clue about.

"No. Um, no." It's his turn to study me, his eyes looking closer than I want him to. "I, uh, I have to bring a team up first. You're going with us," I ad-hoc. Dodge and weave.

"Like hell I am." He laughs and takes a few steps closer.

"Yeah, I think you need to cash in that voucher. I'm not tandem jumping with anyone, so I can strap you on." The words are out before I realize what they sound like, and the full-bodied laugh that falls from his mouth and echoes around the room is worth every ounce of blush that creeps into my cheeks.

"Thanks, Em, but strap-ons aren't my thing, and if they were, it wouldn't be you wearing one."

"I hear pegging is all the rage these days."

The look he gives me says he's having none of this conversation. "It'll be a cold day in hell, my dear."

Oddly enough, all it takes is talking to Grant about strap-ons to put me at ease for the first time all day. My smile feels real instead of forced and brittle. The ache in my shoulders eases some. The box cutter becomes less enticing. The weight of the unremembered dream fades.

"If that's your biggest fear, then jumping out of a plane should be a piece of cake."

"I didn't say it was my biggest fear—jumping out of a plane is. Heights and I don't get along."

"Still traumatized after going on the Ferris wheel, I see," I say, suddenly remembering him screaming to get down and trying not to cry as he clung to his mom sitting between us. The sour look on his face says he isn't thrilled I remember.

"Nice try, but I'm not biting. I hate the feeling of falling, and let's not forget the whole possibility of dying aspect."

"See? That's a huge misconception. There is no feeling of falling when you jump. Not one bit." I offer a huge grin.

"Not buying it."

"Don't you trust me, Malone?" I stand there with my hands on my hips, my head angled to the side, and my eyes issuing a challenge to that manly ego of his.

"No." There's no waffling in his voice when he says it, and while I should be offended, I'm not in the least.

"Oh, c'mon."

"Sorry, Em. Trust isn't going to save me when I'm hurtling to the earth at a million miles an hour and my parachute fails to open."

"Pfft. Such dramatics." I roll my eyes but smile when I realize he really is petrified of the idea. It's in the shift of his feet and the sudden shaking of his head as if he's physically rejecting the idea every time it gets brought up.

It takes a lot to overcome that kind of fear.

I should know.

"Dramatics? Life and death," he says as he pretends his hands are scales weighing each one. In his scenario, death wins. "I'll stay here and watch with my feet planted firmly on the ground."

"Suit yourself." I shrug as I slip my arms into the sleeves of my flight suit and zip it up over my red tank top. "You're gonna miss one hell of a ride."

"I know somewhere else I can get a ride," he murmurs suggestively as I walk past him and laugh.

"Head up. Wings out," I say.

THIRTY-ONE

Grant

THERE ARE HARD LIMITS.

And then there are *hard limits.*

Like watching the specks in the sky above me as they hurtle to the ground and knowing one of them is Emerson.

My hand shields my eyes, and my stomach churns when I think of the feeling of falling. It's total bullshit, there's no way you can launch yourself into thin air and not feel like your stomach shoves up into your throat.

"C'mon, c'mon," I murmur to myself as I wait for what feels like hours to see the parachutes deploy.

"A few more seconds," Leo says and startles me. I was so focused on Emerson that I hadn't realized he'd walked out.

I glance back to the sky in time to see the first parachute explode in a bloom of color. One after the other they open, dragging each jumper higher before slowly floating down again.

I want to say I breathe a little easier, but fuck if I'm not nauseated just watching the whole process.

"You really don't like this, do you?" Leo asks, giving me that look that says I'm a disgrace to the male gender for being such a pussy.

I glare at him from behind my sunglasses, saying, "You people are all fucking crazy."

"Yes, we are."

The phone rings in the office, and he heads back in to answer it while the parachutes continue to get bigger as they glide closer to the ground. From the corner of my eye, I watch the field person get ready to help jumpers if they need assistance, but I never take my full attention away from trying to find Emerson.

I mean, I know she's fine, but I need to see it for my own eyes. And when I do, my feet start moving on automatic to where she is standing amid the long grass of the field with a huge grin on her face.

"Great jump, everyone," she says as she goes from jumper to jumper and pats them on the back or gives them a high five. She takes pictures of a few of them, and some ask her to be a part of the shot with them.

"I have it, Em," Leo says, appearing out of nowhere when she begins to detach the parachute rigs for the clients. "You need to make sure Nervous Nelly over there's heart is still beating."

I open my mouth to make a dig of my own, but when Emerson laughs, it stops the words on my lips. She looks my way and waves animatedly before holding up a finger to tell me just a minute.

Leo may have offered to help, but the control freak in her can't simply walk away without checking all the rigs out. She heads to the pack nearest her and tugs on one part or another before moving to the next.

Definitely a control freak.

Which, of course, was why I let her think she was in control the other night. Anything to make her feel comfortable in the moment and keep what we had going.

And going it did. Very well, too. So well that I pulled the friends with benefits bullshit out of thin air yesterday as a way to get what I want—more of her, in any way, shape, or form I can get her.

She bends over and tugs on the last jumper's pack before laughing at something Leo says to her. And the adrenalized, carefree tone of it stops me in my tracks. Realization hits that I want to be the one who makes her laugh like that.

Christ. I know I want more with her—what that more is, I'm not sure—but until I heard that tone to her laugh, I hadn't realized how much I wanted it.

Studying her as she walks toward me, I know I'll pay whatever cost to make sure that happens.

"You have some serious balls," I say off the cuff the minute she's within speaking distance.

"At least someone does," Leo coughs out, and I lift a finger in his direction, but my attention is focused on Em—the flush in her cheeks, the lines around her eyes where her goggles pressed against her skin, the ear-to-ear grin on her lips.

She laughs and shakes her head. "We both know that isn't true," she says in a voice for only my ears followed by a wink. "You missed a good jump. Perfect conditions. Great visibility. Calm wind."

"I appreciate the hustle, but I'm not buying."

"You don't have to buy; you already have a gift certificate."

"You're relentless."

"And you're handsome as hell."

My feet stop moving as she keeps walking, her comment unexpected and probably one of the first things she's said to me that was complimentary. The thought makes me laugh because to most people that would sound odd, but they're not Emmy and me.

She's sunshine with a little bit of hurricane thrown in, and I'm willingly walking straight into her storm with nothing more than the clothes on my back.

She turns to face me, her brow furrowing as I just stare at her as the realization hits me again that I want to be a part of her beautiful destruction. All of it. Without a damn forecast to prepare me for what's coming next.

"What?" she asks.

"Why do you do it, Em?"

"Do what?" The setting sun plays against the strawberry highlights in her hair and pieces dance in the air like wisps of fire.

"Why do you push the edge?"

"I don't." She smiles and takes a step toward me so we're a few feet apart from each other. Airstrip asphalt stretches all around us, and the excited chatter of the other jumpers coming down from their adrenaline highs turns to background noise.

"What if the chute doesn't deploy?"

"Then it doesn't deploy."

The nonchalance in how she says it pisses me off. "Are you out of your mind?"

"Perhaps." She shrugs, as if it were no big deal. "But we can die at any time. What if I get hit by a car? What if I have a heart attack? What if a meteor falls from the sky and kills me? What if, what if, what if. No use going through life living scared."

"But jumping increases your risk."

"Living every day increases my risk." She laughs, but it's the look in her eyes that shuts me up. "Look, I could wake up tomorrow with cancer and never get to jump again. I'd rather take the chance, Grant."

"Em . . ." I know she's thinking of her mom.

"Look, the probability that something will malfunction is so small that it isn't worth even thinking about. Besides, I pack all my own gear, and unlike you, I trust what I do."

I take the jibe because I deserve it, but it doesn't help me process how casual she is being about this. "If it doesn't work, no one can save you."

"I'm well aware of that," she says as her shoulders straighten, telling me I've activated her obstinate defiance. I'm too pissed at how she can be so careless with her own life to care, though.

"Every time you jump, that probability increases. Don't you think that's something to consider? It isn't as if I could do anything standing here on the ground to help."

"There goes Grant Malone and his hero complex."

"I saved—" *I saved you once, and I'll save you again in a goddamn heartbeat without thinking twice.*

The thought screams in my head, but I stop myself from saying it, from bringing the past into the present. From treating her like the girl she no longer wants to be.

Yet, I remember.

And I wonder.

And I worry.

Just like that fucking case file sitting in my house.

"You saved what?" She grits out the words as she takes another step closer, posture defensive and full of challenge. Sure, she's angry with me. I'm questioning her, but fuck it, she needs to know I care. Too bad I'm a guy and am not sure how to get that point across without setting off that magnificent and infuriating temper of hers.

"Nothing."

"I can save myself just fine, Grant Malone. And not just in skydiving. At least in jumping there's a reserve canopy in case the first one malfunctions. Wouldn't it be great if life had a backup chute for those moments when you're falling without anything to catch you?" She shrugs with her hands out to her side.

"And if the backup chute fails?"

"Like I said, life fails all the time. The only way to deal with it is to roll with the punches. Besides, *living safely* is dangerous. It isn't good for the soul or the psyche." She flashes me a huge grin before turning on her heel and saying over her shoulder, "Come on, I've gotta close up."

Standing on the tarmac, I watch her stride toward the office of Blue Skies.

Living safely is dangerous.

Well, shit.

Just as I'm about to walk after her, my phone alerts a text. I groan when I read it and realize I just screwed up royally.

Talking about sex possibilities with Emerson or fulfilling obligations to my family.

I know which one I'd rather choose, and I currently can't take my eyes off her.

THIRTY-TWO

Emerson

"You don't have to do this," Grant says as he pulls down the street I know so well from memory but have lacked the courage to venture back to since I returned to Sunnyville.

I'm not ignorant of the fact that he took the long way through the neighborhood. I am, however, silently relieved not to have to deal with seeing my old house for the first time since I left it twenty years ago.

I risk a glance his way, the anxiety I know visible in my eyes hidden by my sunglasses. "I know."

I don't know.

Needing to abate the nerves jittering through me, I slide my clasped hands between my thighs and squeeze my legs together.

Cue the panic.

"My mom is going to be thrilled to have a woman to balance out all the testosterone tonight," he says and reaches over to squeeze the top of my thigh. He doesn't remove his hand, though. I appreciate the silent show of support and wonder if he has any idea of the riot of emotions clamoring around inside me.

"It'll be good to see her," I murmur, eyes fixed on the houses as we pass.

Sally Glendale's house is still there and still that awful green color we used to say looked like puke. Then comes Adam Beecham's house to remind me of the hours we spent on the green transformer box out front playing UNO until the streetlights came on and it was time to go home.

Everything looks the same but so very different from my memories. I bet they've all moved out, moved on, and forgotten about the little girl, Emmy Reeves, two streets down who had the *unthinkable* happen to her.

Did their parents gossip about me for a long time after I left? Did they wonder if I was telling the truth, or did they just think I was making stuff up to get attention from my workaholic mother like little kids often did? Or did they not think of me at all because it was too unpleasant and might ruin the idyllic feeling of their safe neighborhood?

My palms grow sticky as the car slows down. My heart beats faster.

Why did I agree to come?

Because I know all of these people forgot about me a long time ago. I would bet that if I were to ask someone if they remembered the Reeves girl, they'd probably recall her name was Emily or Emma and have to think real hard about why the name sounded familiar.

Maybe I agreed to come because after the nightmare of last night, I don't want to be alone tonight. I'm so exhausted that I fear what other dreams will come when I finally let my subconscious crash.

"Emerson?"

I look over to Grant, only to notice that we were already parked along the curb in front of a place I remembered more fondly than my own, the Malone house.

My smile hides my nerves as I take in the exterior. It's just as I remember it being, but the paint's newer and the flowers are brighter. There's a woman's attention to detail in the colorful pots carefully placed on the stoop, and I can hear the wind chimes tinkle in the breeze as Grant opens the truck's door.

With a fortifying breath, I get out, but doubt shreds me apart with each and every step up the walkway. As positive as I am that most of Sunnyville doesn't remember Emmy Reeves with the pigtails and freckles, I am certain that the Malone family does.

I spent years going to psychologists, and every single one of them had the same exact look when they spoke to me. Pity. They all thought I was broken and irreparable. As soon as I convinced my mom I didn't need to go anymore, I promised myself no one would ever know about my past so that I'd never have to see that look again.

Now, for the first time since I made that promise, I'm willingly walking into a room, knowing full well I just might get that look again.

Grant must sense I'm about to lose my courage because he reaches out and links his fingers through mine, squeezing them in silent reassurance. He doesn't speak. He doesn't even glance my way. He just leads me up the last step as if this is an everyday thing for me.

"Hello?" he calls out as he opens the door, but his voice is drowned out by a cacophony of sound. A loud, baritone bark is echoing around the house, along with the screech of a little kid in what sounds like a tickle war. Laughter reverberates off the walls, and the faint chords of music playing in the backyard competes with the sound of an Indy race on a television no one seems to be watching.

Not only is it complete chaos but also it's exactly how I remembered it.

I follow Grant through the formal living room and stop when I see Betsy Malone. Her back is to me, and she's chopping vegetables on the counter I used to steal cookies from. Her hair may be shorter now, but everything else about her appears exactly the same.

"Mom," Grant says.

"It's about time you showed up," she says, but when she looks over and sees me standing in her kitchen, her lips fall lax. "Emmy Reeves. Well, aren't you a sight for sore eyes." She wipes her hands on a dishtowel and steps toward me since I'm frozen in place. "Grant said you were gorgeous, but leave it to a man to understate the obvious. My goodness. Get over here, you, and let me hug you."

Just like that, Betsy has her arms around me and is squeezing me so tight I can barely breathe, but it's okay because if I breathe the tears that threaten are going to fall. I don't want them to fall. Not here. Not now. Maybe later, but not now.

Her hand smooths down the back of my hair as if I were still a child, and I just close my eyes and sink into the feeling. It's like I've stepped back in time. The familiarity of her voice and the feeling of her arms provided more comfort than she could have ever fathomed. I know I was stupid for worrying about coming here.

Betsy Malone was my second mother.

This is the closet I've felt to being home since long before I never had an actual home to go back to.

"Let me look at you," she says, squeezing me one more time before stepping back and holding my arms out. When she meets my eyes, there are tears swimming in hers, and I enjoy knowing I'm not the only one who feels this overwhelmed being here again.

"Hi." My voice breaks with the single word, and it causes her to smile and pull me in for one more quick hug.

"Wine?" She punctuates the word with a decisive nod, most likely to prevent me from getting uncomfortable. "Wine is definitely what us two women need to combat the five testosterone-laced beings manning the barbecue."

And as if on cue, there's a flash of fur followed by a squeal of delight chasing after him. A little boy with sandy blond hair and dirt smudged on his cheek zooms through the kitchen before skidding to a halt and narrowing his eyes at me.

He looks just like the Grant I remember.

The thought knocks me back as I stare at him longer than I should.

"Who's she?" he asks Betsy.

"That's Uncle Grant's friend, Emerson."

"Cool," he says as he lifts a foot to continue his mad dash through the house.

"Luke," she warns, making him stop and causing Grant to chuckle.

With a resigned sigh like I'm ruining his fun, he turns to face me. "Hi, my name is Luke Malone, nice to meet you," he says in a monotone voice and holds his hand out. He's absolutely adorable, and I have a feeling he's also a bit of a hellion. The boy has Malone written all over him, which makes me like him because of and not in spite of it.

"Very nice to meet you, Luke. Is that your dog?" I shake his hand.

"No. That's Poppy's. He's big and slobbery and nice. His name is Moose and right now, he has one of my Pokémon cards in his mouth, and it's a Pikachu—a really good one—so I need to go get it back before he eats it."

Before I can say another word, he zooms out of the kitchen like his pants are on fire, leaving me with the glass of white wine Betsy's holding out to me and Grant eager to properly introduce me to the rest of the crew.

"See? That right there," Grant says with a laugh, "is why neither of you two bast—jerks have a girlfriend."

"This coming from the authority on women," Grayson says with a roll of his eyes.

My cheeks hurt from smiling so much, which tells me it was the right decision to come here with Grant. It had been against my better judgment, but obviously, I was wrong.

Luke is lying on his back on the grass about twenty feet away from us, Moose curled up next to him and dwarfing the five-year-old in size. The little boy seems to be talking to himself while he makes up stories about the aliens in the stars above him. I smile as I think of how many adventures I had in this backyard. It's the one place that holds one hundred percent positive memories for me, and that isn't easy to find.

"How's your studying going?" Betsy asks Grant, seemingly oblivious to the brief meeting of the eyes between Grant and his father.

"Good. I'm as ready as can be, but you know how it goes, there's always politics involved," he replies.

"Just remember, sometimes the high road can mean lying low," Chief Malone murmurs, piquing my interest.

"Once an asshole, always an asshole," Grayson chimes in, and I get the sense they are all talking about someone in particular, I just have no idea who. Even more peculiar is Betsy's lack of a reprimand over Grayson's comment, since over the course of dinner, most curse words were met with her rebuke.

No one can say this family doesn't have each other's backs.

"I have stronger words than that—"

"But you have a lady present," Betsy interrupts and gives Grant a warning glare.

"Yes, ma'am." Grant makes a show of looking properly reprimanded, which has his brothers snickering.

"Competition is healthy when going for a promotion," she says in the most motherly of tones, "even if that competition is a self-serving prick."

Everyone's eyes widen as they look back and forth at each other to make sure their mother really just said that before bursting out into laughter over her unexpected comment.

"You have a lady present," Grant mimics her.

"Yes, well, I'm sure Emmy's heard those terms before, haven't you, dear?" She pats my hand and smiles wider.

"So, Emerson," Chief Malone says. "Grant tells me you are buying Blue Skies out at Miner's Airfield."

"I'm trying to," I say. "After traveling for so long, it's finally time to put some roots down. It's been an adjustment staying in one place for this long, but it's a good change. Blue Skies has been neglected for a while now so I'm enjoying breathing life back into it. Now I just can't wait to make it mine. Fingers and toes crossed I get loan approval."

"You always were up for a challenge," Betsy says as she puts another piece of chocolate cake on my plate without my having to ask. "Eat up. You always loved dessert . . . but jumping out of airplanes? Really?"

There's something about the way she references how I used to be with such nonchalance that makes it ring in my ears. When Grant mentioned the same thing at Desi's, it made me uneasy. He was revealing a small part of my past to people unfamiliar with it. But this, Betsy bringing it up in the one place that was my safe haven, feels different to me. It's almost comforting to know I existed to someone when I was a child and that they remember me. Moving on a whim and living like a gypsy, often doesn't afford you that feeling.

"Emerson subscribes to the living-safely-is-dangerous theory," Grant interjects as he bumps his knee against mine beneath the table.

"Well, if you're with that asshole"—Grady gestures to Grant—"then you definitely like to live dangerously. He isn't known to be one who sticks around longer than the quick—"

"Grady Malone," Betsy warns in that tone that brings a smile to my lips. "You know better than to talk that way when someone brings a guest over. Your father and I did not raise unmannerly heathens."

"Sorry, Mom," he says with no sincerity before looking at me. "See? Nothing has changed. We still bicker constantly like we did when we were kids. We're just older and the insults are more brutal."

That's the first time our collective past has been put out there in the open, causing an uncomfortable silence. Luckily, I've had enough wine that the mention doesn't trip me up like it might have if I were completely sober.

"Is it sad that I remember that? The names you used to call each other and how when your mom called you by your full name, it meant you really were in trouble," I say to try to ease the unspoken tension. "Being an only child, I never had to deal with that. The flip side was I couldn't blame something on someone else either so my mom always knew if I was at fault."

"How is your mom doing, Emerson?" the chief asks, and Grant tenses beside me.

"She passed away a few years back."

"Oh, Emmy," the chief says. "I had no idea. If my eldest would have had proper manners and let me know that, then we would have known not to ask. I'm so very sorry."

"It's okay. She was sick for a long time, and now her suffering is over."

"What made you decide to move back here to Sunnyville?" he continues.

"Blue Skies."

And possibly your son.

The thought has me lifting my fork and digging into the second piece of cake to clear the startling thought from my mind.

But it's true. I always knew that if I moved back I'd run into Grant Malone eventually.

Hadn't I wanted to?

Hadn't I always looked in every crowd, just in case I saw his face?

"Well, whatever reason it may be, we're glad to see you again," Betsy says, breaking the sudden lull in conversation and patting my hand. "It's like having my daughter back."

Those simple words are like resin being poured onto the cracks of my heart. A protective shield to ward off whatever lies ahead for it.

There's a crackling of a police scanner, and I smile at how all of them fall silent while codes are relayed over the radio. Their bodies still, heads all angle in the same mannerism that reflects they are related. Each so similar, yet so different.

"You're being rude, gentlemen," Betsy says and meets my eyes. "It's a full-time job keeping the Malone men in line and away from work when they're off duty."

"Shame on us for saving lives," Grady replies and has us all laughing.

"Always the class clown," Betsy mutters in jest as she stands up with her plate in her hand.

"Can I help you clean up, Mom?" Grant asks as he scoots his chair back. "Emerson and I need to be getting back."

"I thought you were off tomorrow," Grayson says.

"I am, but I sprung this on Emerson without asking, so I'm sure she has other, more pressing things she needs to do."

Every part of me wants to reject what he's saying. It doesn't matter how much I didn't want to come here, because now I don't want to leave.

There's a feeling here I've missed for so very long.

A feeling I craved in my childhood that this house—that this family—provided to me.

Security.

That isn't an easy thing for normal people to find in this world, let alone people with a past like mine. It's often fleeting and habitually false.

It's here and now that I've found it, I find that I'm scared to lose it.

THIRTY-THREE

Emerson

"HEAD UP. WINGS OUT. WHAT DOES THAT MEAN?"

I smile at Grant's question and lean back on my hands as my legs dangle off the tailgate of Grant's truck. "It was something my mom used to say to me. Originally, she told me that if I keep my head up and put on a brave face when I'm afraid, then the angels will put their wings out and use them to protect me." I smile at the memory. "Over the years, it became shortened to head up, wings out. The first time I jumped, she made me carry it on a piece of paper in my pocket, as if it would ensure I made it safely back to the earth . . . so from then on, I said it before every jump. When she died, it kind of became my way of reminding myself she's looking out for me. That it's her angel wings keeping me safe."

"Head up. Wings out," he murmurs. "I like that."

Silence falls between us for a few moments. "This is my favorite time of day to be here," I muse as I stare at the lights of the runway

"Why's that?"

"Because it's quiet. There's typically no one around, and if there is, it's because they've filed a flight plan ahead of time and I already know about it. There are the lights of the runway and the rustling of the trees from the breeze. It's even better when the moon's full and the shadows are everywhere." I fall silent, feeling silly but, for some reason, wanting him to know about one of the places I find peace.

"I can understand that. I have a place I like, too. It's up in the hills, and when I go there, I can stare at the city's lights below and the stars above for hours."

There's the baying of a dog in the far distance and then a reciprocated one from its echoes. This feels so normal, and I'm not sure why I'm not panicking that this is too close to breaking one of my rules, the one that demands I don't do anything that seems like a date. But there's a comfortable silence that I'm not used to, so maybe that's why the anxiety seems to be missing.

Though, I did feel the same way—normal—at the Malone house tonight, which was far from quiet. With Luke and Moose and their little boy-big dog relationship, the constant ribbing between three brothers close as night but different as day, and the constant love felt between all members of the family, it was the most welcoming chaos I think I've ever seen.

"Who would have ever thought the three of you would be what you are today—a police officer, a firefighter, and a rescue pilot," I muse, only realizing I've said it aloud when Grant's chuckle rumbles through the night.

"I'm thinking I should be offended by that comment."

"No. Not at all. It's just . . . kind of cool." My mind fills with memories I forgot I had. Of shy Grady and his books. Of loud Grayson and his daredevil stunts. Of responsible Grant always looking out for the two of them . . . *and me.*

He shrugs. "My dad instilled in us the need to serve."

"And what does your mom think about that?"

"She's tough."

"Yeah, she is." My smile is automatic when it comes to thinking of her.

"She's a cop's wife. She knows the drill. There have been a handful of times when I have known she has been really worried. Bad calls. Natural disasters. Accidents."

"You sound so casual."

"Like I said, she's tough. Just as any woman who decides to take one of us on has to be." He lifts his eyes to meet mine across the dimly lit night, and the look he gives me says the two words that don't pass his lips: *Like you.*

Chills race over my skin despite the warm night air, and I'm nervous and cognizant that we are talking about ourselves more than I typically allow.

"Thank you for taking me."

"The minute I turned into the neighborhood, I realized it might not have been such a great idea," he says, making me close one of the padlocked doors he'd just opened. "I'm glad you had a good time."

"I did. Um, I'd invite you back to my place, but there isn't much to it . . . but it is clean." It's the only thing I can think to say—when all else fails, talk about the physicality between us to prevent us from talking about anything else.

"You say it's clean as if it's a shock."

"It is." I laugh. "We'll just say it wasn't too pretty a few weeks ago. Or if Desi were here, she'd say *ever*."

I shove up off the tailgate and begin walking to my loft, my mind set on the notion of if he follows, he follows, and if he doesn't, he doesn't.

That's a lie I knowingly tell myself. Truth is, I don't want to be alone tonight. I don't want to give my mind a single chance to get lost in itself and bring me back *there* again.

I have one foot on the stairs that lead up to my loft when Grant's hand lands on my bicep, turning me around. "Emerson."

He rubs his thumb on the inside of my arm, and I can see the confusion on his face the same moment I yank my arm away from his touch.

"Did you get hurt today?" he asks, and I cringe at my overreaction, but that's my ugly, and I don't want him knowing my ugly.

I've escaped him seeing them this far and now I scramble to figure out how to recover and take cues from what he asked. "No, not today. The nylon on the rig rubs me right there for some reason, so I have a few scars from always getting scratched. I'm so used to it that I forget it's even there until someone mentions it."

He stares, gauging whether to believe me or not. "I'm sorry, I didn't mean to . . ."

"No, I overreacted. It's okay." I lean in and do what I've been thinking about ever since we left his parents' house—I press my lips to his.

Grant reacts immediately. Hunger and the mint he had in the car are on his tongue. His hands run up and down my arms as he takes a step closer, bringing us chest to chest since I'm still one step up from him.

We sink into the kiss. There is no rush, just a sense that we are feeling each other out to see where we go from here.

A part of me doesn't want to know that answer.

I just want to enjoy the moment.

Live in the now.

Forget the complications that being with Grant Malone could cause in my life.

"Are we going to do this?" he murmurs against my lips.

A long, slow, mesmerizing kiss that leaves me weak in the knees when weakness isn't a thing I allow.

"Do what?"

A nip of my bottom lip.

"Do this. You. Me. *Friends*."

A hand runs languorously up and down my spine before landing on my ass and pulling me tighter against him.

"Friends don't do this."

His chuckle is muted against my lips.

"You and I have never been anything close to normal, Em."

A lick of his tongue against mine makes me press into him when he leans back.

"You're too sexy, and I'm too horny to walk away tonight without sleeping with you . . ." I murmur playfully. *And truthfully*.

"You're goddamn right . . . so is that a yes?"

"*Yes*," I grunt as his hand on my ass slides inside the waistband of my shorts.

The thumb on his other hand brushes the underside of my breast. A tease. A taunt. A promise of what's to come.

"But there are rules," I say before he goes to kiss me again, and I earn a chuckle as he rests his forehead against mine.

"I thought we already covered them?"

"We did, but—*ahhh*."

His teeth tug on my earlobe and cause an electric current to shock through my system.

"You were saying?" His breath is warm against my skin as he asks.

"Before was a one-night thing," I say, but his lips on my neck are making it hard to string thoughts let alone coherent sentences together. "And now we're agreeing to more."

"Em." It's part groan, part moan when his lips try to brush against mine as I take a step backward up the stairs. It's only a fleeting moment that we're apart before our mouths crash back together in a torrent of greed and need.

"No romance."

It's getting harder to remember the things I want to address as my body ignites with every kind of want imaginable.

"Naturally."

He places open-mouthed kisses down the line of my jaw, drawing goose bumps over my skin as we take another step up.

"No lovey-dovey."

"You're not the lovey-dovey type."

He pulls gently on my earlobe, the heat of his mouth only intensifying the sensation as the ache intensifies between my thighs.

"No overnights."

His hand slides beneath my shirt and begins working on the clasp of my bra as his lips close over the peak of my nipple through the fabric.

"Not unless we're doing this."

Another step up.

"No dates. No dating. No semblance of dating."

"You're talking too much," His words are punctuated with a nip before his lips find mine again and his fingers find the button on my shorts.

"Grant." I step up to get away and stand my ground, but I know it's for show. I'm too far gone, too lost in Lustville to push him away.

"Yes. No dates. Or dating. Or eating. Or talking. Or whatever you want so long as you shut your mouth unless it's kissing me and put your hand on my dick because, baby, I'm dying here."

I lean back and meet his eyes. There's humor there. And desperation.

My fingers find the button on his jeans, and he groans when I find purchase. After I tug the zipper down, I cup him and gently scrape my fingers outside and over the seam of denim, causing the sexiest sound I've ever heard to emit from deep in his throat.

"I know I'm forgetting something," I say as my lips find the curve of his neck, and he climbs the final step.

"Your keys. You're forgetting your keys," he says through a laugh as I go to pull my hand away from his dick, but his fingers are on my wrist in a flash. "That's not going anywhere, Em. Give me the keys, I'll open it."

In seconds, my keys are out of my purse and my door is open and we're standing in the dark with my hand on his cock and my rules wedged securely between us.

"No talking about our pasts. No sleeping with other people—just for safety's sake—"

"Woman, you could ask me to skydive and I'd say yes so long as I get to fuck you again. Shortly. Like in minutes."

He must be dead serious.

I draw his shirt over his head and then pull mine off, my bra falling to the floor as I lean forward and suck one of his nipples.

"More like seconds." His voice is strained and his hands grip tighter on my arms.

"This is such a mistake," I groan as his hands slide into the waistband of my shorts and push them down.

"Mm-hmm," he says against my lips. "You can call the first time a mistake. The second time, it's called a decision. Make the goddamn decision, Em. Please. Before I die of desperation."

I chuckle. "So dramatic." I kiss him again and love how when I pull back, he leans forward to take more. It shows what I do to him. It shows he wants me. "No . . ." I can't think of any more rules because his cock pulses against my hand, growing harder.

"What else can there possibly be?" he asks, exasperated as he shoves his own jeans down his hips so that his cock springs free into my hand.

"This," I say before I drop to my knees and look up to him as I take the entire, rock-hard length of him in my mouth.

"I fucking love that rule." He groans as his head falls back and his fingers sink into my hair, tightening when he hits the back of my throat.

THIRTY-FOUR

Grant

THE WOMAN IS INCREDIBLE IN EVERY FUCKING SENSE OF THE word.

She eyes me from where she stands in the kitchen—if I can call it that since it's little more than a hot plate, a mini fridge, a toaster oven, and a Keurig. It doesn't hurt that the only thing she's wearing is a pair of boy shorts.

No top. No nothing.

Talk about a morning view I'd like to revisit.

That fact makes it that much harder not to stare at her and her perfectly perky set of tits. I can remember so very vividly how her nipples feel against my tongue, and it makes my damn mouth water.

Fuck if my morning hard-on isn't begging to take advantage of everything about her again, but there's so much more at stake right now than coming again.

Like her not realizing that we've broken her first rule, not once but twice.

No overnights.

I would be surprised if she doesn't already realize that and is making her coffee and plotting how to get control of the situation back. I'll gladly give it to her if I get to end up sitting here watching her shirtless in her kitchen again.

"How do you want yours?" she asks.

"I can get it."

"Relax. I'm perfectly capable of pushing a button and not screwing it up. If it were anything more than that, then you could be concerned."

"Black, please."

After putting in a fresh pod and pressing the button to start the machine, she pads to one side of the small loft and fires up her computer without looking at the screen. My attention stays on her as she checks her cell phone and gives it a roll of her eyes over something before flipping a file folder open and making a note in it.

A file folder.

Much like the one in a box on my table at home.

How the fuck can the little girl on that folder's label be this same damn woman in front of me. Shouldn't she be fucked up? Shouldn't she be a mess of issues?

Maybe she is underneath and is simply doing a damn good job of hiding it.

Then again, it's hard to see a thing when her self-assuredness, confidence, and strength roll off her in thick waves.

Thankfully, the jiggling of her tits as she walks to get our coffee steers my thoughts away from any further psychoanalyzing. They mesmerize me as she crosses the distance, and hell if I'm not blatantly appreciating them. It's only when she stops at the edge of the bed and holds the cup of coffee out to me that I meet her eyes.

"You like what you see?" She laughs with a raised set of eyebrows, and I love that she is secure enough she can ask the question and make it sound sexy instead of conceited.

"No complaints here. I'm just trying to figure out how I can see this view more often."

"Such a typical male. You get blown, fucked, then fucked again, but you still aren't satisfied." Her smile is wide as she sits on the bed facing me with one knee bent beneath her and the other leg hanging off the edge. "What's it going to take, Malone?"

"*More of you.*"

There's a silent moment that passes where her eyes soften and her smile slowly falls, vulnerability written all over her features before she throws her head back and laughs as if what I said is the funniest thing in the world.

"Flattery will get you everywhere." She takes a sip of her coffee but leaves her eyes on mine from above the rim.

"It will?"

"It will."

"Good to know," I say as I lean back against the headboard and look around her place. It's small but has a pretty cool setup. The colors are muted, the furniture is modest, but it's a complete reflection of her. Practical and minimalist. The best part is the series of windows that face out to the field and trees opposite the landing strip.

"Who do you rent this place from, again?" I ask, already knowing the answer.

"Travis Barnhardt."

"I think I know him."

"You do know him."

"I do? Oh. Isn't he Dean's dad?"

"Dean?"

"Dean from Mrs. Gellar's class."

Her hand stutters in motion as she lifts her coffee cup to her lips. The quick aversion of her eyes tells me she doesn't like this topic.

I push anyway.

"I don't think so." Her voice is soft as she sets the cup down, picks it back up, and then straightens the sheets some.

"Sorry." I shake my head, hating that the simple mention of Mrs. Gellar's class puts her visibly on edge. "You're right. Dean's last name was Meyers."

I wait to see a reaction from her, but her expression remains stone cold. "Yes, that was it."

Silence falls between us as we both stare into our coffees, but questions nag me more than ever before since running into Emerson. It's her dig about not trusting me that she played off as one thing when she really meant another. It's her need to stay detached even though we're clearly sleeping together.

"About that day . . ." *Fucking Christ.* I'm so goddamn distracted by her incredible body sitting half-naked before me that I blurted out my thoughts.

"No," she snaps as she shoves up off the bed.

"We need to talk about it at some point, Em."

"Actually, no, we don't." She turns her back to me and walks toward the windows.

"Em—"

"Stop!" she shouts. "I've dealt with it. I don't need you bringing it up, so don't talk about it again. Now, *get out* before you break another rule because you're walking a fine line with me, Grant. The spending the night was a mistake. You bringing that up, wasn't cool . . . so, play time's over. The benefits have been used up for now. I have to get to work."

I study her for a moment—a silhouette against the morning light beyond—the curve of her waist, the shape of her legs, her strawberry hair falling down her bare back in tangles. There's so much shit I want to say, but the defensiveness in her posture tells me she won't hear a damn word of it.

In time.

In silence and with gritted teeth, I rise from the bed and pull on my jeans and shirt. All the while, she stares out the window, ignoring the tension settling into place.

With my keys in my hand, I walk toward where she stands. "Your past sure as fuck doesn't define the woman you are . . . and it isn't my business, regardless of how much I care about you and want to make sure you're okay. Em, I was there, and I feel like you hold it against me—"

"Or maybe I'm just this hostile with all men," she whispers, never turning to face me, but I can hear the pain in her voice and hate that I put it there.

I take the final step to her and hear her breath catch as I press my lips to the back of her shoulder. “Nah, I think it’s particular to me.” She nods but doesn’t step away from me. “Can we somehow wipe the slate clean?”

“How, though?” Confusion laces her voice, and her willingness to even ask that question is telling. It doesn’t matter how much I think I know about her past, I don’t have a goddamn clue about the demons she still battles. And battle she does. Even now, she’s fighting them with loud declarations of denial and softly whispered pleas for help.

“From here on out, we forget the memories and just chase the moments,” I say with another press of my lips to her skin before walking out the door.

THIRTY-FIVE

Grant

"IF I HAD A SECRET, COULD I TELL YOU AND WOULD YOU PROMISE not to tell anyone in the whole wide world?"

"Huh? Yeah. Sure." I'm at the good part in my RL Stine book and don't want to stop.

"I'm serious."

She is serious. When I look up from my book, I realize she's been crying. Like red-eyes crying. But she's wearing her favorite purple dress with sparkly black shoes—the one she calls her "pop star" outfit.

"What's wrong?" She doesn't move other than to look over her shoulder toward where her house is and then back to me. "Emmy?"

"Never mind. I'm fine." She smiles as she sits beside me but makes a funny sound when she does. Like she's trying not to cry.

"You okay?" Something's wrong with her. Emmy never cries.

She bites her bottom lip and nods before looking over her shoulder again. Something's wrong.

"Em?" I nudge her with my elbow. "If you're gonna tell me, then you need to tell me quick because my mom's gonna come out soon with my lunch, and then we're going to have to walk to school. So what's wrong?"

"You have to pinky promise, Grant Malone, that if I tell you this secret, you won't ever tell another person, ever, ever, ever. If you do, I'll never be your friend again. Promise me. Cross your heart and hope to die."

"But I—"

"Not even your mom or dad or brothers or anyone." Her eyes fill with tears again. Girls and tears. I'd roll my eyes if she weren't so upset.

"Okay. I promise." I cross my heart and link pinkies with her. "Is that good?"

"Yeah. You really promise?"

"Yes. I promise. What's the big deal?"

"You know how my mom goes to work at night?"

"At the hospital? Yeah. It's super cool she gets to help people."

She nods and licks her lips and then looks down to where she's picking the skin around her thumbnail so it bleeds. "Well, when she goes to work, sometimes my dad hurts me."

"Hurts you? Like he spanks you when you get in trouble?" I'd give anything to have a mom like hers who doesn't believe in the belt on your bottom. My dad says it builds respect. I say it builds a sore butt.

"No."

"No? Then . . ."

"He comes in my room and holds a gun to my head and molests me."

A tear drops on her thumb, but all I hear is the word "gun." I don't know what molests means, but I know guns are serious. The million lectures my dad has given me and my brothers to never touch one fill my head, and I know this is bad, but . . .

"Emmy . . . why would he do that?" I look around the street and wonder if my mom can hear inside the house.

"Because he says I'm pretty and he loves me."

"But . . ." My dad has a gun, too, and he doesn't do that to me. I don't like the icky feeling in my tummy. My book slips from my hands, and I don't like what we're talking about, so I concentrate on the creepy monster on the cover as I shove it in my backpack. "I don't understand. I—"

"I don't, either." Another tear falls, and the way she says it makes tears burn in my eyes.

"We should tell my mom. She'd know—"

"No!" she yells as she grabs my hand and squeezes it so hard it hurts. "You promised you wouldn't tell anyone. He said it would hurt my mommy if I tell anyone, and I don't want her hurt, Grant. He said this is what daddies do and . . ." She hiccups over a sob, and I don't know what to do.

"Grant! It's time to get going," my mom calls from the house. "Oh, hi, Emmy. Look at how pretty you look today. Just like one of the Spice Girls."

Emmy smiles for the first time since she got here to walk to school, and I wonder if maybe she's fibbing. Sometimes she does that. Girls always want attention, or at least that's what Cooper says.

Em stays where she is on the sidewalk as I jog up the steps to get my lunch from my mom. After I shove it in my backpack, I give her a hug goodbye.

For some reason, when I hug her, I have to blink away the tears before she sees them.

"Have a good day, honey," she says and then she gets that line in her forehead like when she doesn't believe what I'm telling her. "You okay? What's wrong?"

Emmy's dad is mean.

"You have to pinky promise, Grant Malone, that if I tell you this secret, you won't ever tell another person, ever, ever, ever. If you do, I'll never be your friend again. Promise me. Cross your heart and hope to die"

"Yeah. I'm good. Just got something in my eye is all."

She studies me again, but Grayson cries inside, saving me from more questions. "Don't rub it then, okay?" I nod before she says the same thing she says every day when we leave to walk the straight shot of a street to school. "I'll watch you guys from here until you get to the school gates, and then I'll meet you at the tree after class to walk home with you."

"'Kay."

When I jog down the steps, I hate that Adam from across the

street is standing there with Emmy and waiting to walk with us. I need to talk to her and ask if she's really telling the truth. Her dad seems nice to me.

And he's not a police officer. Only police officers and bad guys have guns and he's not either of those.

But my tummy still hurts.

"You promise?" Emmy mouths to me from where she stands beside me in the girls' line while I'm in the boys' line. We're in the very back this morning because we were battling in two square and neither of us wanted to quit first and lose.

"I promise."

"If you tell anyone, I'll never be your friend again. I might even 'bad word' you."

"'Bad word me?'"

"H-A-T-E," she spells, and I forgot that her mom thinks the words hate and stupid are bad words worthy of television time being taken away.

"I promise, Em. I promise, okay?" I say loud enough that the kid in front of me turns around to shush me like I'm going to get the boys' line in trouble.

Emmy just stares at me like I told her we're getting to watch a Disney movie after lunch instead of doing work . . . I think the word for it is hopeful. I'm not sure, though.

But even as we start our morning paperwork, I can't stop thinking about what Em said.

"*He puts a gun to my head and molests me.*"

Even after our circle time when we move into writing in our journals, I think about it.

But she seems fine. She seems like Emmy. The red in her eyes from crying is gone, and she's pulling out the dreaded composition notebook so she can write about Helen Keller. Just like we all did yesterday. And the day before. I don't care about Helen Keller because I already know the important stuff—that she was deaf and blind.

"Mrs. Gellar?" I shoot my hand up as high as it will go, hoping her answer will be the same as every other time someone has asked.

"I don't know the meaning of this word in our book."

"You know where Webster is," she says, using the class-decided name for our dictionary.

I walk to the corner of the room and open the book, struggling with the paper jacket when it falls off the hard cover. When I glance over my shoulder, no one is near me, but Emmy meets my eyes and smiles softly.

M.

It takes a few seconds for me to find the word.

Molests.

And it takes me even longer to figure out the definition.

To assault or abuse (a person, especially a woman or a child) sexually.

I snap the book closed, my cheeks red because there is the word "sex" in the definition, and I don't really know what that is except for it's what Cooper says only mommies and daddies do and he's never going to do it.

But I know the word assault. My dad uses that word all the time when I get to visit him at work and he talks cases with other officers. So, if he uses the word, then I know it means bad things.

Does Emmy have this same molestation disease these suspects my dad talks about have? But she isn't a suspect. She didn't do anything wrong.

Did she?

The bell for recess rings.

Guns. Mr. Reeves. Molest. Assault.

"Bet I'm gonna beat you at two square again," Emmy says, and I run to follow after her.

"Mr. Malone." Mrs. Gellar's sharp tone—like I'm in trouble—stops my feet from running when I know I shouldn't be running in the classroom.

"Yeah?"

"The word is yes, not yeah. We're working on grammar," she says as she walks toward me with her hand on her back and her big, pregnant belly—that Cooper says you get from having S-E-X—leading the way.

"Yes?" I correct.

"Head on out, Emmy. Grant's going to go back and put Webster in his proper place. He'll be there in a minute."

I grumble and shuffle my feet as the door to the playground shuts, taking the sunshine with it.

Guns.

Picking up Webster, I make sure the jacket is on . . .

Mr. Reeves.

Then I slide it into the bookshelf . . .

Molest.

Finally, I turn to head to the door.

Assault.

"Mrs. Gellar?" I ask, my voice breaking and heart beating so fast I can feel it against my chest.

"Yeah, sweetie? Oh, thanks for fixing Webster," she says, thinking I was trying to show her I did what she'd asked. "You can go play now."

"I have a question."

"You do?" She looks up from the stack of papers she is shuffling through on her desk. "Can it wait until after recess?"

"I'll never be your friend again."

"I don't think so."

She angles her head to the side and stares at me. "What's wrong, Grant?"

She's going to hate me.

"What if someone told you something and made you promise to never tell anyone but you think you should tell someone?"

"Are you tattling on them?"

"No."

"Are you saying something to make someone look bad so you look better?

"No."

"Are you worried about their safety?"

I look down to the smiley face I wrote with Sharpie on my Converse and then look back to her.

Guns.

"Yes."

"Come over here, Grant. Pull up a chair."

With every step I take, I know Emmy is going to hate me that much more. She can't hate me. Dad says it's our duty to help people who are in trouble.

I move a chair toward Mrs. Gellar and sit. "Grant? What is it, honey?"

One of her hands is on her belly, and I stare at it, wondering if I'll see the baby move beneath her black T-shirt if I look long enough.

"Grant?"

"It's about Emmy." My throat is dry. Like if I played really hard during recess and the line was too long at the drinking fountain before coming back into class so I didn't get a drink.

"What about Emmy?" Her hand rubs back and forth and then stills again.

"She told me a secret, and I'm not supposed to tell, but—"

"What is it, Grant?

"She said when her mom goes to work at night, her dad has a gun and he molests her." Her hand jerks on her tummy, but I can't look up because I just broke my promise to Emmy and I'm scared she's going to hate me. "But I don't know what that means other than guns are bad and she's going to hate me and—"

Mrs. Gellar puts her other hand on my shoulder. It makes me stop talking and meet her eyes, embarrassed when a tear slides down my cheek because boys don't cry.

But it's Emmy.

"Grant?" Her voice sounds funny—different—and her throat

makes a funny sound when she swallows. "When did Emmy tell you this?"

"This morning." I can barely get the word out. "Please don't tell her I told you."

"I won't."

I can't look at her anymore.

My tummy hurts so bad.

"Look at me, honey." I take in a deep breath, and I feel like such a wuss when I hiccup a sob, but I look at her. "This is what she told you? You aren't making this up?"

"No." I can barely get the word out.

"You did the right thing by telling me. Did you tell anyone else about this?"

I shake my head. "No. I promised her, and . . . I promised her."

"Oh, sweet boy," she says in a soft voice that makes me think she isn't mad at me for telling on my friend as she stands and gives me a big hug. It takes everything I have not to hold on tighter and cry like Emmy does when she scrapes her knee—super hard so she can barely talk—but I don't do it. Instead, I concentrate on trying to make my arms fit all the way around Mrs. Gellar even though her tummy is too big and my fingers won't touch. She leans back and looks at me. There are tears in her eyes, too, and that makes me worry. "You did the right thing, Grant. I know you're worried Emmy is going to be mad . . . and she might be for a while, but you did the right thing."

"Wh-what are you going to do?" Now that I've told her, I'm not sure what is going to happen next. How is she going to help Emmy without letting Emmy know I told her secret?

"I'm going to make sure she's never hurt again."

"She's hurt?" I know guns are bad, but I'm confused. How is she hurt? She looks fine to me other than having cried earlier.

"Grant, I need you to do something for me, okay? I need you to go out on the playground for a few minutes and get some fresh air. I don't want you to tell anyone else about what you said to me because it's important that Emmy has you as a friend. I'll take care of the rest."

"Are you sure?" How is she going to do that?

"I'm sure. Now, I need you to go out so I can do a few things in privacy, okay?"

I nod and then drag my feet all the way to the door. I swear I hear her sniffle, but her back is to me, so I can't be sure. Why would she sniffle? Just as I push it open, I hear Mrs. Gellar on the phone. "Principal Newman? I have a situation that needs immediate attention."

THIRTY-SIX

Emerson

W*E FORGET THE MEMORIES AND JUST CHASE THE MOMENTS.*

Those damn words replay in my head over and over. All day. Before I close my eyes at night. When I'm staring out the window at the airfield, waiting for the next class of jumpers to get ready. Even while sitting here in a bar with Desi where I came to try to prove to myself that I don't care in the least why he hasn't called or texted me in over five days.

I glance at my phone again sitting on the table next to everyone's empty glasses and then hate myself for giving in to the temptation to look.

This is why I have rules. They are designed so I don't end up sitting here like some needy, whiny chick, which is exactly how I feel.

Maybe he's studying for his test like he should be. You know, he's doing important things. It explains the silence, since I made certain he knew not to count me as one of those important things.

Maybe I scared him off with my rules and shutting him out the other day.

Maybe I . . . shit, I don't know. It's me, so I'm sure I'm the one at fault.

"Earth to Emerson."

"What?" I snap at Desi, misdirecting my frustration at how I'm acting over Grant at her.

"Thanks for coming, but uh, maybe you can act like you're actually having fun instead of looking like I forced you to come," she says.

"You did force me to come." I groan as I stare at the dance floor, which is full of grinding bodies and alcohol sloshing over cups.

"Oh, quit being such an old lady. Live a little. Dance a lot. Drink something new. Pick a guy just for the night. Whatever floats your boat."

I glare at her for what feels like the tenth time in the past hour, but it holds no weight because she's Desi. I let her get away with everything. Case in point, I'm here when I want to be anywhere but.

"What, no guy for the night?" She gives me a double take. "Hottie at two o'clock has had your number since you showed up. He's just waiting for eye contact to make his move."

"Whatever. No he has not—"

Sirens screaming past the bar cut me off, and without thinking, I turn to watch the two squad cars as they navigate through the crowded intersection.

"Uh-huh."

"What?" I ask, realizing I've been caught.

"You do have a thing for uniforms, don't you? That, or you wish it was Grant."

"Hottie at two o'clock is all yours," I say as if she hadn't spoken at all.

"I know your game, Reeves. Hottie at two o'clock has no interest in me, but you're saying he does to throw me off so I don't go over there and play matchmaker. If I did, then you might have to tell him no. And telling him no would inform me, your *best* friend whom you're hiding things from, that you might like Grant a little more than you're letting on."

This time, the glare I level her with is real. "No one said I didn't like Grant." It's her turn to return the look. "He has skills in the bedroom department, and I sure as hell am not complaining about that . . . but I told you that we have rules and we're purely enjoying the physical aspect."

"The physical aspect," she mimics with a roll of her eyes.

"There are other terms I could use that would be more accurate, but I'm trying to be a lady." I smile a big, cheesy grin to let her know I'm going out of my way to annoy her.

"A lady." She snorts. "Well, if there is no commitment, then why aren't you out on the dance floor living it up?"

"Because I don't want to."

"Because you'd rather be with Officer Sexy."

"No." *Yes*. What the hell is wrong with me? "I'll dance in a bit."

"Ha." She scoffs. "You're such a liar."

She's right.

Grant Malone seems to be the only one I'll allow to upend my world.

First to save me.

And now to show me what it's like to feel.

THIRTY-SEVEN

Grant

"WHAT THE HELL, DUDE?"

Nate is barely containing the snicker, his face turning beet red as I stare at the blow-up doll positioned precariously at my desk. Someone—probably one of my brothers—put the thing in a skimpy female cop Halloween costume and used a Sharpie to highlight some of its better features.

"Grady and Grayson, I presume?"

"How could you tell?" He laughs as I finally see their self-portraits horribly tattooed above each one of her boobs.

All I can do is shake my head and take a seat at Ambrose's desk directly across from it . . . her? While I more than admire my brothers' creativity and attempt to make me relax after the long-ass exam, I'm already thinking of ways to get them back.

"Don't worry," Nate says. "All the guys already tapped 'dat for ya." He picks her up, and when he turns her around, there are signatures from all of the guys in the squad on her ass.

"Cute. Very cute. Thanks, guys," I say as everyone around us starts busting up laughing.

Fucking assholes.

"So . . . how do you feel?" Nate asks as if he isn't currently placing a blow-up doll back in my chair so that her feet are propped on the desk. No matter how hard he tries, her legs keep spreading open.

Finally, he gives up and just pushes her out of the chair.

"I see how you treat suspects." I almost don't get the words out around my laughter.

"That's only if they're behaving." We both look down to where she's face down, spread eagle on the floor. "So tell me how it went."

"Good. It was pretty straightforward. None of the questions gave me trouble."

"Like I figured. Is the asshole still in there?" Nate lifts his chin toward the conference room where Stetson and I sat on opposite ends of the table to take our tests.

"Yeah, he—"

"Ah, boys, that test was fucking cake," Stetson says before emitting a whoop to his group of cronies—all of them newer beat cops not schooled in his knife-in-the-back-I'm-a-total-asshole ways yet—as he exits the conference room.

Nate makes the jacking-off motion and rolls his eyes at the sound of Stetson's voice. "May be cake," he mutters, "but Grant's gonna be the one eating it while you tank at the interviews."

"Thanks for the vote of support."

"I have your back," he says. It's his mischievous smile that worries me more than anything.

"I know you do, and I appreciate whatever it is that sick, twisted mind of yours is conjuring as a payback, but don't. I want this on my terms and because I earned it."

"Of course you do, but he's playing dirty. You know he's going to throw everything but the goddamn sink in because—"

I put my hand up to stop him. Not here. Not in the precinct where anyone can hear. The last thing I need is for it to become daily gossip that runs rampant in the squad room. "My record is clean, *unlike his.* Even if we both pass the test and do decent in the interviews, I'll beat him because I've kept my nose clean." It's the truth. Let's just hope the powers that be think that, too.

"'Kay. But if you change your mind, I'd do it in a heartbeat."

"I know you would," I say, rising from my seat and patting him on the back before heading outside.

There are a few texts on my phone that I glance over as I move to find shade from the blinding sun. My dad asking how it went. Grady wishing me good luck. My mom's simple text, asking how my day is so I won't think she is fishing to see how I did instead of just outright asking. Grayson asking if I want to grab a beer after shift.

I shoot them all back quick responses to get them off my back, but I know I wouldn't have it any other way. Family is everything. Even when it's full of nosy fuckers like mine is.

And then I text the one person I want more than anyone. The woman who I've spent far too much time thinking of with my dick in my hand when I should have been studying. She definitely would have been a better diversion, but if I had gotten lost in her body, the only preparation I would have been thinking about would have been how to have her again.

So, instead, I shut her out for a few days. I temporarily gave into her asinine rules and treated us like she said she wanted—bang buddies, which we both know is bullshit. Plus, after the way we left it the other day, I knew she needed time to wrap her head around what I said as I left.

Me: I apologize for not calling this week but calling leads to thinking about you and thinking about you leads to your tits and your tits are one hell of a distraction when I couldn't afford a distraction this week. But, guess what? I just finished my exam. Now, I can be distracted. Wanna meet up and distract me?

THIRTY-EIGHT

Grant

SITTING ACROSS THE STREET IN MY CRUISER, I STARE AT THE house. The lights are on upstairs. I can see Keely's shadow against the curtains as she stands on her bed and pretends to sing into a microphone, which is really a brush, and I breathe a little easier.

I shouldn't be here. I shouldn't be stalking this family. I shouldn't be wrapped around this little girl's finger, but damn it to hell if something about her doesn't remind me of Emerson and make me want to protect her.

It has to be the dream that had me driving this way without thought to where I'd end up. Even after a couple of days, I can't seem to shake the heartbreak I'd felt in my chest reliving the moment when I told Mrs. Gellar about Em.

Of course the dream—the clarity of it all these years later—only made the file folder so much more tempting to pull into bed with me and go through.

I can't do that to her.

Then again, wouldn't it be easier to know what ghosts I have to combat?

Shit.

This woman is fucking with me. I don't get fucked up by women. I date them. I have fun with them. I move on when shit gets too serious.

But Em is . . . Em is different. She always has been.

I scrub my hands over my face, and admit that Emerson is right when she teases me about having a hero complex. Is there something so wrong about that? Maybe if I can save Keely, then I can make up for not saving Emerson sooner?

Even I know that's a whole lot of projecting.

Physical abuse is bad. Sexual abuse is horrid. A child shouldn't have to endure either.

So, I will make sure she's okay.

I pause and try to figure out which of the two females I'm referring to.

Needing a distraction to clear my head, I turn the engine on to leave, but I can't help myself. I can't come here and not look when I promised her I would.

So I'm out of the cruiser and across the street in seconds, trying to look inconspicuous as I jog up their pathway to check on the rock garden.

There's nothing new. At all. It all looks the same, and not just the same, but there has been no new ones added. There's always new ones added.

I'm not sure if that worries me or if it means things have gotten better.

Things never get better.

Abusers just don't wake one morning and stop abusing.

I walk back to the car, slide behind the wheel, and watch the light in Keely's window for a long time while I try to come to terms with all of the shit in my head.

The shit that tells me I need to see Emerson.

The part of me that needs to prove to her that her rules are going to be broken.

One.

By.

One.

Until she sees that sometimes sharing a past means you can build a future together.

It's a bitch that the only girl I've ever really loved is the only one it seems I'll ever really want.

I'm more determined than ever to prove it to her.

Her rules don't matter.

Her past doesn't matter.

It's just her.

It's just the now.

And it's about damn time.

THIRTY-NINE

Emerson

"What are you doing here?" I ask, a little stunned to see him filling the space of my doorway. After his text the other day and our screwy schedules, we hadn't planned to see each other until tomorrow.

But I more than welcome the sight of him.

"I needed to take a break."

"A break from what?" I ask as he waltzes right past me as if I invited him in. I look out the front door and around the parking lot, hoping it will help me understand what the hell he is talking about.

"My brothers. Work. Other shit."

I turn and lean my back against the door I've just shut as he strolls over to the couch, drops whatever is in his hands onto it, plops down, and puts his feet up on my coffee table like he owns the place. He picks up the *People Magazine* on the couch beside him and starts flipping through it without a second thought.

The protest dies momentarily on my lips as I recover from the shock of seeing him. And it's a good shock. The kind of shock that almost made me jump into his arms, wrap my legs around his waist, and kiss him senseless. It feels like forever since I've seen him when, in reality, it's only been a week.

It's just because things were unsettled last time he left here, and I've had time to think it over and know I overreacted.

That, and the sight of him in that dark blue uniform has put butterflies in my belly and a bang of lust between my thighs.

"Don't you have your own house to escape to?" I ask as I push off the wall and cross the distance. He watches me, his stare unrelenting as I sit across from him on the edge of the chair.

"Yeah, but the view here is much nicer." He quirks an eyebrow, and the sweep of his eyes over my body tells me the view he's talking about is me.

I did tell him flattery would get him everywhere.

"Well, what if *I* want a different view?"

"We can go somewhere else if you want. The view I came here to enjoy is mobile." He flashes a heart-stopping grin.

"Good to hear you want to go somewhere else. Go ahead. I'll stay here." I match him smile for smile.

"Suit yourself," he says, tossing the magazine on the coffee table and shifting to lie back on my couch, feet hanging off one armrest while his head is on the other.

I rise and walk to the couch so I can stare down at him with my arms crossed. And as much as I'm playing the hard ass, every other part of my body is sizing him up and wondering how quick I can peel that uniform off him . . . then again, maybe he should leave it on. It is sexy as hell.

"Without you," I warn.

"C'mon. You know you like me." He closes his eyes and settles into the cushions.

"No I don't. I only like your cock."

He snorts and opens one eye to stare at me at the same time he reaches a hand out to rest on the back of my knee. "You like my mouth, too."

His thumb brushes up and down the backside of my knee and sends shockwaves through my body. "It is a pretty damn good mouth."

"Then there are my hands . . ."

"Mmm."

And within a second, he has pulled me down on top of him and his lips are on mine in a kiss to rival all kisses. It's hot and sweet and sexy and all-consuming, and when he pulls back, it leaves me breathless to the point that my chest is heaving and my eyes can't seem to break away from his.

There's a brief moment where I see something in his eyes—sadness, regret, I'm not sure—before it clears away. It makes me want to ask him what happened today that brought him to my doorstep.

I'd like to think he's here because he wants to see me. The kiss he just mesmerized me with says I'm at least part of the reason, but I'm also observant enough to know something is bugging him.

"Officer, is that your baton or are you just happy to see me?" I murmur.

His laugh rumbles through his chest and into me, and there is something about the moment—the ease of it—that makes me feel a bit better about whatever is bugging him.

"I'm hungry," he says, suddenly shifting our bodies so that he's sitting up sideways on the couch with my ass between the V of his thighs.

My laugh is instant. My desire well above a simmer. My body begging him to lie back down so that I can kiss him again. "You're hungry?"

"Yep. Let's go get something to eat."

"What? Where?"

"You're the one who said you wanted a change of scenery."

"I changed my mind." I run my fingertip down the side of his jaw.

"Unchange it. I'm hungry, and from what you've said, I can garner your cooking skills aren't that great."

"Like I offered." I scoff but smile.

"So, it's decided. We're going to grab something to eat. I just need to change first." And without another word, he shifts out from behind me and stands before he begins unbuckling his duty belt.

Then unlacing his boots.

Then unbuttoning his shirt.

Next his bulletproof vest.

When he's standing in my flat in nothing but his unbuttoned pants with a delicious section of happy trail on display, I have no qualms about appreciating the view.

Oh. My.

Sure we've already seen each other naked, but there's something different about watching someone undress when the taste of their kiss is still on your lips. There's a sensuality to it, an intimacy I'm not used to, so I take the time to admire him. His hard lines and tan edges. His broad shoulders and cut biceps.

With his eyes on mine and a smile playing at the corner of his mouth, Grant pushes his uniform pants down and then bends over to pick them up, giving me a very fine view of his boxer-brief clad ass when he does. So he's in my apartment, in nothing but his underwear, fresh out of that hot uniform, and he seriously thinks I'm going to be caring about food right now?

"Grant?"

He looks over to me and stands to full height, every fabulous pack of the six he has rippling for added effect. "What?" he asks with feigned innocence. The man knows exactly what he's doing as he makes a show of folding his uniform in some perfectionist way. Then he grabs the clump he dropped on the couch, which I now know are clothes.

"Food?"

"Yeah." He slips a T-shirt over his head—some Back the Blue competition—and then pulls on his jeans. "I'm starving." His grin appears again as he lifts his eyebrows while my tongue licks out to wet my lips. "You ready?"

"Yes." But I'm starving for a whole hell of a lot more than food.

"Well, Mr. Malone, no one can say you don't know how to charm the pants off a girl when you take her on a date." I take a bite of what's left of my French fries as I push against the sand, making my swing rock gently back and forth like his is.

He glances over to me, eyebrows narrowing as he finishes his own bite of hamburger. "Take-out and the park isn't where I normally take a lady on a date." My back is up immediately, offended by his response. He notices, too. "They're your rules, Emerson."

Those words snap me from the haze of my burgeoning temper. Me and my damn rule about no dates. Can't be mad at the man for listening to me, or for pushing my buttons to get me to realize how dumb said rules are.

"They are," I murmur as I toss the empty fry container into the open bag at our feet before scooting back onto my swing and beginning to pump my legs. Anything to get out the frustration at myself for being upset by his comment when it was my doing.

I lean my head back, close my eyes, tighten my hands on the chains as I swing higher and higher. The rush of the air against my cheeks, the feel of my hair flying behind me . . . there is something about being on a swing that's liberating. I'm under my own power. I'm the one who controls how high or fast I go.

There is no Travis and his to-do lists. There is no dread every time the phone rings over what Chris needs now or what proposition he has for me to assure that I'll get approved. There are no thoughts at all.

It's just the wind, and the effort, and it's just . . . juvenile.

"You can't outswing me, Reeves," Grant says beside me, prompting me to look to my left and see that we are swinging in unison, side by side.

I pump harder, for some reason needing to beat him, needing this release I don't understand.

Our laughter fills the empty park as we race each other. I'm so high now that as I reach the peak of the swing, the rubber seat beneath me falls lax for a second.

I'm not sure how long we race each other or if Grant willingly lets me win, but by the time we stop trying, I'm winded and my cheeks hurt from laughing so hard.

We slowly allow the pendulum of our swings to slow until our shoes are dragging ever so lightly on the sand beneath our feet. And when we come to a complete stop, I rest my head against my hand still holding on to the chain and look over to him.

His hair is mussed, and his eyes are as alive as his smile, but there is something else there that I wait for.

"You want to know why I brought you here?"

"Why?"

"Because the swing set was the last place I remember you before you weren't happy anymore."

My lips part as I stare at him, all the vigor we just used to beat each other gone. I think of that day. Of swinging with him on the playground. Of lining up after recess. Of the intercom call. Of telling him I hate him and that I never wanted to see him again.

My throat's dry, and I'm not sure whether it's because of the exertion or because of what he just said. The one thing I know for sure is that it's the first time that I don't want to run away when he brings up the past.

His reason is actually very sweet. And painful.

And just as quickly, the feeling of betrayal, I don't expect or know how to handle, comes back with a vengeance

"You lied to me," I say in a barely audible whisper.

His eyes fall, as does my heart. "I did." He nods, and the look on his face says he'd do it again in a heartbeat if he had to.

I'm not sure how I feel about that.

"It's hard for me to trust you because of that."

He laughs, but it's a short, gruff sound that dies almost as quickly as it begins. "I think your lack of trust has nothing to do with me and everything to do with what you've been through, Emerson."

"How do you know what I've been through, Grant?"

His head startles in confusion. At least I hope it's confusion. "I don't."

I don't relent on my stare because the sudden racing of my pulse has me doubting myself and if I should trust him now.

Hating this sudden unfounded uncertainty, I stand from the

swing and jog over to the Merry-go-round. I grab hold of a bar and begin pushing it so that it starts to spin. When I think I have it as fast as it will go, I take a chance and jump onto the rusting heap of metal.

It's moving quickly and spinning out of control, but when I get on, I lie down. With one foot hooked on one side of the bars and my hands holding on to another over my head, I close my eyes and let the centrifugal force commandeer my thoughts from where our conversation brought them. I let the world spin out of control around me while I hold on for what feels like dear life.

There's a boost to the spin, and I know that Grant is there. He's pushing me now. I can feel the platform flex as he climbs on and the heat of his body as he lies beside me. I know that when he closes his hand over mine where it holds on to the bar, he's making sure not to let go for the both of us.

He brings calm to the chaos spinning out of control around me and within me.

For the first time in a very, very long time, I allow myself to accept that.

To accept him.

To welcome it rather than push it away.

FORTY

Emerson

"DO YOU EVER NOT HAVE THAT THING ON?"

"What? The scanner?" he asks as he turns onto the highway.

"Yes."

He shrugs. "Does it bug you?"

"Not really. I just don't understand why you still listen to calls if you're off duty." I rub my feet together, and more sand from the playground comes off the soles of my shoes and dusts the floor mat.

"I have a few situations I like to keep an eye on. If a call goes out on one of those, sometimes I like to go so I can make sure what's going on."

"Hm."

"Hm?"

"Sounds to me like someone is attached to—"

"Possible 10-16. 12662 Serenity Court. Officers responding." The scanner interrupts.

"Son of a bitch," Grant says as he slams the heel of his hand against the steering wheel.

"What's a 10-16?" Whatever it is, it obviously isn't good.

"I jinxed it by saying it," he mutters to himself.

"Grant? Are you okay?" I stare at his profile and can see the disconcert in his posture.

"No. Yes. *Fuck*. This is the one case I'm worried about." He glances my way, and I can see the hesitation in his body language. "I need to . . . shit. My cruiser."

"If you're worried, just drive there now. I can sit and wait out whatever you need to do. Don't waste the time taking me back," I ramble, hating that he is so upset about this call.

"You sure?" He eyes me in a way that says he knows more than I do, which is obvious, and yet, I'm not sure why he feels the need to relay it.

"Yes. Positive. Go."

He grabs his cell, punches a few numbers, and then holds it to his ear, waiting. "Dispatch, I'm an off-duty officer responding to the call for 12662 Serenity Court," he says. "Yes. Grant Malone . . . I'm in civilian clothes but want it known to the guys on scene that I'm responding . . . No. It's an ongoing situation. I've been monitoring every call you have listed there . . . Yeah . . . I know, but I'm on my way. 10-4."

It doesn't take long to make it to the address, but that could be because Grant may or may not have completely demolished the speed limit.

When we pull onto the street and park beside two other cruisers, trepidation takes hold. I'm sure it will be cool seeing Grant in action, but at the same time, I feel like I'm eavesdropping on someone else's life.

As if I'm violating their privacy by being here.

"Goddamnit," he mutters as he slams the truck into park, flings the door open, and jogs up the front walkway.

Then I see her.

The little girl sits on a rock in the middle of a planter in the front yard with a teddy bear hugged tight to her chest. She's looking down at her bear's face, fingers picking at its eyes, as a big, burly police officer awkwardly tries to talk to her.

"Keely." I hear Grant say the name, and the minute it is out of his mouth, she looks up. A ghost of a smile turns up the corners of her lips, but something about her face expresses a sadness so strong I can feel it deep in my bones.

Big, burly officer visibly relaxes and has no problem stepping back. Grant lowers himself to the ground and sits cross-legged beside her.

"Oh." My hand flies up to cover my mouth, and tears sting my eyes at the mere sight of them. There is a comfort between them, a gentleness to him I never expected to see. He talks to her, pointing to her bear and the rocks in the planter around her. It's so obvious from the outside how hard he is working to make her smile and put her at ease.

Curiosity has me glancing to the backs of the officers standing at the front door, but I can't keep my eyes away from Grant and Keely for very long. There is something so precious and heartbreaking about their interaction. He dwarfs her, and yet, she seems completely at ease with him. They talk some, his expression so serious when she looks away and then warm when she comes back to him. He works for her smile, and when she grants it, there is a flicker of hope under all the shadows haunting her eyes.

It kills me. In every sense of the word.

Why does this little girl trust Grant so much? More so, why would a little girl know a police officer enough to trust him?

And then I remember the code 10-16—domestic abuse. Grant told dispatch that he'd been to every one of the previous calls to this address.

Every.

One.

How many times has he been here?

I push the thoughts and scenarios from my mind. I don't want to think or assume, but it doesn't stop the sting of tears in my eyes as he reaches out and holds her little hand in his.

Because it's *real.* Grant's hero complex and his need to save everyone is real, and I'm watching it firsthand.

He and Keely are pointing to the smaller rocks around them, and after a bit, I hear her giggle. It's the most adorable sound in the world.

All I can do is stare. And wonder. And hope she's outside because whatever happened inside doesn't involve her.

I'm not sure how long I sit and stare at the two of them, but it's long enough that my feet are numb from their positioning and the sky has slowly faded to black. So lost in thought, I'm startled when Grant slides behind the wheel, starts the car, and pulls away from the curb.

"The fucker's lucky he wasn't home," he mutters under his breath but doesn't elaborate, and I don't ask for more.

I turn some in my seat so I can study him and try to wrap my head around how the man, who seemed so at ease moments ago with a little girl, now feels like a ticking time bomb. The lights from passing cars and streetlamps lighten and darken the features of his face, leaving me to wonder what's going on in that mind of his. I'd also love to pepper him with questions about what the call was all about, but for a woman who doesn't like to answer questions herself, the safe strategy is to keep my mouth shut.

We drive for some time, winding up through the hills around Sunnyville until Grant pulls off the asphalt and onto a graded road. We continue for a ways, and it's only when he pulls into a clearing that overlooks the city and all of its lights below that I know where we are: Grant's place he goes to think.

Our silence stretches, long and thick and heavy, but with the windows down, the sounds of the nightlife around us soften the tension in it. Every part of me wants to ease whatever is upsetting him but I have no clue how to even begin to do that.

"You want to talk about it?" I ask, hoping enough time has passed that he can think rationally about whatever happened.

His sigh is heavy. "I'm not sure that I can."

"Because it's a case?"

Without answering, Grant opens the door and gets out of the truck. I watch him pace back and forth, the moonlight above accentuating the tension seizing his posture. I slip out of the cab and find a flat slope of rock near the front of his truck and take a seat, cross my legs, and focus on the twinkling lights of the city. They almost look like embers burning in the bottom of a fire pit, and I wonder what each of those lights represent.

Is one of them Keely's?

How many of them hide the horror happening beneath their cover?

I shake the thought away. Too much thinking for tonight. Too much delving into a past I don't want to delve into.

"Remember the side of your house?" Everything inside me freezes. The minute I'm determined to get out of my own past, he brings me right back into it. "Remember how we used to go and sit there and play whatever the hell we used to play back then because you wanted to get outside? Sometimes, you'd paint those rocks of yours with silly pictures, other times I'd play Barbies with you. I hated it, but I played because you were always playing cops and robbers with me?"

"No." I whisper the word, not sure if it's because I don't want to remember or because I don't want to talk about it.

Either he doesn't hear me or he doesn't care, because he keeps talking. "After you left, I used to go there. I'd just sit there by myself because I missed you so much. I'd pretend that you were inside and you were going to come out to play any minute."

Every part of me wants to reject what he's saying. I want to cover my ears like the little girl he remembers would have done and shut him out. I don't want to know that he was hurt, too. It's so much easier to think I was the only one who hurt. It's so much easier to remember how much I hated him for pulling my world apart instead of looking at it like an adult and realizing he did the right thing.

But I don't lift my hands. I don't turn to face him. I need to hear this. I need to listen to him. I need to face what I don't want to know and am scared to death to remember.

"I missed you, Em. You were my best friend. You were the one I told all my silly secrets to. You were part of my every day, and then you were gone . . ."

I told him my secrets, too. But mine were far from any secret an eight-year-old should have.

I push up from where I'm seated and walk a few feet away from him, hating the hurt in his voice that somehow I had a part in putting there. But at the same time, I'm angry at him for driving me up here where I can't exactly escape the conversation.

Was this his plan? Trap me here and force me to talk?

"Do you remem—"

"What are getting at, Grant? What's the point to this conversation?"

"I just—" He shakes his head and runs a hand through his hair. "There are so many things I want to ask you, so many things that I want to know—"

"They're none of your goddamn business!" I shout in an explosion of temper I'm not sure he was expecting.

"No?" he shouts back, crossing the distance and getting in my face just as unexpectedly.

"No." I stand my ground.

"Oh, so, what? You'll open your legs for me but not yourself?" His eyes burn with anger as we wage a visual war of contempt.

"Fuck. You."

"That's the point," he sneers. "That's all you want to do."

"And?"

"And what?

"That was the deal, Malone. You agreed to the rules."

"The deal's changed."

"Then the deal's over."

"No. I call bullshit on you. Why can't you let me in? Why can't you just talk to me? I know you went through a shit ton of horror, but I was the one who was there. I was the one who cared about you. *Who still cares.* And maybe I need to talk about it to wrap my head around how you dealt with all of that and turned out so goddamn normal when it still fucks my head up some days . . . did you think of that?"

I fist my hands and grit my teeth as I try to calm the riot of confusion laced anger swirling around inside me. "So you'd rather I be messed up too just so you can feel better? Well, *I am*," I scream at him, hating to admit it but needing the catharsis of saying it. "Did that work? Do you feel better?" I sneer as every part of me vibrates with fury and shame.

"No." His voice is barely a whisper.

"You don't want inside my head, Grant. You don't want to know what's in the dark places there. It crippled me at one time. It sits there and waits for its moment to come forward and cripple me again. So, I shove it away. I don't talk about it. I try not to think about it. *Because if I do, then I can't function*. I can't be the woman you see when I live in the shadow of what happened to the little girl I was. That past doesn't exist to me. *It can't*."

I walk away from him, needing to process my outburst, my confession, and how I can still seem strong to him when suddenly I feel so damn weak. Looking out at the city, Grant at my back, I cross my arms over my chest and dig my nails into my biceps. I welcome the bite of pain. I use it to calm myself and bring me back to the woman I pretend to be.

"Emerson." He says my name again. It's a plea. A request. It's *pity*. "I'm sorry."

"You don't get it do you?" His apology only serves to aggravate me further. To remind me of all those shrinks and their sympathetic eyes and the pity in their tones. The one sound I never wanted to hear again. My temper rages quietly beneath the surface, and I'm not sure if I'm mad at him for pushing me or mad at myself for what I said.

It takes all my effort to make my voice even and calm—unaffected—when I turn to look at him and speak, but there's still a bite to my tone. "Look, I'm sorry you can't talk about the little girl because it's police procedure, but that doesn't give you the right to start poking into my past. Into my life. I don't need to be saved."

"I'm not talking about her because it's police procedure, Emerson." He throws his hands up and laughs but there is nothing amusing in its sound. "Don't you get it? I'm not talking about her because I can't. I'm not talking about her because I don't want to upset you! A lot of fucking good that did me."

I startle at his words. "*Excuse me*?"

"I don't want to upset you," he says softer this time, his voice vulnerable, his body defeated.

"After everything I've been through, I assure you, you can't upset me." And I truly want to believe that, but I already know it's an untruth. Grant Malone serves to be the one person capable of hurting me the most.

"I can't? How is that—"

"Nope. Nothing does," I lie, hoping he leaves it be and doesn't call me on the fact that I just admitted differently moments ago.

He angles his head to the side and stares at me. His silent scrutiny unnerving.

"So, if I told you I think Keely's dad is abusing her but I have no proof to go on, you'd be okay with that? What if I told you I used our rock secret? That I stop by there more often than I should to make sure there is no rock painted like a watermelon, which is her signal to tell me she needs help. You're telling me none of that triggers anything for you?"

I stare at him with my head shaking and my mind rejecting everything he just said, even the stuff I don't understand. All I can think of is that beautiful little girl with the tear-stained face and the haunted eyes and wonder if that was what I looked like to everyone who saw me.

"No." I whisper the word, but my body burns with shame as I dig my nails deeper into my flesh.

"No?" he shouts, finally losing his cool. "How, Em? How is that possible?"

"Because it is, okay?" I yell back, itching for a fight to cover the emotions overwhelming me. "Screw it. Just take me home."

"No." The muscle pulses in his clenched jaw as his body visibly vibrates with anger.

"Yes."

"Why?" he demands.

"Because you make me feel, damn it! You make me feel when I

don't want to feel, Grant. And being numb is how I deal, so please," I say, my voice breaking and almost turning into a sob, "take me home."

I see the minute my desperation hits him. His anger dissipates. His shoulders sag. His eyes fall vulnerable. And then he walks to the driver's side of the truck and climbs in, doing as I asked without saying another word.

FORTY-ONE

Emerson

"WHY ARE YOU OUT HERE?"

I shrug as I look over to Grant on his BMX, gloves on his hands and motorcycle helmet on, and know he's pretending he's competing in the X-Games. "Just cuz," I say, not wanting to tell him it's because my mom just got called into work for a patient and I'd rather be outside.

Outside is safe.

Outside is where I can hide.

"Whatcha doing?" He lays his bike down on the grass and begins to unbuckle his helmet as he walks over to me.

I look at the rocks in front of me, and my cheeks burn because they didn't turn out as pretty as I thought I could make them. The dog I painted on one looks like a big blob of brown. The smiley face I painted on the other is yellow, but the eyes are weird, and I couldn't fix them. Embarrassed, I take what's left on the paintbrush and just draw lines on the rock in front of me.

"Nothing. Just being stupid."

"Oh, those are kinda cool."

"You don't have to say that to be nice."

"No. Really." He drops his helmet onto the sidewalk with a clunk, and I know Chief Malone would get that line in his forehead like he does if he saw Grant treat his things like that. But I don't say a word because I'm too busy chewing the inside of my cheek and waiting for Grant to make fun of me.

He picks up each rock and looks at it like he does his Matchbox cars, and I fidget, worried about what he thinks.

"I think we should make a zombie one, too." I roll my eyes and begin to argue. "No, seriously. We can add stitches to the forehead and . . ." He takes the paintbrush from me and starts adding things to my smiley face rock.

I don't know how long we do this, but by the time we're done, my cheeks hurt from laughing so hard. We have about fifteen rocks in front of us that have all been boy-ified, and I'm okay with that.

"So, why are you really out here, Em?" he asks as we lean against the side of the house where the shade has fallen.

I shrug again but hate that my bottom lip quivers and tears well in my eyes. "I just don't want to go inside." My tummy hurts, and I keep thinking about when it gets dark and I have to go to bed. Hopefully, my mom will be back before then . . . but most times she isn't.

"Is your dad in a bad mood? I always go outside when my dad's in a bad mood about work. That way, when he gets mad, I'm not in the way."

"Your dad gets mad?" I can't remember Chief Malone ever getting mad. Strict, yes. But not mad.

"My mom says he gets stressed when he worries about a case." He shrugs and picks up one of our rocks, stares at it, and then puts it back down. "He has lots of bad people he has to put away, and it's his job, so when they don't get put away, he gets stressed. What does your dad get stressed about?"

When I wet the bed.

When I cry.

When I pretend to be asleep and curl really tight into a ball.

When I don't do what he says . . .

I wake with a start, my own gasp still coming off my lips.

The room.

This is my room.

Not my old room.

In the dark.

There's the runway lights out the window.

There's the hum of the television I left on.

But it's the rocks that are front and center in my mind.

The painted rocks.

The ones Grant keeps talking about but for the life of me I couldn't remember . . . until now.

My hands begin to shake as memories I didn't know I had come flashing back to me.

Going outside to my spot on the side of my house to avoid my dad and finding a new painted rock there from Grant. Something silly that meant everything to me. Something to let me know he was there and checking on me.

To let me know he cared.

To make me smile.

The goddamn rocks.

Grant.

Memories I now remember.

So many more I don't want to.

Oh. Shit.

It's finally happening.

I can't let this happen.

FORTY-TWO

Emerson

THE NIGHT BLANKETS ME BUT DOESN'T PROVIDE THE REPRIEVE that I came out here to find.

There is no escape from my past.

There is no distance from the memories.

There is only the pain.

Only the isolation.

Only the need to make it go away.

I look down to where the blade of the box cutter rests against my scarred flesh. Just the sight of it there allows me to breathe easier. Just the feel of it gives me a tiny sip of control.

Shame has me squeezing my eyes shut. Fear has the tears leaking out. The incessant hurt has me pressing it against my skin.

And cutting.

The sharp sear of pain is instant and yet when I open my eyes and see the bright red blood highlighted by the moonlit sky, I feel like a weight has been lifted for the first time in forever.

The tears fall fast and hot down my cheeks as I watch the red bead up. As I inflict the pain on myself instead of letting someone else do it for me.

I stretch out my other arm, and my fingers itch to repeat the process.

To feel relief.

To gain control.

To match my pain with new pain.

Head up. Wings out.

My mom's voice rings in my ears and has me clenching the knife in my hand as hard as I can.

Don't do it.

The need owns every muscle in my body.

Don't give in.

The want has me vibrating with desire.

My mom's face flashes through my mind. The determination in her eyes. The encouraging murmur on her lips. The warmth of her touch as she'd hold my hand and wait with me for my urge to pass.

The promises I'd made to her that I wouldn't cut myself anymore are now broken. Shame blankets me. Smothers me. I wasn't strong enough to keep them.

My hands ache as I battle restraint. *So does my heart.*

I've let her down.

I promised her I would be strong. I swore to her I'd never cut myself again.

Don't do it, Emmy.

With a wretched sob, I take the box cutter and chuck it as far as I can into the thick foliage at the base of the runway. It takes everything I have not to run in after it.

But I don't. I can't.

The shame is instant.

The regret immediate.

But the want still thrives despite knowing I broke my promise to her.

And to myself.

"I'm so sorry, Mom."

I double over and cry with every part of my body and repeat the words she used to whisper in my ear as she'd hold me after she'd find new cuts on my arms again.

This hurt doesn't take away my pain, only being strong will.

I am in control of me.

I will survive despite it.

I am loved regardless of it.

And at the end of the runway in the early morning, I rock myself back and forth, repeat my mother's words, and hope I can find my strength once again.

FORTY-THREE

Grant

"I FUCKED UP."

"Tell me something I don't know," Grady says as he pulls his attention away from the preseason football game just long enough to glance at me in the kitchen.

"No. Seriously." I look at my phone for what feels like the hundredth time and debate calling Emerson again. Her last text, the one from three days ago telling me she's super busy with a week-long jump class, still doesn't sit right with me. I didn't ask her to do anything. I didn't even text her. So her sending a random text to explain why she can't see me for a few days feels hinky.

Especially after how she asked to be taken home from the lookout and then jogged up the stairs, saying she had a stomachache. I was left to stare at the shut door to her apartment with my apology getting lost in the night around me.

Something is definitely off. Maybe she just needs some space. Fuck if I know.

"Hey, Romeo? You gonna finish your sentence or are you interrupting my date with the 49ers for a reason?"

"Are you in my house drinking my beer, watching my television, and eating my pizza?" I ask, and he nods. "Then shut the fuck up because I seem to be the one footing the bill for your romantic evening."

"Well, then get to the point and stop standing there like someone pissed in your Wheaties. What gives?"

"I don't know." I sip my beer as I cross the distance and take a seat across from him—my view of the backyard while his is of the game. "Watch those files, will you?" I say, pointing to the stack of cold case files I'm working on that are sitting on the opposite end of the couch as him.

"How can I watch them when they're freaking everywhere? On the couch. Falling off the couch. On the floor. On the coffee table. On the desk. I mean, Jesus, do you take them in the bathroom with you, too?"

"You make fun, but when you're sitting outside on my new patio with a built-in barbeque and flat screen television, you'll be thanking me."

"Doesn't seeing this shit every day ever get to you? Don't you need a break from it?"

"Sometimes." I sigh. "Recently, a lot of the time."

For being such a little shit, he's smart.

"Something's going on with her. She's shutting me out."

"I'd shut your ugly ass out, too." I kick my foot out to knock his feet off my table, more to antagonize him than for any other reason. "But considering you just switched topics and left me in the dark, should I assume we're talking about Emerson, again?"

"I'm serious."

"Apparently you are," he says as he smirks.

"What's that supposed to mean?"

"This thing with Emerson. You're supposed to be fuck buddies, right? Well, that was the plan anyway. Either you're getting too deep into it or she is because this is way more complicated than your normal run-of-the-mill one nighter . . . so what gives?"

"It isn't different." *But it is.* "She's not." *But she is.* "We're not." *But we are.* "We're just fucking." *But it feels like so much more than that.*

"Yeah, you keep thinking that's all there is, and I'll start putting money down on the 49ers to win the Super Bowl with this shitty ass team they have this year."

The game drones on, Grady groaning with every turnover—and there are a lot—while I stare out the windows to the backyard and watch the sky change colors as the sun sets. I'm supposed to be relaxing and preparing for my upcoming interview, but all I can think about is Emerson. Did I push her too far and get too personal when she is so obviously used to running away?

"Hey, Grant?"

"Yup," I say distractedly.

"I think I'm gonna head out."

"What?" I look at him, confused as to why he's leaving at halftime when I know the cable is jacked at his house. "What about the second half?"

"I have shit to do." I narrow my eyes at him at the same time he juts his chin toward the front door.

I turn around and find Emerson standing on the other side of the screen. Her face is expressionless and her hair is pulled back, but it's her eyes that are shadowed and sad.

"Em? You okay?" I'm on my feet as Grady opens the screen and gives her a soft greeting before jogging down the path toward his car. "Emerson?"

"I'm sorry. I shouldn't have . . . I just didn't want to be alone." Her voice is barely audible.

"No. Please. Come in." I have my arm around her shoulders and am guiding her into the house. She seems so frail when I've never thought her to be anything but the opposite. We move to the couch, and she sits beside me as if she's on autopilot. Concern rifles through every part of me.

Within seconds, I have the television off and the police scanner on the table beside me silenced. The overwhelming urge to hold her, touch her, soothe that look out of her eyes is too much, so I pull her into me—her head to my chest—and wrap my arms around her.

"What's going on, Em?"

"My head's messed up," she says.

"We all have messed-up heads," I murmur, my lips against the top of her hair, my fingers rubbing up and down her arms. It's only when she hisses that I realize my fingertips have run over the ridge of scars, causing me to jerk my hand back in guilt over hurting her.

"Not like mine," she eventually says.

"Want to talk about it?"

Her chuckle is despondent. "Do you know how many times in my life I've been asked that question? Therapist after therapist until I got so sick of being picked apart I just up and quit going."

"I can imagine," I say but know I have absolutely no fucking clue what she has been through. "Did something happen today?"

"Today? No. The other night? Yes." She lets out a deep breath. Her vulnerability transparent and haunting since I've never seen this side of her. "I can't stop thinking about Keely. I can't stop obsessing over whether her dad is doing to her what mine did to me. I can't stop wondering about what other horrible things he has done to her mother that she's been a witness to. It's messing me up, Grant, and that's really hard for me to admit."

"Sh. Sh. Sh," I say, guilt riding me hard over being the one to bring this all upon her. This is on me. The little girl I see as her, she does, too, and there's nothing I can do to reassure her that Keely will be okay. So, I just hold her a little tighter and press my lips to the top of her head while we both process the turn of events.

Her needing me, and my wanting her to need me.

"I'm going to do everything in my power to save her, Em, but without her mom pressing charges or the little girl admitting anything, I have zero legal rights. My hands are tied."

"And that's why you were talking to her about the rocks."

My hand stills halfway down her back. This is the first time she's reacted to any mention of the rocks. For a while, I thought maybe it was a fake memory I had created to deal with her leaving even though I know for a fact it was real.

"What do you mean?" I fish.

"The rocks. You were kneeling, talking to her, picking up rocks that I couldn't see but that I knew had color on them."

"Mm-hmm."

"I didn't remember, Grant. I didn't remember the rocks until I had a dream about them the other night." I can sense the hysterical confusion in her voice despite how muted it is. "You've mentioned them a few times, and I just thought . . . I don't know what I thought, but I just kind of let it go because it didn't make sense. Then I saw you with Keely and then that night I dreamed of the rocks. Of *our* rocks. The zombie rocks. And the ones you'd leave there for me to find when I'd come out to escape from my house and—" She loses a huge, heaving sob of a sound, her fingers grip into the fabric of my T-shirt, and her body shakes as she fights with every part of her to keep from breaking down.

"Don't be sad. It's a good memory. It was the only way I knew how to let you know I was there for you. It seems cheesy now, but we were eight."

"Not cheesy," she murmurs. "I looked forward to seeing if there was a new one every day."

"I didn't know what was going on inside your house, Em, but I knew it made you sad." I smooth my hand over the back of her hair and just pull her tighter against me, hating myself for doing this to her. "I'm sorry I brought you to the call. I didn't mean for it to upset you."

"You don't understand." She pulls away, her eyes red but not a single tear has fallen.

"Then make me understand." The confusion in her expression kills me. The vulnerability in it even more so.

"If I didn't remember that, then what else do I not remember?"

"It was rocks, Em. That's it. I'm sure there are a million things you remember about what we did or where we played that I don't. It's no big deal."

"It's not—you don't—you're here and I can't stop them," she says, flustered and visibly anxious.

"You can't stop what?"

"Nothing. Never mind." The first tear finally slips over as she runs a hand over her hair, and the chaos of her emotions hit her.

I just stare at her like a deer in the headlights. I can handle hysterical victims, I can manage crazy suspects, but give me Emerson's big green eyes full of tears and have her plead for me to give her answers I can't give her, and I'm a guy fucked in so many ways I've lost count.

"Talk to me."

"I'm so confused," she says. "It's you."

"Me?" *What did I do?*

"No. That's not what I mean." She squeezes her eyes shut for a moment and shakes her head. "I just—I don't want to know anything else."

"What are you talking about?"

She heaves in a breath that hitches as I reach out—needing to touch her—and use my thumb to wipe a tear off her cheek. The simple touch is nowhere near enough, the connection not strong enough, so I lean forward and brush my lips against hers, my hand on the back of her neck, our foreheads touching.

I stay like that for a few moments, caught between the push and pull of needing her to stay and never wanting her to feel pain again. Crushed by the realization that somehow I'm the one causing the discord in her life.

"I don't trust myself, Grant. I don't trust my memory. I don't trust that what I thought happened actually happened—"

"You didn't make it up, Em," I say, hating the defeat reflected in everything about her—eyes, posture, tone. I don't understand why she's so upset over this. "They were silly rocks."

"It's not just the rocks. It's *everything else*." The desperation in the way she says the words twists my heart.

I'd give anything to take her pain away, and for the briefest of moments, I consider telling her I have proof that her abuse happened. That I have the evidence to erase the doubt from her mind. Maybe if she had the choice to know the details, it would be helpful to her and make her feel more in control.

My eyes flash over the table stacked with blue and green file folders and know hers is somewhere in there. I've yet to open it, but I know it holds the detailed history of her abuse.

And as soon as I have the thought, I reject the horrible idea.

"I still don't trust myself," she whispers, the heat of her words warming my lips.

"I trust you," I say, scrambling for anything to take the pain from her voice. I'm far from qualified to give her the answers she needs, but hell, I'd walk through fucking fire if it meant I could make this right by her . . . whatever *right* is.

"It isn't the same."

"People trust you with their lives every day. Every damn day, they jump out of airplanes and put their lives in your hands, trusting that you'll get them back to the ground safely. How can you say they don't trust you?"

"They trust the name on the building. They trust the certificates lining the wall. They trust the reputation that's been around for fifty years. They don't know a damn thing about the woman behind the desk in the flight suit."

She looks lost, eyes wild, body language unreadable besides anything other than scattered, and I hate seeing her like this.

"It's going to be okay, Em. We'll figure it out. It'll be okay."

She pushes up off the couch, agitated and restless. "It isn't going to be okay, Grant. It will never be okay, and it will never go away. Fucking hell, I've gone twelve years without doing this, and now I have and what does that say about me? That I'm not strong anymore? That I'm no longer coping? That I'm just as fucked up as everyone would expect me to be?" She screams leaving me completely lost in regards to what she is referring to.

"Twelve years?"

"This!" She shouts throwing her arms out so the angry red marks on the inside of her right arm scream out to me. "This, Grant. I spent years cutting myself to cope. Years hurting myself because the pain I caused myself overshadowed the pain he caused me. It made me feel in control of something. I was the one responsible. I was the one who knew the ugly on the outside matched the ugly on the inside." Her voice breaks again, breaking my heart right along with it.

I'm out of my seat in an instant and by her side. "Em." I don't even recognize the grief in my own voice.

"You once asked me how I coped. This, Grant. This was how I coped."

"Emerson." My God. How did I not see this? I expect her to fight when I slip my arms around her, I assume she will resist, but she does everything but. Her arms are around my waist, and her head is buried in my chest as we hold on to each other and weather the torrent of emotion that is raging inside both of us.

"Emerson." I say her name again, needing to see her eyes, to know she is okay, maybe to know that I'm going to be okay knowing this, too. Fuck if I know. She tilts her chin and looks at me with red-rimmed eyes full of shame and sorrow before leaning forward and pressing her lips to mine. It's the last thing I expect, but the kiss is slow and hesitant—a woman trying to find her way through the power of the storm swirling around her.

I kiss her back. Gentle and tender. Giving her whatever she needs from me and promising that I'm going to do everything in my power to help her.

Salt from her tears is on our lips.

Her desperate need to lose herself palpable.

There's definitely pleasure in our kiss, but there is also so much more. Her well-being. My sanity. Our belief that we can see our way through to the other side of this.

My normally assured Emerson is anything but. She's timid, hesitant. She may have initiated this, but I know it's because she's trying to lose herself in the physicality like I now see she always has. She's trying to forget the ugly in her.

And that fucking kills me.

For a man who prides himself on being able to handle every situation—womanly or otherwise—I'm at a loss as to what to do.

God yes, I want her. Especially when she scrapes her nails against my abs under my shirt before lifting it over my head. The taste on her tongue. The smell of her skin. The knowledge of how goddamn good she feels when I bury myself in her. They all collide, vying for my focus.

And I may typically be a let's jump right in when it comes to sex, but something is stopping me from ripping her clothes off and giving her the exertion she craves.

If I do that, I'll be giving her exactly what she needs to run away from me again. I'd be giving her the tools to close off, when what she really needs is to know what I see when I look at her.

She needs to see the beauty in her ugly.

The thoughts are clouded with lust, lost in its haze, but when she reaches for the buttons on my jeans, I grip my fingers around her wrists.

"Em," I say, my breath coming in pants as my dick begs me to let her hands stroke it.

"No." She fights my hold, and I just keep my hands cuffed over her wrists as I lead her into my bedroom. "I don't . . . just please . . . I need—" she murmurs between kisses, her lips meeting mine over and over, each time more urgent than the last.

I push her back onto the bed, her mile-long legs working her body closer to the headboard as I crawl over her. She looks up at me with eyes so intense they steal my reasoning. My words. My breath.

Her lip quivers.

Her eyes well again.

When I reach down and pull her arms up so that they rest beside her head, palms up, her breath hitches. With my eyes locked on hers, I lower my lips ever so slowly and press them softly against the fresh and angry red mark on the inside of her bicep. She freezes, and I know it's taking everything she has not to pull her arm away from me. I know if she tries, I'll let her. But if she doesn't, then I'll know she trusts me, if only just a little bit, and a little bit is enough for now.

While I wait for her decision, I can see the shame in her eyes, the discomfort in my knowing, the struggle to let me in. Her inhale is shaky, but she doesn't move.

She puts her trust in me.

I lace a row of kisses across the scars on her right arm, my heart breaking and temper firing as my lips ghost over the ridges that mark her pain. There are so many, and all I can think of is how many times she's felt the need to cut herself to cope with what that fucking bastard did to her.

How much pain was she in that she needed to mar herself? Permanently scar herself to cope? With my lips against her skin and her perfume in my nose, I can picture her huddled in a corner, drawing a knife across her arm. Over and over. Tears falling like the drips of blood were. Alone and isolated from everyone and their help.

And then I realize it's not past tense. It's not how much pain she *was* in, because she just cut herself again. The pain *is* still there. Still prevalent. Still haunting this incredible woman.

My need to show her she isn't alone, that she's beautiful inside and out takes hold.

So I continue to worship her scars with reverent kisses. And when I'm done with the right side, the need to calm my ire leads me to kiss her lips again. To sip and take and soothe and know she's okay before leaning back, looking in her eyes to let her know my next intention, and then pressing my lips to the ridges on her left arm.

Call it my hero complex. Call it her being the first girl I've ever loved letting me love her now. Call it me being a fucking sap. I don't care . . . because put any man in my situation—with a woman who doesn't trust putting one hundred percent of her trust in him when she's at her most vulnerable, and for fuck's sake, it will change him.

Change him in ways he never knew possible.

As I slide my lips down the rest of her arm before pulling her tank up to expose toned flesh and pressing heated kisses across her abdomen, I know I'm changed. I know the taste of her, the sound of her, the feel of her will forever be seared in my goddamn memory.

I told her we should chase moments and not memories.

Enjoy the moment.

So I do just that. I take the trust that Emerson has bestowed upon me and slide my hand up her inner thigh, her flimsy skirt bunching up with it as I go. I lick over the cotton of her panties, prompting her legs to spread apart for me. I suck on her clit, the muted sensation of the fabric and the heat causing her hand to grip the sheets beside me and her hips to buck against my face.

I tug her panties aside with one finger and lick the length of her pussy, circling my tongue on her clit and sliding it back all the way down until I dart into her. She gasps, and her hands move from gripping the sheets to sinking into my hair.

My god. She tastes like heaven, like everything I want and need and desire. My lips are coated with her. My nose is buried in her slit as I lick and lap and pleasure and tease her nerves into a riot of sensations.

As I let her lose herself. As I make her feel. As I help her forget.

I kissed all of her pain away, now I want her to know I desire her, too. All of her. The scars. The beauty. The pain. The past. The future.

And goddamn, the mewl in her throat, the groan of my name, the desperate pleas for more as my tongue and fingers work her into a frenzy are an aural seduction all by themselves. When she gasps as I push her over that cusp where desire burns into bliss, I'm left reeling for her to come so I can push into her and join her.

"Grant." She pants as her body jerks and writhes under the pressure of her orgasm slamming into her. Her pussy pulses around my fingers and against my tongue. I suck ever so gently on her clit, pulling every last ounce of pleasure out of her . . . and fuck me if I don't want to get off the bed, yank her legs open, and fuck her into oblivion.

I just can't.

Not knowing how she came to me.

Not knowing that I'm the one who messed her head up.

Not knowing that she trusts me when it seems as if trust is something she never allows herself to give.

So, as much as my dick is begging to slide into her pussy, I keep my pants on. Fuck yes, my dick aches with the need to take her, and my balls burn for release, but I know this isn't about me. I'll be cursing myself later when I grab the lube and take to my hand, but this is the right thing to do.

With her addictive taste still on my tongue, I press a kiss to each side of her inner thighs then move up to circle my tongue around the rim of her belly button. Inch by torturous inch, I work my way back up her body. Every time my dick even remotely rubs against the mattress or her leg, I want to come like a sixteen-year-old boy.

"So beautiful," I murmur, raining praise between each kiss.

Up the side of her rib cage. Over the peaks of her nipples. Then I bring my lips back to the scars on her arms to let her know even those parts of her are beautiful.

I continue up to her shoulder and then follow the line to the underside of her jaw. It's her sighs that fuel me. Her sudden tensing as she guesses where my lips will land next followed by how she sinks into the mattress when she remembers that she trusts me.

It's when I find her lips again that I know she's calmed some. Her kisses, which were tentative before, are now laced with tenderness and satisfaction. They're still not one hundred percent the Emerson I've come to know, but they're enough for now—they're progress.

"Grant." She murmurs my name against my lips, and when I lean back and look down at her, a tear has slipped out of the corner of her eye and is making its way down to her ear and the pillow beneath.

"Sh," I say as I rest my forehead against hers.

"No one has ever treated me that way," she finally murmurs as she lifts a hand to rest against my heart.

It's only much later when she falls asleep in my arms that I really hear her words. I take pride in knowing I gave her that feeling.

Because while she's never been treated this way, I don't think I've ever paid that kind of attention to a woman before.

But then again, none of them have been Emerson.

FORTY-FOUR

Emerson

I'M SHOCKED AWAKE BY THE DREAM.

I can't remember it, but the sensations linger in my mind. The darkness of the room. The scent of his cologne. The sounds he makes.

Fear consumes me in those first few seconds.

And then I realize it's Grant's arm that's wrapped around me. It's the heat of his body that is cuddled against mine. It's his even breathing that greets the still night air of his bedroom.

It doesn't matter, though. My heart still races from another dream. Another piece of my past unveiled. Another part chipped free.

I shift away from him, needing some space.

As if the distance will help me understand the constant dreams I've been having. Combat the fear that comes with each one of them. Untangle the nightmares where I'm Keely or she's me and my dad is coming down the hall. Things—little things—I hadn't remembered but that are now so vivid and terrifying that I can't breathe around them. I wish they would stay dead and buried.

But the fear reigns. It has owned me every day for the past few days and has taken a toll on everything in my life. I've messed up entering figures on my loan application paperwork, I've given misinformation to students during a class, and I've been scattered when I jumped.

Yet, even with all the distress and all the memories, the one I fear to recall the most remains silent. The blank spots in my memory that hide them taunt me and promise to reveal everything and destroy me in the process.

It's why I don't trust myself.

It's why, when I look at Grant, I know I need some space, and more than the foot of still-warm sheets I just put between us. Some time to think. A few days to clear my head and figure out where to go from here.

I slip out of bed and stand beside where he lies. The moonlight comes in through the window, dashing light across his abdomen but leaving his face in shadows. I take in the beauty of him, the kindness in him, and I know without a doubt I don't deserve him or the patience he has afforded me.

My heart hurts.

For so many reasons. It's why, when I lean over and press the softest kiss against his stubbled jaw, another tear slips over and down my cheek.

He thinks the ugly in me is beautiful.

I don't understand how he can. I don't understand how anyone could look at me and see beauty when it's edged with so much pain. When beneath the surface, I'm a disaster waiting to implode. The notion confuses me. The realization tells me I need to take a breather for myself.

To get perspective.

To figure out if Grant is the remedy or the cause of all the current unrest in my mind.

"Goodbye, Grant," I whisper. "Thank you."

And as I click the front door closed behind me, the tears continue to flow. I'm not sure if I feel vulnerable because I've finally opened up or because I fear I need to say goodbye.

FORTY-FIVE

Grant

"HEY, GRANT. YOU FINALLY DECIDE TO TAKE THE PLUNGE?" Leo asks as he leans back in the chair behind the desk and gives me a knowing grin that challenges my manhood, but I'll fucking let it.

"Nah. It doesn't feel like hell has frozen over yet, does it?" I laugh as I look around for any sign of her in a place where there is always a trace. "Is Em around?" The phone on the desk between us rings, and I make the go ahead motion with my hand.

Leo just glances at the caller ID and rolls his eyes. "The guy's an asshole. He can wait. And to answer your question, no she's not here. She took off for a few days."

Before I can ask where she went, the voice mail picks up and Emerson's throaty voice fills the space around us. "Thanks for calling Blue Skies. We're currently out jumping and can't get to the phone, so please leave a message, and we'll get back to you as soon as we can. Head up. Wings Out."

"Sorry, but the damn volume is broken or I'd turn it down," Leo says as the recorder beeps.

"You're not returning my calls, Emerson. I have a few more things to go over regarding the loan docs and need you to meet me for a late dinner tonight. There's nothing like a little wine to set the stage for success. I expect a call back within the next hour or else your follow-up paperwork might just get lost in the shuffle, if you catch my drift. One hour, Emerson. I don't like to wait."

Every part of me seethes at whoever the prick is on the answering machine. I mean, I know he's the loan guy and it's clear as fucking day what he wants in exchange for loan approval. It's just that he's using his position to try to take advantage of Em, and his boldness makes me think she isn't the first woman he's done this to.

"Fucking asshole," Leo mutters as his face reflects how my temper feels.

"Is this a typical thing?"

"The slimy bullshit? Yeah. It is. The guy's a grade A prick."

"Who is it?"

Leo stares at me for a moment, and I can see him gauging whether to tell me. "Emerson has him under control," he says after a prolonged second, not giving me the answers I fucking want. "If she needs help, I'm sure she'll let you know."

I give him my best cop beat-down stare, but it doesn't faze him. On one hand, I like knowing he has her back, on the other hand, I wish he'd have it a little more so that he'd tell me and I could help her.

"So she has the day off?"

"A few days off."

"Where'd she go?" I ask, hating that the fucked-up feeling I had in the pit of my stomach when I woke up to an empty house is back.

"She said she needed to get out of dodge for a while. She's probably jumping somewhere else for a change of scenery. According to Desi, she's known to do that from time to time when she needs to clear her head. I'm surprised it took this long, actually. With the pressure the Blue Skies owners are putting on her to get loan approval and this asshole holding it for ransom, I bet she just needed some space."

"Huh." His explanation does nothing to explain why my calls and texts to her have gone unanswered. "I thought she never left this place."

"It isn't often, but it does happen."

"Thanks. If she calls, can you let her know I was looking for her?"

"Yeah. I will. But don't expect her to. When she goes off the grid . . . she goes off the grid."

Fucking great.

I walk out of the office and stand with my hands on my hips as I look across the parking lot to where her car should be but isn't.

I have my interview to prepare for and cold case files to go through.

I have a life to live.

So, why I am at Miner's Airfield, wondering where in the hell Emerson is and why she left? I have no idea where she might have gone, but if I were a betting man, I would put money on her leaving having something to do with what happened last night.

Waking in an empty bed sucked.

The worry that followed was even worse.

FORTY-SIX

Emerson

"I MET A GUY—WELL, NOT REALLY *MET*, BUT MORE LIKE SAW HIM again—and I think you'd approve of him, but while you would, he's really screwing with my head. I don't know what to do."

My voice carries on the breeze as it whips through my hair. I tilt my face to the sun, close my eyes, and try to feel her presence beside me. One hand rests on her marker and the other twirls one of the wild daisies between my fingers that cover the top of her grave.

"It's Grant Malone." I smile at his name. "Yeah, I know. You always had a soft spot for him even though I wouldn't acknowledge him or the Malone family when you brought them up. But I ran into him again, Mom, and I'm really struggling like never before."

I watch a hawk soar through the blue sky over where I sit on the hill that overlooks my mom's hometown of Miltonville. She picked her resting place because, according to her, if she were on the top of a hill, she'd be able to watch over me no matter which direction I decided to wander.

"Things I don't remember, I'm remembering. Good stuff. Bad stuff. You were always so proud of how strong I was, but I don't feel so strong anymore, Mom. I feel like I'm losing my grip on reality. One day, all I'm trying to do is keep Blue Skies, get the loan, and keep on top of Travis's to-do lists, and the next day, Grant Malone comes barreling into my life, and it's as if none of that matters anymore."

"*Why is that a bad thing*?" I can hear her asking, just like she always used to, and the common refrain makes my heart twist in my chest because I miss her so damn much.

"It's bad because I need rules and structure and control, but all of that goes out the window when it comes to him, and I can't have that. Without the rules, my mind wanders, and it can't wander, Mom. I can't remember any more than I already do. I just . . . I can't . . ."

I can close my eyes and see her smile as she asks me, "*But why*?" while looking at me above the rim of her beloved cup of tea. If I hold the image long enough, I can even see the way the steam twirls up around her and her hazel eyes squint just a bit, as if she is trying to will the right answer into my mind.

"Because I can't need anyone. I can't trust anyone. You know that. It was you and Desi, and now it's just Desi." I take a deep breath, let it out slowly, and then admit, "I'm scared. I'm so scared because I don't know how long I can keep up the façade that I'm normal and strong when lately I feel like the little girl I used to be. The one who fell apart any time a stranger looked at her for too long and who just wanted to take a knife to her arms to prove that pain was all she ever knew . . . and is all she'll ever know."

I look down and play with a daisy as I struggle with the lie I just told her. How I pretended that taking a knife to my arm was more of an urge instead of a recent reality . . . and then I realize she already knows. Her wings were out that morning. That was why I was able to stop myself from cutting the second time.

Dropping the daisy, I trace the engraved letters of her name and know if my mom were still alive, she would tell me that I didn't mean any of what I said. That I was strong and resilient and beautiful, which was something he saw even if I didn't. She would tell me that was why I was really scared, and that it didn't matter if I remembered some of my past because we always knew it was a possibility.

She would set that tea cup down, reach out, and grab my hand before telling me that maybe I was starting to remember because I finally had someone strong enough to stand beside me and help me through it.

The words I imagine her saying hit my ears but don't grow roots. They're scary and unwanted and against everything I ever thought I'd allow of myself.

To let somebody in.

To share that part of my past.

One of the last things she said to me resonates with me in the moment.

Would she tell me that letting him in doesn't mean I have to stop being resilient and strong?

I smile because she totally would.

"I miss you, Mom. I miss you more than you could ever imagine," I whisper, tears falling as I lie down on my back atop of her grave and think of nights snuggling up in our van while we were between towns. The gypsy girls making an adventure for ourselves.

I stay there for a long while with the blue sky above me, the comfort of my mom around me, a map of possible jump sites circled in purple Sharpie beside me, and my mind fixated on the past and the two men who were such an integral part of it.

FORTY-SEVEN

Emerson

"Stop crying, Emmy." He's irritated and keeps looking at the clock on the wall, but he won't look at me.

"I want Mommy." My hands shake, and my body hurts, and I'm scared and just want my mommy.

"Knock it off. You're fine. Stop crying and get back in bed."

"You hurt me." I stare at him and watch that funny bump on the side of his jaw get hard as he bites his teeth together.

"No, I didn't."

My heart feels like it's in my throat again. The same way it did before I threw up and wet myself. I tell myself not to do it again. I think of the bath he put me in after. The warm water. The weird way he used the washcloth to clean my privates instead of letting me use it myself.

I feel like I can't breathe. "Yes, you did. Mommy would put you in so much trouble for what you did."

"No. You are the one who is in trouble. I don't think you want me to tell your mom about the phone call I got from Mrs. Gellar today about how you keep acting up in class. You know how much she hates when you act up."

"Mrs. Gellar called?"

"Mm-hmm. You and Grant weren't listening again. Do I need to ground you from seeing him anymore? Is he becoming a bad influence?"

Panic hits me. No Grant? He's my only friend. And . . . I don't understand, I didn't get in trouble today. I was good. I'm always good. "Dad, I didn't get in trouble today at school," I barely whisper.

"And I didn't hurt you tonight, now did I?"

"But you—"

"You were dreaming, Emmy." He looks at me for the first time, and his eyes look black to me. Black like the ghost in the Halloween book that Grant let me read that gave me nightmares last week.

Was I dreaming?

"I don't think I—"

"You were screaming. You had a nightmare. You were fighting against me when I woke you because I was holding you to calm you down. Then you peed the bed like a baby. Again."

I blink my eyes and know what he's saying isn't true, but I can't remember it all. I can't remember . . .

"You fell asleep on the couch while I was watching television. I should have put you in bed, but I thought you were sleeping, so I didn't . . . the nightmare you described was the exact same as on the show. You must have heard it when you were asleep, and then turned it into a dream." His voice is getting angry like it does when I don't do what I'm supposed to do.

I shake my head. I fell asleep in my bed. With my Strawberry Shortcake doll under my arm and my rainbow nightlight on the ceiling above me. I never get to fall asleep on the couch.

But my blanket is there. Next to him. Did I bring it out here?

"Mom would be so mad at me if she knew I watched that show with you when you were supposed to be in bed. She's going to be home any minute, and you know how mad she gets when you stay up late on a school night. Do you want me to bring you back to bed?"

"No." I can barely say the word. I don't want him in my room.

"Okay. Come give me a kiss."

I stare at him, my feet feeling like they weigh more than an elephant's. He reaches out and pulls me into him and presses his lips against mine. My tummy feels like it's going to be sick. The feel of his whiskers reminding me of earlier.

Not a dream.

"'Night, sweetheart. Do you love me, Emmy?"

"Yes, Daddy."

"Say it."

"I love you."

"How much?"

"With all my heart."

His smile makes me feel like ants are crawling on me. "Get to bed, now."

I hurry to my bedroom upstairs and shut the door. Then I open it because the darkness brings monsters.

But the monster is downstairs . . .

I struggle for air as I lie in bed and pull the covers tighter around me. The strange surroundings of the hotel room I'm in only add to my discombobulation.

I replay as much of the dream as I can in my head, and one thing stands out above all the rest.

With all my heart.

How could I tell a person who just molested me that I love him?

How could I spend years of my life cutting my arms to deal with the pain a man who was supposed to love me unconditionally caused me?

It all comes back to trust.

The gypsy girls.

I think back to how, while we were on the road, my mom didn't trust anyone. If someone showed the slightest interest in me—even in the most benign of ways—we moved on to the next city. To the next adventure. To the next place where no one would notice us for a while.

It all comes down to trust.

She didn't trust anyone with me.

And now? Now I don't even trust myself.

FORTY-EIGHT

Grant

"YOU'RE SLACKING ON THE JOB, OFFICER SEXY." DESI'S voice comes through the phone loud and clear. It causes me to perk up in my seat at the end of a monotonous day and a monster hangover after a few too many beers with my brothers last night.

"If it isn't my favorite nosy best friend," I say with a laugh, but I am relieved to hear from her. Maybe she's heard from Emerson since she sure as hell isn't returning my calls.

"You got that right. Nosy is better than nonexistent. Have you talked to our girl lately?" she asks, switching topics to exactly why I was drinking heavily last night. Worry does that shit to you.

"Not for seventy-two hours." More like seventy-eight, I mentally correct after I look at the clock on the wall. "But she's like that . . . when she feels like she's getting too close to me, she backs off a bit."

"So is she? Are you? I mean, she just up and took off for three days, should I be worried that you did something to her that I'm going to have to put your balls in a vise for and torture them until you beg for forgiveness?"

"Ouch." I shift in my seat and remind myself to never piss off Desi.

"Well?"

"No. I didn't do anything to push her away. She came to the house the other night upset about . . . a few things, and when I woke in the morning, she had taken off," I explain, not sure how much Desi knows about Emerson's past. If she didn't know anything, there was no way in hell I would be the one to divulge it to her.

"And you just let her go?"

"I was sleeping . . . so I didn't know she'd left."

"I'm going to be nosy here and ask, what are your intentions with her?"

"She's always been the one, Desi." My own answer stuns me. I say it off the cuff and before it's even out of my mouth, I know it's the complete truth.

It's always been Emerson. Every woman was a substitute, a way to pass time, because deep down, I knew she and I would meet again.

God, the fucking woman is gone three days, and I've turned into a sappy, sackless wonder.

Silence fills the connection, and I'm not sure if it's because Desi is letting me process my own epiphany or if she's just as stunned by it as I am.

"Well, it's about goddamn time you realize it. Jesus H. This whole dance was getting old. So, now that you know, what are you going to do about it?"

"I can handle my own relationship. Goodbye, Desi." I laugh as I end the connection and shake my head. I love the woman to death, but she is a royal pain in the ass.

True to my opinion of her, she calls me right back. I debate whether to answer it, but then realize we never got to the part where she tells me if she's heard from Emerson.

"I know you can handle your own relationship, you jackass, but the reason I called was to tell you that I talked to Emerson and something is going on with her."

"What do you mean?" I lean forward, worried and relieved all at the same time.

"She called me last night and she was a mess when normally—"

"She isn't a mess." My mind goes to the angry red scars on her arms, and I hate that I wonder when I see her next if there will be more. If the time away will have helped her cope or made it harder. A selfish part of me wants her to realize it's easier when she's with me. That she doesn't have to run because I'm here for her. To help her. To hold her.

"Exactly."

"What did she say?"

"She wasn't making sense, Grant. She was rambling on about doubt and trust and I don't know what else . . . everything about the conversation worried me. What was troubling her the other night when she came to your house?"

"*Shit.*" I sigh. This is all my fault. The damn ball started rolling because of me. "I took her to a call the other night. She didn't really see anything, but I think the whole scenario affected her and . . . *fuck.*"

"She's home now," she whispers, telling me what I need to know.

"I'm on my way there," I say, standing and grabbing my keys.

"If you break her heart, Grant, you'll break her spirit."

"No one said anything about hearts here."

FORTY-NINE

Grant

"Em?"

Emerson turns to me, her face a startle of shock, hair pulled back in a bun, and there are circles under her eyes. The minute she sees me, she begins to walk the other way.

"Emerson," I call after her and then jog to catch up.

"I don't have time for you," she says as she shakes her head and picks up her pace. "I've been gone for a few days, and I need to get caught up for the owners so that it's in good shape for any potential buyers."

"What?" My gut twists. "You didn't get the loan?" Here I am being an asshole, thinking all of this was brought on by me, and it had to do with her not getting the loan. It has to do with her losing her dream.

"I don't know if I did. It doesn't matter. I'm pulling my application."

What the flying fuck?

"What are you talking about?"

It's the first time she stops walking and turns to face me. "I'm a gypsy, Grant. I don't stick around. I get antsy and need to move on. It's obvious I can't trust my judgment anymore . . . I mean look at me . . ." She laughs. "I'm a twenty-eight-year-old woman trying to buy a sky-diving school with money I don't have. I make rules that I never keep. I sleep with you then run away. I cut myself when I promised myself I was never going to again. I mean . . . who is going to put their trust in me to teach them to skydive, repay a loan, or live a normal life when I can't even trust myself anymore?" There's hysteria ringing in her voice, and the resignation from it is reflected in her expressionless eyes. "I have to get back to work."

And without another word, she turns on her heel and jogs toward the office and the comfort of company to prevent me from making a scene.

Panic hits me like a battering ram.

She can't leave me.

She's fucking crazy if she thinks I'm going to let her walk away and out of my life without a fight.

I guess it's time to make a scene.

"Hey, Reeves," I say as she pushes the door open. I follow her in, and Leo looks up from his desk, his eyes darting between Em and me as he leans back in his chair, watching the show. "Take me up."

It takes everything I have not to sound like I'm choking the words out, but I know the fear currently coursing through my body has nothing on how I'd feel if I lost her again.

"What?" she says as she makes a show of slowly turning around, brow narrowed, confusion morphing into surprise. "What did you just say?"

"I said I'm cashing in my gift certificate. Take me skydiving."

"But you're terrified of heights." She takes a step closer, as if she doesn't believe a word I'm saying, and honestly, I don't, either.

"Everyone has to face their fears sometime, right?" I shrug as she just stands there and stares at me. "Someone once told me that living safely is dangerous . . . I don't want to be dangerous, Emerson. I just want to be with you."

Her breath hitches, and she shakes her head back and forth. Her eyes say she wants to believe me, but her body tells me she's not certain.

I take another step forward, my own pulse racing and mind struggling to believe what I'm asking her to do.

"You're the only one I'd trust to get me down safely, Em," I finally say, my coup de grâce, that she needs to wrap her head around.

"No." It's a half-hearted sound, chock-full of disbelief but laced with hope.

"You don't get to say no." I smile as I catch Leo in my periphery laugh. "I have a gift certificate paid in full, and I'm cashing it in on you. Right now."

"No."

"The customer is always right, Em."

"Once you commit, you can't back out," she says, lifting her eyebrow and straightening her posture.

Exactly. *Once you commit, you can't back out.* I hope she realizes the same goes when it comes to me.

"I won't back out," I say, ignoring the way my feet desperately want to walk the other way . . . but everything about her changing demeanor stops me. The way her shoulders square. How her lips quirk. The placing of her hands on her hips.

She's back in her element, and hell if I'm not going to help her to stay there . . . whether it kills me or not.

Literally.

The growl of the plane's engine roars in my ears and vibrates beneath my ass, but it has nothing on the absolute terror owning my every nerve. Fuck yes, I'm a pussy.

But this is a plane.

And a nylon parachute is about to be responsible for preventing me from falling to my death.

And Jesus . . . I'm about to willingly jump out of an airplane door.

All for a woman.

For Emerson.

To prove to her she's just as fucking strong as she thinks she is. As I think she is. As everyone around her thinks she is.

Trust is an important thing . . . and I'm about to put one hundred percent of mine squarely in her hands.

How fucking stupid am I?

I go to run a hand through my hair but stop when I remember my helmet. I bounce my knee, close my eyes, and berate myself for not calling my mom to tell her goodbye and that I love her.

All of the things Emerson showed me in the classroom downstairs run on repeat through my mind. The initial jump at thirteen thousand feet. The belly-to-earth fall rate of one hundred fifteen miles per hour. Sixty full seconds of free fall. The arch of my back. The yank of the ripcord at twenty-five hundred feet above ground level. And then, of course, there is Emerson's reassuring refrain—if in doubt, whip it out—about the reserve chute in case the main doesn't deploy.

I've seriously lost it.

My ears pop, and I shift my jaw how she told me to equalize the pressure, but holy fucking shit am I nervous.

I can't hear what she's saying, but she's joking and laughing with the pilot as if she is headed to the park to walk the dog. As if she's not even giving this a second thought.

I try to be as calm as she is—which is pretty fucking impossible—and remind myself why exactly I'm doing this. For her. I took the one thing she knew I was absolutely terrified of losing—my life—and put it in her hands, telling her that I trusted her implicitly with its safety.

But doubt still reigns in my mind. Skill is one thing. Equipment failure is a whole other.

There's a nudge against my arm, and I turn to look right into her eyes. They are alive, and I realize in that moment that she needs this like I need my work. She needs the high from jumping just like I need to be the hero.

I guess we both thrive off endorphins and adrenaline but obtain them in extremely different ways.

"You ready?" she mouths, grin wide, eyes animated as she stands so that Leo, who is sitting on the other side of her, can hook the two of us together.

Ready?

No.

I'm not.

I swallow over the lump of fear lodged in my throat and force a smile. My legs are wobbly as I stand, the plane ride rougher than I had expected, but then again, that could be because the door is currently open and wind is rushing into it like a chamber.

The next few seconds are all a blur. My fingers gripping tightly on to the ropes fastened to the ceiling so I can steady myself. Emerson's body pressing against mine as Leo slowly begins attaching our harnesses so that we can tandem jump. The trembling of my hands as I look at the altimeter on my wrist to tell me we're almost at the point of no return. The churn of my stomach as I want to hurl but know there's no way I will be able to save face or my masculinity if I do.

Somehow, as I'm standing unsteadily, her hand finds mine. She links our fingers together and squeezes in silent assurance. It's a simple gesture, but fuck, if it isn't the lifeline I need to take those few steps forward to the open door.

Holy shit.

Holy shit, I'm doing this.

Holy shit, I'm going to step out of the plane.

We make it to the doorway, and Emerson moves my earplug and says, "Get ready to chase the moment, Malone." It's her laugh that rings the loudest. The carefree in it. The freedom. The ease and confidence. "Head up. Wings Out."

And then she pats my side in a signal we'd practiced when our feet were firmly on the earth to let me know it's time.

It. Is. Time.

She turns us around so that her feet are on the edge, her hands are beside mine on the opening of the door, and then before I can even blink, she lets go.

Head up. Wings Out.

Oh. Holymotherfuckingshitthisiscrazy!

Despite feeling like we are falling in slow motion, my brain processes everything—the fear, the euphoria, *my* mortality, the adrenaline—in snapshots of time.

The pressure of the air against my body. The rush of it in my ears. My initial gasp as we begin to fall. The lack of that stomach-in-your-throat sensation I hate, which she promised wouldn't be there. The feeling of being out of control until we hit our arch. The calming presence of Emerson at my back and her arms helping to guide the positioning of mine. Her confidence overpowers my uncertainty.

It's then that I find a few moments of utter peace.

Sure, the sound of the wind is roaring in my ears, but all I see is the whole valley laid out in its greens and browns with the ocean's blue not far beyond. It's breathtaking and eerie and so serene that I forget that I'm falling over one hundred miles per hour.

Then, before I expect it, we are yanked violently upward as the canopy is deployed. It robs me of my breath momentarily, and I have just enough time to wonder what the hell happened before I'm hit with the sensation of floating.

The sound of Emerson's laughter is in my ears, and I follow her hand as she points to a few places for me to look at. And I do look, but my body has such a rush of adrenaline and nerves and disbelief that I just jumped out of a fucking airplane it's hard to concentrate on anything other than this. The moment. The knowledge that I just cheated death.

All I keep thinking as we glide the rest of the way down to the big orange X-marks-the-spot landing zone is: *I get it now*. Emerson's addiction to this high. Her need for it. Her use of it to escape her past that haunts her.

Before I know it, she's shouting instructions in my ear. Pull the guide left to steer us. Right a little more. Feet up so she can take control. Prepare for landing.

The excitement in her whoop is followed by the jolt of her feet as they run beneath us and take the impact of the landing. We are both sitting on our asses, my butt between the V of her thighs as we slide a bit on the ground and the parachute collapses.

Then there is silence around us. My head screams so many

goddamn things, but I'm on the ground. Alive. Whole. And Emerson got me here.

She laughs when I try to turn to face her because we're still harnessed together and then makes quick work of unhooking us. Before I have a chance to process what the hell just happened, I turn around on my knees and kiss the life out of those lips of hers.

I'm riding a high like I've never known before. Cheating death. Proving to her I trust her. Facing a fear. *Everything.* And all I can think about is claiming the goddamn prize of Emerson Reeves because adrenaline definitely has my blood pumping and is intensifying my need to have her.

FIFTY

Emerson

I kiss Grant back with a need more desperate than I've ever felt before. Right here in the drop zone, I deepen the kiss with my hands gripping the lapel of his flight suit and take every damn thing I need from him.

Leo chuckles somewhere near as he gathers his own chute, but I don't care. He gets it. He gets this. Post-jump sex is indescribable. Using the high of the adrenaline coupled with the bliss of an orgasm is a major inside joke amongst jumpers.

And more than anything, right now, I need Grant.

He showed up today seeing a broken woman ready to give it all up. Then with his simple request, he started putting my bricks and mortar back into place to prove that I am as strong as I thought I was. Sure there is doubt, and there always will be. But he knew that was what I needed—to be pushed back into my comfort zone so I'd find my confidence again. So, I'd wipe out my skepticism.

Grant leans back, the gold in his eyes dancing with excitement and lust, and I know he feels the same way I do. We shared something up there. I've jumped hundreds of times and have had the trust of the people I jumped with, but this was different. We both took what the other offered and used it to conquer something we feared.

I shove the rig off my back, leaving the parachute billowing in the breeze to pick up later, and without care of who else might be looking,

I jump into Grant's arms and wrap my legs around his waist.

Between spurts of laughter, our lips find each other's, and God, how good it feels to laugh with him and kiss him. How good it feels to know my mom is looking down on me, approving of my taking a chance. How funny it seems that I want him to save me after all.

"I need you," I murmur against his lips as my hands thread in his hair and the heat of the sun does nothing to rival the fire in my body already burning bright.

"My dick's already five steps ahead of you." He chuckles as he begins to walk across the field with me wrapped around him like a monkey.

I wave over Grant's shoulder to Leo, who just shakes his head at us and rolls his eyes. I think he says something sarcastic like, "Sure, I'll take care of your parachute while you fuck," but I don't care, and I don't have any shame because it isn't like he's never experienced this feeling before.

"Hurry," I murmur as I nip the tip of his earlobe.

"Where? Keys?" His cock presses against me with each step he takes and makes the walk across the strip tortuous.

"Shit. My keys are in the office." I laugh as my mind scrambles. "Go to the left. Red hangar. Far side."

"Christ," he mutters, but only because with each rub over his dick he lets out a little groan. "Here?"

"Mm-hmm. The door slides," I say even though he's already pulling open the large barn-type door. Then we're into the shadows of the red hangar and he's shoving the door shut and slamming me back against it. His lips are on mine in a savage union of lust and greed and want and need and every one of the seven sins mixed in there.

There is no finesse. There are no niceties. We are all about how fast we can unharness ourselves from our rigs and step out of them so we can feel and enjoy each other's skin.

"Christ, Em."

"I know. Hurry." A laugh falls from my lips. "Post-jump sex is the best kind of sex there is."

"Oh really?" he says, leaning back to meet my eyes. His have darkened with lust and suggestion.

"Mm-hmm."

"You were holding out on me." A brush of his lips against mine. A cup of his hand against my ass pulling me against his hardened dick.

"Can't hold out on someone when they are the one refusing you." I quirk my lips, but then they fall lax as he tugs down the zipper of my suit and yanks down my tank so he can suck then graze his teeth over my nipple.

"I'm not refusing you now, am I?"

"I wouldn't let you," I challenge.

There is a quiet moment where our eyes lock and our bodies vibrate from our connection – mental, physical, emotional—and then within a beat, we are back into frenzy mode. Zippers on flight suits sound off. The shimmy of clothes being pushed down. The squeak of shoes on concrete. The begged pleas to hurry. Quicker. I'm desperate.

And then, as we stand in this massive hangar buck naked, his body a mouth-watering sight only serving to encourage my urgency for him, I realize there isn't really anywhere to have sex in here except for the concrete floor. The walls are lined with industrial shelving units. The tables are covered with plane parts.

"Where are we going to . . . crap."

He takes in the sparse space save for the Cessna in one corner and a Piper in another before turning back to look at me with a gleam in his eye.

"What?" I ask.

"Guess there's no time like the present to join the mile-high club, huh?"

Before I can process what he means, he lets out a whoop, swoops down, wraps his arms around my thighs and hoists me buck ass naked over his shoulder.

"Red or blue?" he asks, and I can only guess he's making me choose a plane. I don't have the heart to ask how he plans on joining any kind of club when there is definitely no room in either of them to have sex. "Decide."

"Blue," I say, and then cry out in shock when his hand smacks my ass as he makes his way over to the Piper. "Grant. What are—"

"Shush." He slowly lets me down so that I slide down the length of his body. The friction of my slow descent makes my nipples bud so hard they hurt, but it has nothing on the ache banging hard between my thighs. "We're chasing the moment," he says, flashing a smile before his lips are on mine again.

The trailing edge of the wing is at my back and he pushes my ass against it while we speak with tongues and moans instead of coherent words.

The adrenaline is a high, but so is the taste of Grant Malone. And, Christ, how I want more of him.

Our hands are everywhere and not enough places on each other. His fingers find their way between my thighs, and the groan he emits when they find me wet, willing, and wanting for him is enough to make me come on the spot.

But that's cheating.

If he wants to make me come, he'd better work harder than that to earn it.

"Turn around," he demands.

"Should I assume the position?" My eyes flash up to meet his, my bottom lip between my teeth as I make a deliberate show of turning around. I lay my torso and breasts against the wing and wiggle my ass in a tease as I hiss at the cool metal beneath my bare flesh.

"Christ, Em."

"Are you gonna frisk me, Officer Malone?" I say in my huskiest of voices.

His chuckle rumbles through the space as I wait for him. The sound of his hand working over his own cock is chased by his groan of appreciation, and just knowing he's doing that because he likes what he sees is fire to my blood.

"Frisking someone has never been so tempting." His foot knocks my feet farther apart before he leans forward. "Spread 'em," he says in my ear, the scrape of his chin against my shoulder as he retreats again causing chills to race over my skin.

Then there is an anticipatory silence as he stands behind me and I wait. Adrenaline begs me to rush this, my need paramount, but there's something about how sexy this is that has me biting my lip as I stand there, bare to him, aching for him to satisfy me.

I startle when his hands hit both sides of my right ankle before slowly sliding their way up my leg. When they hit the apex of my thighs, he rubs his thumb back and forth along my slit before pressing into me. The only sounds in the hangar belong to my hitched breath, his labored groan, and his thumb working me at a leisurely pace. And once he has me wanting enough that I'm pushing back against his touch, he stops, repositions his hands, and then starts his ascent up the other leg. But this time when he reaches the top, I groan when he removes his thumb without stroking me.

Then gasp when his tongue does it for him.

His tongue is hot and I'm wet and . . . holy hell. My eyes flutter closed at the feel of him. The tease of what's to come. The desperation for all of him.

I wriggle under his manipulation and plead when he stops. He takes one long, last lick with a libidinous groan before stepping back so that our only connection is where his hand runs back and forth over the curve of my ass.

Every part of me wants him.

"Is there a problem, Officer," I ask coyly, so very aware that he's allowing me to continue this charade of control he's afforded me for the past few hours.

I don't think he realizes that he could ask me for anything right now, and I'd give it to him.

Something changed between us today. Shifted. The fear I had over him, about him, is gone. I just need to accept it. Everything in me is whispering that a jumping-high orgasm slamming through my system to remind me how incredible his cock is will help do the trick.

"It seems I have forgotten my handcuffs." He chuckles and lands a smart slap on my ass.

"Oh, am I under arrest?"

"Definitely."

The palm of his hand slides down the line of my spine.

"What's the charge?"

"Making me want you. Every minute of every goddamn day."

His hands spreading me apart and then his mouth blowing ever so softly over me.

"What's the punishment?" I'm breathless, spent before we even start.

"I'm going to fuck you. Thoroughly. Properly. And hopefully slowly . . ." His words seduce me, but it's his dick slowly slipping into me that consumes me. It's the feel of his thumbs caressing over my ass before one of them presses unexpectedly against the tight rim of muscles above it that excites me. I part moan, part wriggle back against his fingers to let him know I want him. "But the way you feel right now, I can't promise the slowly part."

I purposely tighten my muscles around his cock and moan at how full he makes me feel. "No woman complains about thoroughly and properly," I murmur, the cool of the wing beneath me and the heat of what his dick is doing within me driving me to distraction.

"Good," he says as one hand twists around the length of my ponytail and tugs my hair back some to hold me in place as he drives into me harder this time.

"Yes." The word is a drawn-out sigh and each thrust brings a new round of pleasure, a new way to sustain the adrenaline of the jump.

"You like that?" He grunts as his thumb rubs circles to stimulate the nerves in my ass while the head of his dick expertly manipulates and taunts and teases the ones within me. With each touch, each graze, he pushes me up that welcome precipice between pleasure and pain.

"Please," I beg, and it's the last thing I have to say because he's as primed and desperate as I am and ready to take the fall.

Again.

"We are lucky everyone was gone so we didn't have to take the walk of shame back here," he murmurs against the crown of my head.

He is leaning against the headboard of my bed, and I'm resting my head on his chest. I'm comfortable and more peaceful than I have been in days . . . and I know it's because of him.

"Do you always take your suspects back to their place after you frisk them?" I murmur.

"No, but it sounds like you skydivers do after a jump." He chuckles, its vibration rumbling against my chest.

"Adrenaline has a way of doing that to you—making you need that extra release."

"Is this an occupational hazard I should be worried about?"

"No. God no." I pause and then add, "But I won't deny that all of my staff have had their fun at one time or another."

"And that's why Leo was laughing."

"Ha. At least we left plain sight," I say with a laugh as I think about Leo and that hot little number he all but mounted against the side of the Blue Skies shed after a particularly thrilling jump.

"I don't think I want to know."

"No, you don't." I can still hear the rest of the jumpers hooting and hollering for him to get a room, but the sweet, little thing he was with was so excited to have a catch like Leo, she had no shame.

We sit in silence for a bit, his fingers trailing up and down the line of my spine, moving the towel, which is still damp from our shower, down a bit more with each subsequent trace of his finger. I think of the day. Of how I came back determined to pick up and "go gypsy" to escape the feelings and the memories I can't seem to stop. Oh how quickly that changed when he put his trust in me. He gave me his biggest fear and didn't walk away like I wanted to do to him.

Shouldn't I be able to face my biggest fear then, too?

"Thank you for getting me down safely," he murmurs as if he's reading my thoughts.

"Thank you for trusting me to do so."

"You needed a leap of faith, Em. You needed someone to prove to you that they trust you, so in turn, you should trust yourself."

"There are so many things you don't understand . . . things I wish I could . . ." My fingers draw absently on his chest over his heart.

"No. It's okay I don't need to know."

"I'm just not ready to explain—"

"You don't need to. I've done enough damage. I pushed you when I didn't realize I was. I guess I just want you to understand that I'm here for you. That I care about you. That whatever it is you need from me, I'll try to give you, so long as you tell me. I can't read your mind."

I draw in a long, deep breath as if I'm trying to digest and believe what he is saying to me. As if I'm willing myself to whole-heartedly trust him.

"Trust is hard for me," I whisper, feeling as if I just peeled back my soul and opened it to him. In reality, my revelation is nothing new but it's still huge for me to admit.

"Understandably."

Another deep breath. Another confession that needs to be expressed but that is totally unfounded. "I blamed you for the longest time you know."

"Blamed me for what?" he asks, trying to pinpoint what of the many things I could pin on him.

"My lack of trust." His fingers still for just a beat before they move to my chin and tilt my face so I'm forced to look at him. His eyes question me, but his lips refrain from verbalizing. "It was so much easier to blame you for everything than to blame the man who was supposed to love me."

He nods ever so slightly; the compassion in his eyes is truly overwhelming. "I can't tell you I understand, Em, because I haven't walked a day in your shoes, but I can tell you that I respect what you are saying. That I hear you. That I'll prove to you that you can trust me."

I feel so stupid, needing to hear him say those words, but now that he has, I feel as if a weight has been lifted off my chest. "Where do we go from here?"

"What do you mean?"

"I mean . . ." I pause and try to figure out how to put what I want to say into words. "Never mind."

He pulls me in tighter against his chest. "Where do we go, Emerson? First of all, you're not going anywhere. I love that you're a gypsy and free spirited—I wouldn't change that for the world. I'd never take that away from you. Though, I'd appreciate it if you keep the taking off without telling anyone where you are to a minimum. It makes the cop in me want to track you down to make sure you're okay."

"You wouldn't . . ."

"Don't tempt me," he teases but with a hint of an edge that tells me he'd do just that if need be.

"I won't. Remember, we're working on trust here," I say dryly.

"I'm aware." He plants a noisy kiss on my forehead. "Since you're staying put, then we keep doing what we're doing. You get your loan despite how much I'd like to punch that slimy fucker you're getting it through. I get my promotion despite the asshole trying to take it from me . . . and we . . . move forward. Together."

"This is all a huge change for me." I try to wrap my head around how two months ago, I was thinking about the next flavor of the month, and now, I'm sitting here discussing tomorrows with Grant.

"What is? The having someone care about you part or the feeling settled in one place?"

"Both. None. All of it." I laugh as I hook my leg over his. I meet his eyes and find myself admitting things to him I haven't yet digested myself. "I've survived this far by closing myself off and not allowing myself to feel . . . and then you enter my life with your lights and sirens blazing, and it's as if you've handcuffed me so that I can't escape from you. So that I'm forced to feel. So that I think in wants and needs. So that I wonder how I ever lived without it. I love it. I hate it. It's overwhelming, and it's just . . ."

"Well, get used to it because I'm not going anywhere and neither are you, even if I have to handcuff you and your gypsy ways." There's humor in his voice, but there is also an earnestness that tugs on my heart. It makes me just that much more thankful that he showed up today.

"Better make sure you bring them next time," I tease as my body reacts to the memory of earlier in the hangar.

"I'll make sure to put my extra set in the nightstand."

"Promise?"

He leans forward and presses the most tender of kisses against my lips. "Promise."

Our eyes hold for a moment. "You've pretty much obliterated my rules, you know that, right?"

He makes a non-committal sound. "I was wondering how long it was going to take for you to realize that."

I shrug. "I have a selective memory."

"Is that what it's called these days?" The way he says it makes my body become all too aware of how thin the towels wrapped around us are and how easily we might be able to slip out of them. He kisses me again as my fingers reach for the towel at his waist. "There is one thing I forgot to do earlier—you know, proper police protocol."

"Falling down on the job again?"

He chuckles against my lips. "Only if I'm falling on top of you."

"Cute," I say and then sigh as his fingers find their way between my thighs. "We were talking about following proper police protocol." It's hard to get the words out.

"Then I guess it's time to get this strip search under way," he says before his lips meet mine.

And just like that, we slip into something beyond my rules.

It should terrify me after the past week I've had, which was filled with doubts and questions, but there's something so comforting about the moment.

About being with someone who sees my scars and still thinks I'm beautiful.

FIFTY-ONE

Emerson

Roll your eyes all you want, but I'm breaking the rules again. Have a good day. – Grant

I look at the card in my hand again and then back to the arrangement of dahlias that were just delivered to Blue Skies. It's strange and sweet and crazy that he's sending me flowers on the day of his interview. Shouldn't it be me who is taking care of him today?

I smell them again. I want to be mad and say they're ridiculous, but I find it hard to stop staring at them. My cheeks actually hurt from smiling, and I know by the side-glances Leo keeps giving me, he's noticed.

"Did someone die?"

I look up to see Travis standing in the open doorway, ball cap in hand and eyes curious.

"Seems to me someone has taken a liking to Em," Leo says.

"Humph." Travis looks at the flowers again, then to the card in my hand, and then back to me with obvious curiosity. "When you get my age, you look at every flower like it's waiting to adorn your casket . . . so don't bring no flowers around me and jinx me."

"I won't." I laugh. "I promise."

"Well, you enjoy those then." He nods and offers a smile before leaving the office.

Leo and I both watch him retreat across the tarmac to the Skies' hangar. It takes a while at the pace he walks.

"What's going on with the loan and the prick?" he asks as he rubs his hands together in mock anticipation of when I own this place. "It feels like it's taking forever. When will you know?"

I blow the hairs that have fallen out of my ponytail away from my face and shrug. "Two, three more weeks? Your guess is as good as mine. We had to file an extension and get approval from the Skies family to do so because some paper had to be resubmitted or something like that. Honestly, I have this sick feeling that he's holding out, thinking the more desperate I get to have this close and fund, the more willing I will be to sleep with him." I roll my shoulders. "I'll never be that desperate," I say with a laugh as I look back down to the card in my hand and smile. "Thanks again for not telling Grant who the loan company was when he was in the other day."

"It isn't my business to tell." He shrugs. "Although, I'd gladly watch him go all badass cop on the fucker, if for no other reason than to prevent him from doing it to someone else. I know you can handle yourself, but you're a badass in your own right."

I look at him for a beat, his words striking me. Here I stand, always a mix of uncertainty beneath the surface, and yet, Leo is telling me he sees anything but.

His words remind me of something my mom might say to me and it makes me smile at the thought.

"You know what, Leo?" I ask, turning the card over in my hand again.

"Huh?" he says without looking up from whatever he's doing on his laptop.

"Can you cover my classes today?"

"Sure. Is everything okay?"

"Yeah." My grin widens. "I'm going to take the day off."

"*You're going to what*?" He looks as if I just punched him.

"I'm going to take the day off," I say as I grab my keys from my desk drawer.

"Take off or 'take off'?" he asks considering I did just disappear for three days.

"Take off as in the afternoon. Life's too short not to. I deserve it."

"You do." His laugh follows me all the way out of the office until I hit the stairs of my apartment.

I'm dialing my phone before I even take the first step up.

"Em?"

"Hey, wanna play hooky with me, Des? I need your help."

There's a chorus of barks in the background as she sputters. "Where is my friend and what have you done with her?"

"So, a week ago you were a wreck and now you're a damn ray of sunshine. Let me guess, you found a great new sex toy that's rocking your world and you haven't told me about it yet? Hm? Or should I guess his name starts with G and ends in a T with a whole lotta hotness in between?"

"Shush," I say as I laugh and lower my head as the elderly lady down the pasta aisle stares disapprovingly our way.

"She'll get over it." Desi waves a hand her way. "Well? The answer, please."

"What if they are one in the same?"

"God. Damn." She hoots throwing her arms up in a touchdown sign as we push the cart toward the end cap. "I knew he was packing. He is packing, right?"

"You're perverted."

"And there's a problem with that why?"

"Because you're supposed to be helping me shop for food, not getting me kicked out of the grocery store for offending the customers."

"Sorry. Not sorry." She shrugs unapologetically. "Grab that beef consommé there. We'll use that with the roast."

I follow her pointing finger and put the can into the cart. "You sure I'll be able to cook this by myself?

She stares at me like a mother does a child. "Is that your way of asking me to come over and make it for you and then leave so you can pass it off as your own?"

"I'm not saying the idea hasn't crossed my mind, but no. I want to do this for Grant on my own."

"Okay. Now we need vegetables." I scrunch my nose up in disgust. "It adds flavor. And while you may hate them, he may like them. He can't have all those rippling muscles eating crappy food all the time."

She grabs a plastic bag and begins putting some potatoes in it.

"So are you going to tell me why the sudden about face? I mean you went from running away from him, to struggling for control, to being a wreck last week, to being a giddy female when you're not a giddy female. I'm getting whiplash here, Em . . . but hell, I'll take it."

I want to argue with her and tell her there hasn't been a huge about face but realize she's right. I've been all of the above.

"This isn't like me, is it?" I ask but know I wouldn't change it for the world because it feels liberating.

"No, it's not." She holds up a rather large cucumber and giggles like a schoolgirl when she wraps her fingers around it and strokes it.

"Put that down!" I glance around, mortified that someone might be watching her.

"Can't blame a girl for liking a little girth." She sets it down. "I like this new you, though. I like the smile that's plastered on your face. I like the laugh on your lips. I love the confidence that's back with a vengeance but is still different. Care to explain?"

"I just feel like things are falling into place," I say over a mountain of apples.

"Okay." She draws the word out to let me know I'm making zero sense.

"I'm feeling confident about getting approved for the loan. I went and spent some time with my mom when I was a wreck, and it kind of cleared my head and helped me focus. I let Grant break every single one of my rules and—"

"Every single one?" she asks, voice incredulous, eyes wide.

"Yep." I flash her a huge grin.

"What prompted this?"

I contemplate how to answer her. While she knows I had a screwed-up past, she has no clue just how screwed up. I've let her assume what she wants to assume to avoid her putting a label on me like anyone else who has ever found out has. So, without giving her the correct context, there's only one explanation I can give her that she'll buy.

"You were right."

She accidentally drops the onion in her hands onto the floor. "Excuse me? Did I hear you correctly?"

I nod and let her have her moment of glory. "I let him in, Des. Instead of pushing him away, I let him in."

"You trust him," she whispers as if she's just unearthed the damn Rosetta Stone. She understands how huge this is for me.

"Yeah, I do." It feels so good to say it. It feels even better to think back over the past two weeks and remember all of the laughter Grant and I have shared. Whether it be taking his nephew, Luke, to an extra innings baseball game between the San Francisco Giants and the Austin Aces, or strolling hand in hand at the mall while eating ice cream, or snuggling up next to him while he prepares for his oral interview while I try to make sense of the Blue Skies financials to see where I can cut and expand once it's mine. Dare I say, we've felt normal?

And with the normal has come the cessation of more memories breaking through. It's almost as if the more I fought them, the harder they tried to make themselves known, and then when I decided to own whatever ones came my way, they stopped.

"Earth to Emerson," she says breaking through my own self-realization. "You were saying before you drifted off to thoughts of Grant and what he's packing . . ."

I scramble to remember exactly what I was saying so I ad-hoc. "I've been so busy trying to hide who I was and Grant wouldn't allow it. Instead he stepped in and told me that it didn't matter who I was—what had made me who I was—because I was who mattered. The moment was what mattered. Not the past." I groan and roll my eyes. "That's not right . . . it's hard to explain."

"I think I get it." She shrugs and laughs. "Basically, Grant is me, *but with balls*."

I laugh so hard I snort. "Can we scrub that visual from my mind with bleach and finish getting the ingredients I need?" I glance at the time on my phone. "I need to make sure I have plenty of time in case I screw this meal up."

FIFTY-TWO

Emerson

"THANK YOU. I APPRECIATE IT."

"You need anything else?" Grady asks as he stands in the entryway of Grant's house.

"No. Here's to hoping I don't burn the house down." I laugh, knowing my attempt to cook anything could end up in a dire situation.

"At least you know a firefighter to call," he says before tossing me a wink.

"True."

"Well, I have to get back."

"'Kay."

He turns to walk out the door. "Hey, Em?"

"Yeah?" I look up from where I'm unloading groceries onto Grant's kitchen counter and hope I look somewhat competent.

"This is a really cool thing you're doing."

"I wouldn't say that yet. My post-interview, celebratory dinner hasn't even been started, so let's not jinx me. Cooking is not my strong suit."

"No, I mean it," he says, looking outside and then back toward me. "You mean a lot to him . . . and the fact that you're taking the time to do this is pretty cool."

I smile as he gives me one last nod and then closes the door behind him, leaving me to do this all by myself.

Sort of.

As soon as I know Grady has driven away, I FaceTime Desi.

"Are you sure you don't want me to come over there and help?" she greets me.

"No. I'm capable and competent." There is far more gusto in that statement than I feel. Inside, I'm secretly wishing she would. She may have written down step-by-step instructions, but even that isn't foolproof when it comes to me.

"He better appreciate the fact that you're risking life and limb to do this for him."

"It's cooking, Desi."

"Exactly. For you, that means life and limb."

"Hardy, har, har."

Oddly enough, the house actually smells delicious. And not the delicious that's really a cinnamon scented candle I lit so I could pretend I'd been baking desserts, but like real, honest-to-goodness, meat-and-potatoes type of food.

And despite how great the aroma is, I'm suddenly nervous. It sounds stupid that I've let the man see me naked, strip me bare, but letting him eat my cooking makes me anxious. Most likely because I half expect him to keel over and die because I screwed it up so badly.

So, I busy myself with straightening the stacks of case files on the coffee table. Then I shift the plant sitting in front of the window so the opposite side grows stronger toward the light. I wipe the counters down for the umpteenth time. I fiddle with the place settings on the table and debate over whether that seems too stuffy, but decide the candle I put in the middle negates that.

I pace the room a few times and then decide to fluff the couch pillows when I've never even fluffed my own. I'm putting a pillow back and pulling a throw blanket off the corner to fold it when the green of a case file catches my eye, and I smile. Considering how many times I have caught him nodding off amid reviewing stacks of them, I'm not surprised one has fallen into cushion oblivion.

But it's only when I dislodge it and go to set it on the table where the other stacks are that my heart stops. I shake my head to reject what I'm seeing.

It can't be . . .

My heart races, and my mind tries to comprehend what my eyes are seeing.

Closed File #713920: Emerson Reeves – Sexual Abuse – 10/23/1997

But I know what it is.

This is me. *The old me*. The little girl I was and don't want to be. It's the past I don't want to be reminded of, and yet, my file is sitting here—in Grant's family room—hidden in plain sight so I wouldn't see it.

These are the answers that could simultaneously cure all the doubt that plagues me and knock me so far down the rabbit hole I might not be able to find my way back.

Fuck having ownership of memories should they come. This is proof. Proof in ways I can't comprehend. There is no ownership of it now. There is only falling victim to it when I've been a victim enough in my life and . . . Oh. My. God.

Shock burns its way into anger. The fuse is so short it's combustible.

My hands tremble as I throw it down on the table like it's burning my skin. It hits the wooden edge and falls to the floor, causing a few items to dislodge.

Every part of me screams to turn around and run out of the house while my feet remain rooted. A little voice in my subconscious tells me, "*Look at them*."

Trepidation courses through me as I take the dare and bend over to pick up the piece of paper that taunts me.

What am I doing?

I turn it over, and it takes me a few seconds to have the nerve to open my eyes and look. What I see has a sob falling from my mouth as I sink to the floor.

The top of the page is labeled "Child Assessment - Emerson Reeves - Age Eight." Memories ghost through my mind of when I drew this—the light blue room that was cold, the nice lady with the gentle voice who asked me to draw a picture to show her what happened, my tears hot on my cheeks as I looked around for my mom.

The drawing depicts what I saw through my innocence. Now, I look at it with the knowledge of an adult. Tears well as I take it all in. There is a bed where two stick figures lie, one bigger like an adult with short brown hair and the other smaller with red hair. The red-haired figure, me, has blue dots falling from her eyes and making a puddle on the floor. The brown-haired man, my dad, has his hand over where the legs on my rendition meet. There's a black L-shaped thing on the top of the bed, a gun, and words line the left side of the page: No, stop, hurt, all my heart, I love you, daddy.

It hurts too much. *This* hurts too much.

I want to cover my ears and squeeze my eyes shut and block this all out so I can forget that I remember that day.

In haste and with a scattered mind determined to get the drawing out of my sight, I shove the piece of paper under the file's cover where it is on the floor. I pick it up to put it on the table, and when I do, I see the Polaroid beneath it.

I forget every intention I just had when I'm met with a picture of myself in a hospital gown. There is no smile on my lips. There is no happiness that every eight-year-old should have. Everything about me—my posture, my expression, my eyes—look defeated and scared.

I stare at the little girl in the photo and tell myself I am not her anymore. I will never be her again. But every part of me feels like her right now. Lost. Withdrawn. Petrified.

Betrayed.

A tear drops on the picture, and I realize for the first time that

I'm crying. Tear after tear tracks down my cheeks as parts inside me I thought were whole again slowly crumble to rubble.

I tell myself to close the folder because I don't need to see this. I don't need to know more details. Don't I already know them somewhere in my mind?

FIFTY-THREE

Grant

IT'S AS IF MY DAY JUST KEEPS GETTING BETTER AND BETTER. I nailed my interviews and now I come home to find Emerson's car in front of my house and music floating out of the windows.

Grady's cryptic text earlier of "I let her in" makes perfect sense now.

Tonight seems like it's going to be even better than today.

What did I do to deserve this?

"Emerson?" I call when I open the door, but I see her before the word cuts through the room.

When she hears my voice, her body stiffens where she's sitting on the floor behind the coffee table. Her head rises slowly and the look in her eyes—a mixture of devastation and anger—is enough to have the hairs on the back of my neck bristling.

"Em?"

"So, what? I don't tell you what you want to know, so you figure, fuck my privacy. Fuck my need to quiet my own mind and deal with my own shit as I see fit . . . and take it upon yourself to figure it out on your own?" Her voice escalates in pitch with each word and warns me to proceed with caution.

"What are you talking about?"

"*I trusted you!*" she screams at the top of her lungs, and it isn't the sound of her desperation that kills me. It's the depth of grief in her eyes.

"I don't . . ." I step into my own house and begin undoing the knot of my tie. I'm fucking suffocating all of a sudden and have no clue why all the oxygen has been sucked out of the room. "I don't understand."

"Exactly. You didn't understand," she says as I round the couch and see it at the same time she speaks. "You didn't understand, so you dug up my old case file so you could."

Oh. Shit.

The green file folder—her file folder—is sitting squarely in the center of her lap, causing dread to drop through me like a lead weight.

"You had to call it up from wherever the fuck it was so you could pour over every goddamn detail there was about me. *About what he did to me.* Anything you could find so you could satisfy that hero complex of yours and come to the rescue with your cape and save me." She stands and slams the folder down on the table with a smacking noise that sounds just like I feel. "Well, *fuck you*, Grant Malone. Fuck. You. If you think he violated me, what the hell do you think you just did to me?"

For the first time in my life, I'm at a complete loss for words, and yet, I know I need to find them.

"It was a mistake—"

"*So were you.*" Her voice is as cold as steel.

"It isn't what you think." I backpedal, trying to explain. "The file. It was a mistake. I had a list of files to pull to work on for Ramos. I was thinking about you. I doodled your name down—"

"And then what? Then you got the file and kept it? I've seen you move boxes in and out of here after a few days . . . but you kept mine. Why, Grant? Face it, you couldn't handle me not telling you what you wanted to know." She paces like a caged animal begging for either an escape or an attack. I guard the door, willing to take whatever she throws at me as long as it means I can explain what happened.

"At first, yes." My confession is barely audible.

"I hate you." The tears burning so bright and pain so raw in her voice it shatters every part of me.

"No, Em. No. It wasn't like that. I wanted to know. And then I realized that—"

"You don't get it, do you?" she shrieks, hysteria bubbling over in her erratic movements and flailing arms. "*I don't want to know*. I don't want to know every little detail. I don't want to hate the dark again like I used to. I don't want to lie in bed at night and listen for every damn noise because I think he's walking down the hall to '*love me*' again. I don't want to remember the feeling of the hair on his legs scraping against my bare bottom when he sat me on his lap." She covers her hands over her ears and emits the most horrid sound I've ever heard. It's part sob, part yell, part protest, and if I never hear it again, I'll be good with that. It renders me helpless. "I was fine until you, Grant. I had the memories I had and those were enough nightmares for a lifetime. But that wasn't enough for you, was it? My lack of answers wasn't enough?"

"Em—"

"Don't you get it? I don't want to remember what happened after the feel of his hair scraping against my skin. It was obviously so bad that my own mind has shut the memories out—repressed the fuck out of them *to protect me* . . . and yet, *you know*. I don't even know, but you know." A heart-wrenching sob breaks free from her chest.

I fumble for words, for a way to get her to see that I never opened the folder, but the truth she just told me is more staggering than that.

It was *so much more* than her remembering the damn rocks the other day.

She doesn't remember *anything*. At all.

How could I have been so stupid not to pick up on that?

"No, Emmy. No—"

"Don't you dare call me that! Just don't." She takes a step back as I take a step toward her. "Please don't." Tears continue to streak down her cheeks, and her mascara paints their paths. She's a broken woman, and I've done this to her. "Knowledge isn't power in this case. You can't use it to your advantage to save me from what already happened."

"Will you fucking listen to me? I did *not* look at it."

"I don't fucking believe you!"

"Christ." I blow a breath out and run a hand through my hair to stop myself from reaching out to touch her like every part of me wants to. "Will you quit being so goddamn stubborn and hear me? I did not—"

"How can I ever let you look at me again without thinking about how you know things about me that I don't even know? How can I ever be with you when you cared more about feeding your own need to be the hero than how it would make me feel?"

Her words cut into the room and ram like daggers into my heart.

"I trusted you, Grant. You pinky promised," she says, her words quietly followed by a hiccupped sob. "And you broke it. *Again*." With that, Emerson rushes past me out the door.

"Em. Wait." I jog down the path after her.

"I hate you. I never want to see you again."

It's those words—the ones repeated twenty years apart that hit their mark. I don't have the heart to stop her from going . . . because she's right.

Shell-shocked, I watch her get in her car and drive away without looking at me. I stare down the empty street long after the glow of her taillights have faded and the crickets have settled into their space in the night.

At some point, I walk into the house, turn off the oven, and blow out the candle as if I'm on autopilot. My eyes burn. My stomach churns. The pressure in my chest makes it hard to breathe.

Because she is right.

I wrote her name down. It may have been a doodle, but her name was there on the top of the list.

I held on to the file when I knew I shouldn't. My initial intentions might have been pure behind it—find out what exactly she experienced so I could . . . so I could be the goddamn hero.

Fuck.

I'm such a damn asshole.

I didn't want to screw this up and look what I just did.
Trust is hard for her.
And I just went and fucked that up.
I clench my fist and beg for something to hit.
The problem is, the only thing worthy of being punched is myself.

FIFTY-FOUR

Emerson

I DRIVE.

I press the pedal to the metal and push the limits of the engine as I roar down the rural road. I use the rush of the air through the open windows to fill my ears and drown out my thoughts. And to dry my tears.

I don't know where I'm going.

I have no clue.

All I know is I need space and freedom and air that Grant Malone doesn't breathe.

All I want is to lose myself in something—*possibly in someone*—so I can remind myself why I don't let my guard down.

All I need are my rules back in place.

All I want is my chest to stop hurting and my heart back.

I know that, regardless of how determined I was to hold on to it, I left it back at Grant's house.

I gave my heart to him, and I gave my trust to him.

And he has just broken both.

FIFTY-FIVE

Grant

"YOU WANT TO TELL ME WHY YOU'RE BEATING THE SHIT out of the heavy bag like it has done something to you?"

I don't have time for Grayson or his shit right now. "I can punch you instead."

I grunt as I connect again. The jolt of my fist against the bag ricocheting up my arm and slamming into me is nothing compared to what I deserve.

"Who pissed you off?"

"No one."

Another grunt. Another unsatisfying slam against the bag.

"Ah, so then you pissed yourself off." He chuckles, and I don't respond. "Oh, shit, I'm sorry, man," he says suddenly, as if the wind has been knocked from his sails. And it's just enough to catch my attention that I glance his way.

"What?"

"Did you blow your interview?"

"No." I hit the bag again. "I killed the interview."

"Then what the fuck man?" A few seconds pass. "*Oh.*"

"Yup." A one-two combo.

"How'd you fuck it up?" I love that I have brothers who understand what's going on without my ever saying a word, but at the same time, it's annoying as fuck when I want to be left alone. A blessing and a curse.

A jab combo. An uppercut that I pretend is Grayson if he doesn't leave me the hell alone.

"Because I am a dumbfuck, is how."

"Tell me something I don't know," Gray says and dodges to his left as I miss the bag on purpose and come a little closer than I should to his chin.

My arms ache, but there's nothing I can do but blame myself.

"So? What did you do?"

It's his question that steals my air. I throw one more punch and then let my arms hang as I rest my head against the bag and try to catch my breath.

"I broke her trust," I murmur, not even sure I want to tell him. How could I have been so damn stupid?

"You *are* a dumbfuck." He slaps me on the back, and I jerk my shoulders back to get him off me.

"So we've established." I step away from the heavy bag and walk toward the bench where my water bottle sits, gritting my teeth when he follows.

"Considering you're here and beating the shit out of a bag instead of figuring out how to make it up to her, I'd say it's definitely been established."

"Leave me the hell alone, Gray. I can handle things on my own."

"You sure about that?" *Not at the moment.* "Because I may not know what the fuck you did, but the big brother I know doesn't give up without a fight. You're the hero. The guy who saves things . . . so, go save this."

I glare at him.

"I'm out of the hero business."

"Like hell you are."

"C'mon, Em. Open up." I pound my fist on her door. *Again*. The same as I've been doing for the past ten minutes.

"She obviously doesn't want to talk."

Leo's voice startles me, and when I turn, I find him leaning against the wall of the next hangar over, arms across his chest, eyes hidden beneath the shadow of a ball cap, body riddled with irritation.

"Thanks, but it's none of your business, Leo," I say and turn back to the door.

"It actually *is* my business."

I'm not in the mood for this shit. "You know what?" I say as I take a few steps down the stairs. "I love that you watch out for, Em. I do . . . I love knowing that when she's here alone, you have her back . . . but I'm not the prick from the loan office trying to get in her pants. I appreciate the whole big brother thing you have going, but it isn't needed. So, do you mind?"

Leo stands to his full height and takes a few steps toward me. Christ, here comes the macho bullshit.

"Choose wisely," I say with a lift of my brow. While I may not be in the mood to fight after hitting a heavy bag for over an hour, landing a punch on a real, live person might feel a lot more satisfying.

We stare at each other for a few seconds before he nods slowly.

"She isn't here."

"Where is she?"

He shrugs. "Not sure." *He knows where she is.* "She took off outta here like a bat out of hell."

"Christ." The gypsy girl has gone, and I have no one to blame but myself.

"You're a good guy, Malone, but cop or no cop, you hurt her, I have no problem throwing a punch in her honor."

"I think she'd have no problem throwing one herself."

The entire day replays in my head. Over and fucking over.

Killing the interview. I nailed every question with such precision that when I walked out of there, I had no doubt I was going to get the promotion.

The highest high.

Coming home to what I thought was perfection—Emerson's car in my driveway and her waiting for me in my house—and then it turning to shit.

The look on Em's face. The accusations she hurled. The goddamn fucking everything I did to her all because I kept the file. If I wasn't going to look at it, then why did I keep it?

The lowest low.

Fuck me.

The rest of the night is a blur. The gym. The showdown with Leo. The coming home to see the file sitting on the table and knowing I'm to blame for all of this but having no clue how to fix it.

If she thought I broke her trust before—twenty years ago—and she had a hard time getting over it, then she sure as shit isn't going to get over this.

But what kills me more than anything is what happened this afternoon when I went to move her file into the storage box. I can't get it out of my head. The loose picture that slipped out and fell to the floor. The one of an eight-year-old Emmy Reeves—eyes haunted, skin pale, body language withdrawn, scared as hell—staring back at the camera.

The sight staggered me. My memory may have remembered a little girl with bouncy pigtails, freckles, a smile with missing teeth, and a laugh that came from her belly, but that was only the reality a naïve little boy could see. A little girl who looked so scared she might break if you push her shoulder with your finger is what she was.

And even two hours later, I can't get the image out of my head because that haunted look she had in the photo was the same one Emerson looked back at me with today before she left.

"Earth to Grant," Grayson says, throwing a pretzel at me. I don't react.

Leave me the fuck alone. I repeat it in my head for the millionth time but don't say a damn word. I want to wallow in my pity. I don't deserve to, but I'm going to.

"It must have been really bad," Grady says.

"You think he cheated on her?" Gray asks.

"I'm right here, assholes. I can hear everything you're saying, so why don't you just ask me yourselves?" I say it, but I don't want them to ask. I just want them to shut up. So, I slump farther down into the lounge chair in my backyard and stare up at the stars above.

"You're not responding when we came here to try to cheer you up, so . . ." He shrugs. "We're gonna keep guessing until you start talking. You know it'll make you feel better."

"I didn't cheat on her," I mumble as the words she said ring in my ears.

"Well, that's good because that's one fire I wouldn't be able to put out," Grady says and then looks at me when I don't respond. "C'mon, you know that was a little funny?" He holds his thumb and forefinger an inch apart. "Just a bit?"

"Shit. He thinks he's Chris Rock now with the jokes," Grayson chimes in as the *crack* of a bottle of beer opening sounds off.

"Thanks for the visit, but you guys can go now." Their banter is not what I want to deal with right now, but it's obvious my statement falls on deaf ears. They don't move. "Okay, then I'm going to ignore you guys like you aren't here."

Grayson swears at me when I reach over and snake his fresh beer from his hand without asking. I take a long pull on it, lay my head on the back of the chair, close my eyes, and tune them out.

And think of Emerson.

It works for a little bit until something Grady says breaks through my thoughts and catches my ear. If he's purposely trying to get me to talk, it works.

"I bet you anything he couldn't handle it," Grady says.

"Couldn't handle what?" I ask, lifting up one eyelid to look at them

"You think?" Grayson interjects as if I'm not even here and hadn't spoken.

"Yeah."

"What the fuck are you two talking about?" I growl. I'm tired. I'm drunk. And fuck me, I miss Emerson, and for more reasons than just because. This guilt and regret are eating away at me from the inside out.

"You looked her up, didn't you?" Grady says, prompting me to close my eyes again and exhale. "Curiosity got the better of you, and you looked her up. Pulled her file or whatever the fuck you cops do so that you knew what you were facing."

Ignore him. He's just trying to goad you into talking.

"Just like *our Grant* to need all his ducks in a row so he knows exactly how to handle a situation, especially when that situation is a feisty, sexy handful who doesn't just fall into his arms like every other woman on the planet," Grayson adds with a chuckle that grates on my last nerve.

"Too bad a person isn't a situation," Grady says, the statement hitting its mark. Good thing I've had enough to drink that I'm mellow or I might just have landed that punch I was jonesing for yesterday.

Don't take the bait.

"True," Grayson muses. "I'm not saying that I'd ever follow through with it, but I can't say I blame him."

"What do you mean?"

"It's natural to want to know what you're dealing with. I mean . . . we all know whatever happened to Em was fucked up . . . so, maybe Grant was being a good guy and wanted to know what triggers to avoid or some shit like that for her own benefit."

"You're giving him too much credit," Grady says, and I clench my jaw. They may be enjoying making their damn point, but that doesn't mean I have to react to what they are egging me on to. "You know *our Grant*. He just wants to swoop in and save the day like always."

Another dig. Another bullshit dig.

"He did save our asses a few times," Grayson says.

"But this is different."

"It *is* different. It's Emmy. And Grant's in love with her."

Grady snorts. “Hasn’t he always been?”

Patience snapped. Buttons pushed.

“Will the two of you shut the fuck up already? You’ve made your goddamn point even though you have no fricking clue what the hell happened,” I lie because they nailed it on the head, which makes it even worse. That I’m that fucking readable and predictable. I shove up out of the chair to pace, and it takes me a few seconds to gain my balance. The beer is hitting me, and I already know I need it to hit a lot harder.

Because they’re right.

I am in love with her.

Jesus Christ, when the fuck did that happen?

Probably about second grade.

FIFTY-SIX

Emerson

I LOOK AT THE LIST OF TEXTS ON MY PHONE.

Grant and his apologies and explanations and hurt I don't want to deal with.

Christopher and his promises that we should have loan approval in a week or two, and since he's charging me a below the rate fee, how about I repay him by going out for a few drinks. At what point will the man understand that it isn't going to happen?

Desi and her daily check-in to make sure I'm okay and that I haven't fallen off the face of the earth.

Leo and his questions about the classes over the next few days and how to arrange staff since I'm the one who typically does it.

I scroll through them again and then toss my phone to the end of the bed before snuggling deeper under the comforter. It smells too much like Grant and so I pretend the world outside and everything that happened doesn't exist.

I know they all think I'm out jumping. That I closed my eyes and put my finger to the map and drove to that spot. That I'm chasing the wind and being the gypsy I typically am.

But I'm not.

My car's in the red hangar where it can't be seen.

And I'm holed up in my apartment. *Alone.*

The person I've become fighting the urge to cut myself, while the little girl underneath screams for more of the pain she knows. The pain she needs to feel again to know she's alive.

But I haven't cut myself.

And I won't.

If there's one thing I'm going to win in this whole damn situation, it's going to be that.

I don't even have a desire to jump.

Grant stole that from me.

Just like he stole my heart.

My trust.

But both of them have been broken before. Both of them have wounded me, and I have survived.

The only difference this time around is my ability not to feel *anything.*

Because hell if right now I don't feel *everything.*

So much so that it hurts.

It pisses me off more than anything because I can't turn them off.

That I can't run away from them when that's all I've ever known how to do.

FIFTY-SEVEN

Grant

"YOU'RE RESTLESS."

"No shit." I look over to Nate, who has obliged me with a drive by of Miner's Airfield for no other reason than to see if Emerson is back.

"Just go talk to her."

"I've tried."

"Well, try harder. It's not as if she isn't going to notice the cruiser driving by several times this week."

"I know. It's just . . ."

"I know, I know. There's more to it that I don't understand other than you fucked up royally . . . well, royally unfuck yourself," Nate says and shakes his head.

"Gee, thanks, Dad." I roll my eyes and turn back onto the highway.

"Did you call her?"

"She won't pick up."

"Did you text her?"

"She won't reply."

"Did you stand there and pound on her door?"

"Ha." The image of Leo flexing his muscles comes to mind. "Yeah. Something like that."

"Did you send her flowers? Chicks always love flowers."

"Not this chick," I murmur, thinking I won't test fate by sending them to her twice.

"Then what is it she likes? What is it that is unique to you two? Use whatever that is. Chicks dig uniqueness."

"According to you, chicks dig everything."

"Be original," he repeats.

And I laugh. But as I glace at the Blue Skies sign one more time before we leave, an idea starts to form as a call comes across the radio.

FIFTY-EIGHT

Grant

"GRANT?"

"Mm-hmm."

"Don't you want to go out front and play?"

"No. I don't feel like it."

The screen door creaks. The wood of the porch flexes with each step she takes. The smell of her perfume fills my nose when she sits next to me.

"You miss her, huh?"

I nod instead of talk because my throat burns from trying to hold back the tears. Boys don't cry over girls, but she's gone, and all I want is to cry because I miss her.

My mom slips her arm around me and pulls me against her side. I concentrate on pushing the rocks on the porch beside me around with my finger instead of crying.

"Why did she have to go?"

I'm the reason she left.

She made me promise, and I told.

I'm the reason she left.

"She's gone for just a bit. She and her mommy are at the hospital for—"

"Is she sick?"

"No." My mom makes that one word sound so sad. "She's just

not feeling well."

"But why—"

"And then after they leave, they are going to go on a big adventure," she says in that funny voice she uses when she tells us the dentist is going to be fun. Like I'm supposed to believe her when she's not telling the truth.

"Where?" I ask, my hopes getting up that she'll send me postcards.

"I don't know," she murmurs and then sniffles as if she is crying, but when I look up to her, she shifts suddenly so I can't see her face. "Are these the rocks you were painting?" The dentist voice is back again.

"Yeah. I painted them for Emmy."

"That was nice of you."

"She likes rocks. Even ugly zombie ones. She's been really sad, so I've been painting them and putting them in her planter. She said they make her smile." I push the rocks around some more. "She's not going to have any more of my rocks, Mom. How is she going to smile now?"

"Oh, Grant." My mom hiccups real loud, and it sounds like she's crying again. Before I can look, she grabs me into a hug and holds so tight I can't breathe.

But I cry, too.

I miss my best friend.

Her and her yucky purple backpack and her Barbies and other girly things I hate but would play with her a hundred times if she would just come back home.

Bye, Emmy.

I'm sorry I told your secret, and it made you go away.

If I had kept my pinky promise, you'd still be here.

I'm sorry. Will you forgive me?

FIFTY-NINE

Emerson

THE KNOCK ON THE DOOR TO MY OFFICE STARTLES ME. THE person standing there does even more so.

I look like hell.

That's the first thought that glances through my mind when I look up to see Grant's mom in my doorway. My second is it's her son who made me feel this way.

"Betsy."

Is it bad that just the sight of her—my second mom—makes me want to hug her and just sob? I fight the tears burning my eyes because I will not fall apart. Not here in the office. Not at home. Not anymore.

"Em? You okay, honey?" She steps into my office.

"Yeah. Just . . . it'll be okay."

For a moment, she studies me as if she's trying to figure out whether to believe me. "I'm sorry for stopping by unannounced, but I called earlier, and it went to voice mail. I hope you don't mind."

"No, of course not. Come in and have a seat," I say as I stand from my desk and shut the door to my office behind her. The last thing I need is for the staff to hear any part of this conversation. I'm certain they're already wondering what's wrong with me since I've been snapping at everyone. I wait for her to get settled and sit in the office chair next to her.

"It's a wonderful little space," she says with a sincerity I know she means. "I can't wait to see how you improve it when it's yours. I won't stay long. I just . . ."

"What is it?"

"Grant will kill me for meddling, but I couldn't stand by and not say anything." I hold back my sigh when I realize why Betsy has come to see me. "He told me you've been remembering things you hadn't before."

I thought her opening statement was going to be about the file folder or some grand pitch about how I need to give Grant another chance—the same spiel I'm getting from Desi. So I'm a little taken aback by her statement. With anyone else, my guard would be up, but I find myself needing someone to talk to.

"Yes, they have. Ever since I saw Grant on the Fourth."

"And you assume it's because of him?"

I nod, curious but uncertain about where this conversation is going. "It isn't a coincidence."

"You know, sometimes it doesn't take a reminder to trigger a memory. Sometimes your mind just knows you can finally handle it. It knows you've found the right people, the right support network to protect you from the fallout of the memory—keep you safe—and your subconscious just wants to rid itself of all of it and start fresh. Sure, the memory is going to screw you up. The devil is in the details after all . . . but sometimes, what you imagine might have happened is worse because your imagination magnifies it." She shakes her head and corrects herself. "That isn't what I meant. What happened to you was horrific. All I meant was that, maybe by knowing the truth, you'll stop feeling the need to run from the constant and probably nagging unknown. Because I don't want you to run anymore. You're the only daughter we've ever had, Emmy. You left such a big hole in our family when you left before, and we don't want you picking up and leaving again."

I feel like something inside me breaks from her words. I spent months missing Grant and his family after we left Sunnyville. They were the one normal I could count on, and then they were taken away from me when I needed them the most. She has no clue how long it's been since I felt like I belonged somewhere or how her words are like salve on an open wound. They aren't enough to heal, but they are enough to soothe.

"I don't want to leave again, either," I find myself saying. The truth behind why getting the loan means so much.

"And since I'm being pushy, I might as well just get it all out. You can't leave Sunnyville. Plain and simple. Grant is the one for you, Emerson. He always has been." The stubborn lift to her chin is so similar to Grant's that it makes me smile. "He's patient and strong-willed and will put you in your place if need be, but he will also be the first one to pull you into his arms and hold you so tight that your demons have nowhere to go but out. I know you'll keep him on his toes and make him work harder to be a better man because that's what he thinks you deserve . . . but what do I know?" she says as she waves her hand dismissively. "I'm just his mom."

"I wish it were that easy, Betsy. Grant's a great man . . . but I have things I need to figure out first. Things I need to work through. I need to be able to trust him and . . ." I shake my head and exhale, unsure of how to explain it all to his mom.

"I know my son, Emerson. If he had looked at that case file, he would have been eaten up alive by what is in there," she says so matter-of-factly that it takes me a second to process he told his mom about the file

"You know?" My words are barely audible.

"Of course I know," she says, her eyes never breaking from mine. "You were like mine, Em. Your mom and I spent many nights together on the phone, sobbing one minute, screaming the next, and sitting in silence between so the other wasn't alone."

I blink rapidly, forcing back the burn of tears as my mind catches up with her words. With the piece of truth she just gave me.

I *remember.*

The murmured conversations in the back of the van when my mom thought I was sleeping. My eight-year-old self assumed it was my dad she was talking to, that she was apologizing to him because I had been such a bad girl, but it was Betsy.

"I didn't know."

"We both blamed ourselves, Em. How could the two of us—two intelligent, educated women—not see the signs that were sitting right in front of us? How could we be so busy with life that we failed you?"

"It isn't your fault," I say. My need to rid the pain in her voice all-consuming.

"You're right. It isn't. Just like it wasn't yours and it wasn't Grant's. Though, to this day, I think he blames himself for not saving you sooner."

Why would Grant blame himself?

The thought is staggering, and my head is so full of these new revelations all I can do is keep listening to her. "It was your father's fault. He was pure evil. To make you feel like it was your fault? To trick you into thinking it was all dreams? He was evil to the core."

My heart drops. How does she know this? How does she know the doubt I have and my mistrust of my own memory? "You knew about that?" My voice is barely audible.

"Who do you think sat and held your mom's hand as we watched you with the detective and therapist on the other side of the two-way mirror at Children's Hospital? It was me, sweetie. I know he tricked you. I know you doubted back then, and probably sometimes still do today, whether you were at fault or to blame. After all the games he played with your mind, that's more than understandable. Let me tell you that you weren't."

"I didn't realize that you were there after . . ."

"Do you think I would leave you and your mom when you needed me most?" She smiles a sad smile as she remembers. "I'm sorry for what happened to you. I'm sorry that you're remembering some of it. Will you keep remembering? I don't know. Your mind might continue to protect itself from the trauma . . . or it might not. Just know that we are here for you if you need us. You can call me any time, day or night, and I'll come to you, even if it's just to sit with you in the darkness and so you know you aren't alone with a new memory rattling around in your head. You're not alone anymore, Emerson. You never were."

"Betsy, I don't know what to say . . ."

"Don't say anything," she says as she reaches out to squeeze my knee. "Obviously, if you stay and want to be a part of our family—in all our craziness and bantering—it will be on your own terms, your own time frame. And the offer remains regardless if you are or aren't with my son." She stands. "But I have to tell you he's downright miserable right now. My bet is it's because he misses you."

SIXTY

Emerson

Y*ou're not alone anymore, Emerson. You never were.*

Betsy's words still linger in my mind when Desi walks in a couple of hours later.

"You look like shit."

"Thanks," I say with a sarcastic smile as I brush past her without saying anything else.

"You talk to him yet?"

Jesus. Is this the Save Grant brigade? First Betsy. Now Desi. If Leo joins the party, I might just leave after all. It's really hard not to think about someone when they keep getting brought up.

"I have shit to do, Des. I have this class coming in to jump. I have . . . I just have shit to do."

"You think that's smart, Em?"

"What?" I busy myself with papers so that I don't have to meet her eyes.

"Jumping. *From an airplane.* You know, thousands of feet above the ground. I sure as hell wouldn't trust you to take me in the state you're in. Like I said, you look like hell. And distracted. Exhausted. And if I'm honest—"

"By all means, don't hold back."

"Sketchy."

"Sketchy?"

"Yeah," she says and then falls silent until I meet her eyes for the first time. "You look like you couldn't complete two tasks if your life depended on it."

"That's just because I'm trying to avoid talking to you."

"Well, at least you're being honest."

I stop fidgeting and sigh. She's right, and I don't want to admit it. "Look, Des. I'm dealing with a lot of shit. I appreciate you coming to check on me, but nothing has changed. Nothing is going to change."

"So, you're going to shut me out just like you're doing to him?" she asks, hands on her hips, eyebrows raised.

"How do you know I'm shutting him out? Did you talk to him?" My voice escalates in pitch, and when Leo walks in and sees the silent standoff waging between Desi and me, he backs back out of the office without saying a word.

"I didn't say I spoke to him."

She implied it, though.

"I'm not shutting you out. I'm just . . ." I look out the window to where I've noticed a cruiser drive by several times over the past week and hate that I hope to see it.

"Correction. You're not shutting me out, you just aren't dealing is what you're doing. In that head of yours, you're trying to figure out how you can rabbit out of here without messing up everything you've worked so hard for. The loan. Blue Skies. Me, your only family." Her voice softens. "I'm not going to let you run, Em."

I hate that my eyes burn with tears. I hate that the chocolate cake she brought me holds no appeal. I despise that as much as I hate Grant right now, I also miss everything about him.

"He hurt me," I whisper, the words barely audible, as if it pains me to admit it.

"Yeah, I know he did. And I'm sorry for it. I'm sorry you're hurt, but sometimes, when you're in a relationship with someone, that happens." I start to reject her notion of relationship, but she holds her hand up and nips it in the bud. "Have you considered giving him the benefit of the doubt?"

"Why does he deserve it?"

"That's up to you to decide, but in the meantime, you're miserable as hell, you look like shit, and in the end, you're only hurting yourself by not listening to him. Have you stopped for a single second to consider that maybe you're wrong? That maybe Grant is telling the truth about pulling the file accidentally and never opening it?"

I shake my head, not wanting to hear her reasoning because she should be the one supporting me. She should be the one telling me I'm in the right and to dump him.

But she isn't.

"I'm not wrong," I say, using anger to fuel my denial.

"Maybe you are." She shrugs with a challenging lift of her eyebrows. "Maybe you're willing to believe he hurt you because it's so much easier for you to be mad and shut people out than it is to believe them. Because believing him means you might have to put yourself and *your heart* on the line."

"I have my rules, Des."

She's wrong. She has to be.

She laughs, and I hate the condescending sound to it. "And look what happened when you threw them out the window. You came to life, Emerson. He made you feel alive. Anyone who can do that to you shouldn't be confined to your self-preservationist rules. They deserve the benefit of the doubt. They deserve a second chance."

"I have to get to work."

"Don't jump today."

"Head up. Wings out," I say as I walk into the conference room and away from the truth she's telling that I don't think I'm ready to hear.

And straight into Christopher.

Startled, I jump back, but he keeps his hand firmly on my arm.

"How did you get in here?" I ask, completely uncomfortable as I yank my arm away from him.

"The side door was open. I didn't want to interrupt your girl time."

My skin crawls with the knowledge that he was eavesdropping.

"Next time use the front door please."

"Or you could answer my calls when I make them, or were you too busy sleeping around with the Malone boys?" He tsks. "Big mistake on your part."

"Mistake or not, it's none of your business." I grit my teeth for the umpteenth time. Patience.

Only a few more days, and I'll never have to deal with this slime bag again.

His hand is back on my bicep without warning. "Apparently, you don't want your loan, Ms. Reeves?" he says, purring out my last name and causing my stomach to revolt.

"You asking me out for dinner has nothing to do with my loan."

"It has everything to do with your loan."

"Excuse me? I wasn't aware that when I signed the loan application with you that prostitution was part of the deal."

He runs the tip of his finger down my arm, and I want to slap his hand away. "*You* have everything to do with the deal. Don't forget that I am the only one willing to take a risk on you, Emerson. I'm the only lender even remotely willing to issue a loan with your credit history . . . so, I think it's *you* who should be bending to me."

"*No*. I don't bend for *anyone*. It's as simple as that."

"No?"

"You heard me, Chris. Your sexual harassment bullshit doesn't fly with me, and I'm sick of putting up with it. I'm sure the board of ethics wouldn't approve of it, either," I say without even knowing if there is such a thing as a board of ethics for lending practices. "Get the loan approved. Fund the money to the owners. Close the deal. Do your job."

His chuckle scrapes over my skin like nails on a chalkboard. "Your loan was denied this morning."

"What?" If I could get whiplash from the change in conversation, I would have it. "What did you just say?"

Is he fucking kidding me?

"Yep. It was rejected today. If you would have answered my calls or listened to any of my voice mails, you would have known that already . . ." He crosses his arms over his chest and leans one shoulder against the wall. "Don't worry, though. When the lender notified us, the Skies' broker said they were going to move forward and accept their backup offer. I'm sure if you ask nicely, they'll put in a good word for you with the new owners. Maybe they'll give you a job."

"How is that even possible?" I shout as every part of me rages in a disbelief I can't even process.

"Well, when you drag your feet and don't provide your loan officer the things he needs, it can happen quite easily." His smarmy smirk matches the tone in his voice. "One missing piece, one mistyped figure, is all it takes for the lender to throw it out."

"You bastard."

"Not from where I stand."

"You knew my loan was denied, and you pretended it wasn't to try to get me to sleep with you." My fists clench and body vibrates with anger. "Get. Out."

"Too bad, this place could have been all yours." He holds his hands out to his sides and winks. "Good luck finding someone to lend you the money now . . . but then again, it doesn't matter. Your dream is already being sold to someone else."

And with that, he slams the side door shut as I stand there and just stare at it.

With each breath, each beat of my heart, each tremble of my hands, the anger slowly morphs into disbelief.

Then disbelief gives way to shock.

Then shock to devastation.

"Em, you okay? It sounded like something fell," Leo says as he clears the doorway and looks around, his constant movement faltering when he sees me.

"Emerson?"

I just lost my loan.

"I'm fine. I just . . ."

I just lost my fresh start.

"I just need to get out of here for a bit. Can you handle everything?"

"Sure. Yes. You sure you're okay?" Concern laces his tone.

"Yeah."

I just lost my dream.

SIXTY-ONE

Grant

"HOW LONG YOU GOING TO DO THIS, MAN?"

"Do what?" I ask as I turn down Serenity Court.

"You're too close to this case," Nate says as I pull the cruiser to the curb and put it in park. There are cars in the driveway, the garage door is closed, and there are lights on inside. "How are you going to explain why you're in their front yard if Davis comes waltzing out? That doesn't exactly look good. I mean . . . what if he is abusing them, you snooping around constantly looks like a perfect case of police interference, planting evidence, discrimination—Jesus, just about anything people accuse cops of these days."

I hang my head and drum my thumbs on the wheel, knowing he's one hundred percent right.

"I promised her, Nate." It's the only explanation I can give before I hop out of the car and jog the few feet across the street to the driveway.

This is the last time.

Nate's right.

And just as I agree with myself, I turn the corner of the walkway and freeze. Sitting there in a garden of rocks that hasn't had a new one added to it for the past three weeks is a freshly painted rock.

It's red with black seeds.

Oh, shit.

And it's sitting prominently on top of all the others.

It feels like it takes me a second to register what I'm seeing, but I damn well know what it is because my fist is banging on the door without a second thought.

"Sunnyville Police, open up."

Bang. Bang. Bang.

"Open the goddamn door."

Bang. Bang. Bang.

"Mr. Davis, open the door. I know you're home."

Bang. Bang. Bang.

"What the fuck is going on, Grant?" Nate says, already out of breath as he runs up behind me.

The turning of locks startles me, even though it's exactly what I'm asking for. My hand is on the butt of my gun, my temper a rush of adrenaline that has that hand trembling.

"Keely, don't open the door—" Davis shouts from somewhere inside the house, but the sound drowns out to a white buzz when I look down to see her standing there.

Her cheek is bruised beneath her eye.

Her bottom lip is cracked, and there is some dried blood smudged in the corner.

And more than anything is the way she looks at me.

Haunted.

Like I failed her.

Withdrawn.

Like I didn't get to her in time.

Petrified.

Like I didn't save her.

For a second, the picture of Emerson that fell from the folder flashes in my mind and the two of them meld together.

Emmy and Keely.

Keely and Emmy.

They could be one and the same.

"Don't do it, Grant," Nate warns, already grabbing my arm and trying to drag me back a step. "Don't do it."

"Do you have a warrant?" Mr. Davis says as he stands there with a cocky smirk.

"I have probable cause," I say, lifting my chin toward his daughter.

"You don't have shit," he sneers. "She fell running up the stairs earlier. Got banged up real good, too, but we kissed it and made it all better. So, since you have no authority to be here." He strides the short distance to the front door. "Then good bye."

My palm is on the door slamming it back to prevent it from closing. Keely shrinks at the sound, and Davis curses at me.

"Grant," Nate cautions, but all I can think of is willingly letting this little girl go back into this house.

Her blood is on my hands.

Keely isn't Emmy.

I don't have probable cause.

She asked for help.

Emmy isn't Keely.

I don't have any cause other than a rock painted like a watermelon.

"Get inside, Keels," he demands, but never once looks at her. Tension ratchets with each second that we stare at each other, the predictability of what's going to happen next changes with each and every one of my thoughts.

"No." My hand is on her shoulder, keeping her put as she swivels those big, blue eyes of hers from her dad to me and back again, both of us wanting her for different things—I want to protect her, and he wants to hide his abuse.

"Man, we don't have the auth—"

"I don't care about parental privilege."

"Get inside the house," Davis growls.

I look at Nate and then back to Keely. I couldn't give a rat's ass about her piece-of-shit father, but I know what I have to do, and Nate is going to kill me for it.

Without warning, I stoop down and pick Keely up. "She isn't going back in there." I half expect to be attacked from behind as I walk down the path. I prepare for it, but it never comes. Though, Nate is swearing and Davis is shouting.

Or possibly Nate is holding Davis back while I jog away with his daughter.

With the evidence.

I don't have a plan. I don't have anything thought out other than there is no way in hell I am letting her go back into that house with that jerk and her compliant mother. Keely's little hands grip my neck, and her sniffles fill my ears.

All I can say is, "I've got you, sweetheart. I've got you."

I press my hand to her back and make it as big as possible so she feels protected, but I fear there will never be enough protection for her.

The system fails.

Look at Emerson.

Nate's call from his on-person radio goes out for backup as Davis's shouts fill the quiet cul-de-sac.

By the time I reach the cruiser, my hands are shaking. I know I'm in the wrong, but I don't fucking care.

"What are you doing, man?" Nate says as he jogs down the path, out of breath and more than flustered.

"Where's the mom?" I say, worried about what else we'll find inside.

"Not home."

"Bullshit. Search the house. Make sure she's all right."

"On what premise? You know we can't do that." Nate blows out a breath as neighbors start coming out from their houses and standing on the curb as the blue and red sirens light up the night like a carnival attraction.

"Well check."

Keely clings to me, her whimper at the sound of her dad bellowing is all I need to hear to know I'm doing the right thing.

"Hey, sweetheart, is your mommy home?"

"She's in the shower," she barely whispers in my ear.

I glare at Nate as another cruiser burns down the street and comes to an abrupt stop beside us.

"Hey, Keely?"

"Yeah."

"I know you're scared right now. There's lots of shouting and lights flashing, and I know you're confused, but I need you to trust me," I say into her ear as Nate gives the new officers on scene a run-down of what's going on. "Have you ever wanted to see the inside of a police car?" She nods ever so slightly without lifting her head from my shoulder. "It's super cool. Can I show you mine?"

Another nod as I open the back door and slide into the backseat with her still clinging to me. It takes a minute for us to adjust and get comfortable, but her fingers never let go of their grip.

For a little girl used to seeing the worst in people, she is so trusting. The thought kills me. Her innocence has been tainted. Her ability to believe in happily ever after skewed.

"See? Nice and cozy." Outside the open car door I see Officer Lou talking to Davis on the sidewalk and assume Amelia is inside talking to Lou's partner. Nate's at the trunk of their car on his cell with someone—probably CPS.

"Maybe when you're not so scared I can let you turn the lights on and off and sound the siren." She doesn't respond. "Can I ask you something?" I say smoothing a hand down her hair. "How'd you get that bruise on your cheek?"

I feel her chest shudder against mine, and her fingers slowly release from around my neck as she voluntarily crawls off my lap and sits in the seat beside me. She studies her fingers for a long time before finally speaking.

"I fell on the stairs and hit my face," she murmurs.

"That's a big fall. Did you cry?" She nods but doesn't look at me in the eyes. "If you didn't fall on the stairs . . . you know, like if you got hurt in some other way, you could tell me and I wouldn't be mad."

"'Kay."

We sit in silence as I figure out how to get the truth from her. If she doesn't talk and if her mom protects her dad, then we have no grounds to keep her out of the house. Silence eats up the car as the crowd of onlookers grows.

"Keely?"

"Hmm?"

"Why did you use our secret code?" She shrugs, but I can see her bottom lip trembling. "Did something happen that made you think you needed help?"

Another shrug.

Another loss for how to talk to her.

"Is my daddy in trouble?" she whispers, and I fumble with how to answer.

"If he hurt you, then yes. Just like in school, you can't hurt people without getting in trouble. It's the rules." She nods. "Did he hurt you, Keely?"

She looks at me for the first time since I picked her up. Those eyes so wise beyond their years as she stares at me. Tears well until she finally blinks and releases them down her cheeks.

Tell me, please.

Car doors shut around us. Nate yells something to Lou. But I sit in the back of my cruiser with this little girl and will her to let me protect her.

To save her.

To do what I couldn't for Emerson.

After a few moments, she pulls her knees up to her chest, curls into a ball, stares out the window, and slides her hand into mine.

If I thought my heart was broken before, she just shattered it.

SIXTY-TWO

Emerson

I NEED OPEN SPACE.

I need the wind in my hair and the roar in my ears to drown out the devastation owning my soul.

I didn't get the loan.

I'm not going to get Blue Skies.

I tried to start over. To build a life. To stay put. To trust someone.

But it doesn't seem to be in the cards.

All this hard work. All this busting my ass, and I have nothing to show for it except that I'll probably be out of a job and most likely out of a place to live.

The thought hits me hard, and I press the pedal down even farther.

Anything to quiet my head, but it isn't working.

Nothing is working.

Me. Grant. Blue Skies. My attempt to make a life for myself. Maybe it just isn't meant to be.

So I drive. Push the limits of reason with a pedal and a full tank of gas and wonder what's next.

The sirens cut through my thoughts, and red and blue lights up the dark night.

"Goddamnit!" I shout to myself as I thump the steering wheel with the heel of my hand, and for just a second, I imagine flooring the gas and taking off.

Was he just sitting here waiting for me?

Nothing like abusing his power.

Because I'd bet anything it's going to be Grant walking up to my car and asking for my license and registration. It's going to be Grant trying to reel me in when all I want to do is run.

As I pull over to the side of the road and put my hazards on, I force myself to acknowledge that a small part of me yearns to see him. After the visit from his mom and the doubts Desi lit the match to in my mind, I finally feel ready to face him. The hurt is still there, still raw, but what if I was wrong?

I lean back in my seat and watch the swing of the flashlight as he walks, curious how he's going to play this. We still have a lot to say to each other, and the side of the road isn't exactly the place to do it.

Then again, he's the one who pulled me over.

I squint when the flashlight hits my eyes.

"License and registrat—ah, so we meet again," the officer says, startling me. It's the same officer who pulled me over before. The one who started the whole Tampax adventure.

"Hello, Officer."

"Do you happen to have lead in that foot of yours, Ms. . . ."

"Reeves. Emerson Reeves."

"Ah, yes. Emerson. Where's the fire tonight?"

I stare at him for a second, ready to bullshit my way through it but don't. "You know what? I had a really crappy day. That's it. No excuse. Sometimes there's nothing better than an open road and the windows down."

He chuckles. "Honesty. I like that." He nods as he leans his forearm on the top of my window. "So, what am I supposed to do with you—"

"Officer Roberts, what's your 10-20?" His radio interrupts.

"I'm out on Highway 43."

"We have a situation that needs assistance out on 12662 Serenity Court."

That address.

How do I know it?

"What's the 10-13?" he asks as he steps back from my door and walks a few feet toward the front of the car so he can watch me and also have some privacy.

"Malone and Nunez are on scene. The situation is escalating."

The minute I hear Malone, my heart jumps in my throat. "*Grant.*" I don't know if I say his name aloud because all I hear is "situation is escalating" and dread drops like a lead weight through me.

"10-4. En route."

Is he okay?

"What's your ETA?"

What does escalating mean?

"Five minutes."

Please let him be okay.

Officer Roberts strides back to my window. "Today is your lucky day. Try to keep it below seventy."

I watch the beam from his flashlight as he jogs back to his car. The siren joins the lights as he pulls away from the shoulder and screams down the asphalt.

Grant.

SIXTY-THREE

Emerson

MY HANDS TREMBLE ON THE WHEEL AS I TURN DOWN Serenity Court where blue and red lights explode in their dizzying array of patterns. They flash over the houses and cars and people gathered to watch the activity at the end of the street.

It's been nine minutes.

Nine minutes where I don't even remember purposefully taking the turns to get here.

Nine minutes where I mentally ran through every scenario possible and none of them were good. In every single one, Grant was hurt, and all I could think of was that I'd been stubborn and hadn't spoken to him. I hadn't made things right.

I haven't told him I want to take a chance.

Funny thing is that I didn't even admit that to myself until just now.

Tears blur my eyes as the realization hits me that this is his reality. His every day. His way to be a hero. I'm out of the car and running to where the crowd of looky-loos stands. My heart is in my throat and hope is in my hands.

"C'mon, Malone. We have to let CPS deal with this."

"CPS? Really, Nate?" Grant's laugh echoes off the houses just as I break through to the front of the crowd. I'm not sure what I expect to see—a standoff, weapons drawn? I don't know, but this isn't it. Grant is standing in front of his cruiser, arms crossed and body taut, as Nate, the officer who was with him on the Fourth, and another face him. The tension between them is so palpable that if I didn't know better, I'd think Grant was holding someone hostage. Murmurs roll through the crowd about the little girl in the car, and there are questions about whether Grant is going to do it, whatever "it" is.

"CPS?" he says again, punctuating his incredulity with a shake of his head. My breath catches when I realize he actually *is* holding someone hostage in a sense. But only to protect her. *To help Keely.* "CPS's response was to put her back in the house so they could come and assess the situation at a later date because there is no immediate threat. Tell me that's not a fucking joke."

Nate rolls his shoulder, frustration evident. "I know, Grant, but there is nothing we can do. Without proof or her saying he did it—"

"Proof? You want proof?" Grant shouts. "Look at her cheek and lip. That's all the proof I need."

"It's her words we need to hear. We can't take her. We can't arrest him. We technically can't even be here since there wasn't even a call we were responding to! Nothing we charge him with will stick."

"I don't fucking care. When I leave here, she's either coming with me or she's going with someone from CPS. She is not going back in that house."

There is a determination in Grant's stance that matches the tone in his voice. The little girl in me roots for him. The grown woman in me can't tear her eyes away from him.

"You're too close, Malone."

"Did you see her face, Nate? That's not from the stairs. That's not from a fall. She's terrified. Of course she isn't going to rat her dad out. *He's her dad*!" He rakes his hand through his hair. "She still loves him regardless of how big a piece of shit he is. Then there's her mom, who sits by and lets it all happen. She's five. *Five*. Someone has to stand up for her, and fuck if I'm not going to be the one to do it."

"C'mon, man," the other officer says as she takes a step forward. "All you're doing is making a tense situation worse. We can stand out here all night long, but in the end, we're going to end up with the same result. Her back with her parents. Parental privilege."

"Just unlock the doors so we can get her out," Nate says, reaching out for Grant's arm, but he yanks it away.

"*Don't touch me*." The two men face off, inches apart, duty versus morality.

"Grant, think about what you're doing here," the other officer says to try to cool the tension.

"I know exactly what I'm doing. I'm protecting and serving. I'm upholding my oath. I think you're the ones who need to ask yourselves the same question." Grant looks back to the car and shakes his head in disbelief. "Let me just take her to the police station. I'll sit with her all night until CPS can fit her in their schedule tomorrow. Anything. It's better than her being here." There's a desperation in his voice that brings tears to my eyes.

The man who blames himself for not saving me is trying to save her.

"Her parents are one hundred feet away."

"And they like to hit their little girl," he says.

"They are threatening kidnapping charges. Really, Grant? Is it worth it? Is your career worth it?"

"Yes." The answer is instant and unwavering.

Nate's shoulders fall as he pinches the bridge of his nose before saying something I can't hear to the other officer and taking a few steps away. Grant takes a step toward Nate and then thinks better of stepping away from the car. "The only way I'm leaving her is if you arrest me."

Minutes pass as Grant stands guard. He looks into the back of his cruiser and makes funny hand signals. The entire time, his face is a mask of calm, when I know he's feeling anything but.

The onlookers around me buzz about the standoff between officers. Opinions flow freely. Bets are wagered. Comments about how the little girl always looks so sad.

But it's Grant I stare at. It's Grant I want to look my way. It's Grant

I want to know I think he's in the right.

Memories of when the police took me away for my evaluation ghost through my mind. The hard chairs. The white walls. The scary guns on belts I couldn't stop staring at. The perfectly sharpened crayons I made my drawing with. The constant fear that my mom was going to leave me there. Alone. The promise that she wouldn't.

Is Keely feeling any of this fear right now or is she just confused?

"I'm sorry, Grant, but I have to." Nate's voice startles me from the unexpected memory that has me shivering and pulling my arms around myself. He steps toward Grant, his hands going to his cuffs on his belt.

"Don't do it, Nate." Grant shakes his head.

"You've given me no choice. It's orders from the chief."

Grant stares at his partner as he reluctantly turns him around and pulls his hands behind his back. The first cuff clicks, and its then that Grant looks up.

It's as if he knows I'm there because he looks right at me. Our eyes lock, and I can see the fight in his gaze. The defiance. His want to be a hero for this little girl, and God, how I want him to save her. I want to wade through the ocean of emotion swelling between us and tell him he's standing for the right cause.

The cuff goes on his other wrist.

"I'm sorry," he mouths to me, and I don't know if he's apologizing for back then or for right now, but it doesn't matter. He doesn't have to apologize for anything.

Nate turns Grant so his back is to me and removes Grant's gun from its holster.

"Her blood will be on your hands," Grant says, causing Nate to falter; his statement making what his fellow officer has to do that much harder.

Nate pulls Grant's keys from his pocket and unlocks the cruiser, allowing the female officer to open the car door. The whole scene is hard to watch, but it's the look on Grant's face as he turns that breaks my heart.

Compassion. Grief. Anger. Disbelief. All four flash across his expression when Keely climbs out of the car. She's in a pink nightgown with a unicorn on the front of it. Her hair is a tangled mess, and she looks around shell-shocked at all of the strangers staring at her. Despite her hand being in the officer's, her eyes are big and terrified as they search for a familiar face.

I can sense her fear. Her confusion. Her uncertainty. And somehow, I remember the feeling of being lost in a maze of people when all I wanted was to be home curled in a ball on my bed.

Her terrified sob cuts through the air as she sees Grant and runs toward him, her arms wrapping around his thigh like he's her lifeline.

"Grant," I cry his name out, my heart shattering in a million pieces as she clings to him. And for a split second, he meets my eyes, and the look we exchange claws its way into my damaged soul and warns it that he's going to help heal it. The connection is quick and ends when he kneels down and says something in her ear.

Reassuring her.

Telling her it's all going to be okay when it isn't going to be.

Her life will forever be changed.

I remember the promise of a trip to Disneyland to try to dissipate the upheaval in my life. Every little kid loves Disney. I don't blame my mom for the fib, but I remember thinking back then how I didn't care where we went as long as she didn't leave me. And so long as my dad didn't come with us.

I'm jostled by the person behind me and it snaps me from the memory just in time to watch Nate grab Grant's elbow to help him stand. The female officer has the tough task of picking up a petrified five year old and walking her into a house that seems to be filled with fear instead of comfort.

Grant watches, too, defeat owning every part of him.

As Nate leads him to the police cruiser, opens the door, and guides his head so he doesn't hit it on the way in, Grant never once takes his eyes off Keely.

Officer Roberts slides behind the wheel, and the cruiser leaves with Grant in it.

I stare until I can't stare anymore.

I've only ever loved two men.

Both were taken away in handcuffs.

One because he hurt me.

The other because he tried to save her.

And in the end, save me.

SIXTY-FOUR

Grant

My dad pulls the blinds shut on each window in the conference room. As he pulls the cords, one by one, the metal slats drop down with a resonating thud. The sound of my fate being sealed.

"I'm being interrogated now? I thought you were retired." I'm being a sarcastic ass, but I'm tired, and fuck, if I care about this police department right now when "To Protect and Serve" feels like a baseless catchphrase.

"This is professional courtesy extended to me by Chief Ramos to let me come down here and level with my son over why he was put in handcuffs tonight. You do realize they could haul you off to booking and charge you with obstruction, right?"

I slump back in my chair and sigh like a ten-year-old kid waiting to have his ass handed to him. "By all means. Let's get this party started."

"Would you rather do this out in the precinct where everyone can hear me ask you what the fuck you were doing?"

"Does it really matter? They all know why you're here so . . . ask away." I direct every ounce of anger I feel over the situation toward my dad. It's unfounded, and he doesn't deserve it, but the only thing that would calm my nerves right now is to know that both Keely and Emerson are all right.

Keely for the obvious, and Emerson because the last time she saw Keely, it messed her up. She doesn't deserve to be messed up any more than she already is.

When the last blind falls, he takes his time moving around the conference table before sitting directly across from me.

"What the hell were you thinking?" he finally asks as his brow narrows and his eyes demand an answer.

"My job," I state matter-of-factly.

"Your job?"

"Don't come at me, Dad, with the holier than thou bullshit. I did what I had to do, and I'd do it again in a heartbeat. You're lucky I didn't do what I really wanted, which was to beat the shit out of him, because I don't think I would have been able to stop once I started. So, yeah, it's a lot better than the alternative could have been. It's been a rough night, so if you came to give me a lecture, thanks but no thanks. I'm not in the mood for one."

He sighs and leans back in his chair shaking his head. "What you did was incredibly stupid and profoundly valiant."

I grunt, not feeling too valiant at the moment since I didn't accomplish anything. "I don't think Ramos is going to look at it that way."

"Probably not." He raises his eyebrows. "What did he say?"

I shrug, not wanting to think about the consequences when the actions were damn well warranted. "I haven't spoken directly with him yet."

"You suspended?" he asks.

"For starters."

"Your promotion?"

I laugh. "Most likely gone, too. Insubordination and obstruction aren't exactly looked upon in a favorable light when you're competing for a promotion."

"True."

"Sorry I didn't live up to the Malone family standards," I say with sarcasm he doesn't deserve.

"I don't give a shit about the promotion, Grant," he says, irritated by my cheap shot. "I care that you stand by the right principles and make the right choices. I care that, at the end of the day, you can hold your head high. So you tell me, if you had to do it all over again, would you do the same thing?"

"In a heartbeat," I say without hesitation. "It was the right thing to do."

I think of Emerson highlighted by red and blue lights. The look on her face solidifying I was doing the right thing. Her presence telling me the time she needed is up.

God, I need to know she's okay, but instead, I'm locked in this damn room.

My dad continues to stare at me, study me, mull over the thoughts I can see clear as day in his eyes.

"This doesn't have anything to do Emerson, does it?"

"Christ, yes, it does," I say with a disbelieving laugh, nervous energy eating me up. Too anxious to sit still, I shove up from my chair and pace the length of the room.

"Is she worth risking your career over?" I fall silent at his question, knowing the answer and not knowing it all at the same time. Certainty versus uncertainty. My routine versus her chaos. Alone versus loved. "Grant?"

"I didn't save her," I say, not answering the question, my voice breaking as the one truth that has eaten at me over and over finally has a voice. "I was her best friend, and I knew she hated being at home . . . and I did not save her." The guilt is real and raw, and I know that every time I've seen Em suffer through something, was because I didn't help her in time. It's my fault.

If only I had saved her sooner . . .

My dad sighs as he approaches behind me, his hand patting me on the shoulder and then squeezing there. "You were eight, son. There was no way you could have known."

"But still . . ."

"If anyone is to blame it's me. She was in our house day in and day out. I was the chief of police for Christ's sake, and I didn't see the signs because monsters aren't supposed to be your son's friend's dad."

I know he speaks the truth, but it's also hard to let go of the feeling that I still failed. Emmy then and Keely now.

"I saw Emerson when I looked at Keely tonight," I confess with a shake of my head. His exhale is long and steady and says his assumptions were correct. "I've seen Emerson in her all along, but tonight . . . she opened the door and had a bruise on her cheek and blood on her lip, and I lost it. They had the same haunted eyes. The same timidity. All that was different was the hair color."

"In order for you to draw conclusions, should I assume you opened Emerson's case file?"

His words stop my feet in place. The fuckers. Gray and Grady told him what I did after promising me they wouldn't. So much for all for one and one for all. "You gonna ride me for that, too?" I snap.

"Just asked a question," he says in the calm, probing way of his that tells me he's nowhere near finished.

And the longer he stares at me, the shorter my fuse becomes, until finally, I give into the pressure to explain.

"No, Dad. I didn't open the file. At first, I wanted to. I thought if I could just see the things she faced, then it could help me know how to best approach her."

"And it was your right to do that? Shouldn't you have waited to see what she did or didn't tell you? Wasn't that her choice?"

"Christ, yes." I shove my hand through my hair, hating the next words and knowing damn well they are truth. "I was afraid I was going to *hurt her,* Dad. We were sleeping together. How am I to know if there's something that bastard did to her that is a trigger? Something stupid and simple, but if I did it unknowingly, it would affect her? I've seen enough of these cases to know the kids are scarred for life . . . so fucking sue me if my first thought was how to protect her. How not to hurt her. Fuck it," I say as I sit and then stand again. "I'm so sick of explaining this."

The intensity in my dad's eyes matches how I feel inside. "I commend you for caring enough about her to think that far ahead. I can understand where you are coming from . . . but she doesn't get to look inside your darkest secrets without your consent, so can you blame her for feeling violated that you did hers?"

"But that's the thing." I throw my hands up. "I never opened it. I thought better of it, even when she was pulling away from me, I thought better of it. I only saw the picture because it fell out of the folder when I moved it to get it out of the house, but it isn't like she believes me."

"Can you blame her?"

I scrub my hands over my face and sigh. "I don't blame her for anything, Dad. Not a damn thing."

"But it makes you feel better if you blame yourself?" He gives me the same slow measured nod he's given me my whole life. It's the one that tells me he thinks I'm being dense and is waiting for me to see what's right in front of me.

"*Better*? Seriously? You think I feel better knowing nothing I did tonight matters because Keely is back in her toxic house where who knows what is happening to her because I can't get CPS to make time to help her out?" I pace the room. "I have to sit here, knowing I probably threw gasoline on the fire. If something happens to her, you're damn right the blame is on me. Add to that, there's all the hard work, the overtime, the everything, I put into getting the promotion, and now my chances are fucked. If those aren't enough, I hurt Emerson. I violated her trust, and I don't know how the fuck to make it right again . . ." I push out a deep breath and try to think around the chaos in my heart. "So, yeah, I'll wear the blame like a goddamn coat, but it doesn't mean shit because I can't do anything about anything to make it all right again."

"The Keely situation. The department will do right by her. It might not be tonight, Grant, but you made a big enough scene—reporters and all—that CPS wouldn't risk not dealing with the situation because they'd take the blame. It may not feel like it made a difference tonight, but you got the ball rolling and the attention piqued . . . so you did what you had to do."

"Not soon enough," I grumble but take a little bit of what he says to heart. Maybe I did make a difference.

"And the promotion." He shakes his head. "I'm not Chief Ramos, but I have walked in his shoes a time or two. You were technically in the wrong, but if the department is smart, they'll take the attention and turn it into good PR. With all the bad cop stories surfacing constantly, they'll have no problem highlighting how they had an officer who went above and beyond to protect and serve."

"I don't want the limelight dad. I just want my job." I sigh.

"You'll still have it. Take the suspension, enjoy the time off. I wouldn't be surprised if that promotion is yours within six months to a year. If it isn't, then it isn't. You still get to do what you love every day. There will be other chances."

I murmur in agreement, having a hard time believing him when I'm in the midst of the chaos.

"And then there's Emerson. She should be hurt by what you did. Intent matters, but it isn't all that matters. You know that. So, all she knows is your intent, even though she doesn't know your reasons behind it. You violated her privacy, Grant. It'll take time, but you'll redeem yourself."

The sound of Em's voice when she called out my name tonight rings in my ears.

Maybe I redeemed myself a bit already. If I did, it wasn't intentional, but then again, neither was loving her.

"Just remember when you're building a relationship, you need to hear what the other person *isn't* saying. Those are the words that are the most important."

I remember the look she gave me tonight. The pride and the pain. The will and the want. The apology and the blame. So many unspoken words I heard loud and clear.

"Do you love her?" The sincerity in his question throws me.

But the honesty in my answer does even more so. "Yeah, I do."

I'm not sure what I expected his reaction to be, but he just nods as if my answer is no surprise to him and gets a soft smile on his lips. “Then these little blips will be worth it. You’ll recover from the fallout. She’ll forgive you.”

“Trust is a hard thing to earn back.”

“Agreed.” He gives a measured nod. “But remember, you don’t need to know the details of her past to love her heart in the present.”

I fall silent as I mull his words over and know they are truer than I care to admit. I think of all I’ve done thus far to prove to her I want her to stay and all the things I haven’t even gotten to show her yet.

“You’ve always loved that girl,” he says softly, as if he’s remembering back, and I wish I could, but so many of my memories are of her not being there. “Have you told her yet?”

“I’m not sure she’s ready to hear it.”

Or maybe I’m afraid that, if she does, she’ll run.

“You don’t give her enough credit. She’s tougher than you think, and maybe that’s where you’ve underestimated her. You have to be all in or get all out. There is no halfway when it comes to love.”

There’s nothing I can say in response so I watch as he walks to the door of the conference room. “And there’s no time like the present since she’s been sitting out in the waiting room for the past several hours.”

“What?”

“Ramos told me you were free to go when I was done with you.”

SIXTY-FIVE

Emerson

THE LIGHTS OF THE PASSING CARS GLANCE ACROSS GRANT'S face as he drives to his house. They paint a vivid picture of the emotions roiling beneath the surface.

Or so I can guess.

Because other than saying, "Let's go," before he grabbed my hand and led me from the police station, he hasn't said a word.

He's been on autopilot. Get in the car. Start it. Seatbelt. Drive in silence—the pulsing of the muscle in his jaw, the flexing of his hands from gripping the steering wheel so tight, the dancing of his eyes between his mirrors and the road. Pull in the driveway. Park.

The house is dark when we enter, silent except for the sounds of our breathing, and we stand facing each other for the longest of moments.

We don't speak.

We don't move.

We just accept what has happened without ever exchanging a single word.

We absorb the moment and the weight of it.

That I'm here. In his house. Willing to trust him again.

We can barely see each other's eyes in the darkness, and yet, I can tell how emotionally drained he is from tonight and how emotionally stripped he is for me.

Without preamble or pretext, he makes the first move when he steps forward and pulls me into his arms. And just like that, we cling to each other as if we can't get close enough.

"Grant, I—"

"Shh," he says right before slanting his lips over mine. "Please." Another brush of a kiss. "I just need you, Em. Now. Here. All of you."

His lips are on mine again. It's the same man kissing me, but it feels so very different this time around. Something has shifted between us, changing us intrinsically without changing us at all.

It's just him. And me.

No past.

No future.

Just the moment.

I get lost in his kiss. In the feel of his skin and the taste on his tongue. In the unspoken need and unchecked desire.

We don't walk to the bedroom. We remove our clothes in subtle movements, as if we're afraid to ruin the magnitude of the moment, and lower ourselves to the rug.

We react in sighs and moans.

We feel in emotions.

We revel in the connection.

We make love for the first time.

SIXTY-SIX

Emerson

I WATCH HIM.

The sun is barely peeking over the horizon, but I can't sleep.

And haven't been able to.

My mind won't shut off. I try to process everything that has happened in the last twenty-four hours.

I see Keely and the terrified look on her face and wonder if she slept last night. Did she have nightmares? Was she scared of the dark? Will someone show up today and make sure she's okay? In ten days? In six months?

I try to come to terms with the fact that the whole reason I came to Sunnyville is now gone. I wonder what I should do next. If I should let the wind blow me wherever it wishes.

But there's Grant.

I attempt to wrap my head around how I feel about the man snoring softly beside me. I itch to reach out and touch him, make sure the mix of emotions I feel are real, but if they're not, I don't want to ruin them with reality. They're scary and euphoric and I don't think I'm built to handle this.

I revel in how it felt last night to make love to him. To feeling closer to him than I've ever felt before without us having to utter a single word. To moving from the floor to the bed where he gathered me in his arms and didn't let go. To how it took well over an hour for his breathing to even out while I wondered what he could possibly be thinking about.

The clock tells me I need to get to work, my first class is coming in just over two hours, but when I pull open the covers, he reaches out and tugs me against him, my back to his front.

"Uh-uh," he murmurs as the heat of his body warms me in more ways than one.

Sinking into the feel of him, I'm reminded immediately of his raw and honest need last night. I settle my hands atop his on my waist and fill the silence. "Are we going to talk about last night?"

He rests his forehead against the back of my head. "What's there to talk about?"

"Well . . ."

"I did what I had to do, and it wasn't enough."

"It was everything," I say as tears spring to life. "You gave her hope, Grant, when hope is a scarce commodity for her. You showed her there are men willing to protect her instead of hurt her. And while she may have gone back into her house last night because that was what the law demanded, you also made it so no one will ignore her again."

"I didn't save her," he says, the statement holding so much weight in it.

"But you did. You let her know she's worth something." I link my fingers with his and pull his hand up to my lips so I can press a kiss to his knuckles. "You can't go around saving every little girl because you see me. It's honorable. It's admirable. It fills my heart in ways you could never imagine. It's why—" *I love you.*

I can't say the words aloud just yet, their power too much for even me to handle right now.

"Why, what?"

"It's . . . why you need to stop blaming yourself. What happened to me was not your fault. You couldn't have stopped it if you tried. It was my dad's fault. I've accepted that, and I'll continue to deal with accepting it the rest of my life . . ." I fumble with getting the things out

I need to say so that he can stop beating himself up over this. So that we can move forward. "My dad stole so much from me, but I learned a long time ago that I can either let it define me or I can let it fuel me. I choose to let it fuel me, Grant. I choose not to let the fear own me or deprive me of what every woman deserves. Happiness. Some thrills. A good sex life.

"Am I perfect? No. Are there days when a new memory comes back and I'm rattled for a bit? Yes. But when it comes right down to it, I can't keep moving forward, I can't keep *chasing the moment*, if those around me who know about it keep looking to my past to manage expectations. That's not fair to me."

"You don't need to know the details of her past to love her heart in the present," he murmurs . . . or at least that's what I think he does because he says it almost to himself before pressing a kiss to my shoulder.

The words hit my ears nonetheless and give me hope that he heard and understands where I'm coming from.

"I didn't open the file, Emerson."

"I believe you." *And I do.*

"And I'll always blame myself for not saving you—I've been told it's called a hero complex or something." I can feel his mouth curve into a smile as he presses it against my shoulder. "But I'll use it to help others."

I snuggle in closer against him. My head is finally quiet, allowing me to fall into a dreamless sleep.

I wake with a start. For a minute I'm disoriented, but then I realize Grant's still behind me, arm draped over my waist.

Crap.

"I have to get to work," I say but make zero attempts to move.

"Call in sick," he says in a sleep-drugged voice that sounds as tempting as his morning hard-on pressing against my backside feels.

It has never sounded more appealing than right now. "I can't."

"You're picking work over me?" He chuckles.

"I'm picking money over you."

"Pretty soon, the place will be yours, so does it really matter if you're there today or not?"

The pang is instant. Having to speak the words aloud even more painful. "I didn't get the loan."

His body stiffens before he untangles himself from around me and sits up. "What did you say?"

"I didn't get the loan."

His face falls from shock to worry. "What does that mean?"

I slide out of bed. "It means I need to earn my paycheck while I can because I don't know who bought Blue Skies or what they intend to do with it, if anything. For all I know, they're going to raze the place and put something else in its spot."

"Em . . . I don't know what to—"

"There's nothing you can say. It's okay. Really. I'll figure something else out." I force a tight smile, always mindful of how my life goes from one extreme to the next, as I pull on my clothes. I haven't really even had time to process it all, so talking about it makes me itchy.

"If it's a money thing, Em . . . you know I'll—"

"Thanks, but from what I overheard in the station last night, you're suspended, so I assume you're not making a paycheck, either." I shrug and pull my shirt over my head. "I'm a big girl, Grant. I—"

"Can handle yourself," he finishes for me.

SIXTY-SEVEN

Grant

"Chief Ramos," I say, shocked to see his name on my cell. "This is an unexpected surprise."

"So is what you did," he says.

"What can I do for you?" I will not apologize, not even to my boss, for my actions.

"I know you talked to Deputy Chief Castro last night, but I have to give you the official company line. What you did was wrong. You went against protocol. Became the scene instead of managed it. Yadda, yadda, yadda. You got all that?"

"Sure," I say, biting back my smile at his cavalier attitude.

"Good. Now I can say what I want to say, off the record, of course."

"Of course, sir."

"You've caused quite a stir around here. So much so, that I have to have an official investigation, but before it even begins, I can tell you the results will be inconclusive. Were you in the wrong? Yes. Is there anything to charge you with or permanently ding your record with? No." I stand, suddenly needing to move. "Your suspension ends in five days, should I assume you'll be back here the following Monday?"

"What?" This is not what I expected. I expected weeks of internal affairs dragging their feet while I sat home, twiddling my thumbs bored out of my mind.

"Monday? Yes or no?"

"Yes. Definitely yes."

"Good. Now that I have your attention, I need to go over a few other things. Once reinstated you are not allowed to answer any calls—or non-calls—to the Davis residence."

"How is she?" I ask.

"Why are you so attached to this little girl, Malone?"

"She reminds me of someone I once knew." I think of Emerson's words yesterday as she lay in my arms. *Define or fuel*. She chooses fuel.

"She and her mother have been moved to a battered woman's home. They are undergoing counseling there for a bit while their family in Oregon makes arrangements for them to come live with them."

"And the dad?"

"We can't win every battle, Grant. We have to take the victories when we get them and hope the good guys win out the next time."

So, if I can't frequent the Davis residence, that means he still lives there. Still able to meet another woman and mistreat her the same way. The endless cycle.

But Keely is safe.

Keely is saved.

What I did mattered.

"I need your word that you'll avoid the residence in question?"

"Yes, sir."

"Good. Now, on to the promotion. I'm sorry, but I had to give it to Stetson," he says, regret heavy in his voice. "You were clearly the better candidate for the job, but I can't reward insubordination."

"It's on me," I say. Just because I knew this was coming, it doesn't make the sting of it any easier to take.

"It is," he agrees, "but that doesn't mean you can't go for it next time the position opens."

"Thank you, sir."

"Monday, Malone."

"Monday."

I end the call and put my hands on my hips as I look around my house and try to digest what I just heard.

It's good news.

It's great news, in fact.

Especially considering what I'm trying to pull off.

Glancing down at the papers scattered all over my table, I know I can't do this alone. I've been trying to these past few days, and now I need to kick it into overdrive.

I pull up my contacts on my phone and hit dial.

"If it isn't Officer Sexy."

"I need your help, Desi."

SIXTY-EIGHT

Emerson

"SERIOUSLY? THAT QUICK?" I LOOK AT TRAVIS, WHO'S standing in front of my desk, and my jaw falls lax.

"I know. I'm sorry. I tried for more but—"

"Thank you for getting me the two extra months. That's better than immediately." I force a smile as the bottom drops out and reality hits.

Not only is my job most likely going to be gone—because who knows what's going to happen since the new owner hasn't said—but my apartment is, too. I have two months and a savings I know will be gone before I can blink an eye.

"You okay, Em?" Leo asks after Travis leaves the office, shoulders sagging, to begin his task of emptying out the old owner's belongings to make way for the new owner's stuff.

"As okay as okay can be given the situation, I guess." I sigh. "I'm just having a hard time wrapping my head around the fact that this is all over. I've never stayed in one place for this long. I've never thought about tomorrows and futures, and it's like when I finally did, the universe tells me to quit adulting."

He chuckles, but the lines etched in his face tell me he's worried, too. "I'm sorry. I know that slimy bastard had something to do with it. You should have let me punch him, you know."

"You know what they say about hindsight."

He lifts his eyebrows and nods. "We could always try to start something ourselves. We could get Sully to fly for us. He'd give us a decent rate to bring people up. We wouldn't need much. Just some gear and a place to teach."

"I know. I've thought about it, too, but the insurance . . . that would kill us. There's no way we could take in enough to cover all the expenses, and I obviously can't get a loan . . . so, it's a good thought. Thanks for the vote of confidence, Leo." I smile through the hurt.

"I hear they're hiring at Fly High. Their crew had some infractions, so they're looking for a flight instructor and jump coordinator." He nods as he says the words, but I know we're both thinking the same thing: That's two hours away. "We could go as a package. Buy it out some day and make it our own."

"It's a possibility," I say, but my heart squeezes in my chest at the thought of leaving Sunnyville. Of leaving Grant. "Look at both of us getting old." I laugh. "I used to bail at the first sign of commitment."

"And I used to chase the next new city, the next great jump." He chuckles as he looks down at his hands for a moment before looking back to me. "Chasing the adrenaline rush does have that gypsy, will-jump-for-food type of personality it seems we both have."

"Maybe we should say *had* since now we're hesitating."

"True, but hesitating doesn't pay the bills."

"Maybe the new owner will pull through," I say, holding out hope.

"Or maybe he just bought it for the real estate and doesn't give a damn about Blue Skies and is going to demo it."

"Yeah. That thought has crossed my mind, too."

"Would it be so hard for the Skies to tell us if we have a future or not?"

"They don't care. They haven't cared about this place for a long time. Money is all they think about."

And that's the thought that is depressing.

Because I cared. Because I would have put the blood, sweat, and tears into making it work.

Even things that are worn down and ugly deserve love.

SIXTY-NINE

Grant

THE COLD AIR HITS ME AS I WALK INTO SUNNYVILLE TRUST and Loan. I stop just inside and look around the place.

"Hi. How can I help you today?" the receptionist asks in an overly cheerful voice.

"I'm looking for—" And right when I say the words, I see him. The fucker is standing in an office in the back corner of the space, hands on his hips, back to me. "Never mind."

"Sir, you can't go back there!" I walk past her despite her protests and stride across the lobby. "Sir. *Sir*. Christopher!"

He turns around at the sound of his name, words fading, just as I enter his office. "Freddy, I'll call you right back."

Christopher pulls his Bluetooth earpiece off in a slow, measured movement while keeping his eyes locked on mine.

"Can I help you?" he asks, brow furrowed and a ghost of a smile on his lips that says he knows exactly who I am. The fucking bastard.

"Yes, you can." I laugh, but there is nothing even close to humor in its sound as I take a step toward him.

He takes a step back.

We continue this dance until he bumps against the wall at his back. I step well within his personal space so that I can smell the coffee on his breath and hear his startled gasp.

"How many clients did you threaten today, *Chris*? How many

women did you tell that if they didn't meet you for drinks, *if they didn't sleep with you*, that you would pull their application or sabotage their loan? Huh, *Chris*?" I'm as close as I can be without touching him.

"Malone . . ."

"That's Officer Malone to you. Does it make you feel like a big man to play God with other people's dreams, *Chris*? Do you get off on their fear?"

"I do-don't know what you-you're talking about."

"Oh, but that's where you're wrong. You know exactly what I'm talking about." I shake my head very slowly, stretching the silence to unnerve him as much as possible. "Does the name Emerson Reeves ring a bell?"

His eyes widen, and his quick intake of breath is audible. "I'm not at liberty to discuss my clients or their applications."

"Funny how you become so professional all of a sudden when you've been anything but to her." I reach up quickly to scratch my chin and love when he flinches. The asshole should be scared.

"What do you want?"

"You will never, and I repeat, *never*, talk to Emerson, approach her, deal with her, or contact her in any way shape or form again." Our height difference allows me to look down at him with a threatening glare that makes my words more than clear. "And if you do, you'll have to deal with me. And *my whole* police department." That one little lie isn't going to hurt anyone.

He nods rapidly, his eyes blink, and his face turns red.

"And if I catch wind of you ever threatening another woman's loan because they won't sleep with you . . ." I shake my head and chuckle, long and low, as his Adam's apple bobs with his swallow. "The Sunnyville district attorney is a close, personal friend. I'm pretty sure this place would have to shut down after all the legal fees you'll incur trying to defend yourself from the dozens of charges she could pin on you." I take a step back with a cocky grin and cuff him on the side of his shoulder. "Did I make myself clear?"

The same nod again.

"I need to hear it."

"Yes."

"Yes, Officer Malone," I say and wait for him to repeat it.

"Yes, Officer Malone."

"Not so brave now, are you?" He just stares at me without speaking as the armpits of his dress shirt stain dark with sweat. "Good, then this little chat is done."

With another flash of a smile, I turn on my heel and feel pretty damn good with myself.

Time to go pay Leo back with a cold beer. *Or ten*. Thanks to his phone call earlier, I knew where to go to put this asshole in his place.

SEVENTY

Emerson

"THIS IS DEPRESSING,"

Desi sighs from her spot beside me on the top step of my stairs that lead into my apartment. We are currently watching the small crane lift the Blue Skies sign off the top of the office. "I wish there were something I could do."

"There isn't." I take a sip of wine from my red Solo cup. "Sometimes you chase the dream and you catch it, other times you fall short." The words sound good in theory, but they feel like shit when they're reality.

"Are you really going to leave me?" she asks.

And leave Grant.

"What am I supposed to do, Des? In a month, I'm out of a place to live, and I don't have a paycheck coming in to pay rent."

"Easy. You move in with me."

"Thanks. You know I appreciate the offer, but then what? Where do I work? I'm not qualified to do anything other than jump. Sure, I could try, but being chained to a desk . . . not having that rush? It would kill me."

"Then maybe you do something else for a bit—help me with Doggy Style—and wait to see what happens out here with whoever bought this place. They might need help. It might not be jumping, but at least you'd be where you're comfortable."

"I couldn't do that to you."

"Pride doesn't pay the bills, Em."

"Neither does killing your spirit.

"The offer still stands."

"Thanks. It's generous of you, but how long can I hang on? It's as if I've spent all this time dreaming of making this place my own, and now that I have the idea, I don't want to settle. *I shouldn't have to settle.*"

"Have you told him?" Desi says, lifting her chin to Grant's car, which is heading down the highway toward us.

"Told him what?"

"That you love him? That you're leaving? Either or."

Tears spring in my eyes at just her words. "No to both," I whisper.

"I figured as much. You want to tell me why not?"

I shrug, my mental turmoil over the past few days returning. "He's been super busy. Doing all kinds of stuff for the chief to make amends for his suspension."

"Ah, so the truth comes out. You haven't been hanging out with me because I'm your first pick, but rather because you don't have him to hang out with. I don't do well being sloppy seconds." She laughs, and I know this is her way of trying to add levity, but I don't smile. "So he's been so busy you couldn't tell him you were going to leave? That sounds more like chicken shit to me than anything."

"I'm scared to," I say as his cruiser pulls into the parking lot. I know we still have time to talk because he usually has paperwork to finish before clocking off shift.

"Why? Because once you say it, you can't take it back? Or is it because once you tell him you're planning to leave, he's going to lose his ever-loving mind? My bet is you're avoiding telling him you love him but you aren't *in love with him* enough to stick around to save yourself from that hurt?" She purses her lips and gives me an I-don't-believe-a-word-you're-saying look. "Self-preservation."

"It isn't like I'm not going to try to make it work. I'll drive back on weekends—"

"Which are the busiest days for jumps."

"I'll make my off days match his so we can be together."

"Easier said than done."

"Desi, I love him, damn it. I want to make this work. I'm doing the best I fricking can, so stop the guilt trip, will you?"

She smiles. "I know you do. I also know you run when you're scared. You put the pedal to the metal and race the wind and follow wherever it takes you . . . but I'm calling you on it this time. I'm holding you accountable. I'm not letting you leave us without knowing the exact day you are coming back . . . and it better be less than seven."

"It's only temporary."

She stands, saying, "It better be," before walking down the stairs without looking back and stopping when she reaches Grant in the parking lot. She laughs about something, and there's an easiness between them—my lover and my best friend—that tells me I've built something here. A family. A place I belong. Every part of me wishes things didn't have to change.

I watch the crane lift the old sign, its beeping filling the air as it swings it to the far side of the building, and I hate it. Everything about it.

As Grant heads in my direction, I make my way down the stairs.

"Are you ready for date night?" he asks as he closes the distance. "I just have to change real quick and I'll be—what's that?" he asks as he notices the storage containers stacked at the bottom of the stairs.

"Hi." I pull him toward me and kiss him hello with an unexpected desperation that suddenly feels so real.

I don't want to lose him.

I don't want to lose this feeling.

But I also don't want to lose who I am.

"Whoa. Well, if that's the kind of greeting I get when I come here when my shift ends, then I'll be here every day at this time." He chuckles against my lips as I just pull him into me and hold on tighter.

How am I going to tell him?

How am I going to convince him I'm not going gypsy?

"Em, I can put these with my shit when I take this trip . . ." Leo says as he turns the corner, his words trailing off when he sees Grant standing in front of me.

"Trip to where?" Grant asks as he takes notice that the containers are labeled as kitchen, desk, and bathroom. Grant looks from me to Leo and then back to me. "What the hell is going on, Emerson?" He's already shaking his head, rejecting the notion that he already knows.

"That's what I wanted to talk to you about tonight," I say, my voice barely audible. In my periphery, I see Leo slowly slink away and wish I could go with him. If the look on Grant's face is any indication, our date night is about to turn into a blowout fight.

"You're not going anywhere!" The workers pulling down the sign turn to look at us, prompting him to grab my wrist and all but drag me up the stairs so we can have privacy, which is a huge mistake. When he enters my flat and sees everything stacked in partially filled boxes, the hurt is written all over his face.

I could have played it off before. I had planned to tell him I was prepping for the end of the month, but him seeing Leo and knowing Leo is moving on to Fly High is all he needs to draw the conclusion.

He stares at me, a plethora of emotions flickering through those brown eyes of his and every single one of them—hurt, disappointment, disbelief—is paralyzing. "Were you going to tell me, Em? Or were you going to leave in the middle of the night like a gypsy because you were too scared to face me?"

"I told you I was going to tell you tonight." I take a step toward him. "It isn't what you're thinking, Grant."

"It isn't? What exactly am I thinking, then?"

"I'm a restless soul. Blue Skies was my chance to settle, and now it's gone. The new owner hasn't said boo, and for all I know, they're going to raze the place. They've already cleaned out the hangar. It's written on the wall, my days here are limited."

"You don't know what the new owners are going to do. They're already starting to make changes, taking the sign down, what have you. You have a month left on your rent, why not stay here and see what happens first?"

"In theory, it sounds good. But everything sounds good in theory. If it is a new flight school, that takes time to set up. Certifications, insurance . . . I can't wait around for six months to see if I can start my life again," I murmur, as if speaking the words softly will make them hurt him less.

"What about me, Emerson? What about us?" The way he says it—the hurt emanating off every word—makes it hard for me to think.

"We'll make it work. It's only temporary. Hopefully, this will be a flight school and I can come back and figure out a new dream to chase, but in the meantime, it's only two hours away. There are days off and phone calls and FaceTime. We'll make it work." I'm pretty much begging for him to believe me, but the look on his face says he's not convinced.

"It isn't the same, and you know it."

"I know, but it's doable."

"What if I told you that you're not going? That I'm not going to let you go."

Every part of me surges with his words, already knowing he wants me to stay but still needing to hear it. I chuckle. "Then I'd tell you that you know me well enough to know the quickest way to get me to do something is to tell me I can't."

"Is it that hard for you to need someone, Em? Is it that hard for you to need me?"

"No." I'm just so conditioned not to need anything from anyone that my heart twists at the lie buried under all the truth in that one word.

"Then need me, damn it. Use me." I watch the hurt manifest itself to anger. "Stay at my house. Live with me while *we* figure this out. Do anything but run away because running away is the chicken shit way to deal with this situation."

There's the second time in ten minutes I've been called that.

"I'm not running, Grant."

"You sure about that?" His eyes bore into mine as everything about him screams defeat.

"I'm sure."

"Good, then you won't mind if I do this," he says as he steps forward and, before I can even process what he's doing, slaps a handcuff on my wrist and the other on his. "See? It's that simple. You're not going."

And just as quickly as my heart breaks, my temper fires. "Are you kidding me? What are you doing?"

"Did you really think I was going to let you go without a fight? I've lost you once before, Em. You're out of your mind if you think I'm going to let it happen again." Every part of me melts at his words and wants to surrender right here, right now to whatever he asks. I remember the emptiness I felt when I left him before. I remember how lonely I was, and I don't want that ever again.

"So, you're going to handcuff me?" I shriek, eyes wide and disbelief reigning. Amid the stubborn anger I have rioting inside me, a small piece of me wants to laugh at him. This is so *us* that it's ridiculous. But I can't. I won't. At least not outwardly.

"This is just insurance to make sure you're true to your word."

"My word?"

"That you're not running. So see?" He holds our hands up. "Now you can't."

I try to yank my hand away and am met with the bite of cold steel. The smirk he gives me and the feel of the metal is fuel to my temper. "The harder you fight against me, the closer I'm going to pull you."

"Let me go." Doesn't he know he's won?

He takes a step into me so his face is inches from mine, and as angry as I am at him, all I see are his lips. All I can think about is losing him. "This isn't how a relationship works, Emerson. You don't get to decide for yourself anymore. You talk to me. We discuss. Sometimes we fight. But in the end, we decide—*together*. Simple as that."

"And you think kidnapping me is the right way to go about that?" Despite the bite of pain I know it will cause, I yank my hand again, but this time it's more for show than out of anger. The look in his eyes and the determination in his words . . . how could a sane girl walk away from a man that resolute in his love for her?

"No, but apparently, it's the only way when it comes to reasoning with you." He quirks an eyebrow. "Do you think it'll be weird brushing our teeth like this? Or how about going to the bathroom. That might cause some problems." He chuckles and walks over to the couch without telling me so I'm forced to trail behind as he sits and puts his feet on the coffee table. "I could get used to this, couldn't you?" Then he gets back up and walks to the windows overlooking the backside of the airstrip, forcing me to follow again. He turns one way to pull me and then back the other way.

"You're infuriating, you know that?" I say, trying to stand my ground when I'm not really sure what we are fighting about anymore. "We're talking about the same thing here."

"No. We're not. You're talking about going, and I'm talking about you staying. That's as different as night and day."

"It would be temporary."

"I don't do temporary. See?" he says, lifting our hands again. "I like sure things."

"I am not running," I grit out. "I didn't want this. I didn't want to lose the loan and have to leave. I wanted roots for the first time in forever. I want you damn it. That's all I really want. You and my jump school. That's it. So, stop turning this on me. Stop acting as if this is all about me. *I love you*, and as much as that scares the shit out of me, not having you terrifies me even more. *You win*. Tell me what you want me to do, and I'll stay." I heave in a huge breath because I used it all. When I look at him, he's blurry because tears are in my eyes, and I don't care. This . . . he and I . . . is what matters.

But his fingers on his handcuffed hand link with mine. He stares at me, eyes blinking, a ghost of a smile on his lips and relief easing the lines etching his features.

"It's about time," he whispers.

"What?" My head spins from the mental whiplash.

"I don't need convincing about how you feel about me, Em. Hell, I don't even need the words. I already knew. I just needed you to know. I needed you to admit it. I needed you to believe it. You're the most honest when your back is against the wall . . . so, I pushed your shoulders some to get it there."

"You maneuvered me."

"I believe the correct term is positioning," he says as his smile inches up a bit more. I want to be indignant that he can read me so well, that he knows me so well. And then I realize that I told him I loved him. He sees it the minute it hits me and reaches out to pull me against him.

"It's okay to need me, Em. It's okay to love me. God knows I think I've been in love with you since we were six years old. You're maddening and frustrating and stubborn and the biggest challenge I've ever faced, but seeing you is the best part of my day and where you are is the only place I want to spend my nights. Losing the loan was a curve in the road we didn't see coming. But you like to speed, so we can ride this out. We adjust the wheel and take the curve. We talk, and then we work together to create another dream for you to chase." He leans forward and presses his lips to mine in a kiss to rival all kisses that I feel all the way out to the tips of my toes and back. "Two hours is too far away from me when we have twenty years to make up for . . . so, please trust me when I say we can make this work. Trust me when I tell you that making this work might be the hardest thing we ever do, but the payoff will be worth it and then some."

I'm rendered speechless. I open my mouth to speak but know words won't do any justice. So, instead, I press my lips against his.

"I love you."

God, it feels good to say it.

To know it.

To know it's returned and then some.

Grant Malone loves me.

We stand like this for a few minutes before there's a honk of a horn somewhere outside that interrupts our moment.

"Seeing those boxes really upset me," he admits. "Can we bring them inside now? Can we tell Leo you're not going?"

I roll my eyes and shake my head at the silly request after such a poignant moment between us. "If it makes you feel better."

My laugh turns to a shriek when, without warning, Grant swoops down and picks me up and hauls me over his shoulder, our handcuffed hands making it a tad more difficult.

"What are you doing?" I laugh.

"I told you, we're going to get the boxes."

"Right now? Wouldn't it be easier if we had both of our hands free?"

He smacks me on the ass. "Yeah, but I kinda need you to get used to the fact that you aren't going anywhere before I take them off."

"You're being ridiculous. After what you just said to me, any woman would be stupid to walk away."

"That's good to hear." He laughs as he makes his way down the stairs. "But it doesn't hurt to have a little insurance." He sets me down on the ground and then says, "And a backup plan."

"A backup plan?" I ask, using my free hand to flip my hair out of my eyes so I can see. And when I can, he lifts his chin in the direction over my shoulder.

I turn to look at what he's talking about and blink. It takes a few seconds for it all to register. To understand what it means.

The new sign on top of the office. It's a deep purple with the words "Wings Out" written in some fancy font atop a pilot's wings.

"Grant?" I take a few steps forward, my free hand to my chest, my lips parted, my mouth dry, and my mind spinning.

The door opens, and I watch all the important people in my life walk out. Desi. Leo. Grayson. Grady. The Malones. Sully. Travis. One by one, they file out and stand beneath the new sign.

I blink several times to make sure I'm really seeing what I'm seeing. "Grant?" I ask again as I look at him standing beside me.

"It isn't a painted zombie rock, but I think it will make you happy all the same."

"This can't be . . ."

"My backup plan." His smile is wide as his eyes dance with excitement.

"What did you do?"

"I've been doing a lot of overtime for the department, so I figured why not use it as a down payment on a new business venture. It's always been a dream of mine to own a business. You know, have something to fall back on when I retire from the force."

"Grant," I say his name again as I shake my head in disbelief. I must be freaking dreaming right now.

"I have some confessions to make," he murmurs as he shifts and wraps his arms around me from behind as we both stand and stare at the new sign. "They were all in on it. Every single one of them, even poor Leo. I haven't been working late because of the station, I've been madly scrambling to convince the owners of Blue Skies I'd be a better fit than the backup offer they were just about to sign on. That, and paying them a little above asking price had them changing their tune on which person they thought would be the best buyer. Then I had to get paperwork for loan docs. Desi was enlisted to keep you busy and away from my house. Leo has known for the last few days and played along so he didn't spoil the surprise."

"So, there is no Fly High?"

"There is, but not with you two. I've already called them and told them you wouldn't be showing up."

"Grant . . . I don't know what to say."

"You don't have to say anything."

"I need to say everything." I laugh as none of this sinks in.

"No, you said all I needed to hear upstairs." He presses a kiss to the back of my head as Leo whoops at something, and Desi's cackle rings across the tarmac.

"This is too much, Grant. I can't—the money—"

"I figured I didn't need a new patio after all."

"But you put in all that overtime."

He shrugs sheepishly. "I assumed if you had a place of your own, you'd be stuck with me. You can't go gypsy when you have roots. And

I want you to have roots, Em. Here. With me. Ones that tangle with mine and can never be ripped out. Lazy Sunday together ones and white picket fence ones."

"I'm stunned. Shocked. Overwhelmed."

"This is yours, Em. Your school. Your dream. Yours. My dream has always been you, and I have you. Your dream is the school, and now you have it. Oh, but there's one caveat."

"Anything," I say, still thinking I need to pinch myself.

"The new owner says it's against code to have someone living in the hangar."

"He does, does he?" If I could smile any wider, I would.

"Yeah, he's a stubborn SOB, so I don't think I can get him to change his mind . . . but I happen to know one half of a king-sized bed that's unoccupied."

"I snore."

"I know." He laughs.

I turn to face him for the first time and know I could never repay him for what he's given me. The safety. The security. The love. The friendship. The humor. The opportunity.

"I'll pay you back. I'll work harder than—"

"I'll count on it," he murmurs as he presses his lips against mine.

"I'll sign an agreement to—"

Another kiss.

"No worries, I have insurance." He laughs as he holds our handcuffed hands up. "You're not going anywhere."

EPILOGUE

Emerson

Eighteen Months Later . . .

THE CITY'S LIGHTS BEGIN TO COME ALIVE AS THE NIGHT grows darker. I sit and stare at them because it's all I can really do since Grant is sitting solemnly beside me without saying a word.

"Do you want to talk about it?" I ask, knowing the case he's investigating has been upsetting him. He won't admit it, but it's in his snap of temper and silence when he comes home after work.

It's taken some getting used to him being a detective and having cases to become invested in versus his old job where he responded to a call and then left.

"I'm fine."

When he asked if I wanted to take a drive and we ended up here, I wasn't surprised. His thinking place. His temporary solace.

"When you look at those lights," he finally says, voice gruff and eyes fixed ahead, "what do you think of?"

I look at him with a narrowed brow and try to figure out where he's going with this. We've been up here dozens of times, and this is the first time he's ever asked me that.

"I think each light tells a story of the person living beneath it."

He nods slowly and falls silent again for a bit. "You know what I think? I think each one of those lights represents someone's dream. Sometimes they flicker and fade and die out, and other times they grow brighter and stay lit forever."

I startle at his statement, finding his thoughts to be quite profound. "I like that," I say softly and lean my head gently on his shoulder.

Grant points to the far west where the skyline is lit up with lights. "What dream does that sparkle over there represent for you?" he asks.

"There are thousands of them." I laugh. "How do I know which one you're pointing at?"

"Just pick one."

I do as he says and stare at it for a beat before I answer. "Wings Out. That's definitely Wings Out because it's the brightest one."

He nods in acceptance of my answer. "And the sparkle over there?" He points to the east.

I play along and pick one out and stare at it. "That's happiness. I never thought I'd find it and I have. You've helped me find it."

"And that sparkle?" he points straight ahead of us.

"Wait. That's not fair. It's my turn to ask." I pick a location he hasn't done yet and point. "What dream of yours does that sparkle represent?"

He falls quiet for a moment as if he's deep in thought. "*You.*"

"What? *Oh.* Grant. That's so sweet." I press my lips to his shoulder, my heart a jumbled mess of love for the man beside me.

"What about that sparkle over there?"

"You." I smile, wanting to return the comment because I really do feel that way.

"Nope, you can't steal my idea. I get to win the romance award tonight," he says and chuckles as he presses a kiss to the top of my head. "Pick another dream."

"Hm. It's stupid and isn't realistic . . ." I begin to explain.

"It's a dream, Emmy, there is no such thing as reality. There's just possibility. What is it?"

"That no one ever has to go through what I went through." My voice is barely a whisper, but I know he heard me.

"I agree."

"Okay. My turn," I say, wanting to keep this mood upbeat so I can help cheer him up and pull his mind from work. "What dream does that sparkle represent for you?"

"You."

"You don't get to repeat the same one."

"Says who?"

"Says me."

"Well, since I made up the game, I get to make up the rules, and I say I get to repeat the same dream." He purses his lips and lifts his eyebrows, looking like the defiant little boy who saved me so very long ago.

"You never did play fair." I laugh while he just grins. And I love the sight of it since he's been so serious lately.

"Next one," he says as he peruses the skyline for a location and points. "What dream does that sparkle represent?"

"Endless possibilities," I murmur.

"Getting all philosophical on me, are you?"

"Yep. My turn." I point to the south. "What dream does that sparkle represent?"

"You," he says again, and when I look up to scold him, his lips meet mine. They're warmth and comfort and familiarity and desire. Everything I could ever want. I melt into him as his hands frame my face and our tongues dance intimately. When the kiss ends, he presses his forehead to mine and we just sink into the silence of each other for a bit.

"I want to pick one more sparkle that you need to pick your dream for."

"Can't we just sit like this and ignore the sparkles?" I murmur, loving the feel of his hands on my face and the warmth of his body against mine. I almost groan when he removes his hands and runs them down my arms.

"What about this sparkle?" he asks as he leans back, eyes locked on mine for just a second before he glances down.

I see the ring immediately, the sparkle of the diamond off the moonlight, the shine of the platinum against it, but I'm unable to form words.

I have so much passion and joy and every indescribable emotion inside me that I'm not sure how to manage it. So, I do the one thing I know will calm me. I thread my fingers through his hair and press my lips to his until I've knocked him backward onto the ground with me on top of him.

"Yes." Kiss. "Yes." Another kiss. "Yes times infinity," I tell him as I smother the laughter on his lips and deepen the kiss.

"Is that a yes?" he murmurs when I finally let him up for air.

"Yes." This time, I yell it so loud that he winces before laughing as I kiss him again.

When I lean back and sit astride his hips, all I can do is stare at him. At his mussed hair and his crooked smile. At his eyes that hold more than I could ever ask for. I see love in them. I see pride. I see tomorrows.

I see forever.

"You know I had a whole speech planned out, right?"

"You did? I'm sorry."

"I should have accounted for the squeal factor."

I swat at him and then lean forward and kiss him before sitting back up. "This is far beyond the squeal factor. This is more the best-day-of-my-life-need-to-tell-you-yes type of urgency."

His grin grows wider, and the gold in his eyes lights up. "The best day, huh?"

"By far." I lace my fingers with his, needing more of the connection we already have.

"How about I tell you this is only the beginning. From here on out, you're going to have best days top best days top best days because that is what you, Emmy Reeves, deserve."

"Grant—"

"My turn," he warns as he lifts his eyebrow and a ghost of a smile pulls at his lips. He sits up so that I can settle onto his lap with my legs wrapped around him. We are face to face, and the temptation is too hard to resist. Another brush of lips. Another chance to get lost in him.

"Emerson Reeves, you know I've always loved you. What you don't know is that since you've walked back into my life, I've realized just how ready I was to settle in all things—relationships, jobs, *life*. You always say I'm the hero, but you're the one who saved me. From a life without passionate fights and incredible make-up sex. From a life without nonstop laughter and friendship and unconditional love." He leans forward and brushes the most tender of kisses to my lips that makes every part of my body want to sigh. "From a life without you, Em." The sincerity of his words weaving their way through my heart and wrapping themselves around my soul.

"Grant . . ." His name is a plea. A promise. An answer.

"I love you, Emmy. I want to spend a lifetime chasing moments with you. I want infinity to love you. I want you to know you're my sparkle. My dream come true. I just want you. Will you marry me?" he asks, every part of my body captivated by the sound of his voice and the words he speaks.

His eyes are swimming with emotion as he waits, but I take a moment to take it all in. To take him in before I give him my tomorrows. "Yes," I say on a whisper. "Yes to infinity and sparkles."

I wrap my arms around him and cling tight. My face is buried in the crook of his neck, and all I want to do is breathe him in.

Breathe the moment in.

Tears blur my vision as I lean back and look at him. My rock. My sparkle. My everything.

To think I wanted to run from this. From him.

To think if I had never taken the chance.

Head up. Wings out.

NOTE FROM THE AUTHOR

Dear Reader,

Often times, authors use events that have happened to them in real life and tweak them to fit in a story. How better to write about a situation—to get the emotion across to the reader—than to have actually walked in the shoes of your characters. From there, the author takes the situation and builds on it by adding the fiction to complete the story.

Cuffed is that book for me. I may have changed the names, but when I was in elementary school, I knew an Emerson.

And I was the Grant.

No, we weren't best friends who basically lived at each other's houses like Emerson and Grant do in *Cuffed* (that's my added fiction), but we were friends nonetheless. I will never forget the day we were walking around the playground and Olive (that's what I'll call her for this) told me the exact words Emerson told Grant. "When my mom is gone, my dad holds a gun to my head and molests me and my brother." I can still picture the look on her face and the sound of her voice. And then, of course, she went on to say he'd told them he would hurt them if they told anyone else.

It's been over thirty years since that day, but I still remember so much about it. I remember going home and asking my mom what "molest" meant and her shocked reaction when I wouldn't tell her why I'd asked the question (there is a lot more to this part but for the sake of this note, I'm keeping this short). I remember worrying about my friend all night long because, while my mom's explanation of the word wasn't scary (remember she was explaining to a young child), I knew "gun" was a bad thing. I remember going to school the next day and Olive telling me that it happened again.

And then I remember telling my very pregnant teacher when everyone was out at recess that I had to talk to her. That in and of itself was hard to do, so you can imagine how nervous I was telling her what Olive had told me. I can picture her face when I told her and how when she hugged me, I couldn't fit my arms all the way around her pregnant belly.

What happened next was the same as the story. The principal came over the intercom, called Olive to the office, and as she walked out the door, she turned to me and said, "I hate you. I never want to see you again."

Over thirty years have passed, and I still think about Olive off and on. I never saw her after that day when she walked out of the classroom and told me she hated me. She never came back to the school. Through the grapevine, we'd heard she and her brother were removed from the home and adopted, but we never knew more than that.

When I think of her, my main hope for her is that she has had a good life. I wonder if she ever thinks about the chubby little girl whose name she probably doesn't even remember but who pinky promised her she wouldn't tell and then broke that promise. Does she still hate me for tearing her family apart despite getting her out of that situation? Even if I found her again, I would never approach her but rather would just want to know she's okay. That she's happy.

That she doesn't blame me.

Or hate me anymore.

Sound familiar? There's a lot of how I feel in Grant.

In a perfect world, there would be no Olives, but unfortunately if there is one, that is too many.

This book is dedicated to all of the Olives out there. Wherever you are, remember we are rooting for you. To succeed. To thrive. To battle. To overcome.

And to my Olive, I hope you have found happiness.

STAY TUNED

Want more of the Malone brothers? Stay tuned for the next book in the Everyday Heroes series. Firefighter, Grady Malone, has met his match with songwriter, Dylan McCoy. *Combust* is coming January 29th, 2018.

And in Spring of 2018, you'll meet the final Malone brother, Grayson, in *Cockpit*.

ABOUT THE AUTHOR

New York Times Bestselling author K. Bromberg writes contemporary novels that contain a mixture of sweet, emotional, a whole lot of sexy, and a little bit of real. She likes to write strong heroines, and damaged heroes who we love to hate and hate to love.

A mom of three, she plots her novels in between school runs and soccer practices, more often than not with her laptop in tow.

Since publishing her first book in 2013, Kristy has sold over one million copies of her books across sixteen different countries and has landed on the *New York Times, USA Today, and Wall Street Journal* Bestsellers lists over twenty-five times. Her Driven trilogy (*Driven, Fueled, and Crashed*) is currently being adapted for film by Passionflix with the first movie slated to release in the summer of 2018.

She recently released a two book, sports romance series, *The Player* and *The Catch*. *Cuffed* is the first book in her new Everyday Heroes trilogy. This three-book series will be about three brothers who are emergency responders, the jobs that call to them, and the women who challenge them. The remaining standalones in the series are *Combust* (January 29th) and *Cockpit* (Spring 2018).

She loves to hear from her readers so make sure you check her out on social media or sign up for her newsletter to stay up to date on all her latest releases and sales: http://bit.ly/254MWtI

Connect with K. Bromberg

Website: www.kbromberg.com

Facebook: www.facebook.com/AuthorKBromberg

Instagram: www.instagram.com/kbromberg13

Twitter: www.twitter.com/KBrombergDriven

Goodreads: bit.ly/1koZIkL

CPSIA information can be obtained
at www.ICGtesting.com
Printed in the USA
LVOW07s1629231017
553452LV00011B/1486/P

9 781942 832096